Praise for *New York Times* bestseller Grace Burrowes's rule-breaking, unforgettable Regency romance

"Delightfully different… Burrowes brings to life a deeply moving romance that's sure to be remembered and treasured."

—*RT Book Reviews* Top Pick, 4.5 Stars

"Exquisite… breathtaking and heartwarming."

—*Long and Short Reviews*

"Steamy… very compelling… a scorching tale of seduction and intrigue."

—*Night Owl Reviews* Reviewer Top Pick, 4.5 Stars

"Brilliant… The plot was unlike any romance novel that I have previously read and yet the romance arc was both realistic and believable."

—*The Royal Reviews*

"Heart-wrenching… an incredible love story that will stay with readers."

—*Romancing the Book*

"Ms. Burrowes continually presses the bar and goes above and beyond the normal to give her readers phenomenal love stories that keep us manic for more."

—*Romantic Crush Junkies EZine*

ANDREW

GRACE BURROWES

sourcebooks
casablanca

Published by Sourcebooks Casablanca, an imprint of Sourcebooks,
Inc.
P. O. Box 4410, Naperville, Illinois 60567-4410
(630) 961-3900
Fax: (630) 961-2168
www.sourcebooks.com

Printed and bound in the United States of America.
VP 10 9 8 7 6 5 4 3 2 1

To Delray the Wonder Pony,
and all the Wonder Ponies.

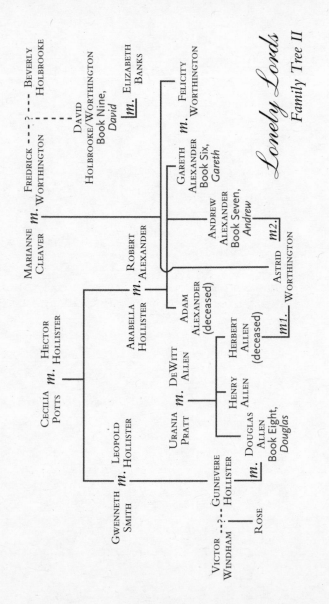

Lonely Lords
Family Tree II

One

I WILL NOT RUN FROM THE SIGHT OF MY BROTHER'S front door—I hope.

Andrew Alexander's composure felt as tentative as if he were facing another Channel crossing under stormy skies, though he nonetheless rapped the lion's head knocker stoutly three times against its brass fitting.

"Have you a card, sir?" The butler posed his question with that precise blend of hauteur and deference appropriate in the household of an English marquess.

"I'm afraid you have me at a loss," Andrew replied. "My cards went missing somewhere between the Levant and Gibraltar." He'd pitched them overboard at a point in his wanderings when he'd been so homesick that, despite all his misgivings, despite the sea voyages involved, and despite the prospect of renewed proximity to Astrid Worthington, he'd turned his sights for England.

Not Astrid Worthington. Astrid *Allen*, Viscountess Amery.

Andrew had something better than calling cards, however. He had a pair of dark eyebrows, which when lifted at a certain angle over eyes of a particularly brilliant blue, proclaimed him—to those possessed of a modicum of perspicacity—the younger sibling of the marquess.

The butler apparently numbered among such noticing souls. "My apologies, my lord. I will see if the family is receiv—*Lord Andrew*?"

Andrew assayed a smile, though he did not recognize this man.

"It's Hodges, your lordship. I was the newly hired underbutler when you left on your travels four years ago. Welcome home! Welcome home, my lord!" The fellow—whom Andrew still did not recognize—was bowing so enthusiastically his wig nearly came down over his ginger brows.

"Thank you, Hodges. It's good to be home." Andrew had rehearsed that very line, and thought it came out rather well.

To be on dry land was always good. Always.

"Lord Heathgate has been on a tear ever since we got your letter, my lord," Hodges declared as he divested Andrew of hat and gloves. "Her ladyship, too. Please do come along. The master is in his library."

Hodges bustled down the hallway, while Andrew sustained a sensory blow that had to do with the scent of beeswax and lemon oil, the sight of red roses in a silver bowl on the side table, and the jingle of a passing carriage.

He was as much at home as he was ever going to be.

Hodges tapped three times on the library door, a small sound that guaranteed for a while, at least, Andrew would remain at home.

"We'll surprise him, eh, your lordship? And I'll let

the marchioness know the happy news." Hodges was fair to bursting out of his silver and blue livery to tell Heathgate's lady that the prodigal was home, while Andrew felt a sense of frigid waves closing over his head and brine filling his belly.

Though beneath those reactions also dwelled a stubborn joy. Andrew seized the joy with both hands as Hodges announced, "a visitor," then promptly dropped it when he found himself standing in his brother's library.

"You'll have him to yourself," Hodges whispered with a cheeky wink.

Which was exactly what Andrew did *not* want.

Will he, nil he, the door clicked quietly shut. Andrew's only surviving brother stood in quarter profile by a set of French doors that led out to the back gardens. Gareth looked the same, no gray in his sable hair, no age creeping into his face, no dimming of his icy blue eyes. If anything, the man looked... younger, and the sight of him hale and whole comforted unbearably.

Gareth shot across the room and enveloped Andrew in a silent embrace, as a queer feeling suffused Andrew's chest, then his whole body, a kind of chill and heat that left him weak-kneed and resting his forehead against Gareth's shoulder. He did not deserve this unseemly display, but he held fiercely to his brother a moment longer.

"Squeeze me any harder and you will make me cry," he said, stepping back when Gareth's hold eased. A boyhood taunt between brothers was nothing less than the God's honest truth now. Andrew tried for a smile—and mostly failed.

"You have damned near made your brother cry," Gareth growled. "God's balls, you're skinny. Between Felicity and Mother, you will soon be fat as a market hog." He went to the sideboard and gestured with a decanter. "A celebratory tot?"

Andrew avoided strong drink as a matter of course, particularly whiskey, because it—along with sea voyages and introductions to any woman named Julia—seemed to fuel the nightmares.

"Of course," Andrew said, still feeling strangely weak. "Brandy will do. I have missed your cellar." He had missed his brother far more. He propped himself against Gareth's huge desk in what he hoped was a nonchalant pose. "We can drink to the health of your lady. Your last letter said Felicity is once again blooming, to use your words, in anticipation of a happy event."

Given her condition, Andrew would need the fortification of his drink before he saw his sister-in-law again.

"She does the blooming, I do the anticipating," Gareth said, handing his brother a bumper of brandy and clinking his glass against it. "To homecomings."

"And your wife's continued good health," Andrew countered, raising his glass. The taste of Gareth's bribing stock was more proof of homecoming, the brandy smooth, fruity, and subtly complex. Andrew sipped once and set his glass aside. "You do serve the very best."

"Only to my most honored guests," Gareth shot back. "Do you know, Andrew, how badly I have missed you? Worse than that, *Felicity* missed you, and Mother missed you, perhaps more than all of us put together."

Astrid had missed him too. She'd put that in writing a time or two, and Andrew still had those notes.

"And how fares our good dam?" Andrew rejoined. Yes, he'd missed them as well, and he'd been gone too long—and not nearly long enough. On that thought, he sank into the comfortable depths of Gareth's sofa.

Gareth appropriated an armchair, looking very much the lord of the manor. "Mother is well, having had great fun shepherding Astrid through two seasons and a wedding. We've also had the sense to present her ladyship with perfect, brilliant, adorable, et cetera grandchildren whose precociousness flatters her endlessly. With another—at least—on the way, her cup runneth over. Seeing you, however, will make her truly happy, and not simply busy with other people's happiness."

Something in that litany—besides the casual mention of Astrid's name—caught Andrew's ear. "Is Felicity expecting twins, then?"

"I hope to God not," Gareth said. "Astrid intimated to Felicity right before the funeral that she may be increasing as well. Felicity hasn't wanted to question her about it in light of her bereavement, but we're hopeful she will have that consolation at least."

Andrew turned a hard stare on his brother, feeling internal upset lurch toward complete chaos. "Gareth, what are you talking about? *What* funeral, *what* bereavement?"

Gareth set down his glass on the stones of the raised hearth. "I sent a letter to intercept you at Gravesend and another to our office at the Pool, but I gather neither one reached you. Astrid's husband was killed in a hunting accident two weeks ago. She stayed here for the first week, but was determined to return to her own household thereafter."

"This is unhappy news," Andrew managed. Damned rotten, unhappy news. "Sad for Astrid." Tragic, if she'd loved her husband, and Andrew fervently hoped she had.

And not at all convenient for him. He battled the impulse to get off the couch, walk out the door, and up the gangplank of the nearest departing ship. Astrid—lovely, dauntless Astrid—was alone, grieving, and possibly expecting her late husband's heir. Could there be a less felicitous set of circumstances?

"How does Astrid fare?" He couldn't keep that question behind his teeth for all the calm Channel crossings in history.

"I don't know, Andrew," Gareth said, and those were not words the Marquess of Heathgate uttered frequently. "She's young, and she's sturdy in her own way. Her brother, David, is keeping a close eye on her, but I get the sense she's not grieving well. Felicity claims her sister has yet to shed a tear on her late husband's behalf."

Andrew considered Gareth's words rather than consider the unlocked French doors. David, Lord Fairly, was an astute man and a conscientious brother, and that was some consolation. "She loved her husband?"

He should not have asked; he should never have even wondered. Astrid's domestic affairs were none of his business, and they never would be.

"I think that's part of the problem." Gareth rose and refilled his glass with a half measure. "She was fond of him, but Fairly and I, and Felicity too, were puzzled by her choice of him. Amery was a great puppy dog of a fellow, jovial, doting, and without intellectual pretensions. Astrid played him like a fiddle, if you ask me, but I couldn't figure out why she'd chosen him in the first place. I don't find boredom much of an aphrodisiac," Gareth concluded, resuming his seat.

Andrew had forgotten how frank his brother could be—and how perceptive.

"Astrid's father was a bounder, and her brother is an odd duck. That she'd want a steadier sort for the father of her children makes sense." A steadier sort than he, of course. Andrew had told himself this through twelve countries and three sea voyages. He'd told himself this when he'd been unable to burn the notes she tucked into his brother's letters, and told himself this again when her notes had stopped coming.

"You may have the right of it." Gareth might have intended to say more, but he was interrupted by a knock on the door.

"Gareth? *Andrew?*" Felicity, Marchioness of Heathgate, came in sporting a fulsome smile and suspiciously bright eyes—also carrying a silver tea tray which she set on the table in front of the sofa. For a progression of moments, Andrew experienced a resurgence of joy mixed with unease as Felicity fussed, hugged him, dabbed at her eyes, and fussed some more.

And her ladyship was visibly gravid, which did nothing for Andrew's nerves.

She ensconced herself next to Andrew, right next to him, in the friendliness Andrew associated with both Worthington sisters.

"Are you interrogating my brother-in-law, sir?" she asked her husband. "I won't have it. That prerogative is reserved for females, among whom you do not number. Who would like tea?"

Gareth returned her smile, his saturnine features acquiring a softness when he beheld his wife. "None for me, sweetheart, I'm drinking the good stuff."

"None for me either, sweetheart," Andrew said. "I'm drinking Heathgate's good stuff, which I have sorely missed." He had not missed the little lies Polite Society required in the name of manners, but he could hardly say he'd missed his brother to a point approaching lunacy.

"Leaving the entire pot for me," the marchioness said. "While the tea is steeping, would anyone like a sandwich?"

Andrew considered the question and realized that with the anticipation of this homecoming behind him, he was starving. He accepted a heaping plate—two sandwiches of sliced beef and cheddar on white bread with a pale French mustard—and caught the look Felicity exchanged with Gareth. Their brief glance was domestic; a bit of wifely smugness at having guessed correctly at Andrew's appetite.

"Eat all that," Gareth remarked, "and we will have to change your title to Earl of Shoat. I wouldn't mind a sandwich myself, Wife, if there are any left, that is."

"Now, children," Andrew chided between bites of simple English food. "I will eat as much of this delicious fare as I may, and would appreciate it if we did not apply any titles to me, even in jest."

Another look passed between Gareth and Felicity,

but it wasn't domestic or smug. Felicity was puzzled, and Gareth was... uneasy.

"What?" Andrew asked, pausing with a sandwich halfway to his mouth. Astrid was now widowed, possibly an expecting widow. What development could be more disconcerting than that?

Gareth appeared to find his sandwich fascinating. "You do have a title, or two, actually."

Foreboding settled into Andrew's stomach, swirling about in a queasy mess with his brandy, his half-eaten sandwich, and the upheaval of Gareth's various disclosures.

"What do you mean, I have a title, or two—*actually*?"

"You will recall our maternal grandfather was a baron," Gareth began. "But you may not recall he had a second cousin who was Earl of Greymoor. The earl died without surviving issue, and after some roundaboutation, that title devolved to grandfather the year before his death. He made nothing of it, and I wasn't even aware it had happened until I was tidying up his estate and cousin Gwen informed me. By then, Privileges was looking about for someone to foist the barony and the earldom onto. Because I am already overburdened with titles, they saw to a special remainder, or a re-issuance of the letters patent, something of that sort—it was one of those titles that could be preserved through the female line—and settled the honor on you."

Andrew shot out of his chair and whirled on his brother, who was very likely the *something of that sort* responsible for this fiasco.

"How could you let that happen, Gareth? I trusted

you to watch my back while I was gone, and I come back to *this*? I want no titles, do you understand? Privileges will have to look about for someone else to honor, but it won't be me."

The damned man remained seated, regarding his wife, then his glass of spirits, when what Andrew wanted was the sort of set-to they'd indulged in as adolescents, before the accident had made them so blessed careful with each other.

"I knew you'd resent this," Gareth said. "If you don't want to administer the estates, we can hire a steward or two. The titles need not burden you, Andrew."

Felicity's expression was worried, so Andrew forced himself to sit back down beside her.

"You will pardon my lack of manners, Felicity," he said. "I do not mind the burden of the estates, Gareth." Not much. Not yet, though he would and soon. "The burden of the succession is the untenable obligation." He managed a sip of brandy and tried to batten down his anger—his panic, to apply the more honest term.

Felicity put two frosted tea cakes, one pink and one blue, on his already full plate. "You needn't worry about the succession, Andrew. Your nephews can inherit if all else fails. Would you like to meet them?"

Nephews. Never did a word bring a greater sense of relief. *God bless all nephews, the more the better.* "I would like very much to meet them, and I'm warning you both now, I will spoil them rotten every chance I get."

And guard their lives with his own.

❦

The clock ticked in the otherwise silent house.

And ticked.

And ticked.

And ticked.

Sitting in her front parlor, a cup of tea growing cold in her hands, Astrid Worthington Allen, newly widowed Viscountess Amery, considered getting up, crossing the room, and pitching the clock through the window.

She contemplated this maneuver with the small, detached part of her mind still capable of ratiocination. The clock was safe, of course. Smashing it would take action, and action took willpower, and Astrid had used up the available quotient of that precious commodity dressing and getting down to this sitting room. Most of her, however, was still upstairs in bed, unwilling to face another day.

In the privacy of one's thoughts, one could be brutally honest: she was all but *unable* to face another day.

That bluff, genial Amery had died in his thirtieth year was unfair. Not fair to Amery, and most assuredly not fair to Astrid. She had loved her husband, truly she had. He had been—oh, how the pluperfect tense oppressed!—he'd been a pleasant, harmless young man. Not strikingly handsome, not particularly quick, not flashy in any sense. But she'd chosen him for that very solid, undramatic, pleasant quality… and now *this*.

Every corner of the house held memories of Herbert, every space had a deserted quality, where he should still be sitting, standing, laughing, lounging with a drink, or tracking mud. Herbert had tracked a deal of mud, never caring for the carpets when he'd come in from a hard ride or a morning's shooting.

Astrid had hoped they could become friends, in time. But they weren't to have time. No more time at all.

Out in the hallway, voices sounded. Astrid recognized not the words but the smooth, quiet cadence of Douglas Allen's greeting and instructions to the footman. As the present Viscount Amery, Douglas could do that—order Astrid's staff about, visit any time he chose, and generally intrude on her grief with the best of stated intentions.

Between one tick of the infernal clock and the next, energy suffused Astrid in mind and body.

Douglas could interrogate the staff all he wanted, but Astrid could not bear the prospect of him oozing cool sympathy while his chilly blue eyes gave away no grief of his own.

Not today.

Before Douglas could finish his interrogation—for Astrid had no doubt he was again questioning the staff about her daily habits—she slipped out the parlor's side door and kept walking, toward the back of the domicile in which she'd been entombed.

She grabbed a black cloak and a heavily veiled black bonnet from the hooks in the back hallway, finding them appropriate, not to her grief, but to her *anger*.

Amery should not have died as he did.

He should not have left Astrid alone to bring a child into the world, not after last year's miscarriage.

And he most assuredly should not have left Douglas with the authority and assets of the viscountcy.

Astrid fairly charged out into the mews and called for her coach while she tried to think of where she might go to be alone with her anger and with the endless, painful lump in her throat that would not turn into tears.

❦

When she let herself into the kitchen of her girlhood home, Astrid saw that the Crabbles were taking very good care of the place, indeed. Not one corner sported a cobweb, not one surface a speck of dust, not one carpet was in need of a thorough beating. The whole house, in fact, lacked the hollow, empty feeling Astrid had expected as she made her way up to the attics.

The state of the house, the dearness of it, cheered her considerably.

Astrid found the appropriate trunk immediately. The latch was sticky, and when she opened the lid, camphor and lavender assailed her nose. Taking off her bonnet and gloves, she knelt before the trunk.

A lace-attired doll she remembered from her earliest childhood was the first thing she encountered, followed by very small dresses. Toward the bottom of the trunk, she found even smaller clothes, as well as a soft wool receiving blanket with mock orange boughs beautifully embroidered on the borders. The sight of it, something her own mother had made while carrying her, brought tears to Astrid's eyes.

Mock orange symbolized memory, and of her late mother, she had none.

Finally tears, for a mother she'd never met, who had loved her before she'd even been born. The thought caused an upwelling of sorrow, a flood of misery that had Astrid crying noisily into the blanket. She didn't know how long she remained kneeling on the floor, crying like a motherless child, but eventually she became aware she wasn't alone.

Hands settled gently on her shoulders.

"Astrid." The voice was masculine and dear to her, but what Astrid responded to was the wealth of caring she heard, even in just her name. "Astrid, hush." A pair of strong arms turned her and scooped her up, then settled her against a broad masculine chest.

Andrew. Andrew was home, he was here, and why that should be she could not fathom, though she knew without reservation, she was glad of it.

"I want my mother," she confessed miserably, clinging to the comforting embrace. She heard no reply, though her admission had intensified her sense of loss and expanded it to include the child she'd conceived and then lost the previous year. If she'd had to choose, she would have said she was crying more for her mother and baby than for her departed husband.

Comforting hands caressed her back; gentle fingers stroked her hair; soft lips pressed to her temple. The great knot of pain inside her gradually eased under the onslaught of tenderness, and she was able to take the first deep breath she'd inhaled in weeks. Without looking up, she traced her fingers along the strong jaw of the man who held her.

He'd have the same dark hair, the same blue, blue eyes, the same charming, even tender smile.

"Andrew… Oh, Andrew. My dear, dear friend," she murmured against his chest. "I have been so worried for you."

Two

ANDREW HELD THE SLIGHT WOMAN IN HIS ARMS securely, but even as his heart ached for her, he felt a growing sense of consternation. Astrid wasn't going to berate him for departing from England without taking a proper leave of her. She wasn't going to castigate him for never acknowledging her letters. She wasn't going to scramble off his lap and huff out of the room in a cloud of sorely tried dignity.

She *was* going to let him hold her and torture himself with the feel and scent and reality of her.

And he was, just this one more time, going to take advantage of her generosity. Had Andrew known borrowing the unoccupied Worthington domicile would result in this encounter with Astrid, he would have slept in the street instead. His own town house was still in use by tenants, though, and Felicity and Gareth had insisted.

He let out a breath, then inhaled Astrid's scent on the next in-breath. She felt smaller than ever in his embrace, though she still had the same thick masses of blond hair, the same luscious, rosy scent.

"Having a good cry, are we?"

"You seem fated to come upon me in moments of weakness," Astrid replied. She referred to the first time they'd met, when Andrew had accompanied his brother to the Worthington household in the aftermath of a potentially deadly fire. "And yes, I would say that undignified display qualifies as a good cry." She paused on a shuddery breath. "I haven't yet, you know… Cried, that is, until now."

Astrid had ever been one to posit confidences and trust where they had not been earned.

Andrew shifted her against the arms of the rocking chair and loosened his neckcloth. He handed it to her in lieu of a handkerchief, then resettled her in his lap.

"You fear if you start crying, you won't ever stop."

Astrid looked up at him, the expression in her great blue eyes arrested. "I might have feared that, Andrew, but I couldn't make the tears come. I was feeling things, but not experiencing my own feelings, if that's possible. Though just now, I found this blanket my mother made for me before I was born. I killed her, truth be known. She died right after giving birth to me. I've never missed her more than I do right now."

Andrew set the chair to gently rocking again and cradled her silently in his embrace for long moments. She remained peacefully in his arms, a boon he didn't deserve and shouldn't want.

"Tell me about your husband." He chose this question deliberately, hoping a grief-stricken recounting of Astrid's love for the man might be adequate penance for the liberties Andrew took.

"Amery was a decent fellow," she began, her tone

as prosaic as if she'd been discussing a stable mouser sent to his reward by a passing beer wagon. "He was pleasant and easy to be with. Undemanding, tolerant, affectionate to hounds and horses, and patient with the elderly. I loved him." She fell silent, though Andrew heard the self-doubt in her voice. "Most of the time, I liked him as well. I hoped we would grow close as our marriage matured."

This was not going to help Andrew one bit, for clearly, Astrid had not been *in love* with her husband. The thought disappointed and pleased at the same time.

"You respected him."

"Mostly, though he also had a… he could be unimpressive," Astrid said, fingering the border of the receiving blanket. "Herbert wanted everybody to get along, and sometimes that isn't possible. Confrontation can be a good thing, but not among the Allens. That was hard for me, not speaking my mind *ever*, not being able to discuss difficult matters even with my own spouse."

Hard for her? She'd described her version of hell, and made it sound convincingly trivial. But what to say?

"I think most couples find the first few years of marriage a challenge. Learning how to communicate with one's spouse takes time." Though what Andrew knew about marriage could fill a small thimble, and that gained mostly from his dealings with wives more vocal than faithful.

Astrid blew a stray lock of hair off her forehead. "Not for your brother and my sister. Have you seen how those two *look* at each other?"

"It's nauseating," Andrew agreed, speaking more literally than Astrid could know. "Also dear. Have you considered making your household with them, Astrid? I don't like to think of you alone."

She folded the blanket on her lap, a soft pile of pale wool with embroidered satin borders. "I honestly could not stand to live with those two right now, much less the demon brats who are our nephews. I haven't the energy to deal with a happy family and their well-intended concern."

"Speaking of concern, you feel skinny to me, Astrid. When was the last time you ate?" How easily they reverted to simple honesty with each other, something Andrew had missed more than the very shores of England.

She folded his cravat—now hopelessly wrinkled—on top of the blanket.

"That long?" Andrew answered himself. "I find myself in want of sustenance, so you are invited to raid the kitchen with me." He didn't move to rise out of the chair until Astrid had scrambled off his lap, but when he saw she was unsteady on her feet, he stood and secured an arm around her waist.

"Astrid—" Women could be carried off by grief, and she weighed less than thistledown.

"Don't scold me, please, Andrew. I am simply light-headed. I don't sleep so well, and I haven't much appetite, is all. I'll be right enough when I get some food in me."

"I'll send a maid up here to tidy up. Would you like the trunk taken over to your house?" he offered as he ushered her out of the room. He took care to walk slowly and kept his arm around her as they traveled down three flights of stairs to the kitchen.

And Astrid allowed this familiarity, when Andrew knew she shouldn't. She ought to slap his face and deliver the blistering lecture he had coming after four years of larking around anywhere but where she was.

"Don't send the trunk over just yet," Astrid told him as they progressed through the house. "It's safe enough here, and Felicity may not have a girl, despite Gareth's autocratic pronouncements."

Maybe not so honest after all; though it occurred to Andrew he was in the presence of an expecting female, and for once not the least bit upset by it. "You were on a mission for your sister?"

She paused at the top of the last flight of stairs. "I could tell you I was, Andrew, but the truth is I have reason to believe I might be increasing. I am hesitant to share this news, however, because I've already had one disappointment, and it would not be fair to Amery's family to get their hopes up."

He'd heard about the miscarriage—a half sentence in one of Gareth's letters, a half sentence Andrew had read and reread, between prayers for the aggrieved mother.

Andrew turned her by the shoulders to face him. "If you are increasing, you must take special care to eat, to rest, to keep up your strength. You cannot go all day without eating, and all night tossing between the sheets. You know better," he chided gently.

She ducked out of his grasp and trundled down the steps.

"I tell myself the same thing, Andrew, but in truth I

am not sure I want to have this baby—and yes, I know that sentiment is at least eight kinds of blasphemy."

Astrid could torture him with her physical proximity, and she could torture him with confidences too. "What do you mean?"

"If I present the Allen family with their heir, then I am tied to them for the rest of my life. The new viscount, Douglas, will have the raising of my son—who will depose Douglas as viscount—or the guardianship of my daughter, and Douglas's views on many things are not entirely consonant with my own. I have tried to like Douglas, but he is a cool... a *reserved* fellow. He will bear the title with more credibility than Herbert ever did."

Andrew tucked her hand around his arm and continued walking her toward the kitchen, wondering why nobody—nobody named Gareth—had seen fit to provide him information about this Douglas fellow earlier.

"You know Gareth will take a hand in the upbringing of any child of yours, if you wish it—and probably if you don't. He can't help it, and he is a marquess, not a lowly viscount. Then too, I apparently hold the titles of both baron and earl, thanks to my brother's well-intended, if egregiously misguided, machinations. So both of us outrank Amery, and could at least tie up a guardianship in years of knots."

The idea that he could champion her causes loomed like a worthy penance—and like an excuse to spend time with her.

"True enough, Andrew, but you are not related by blood to my child, and Douglas is. And it isn't only the thought of being tied to the Allens that daunts me," she admitted as they reached the kitchen.

Andrew watched as Astrid went about gathering the tea things, setting out bread, butter, cheese, a jar of brandied pears, and cold slices of roast beef. She had been raised in this house and with few servants. This was *her* kitchen, and the competence of her movements underscored that fact.

"So what else concerns you about your delicate condition?" Andrew asked, getting down mugs for tea and bracing a hip against the sink.

Astrid stopped fussing about and considered the jar of raspberry jam in her left hand. "I never told Amery we could be expecting a child."

Abruptly, her unshed tears, her dispassion where her husband was concerned, made sense.

"Guilt plagues you. You don't deserve motherhood because Amery is not here to enjoy fatherhood."

"Yes." Astrid glared at him across the kitchen even as another tear trickled down her cheek. "Guilt. I told my sister, and I've told you, but I never t-t-told Amery. He would have died happy."

Andrew was at her side in two strides, his arms around her.

"He would have died happier, perhaps, Astrid, but he also would have died worrying." Andrew snatched a towel off a rack behind them and handed it to her. Weren't widows supposed to carry black handkerchiefs and flourish them at such moments?

"How did your husband die, if I might ask?"

She pushed away from him, to his regret and relief. "He was out shooting with his youngest brother,

Henry, and some of their friends. Amery was quite the sportsman. His gun misfired, and he lost too much blood from the resulting injury. He died the same day, before anybody could get word to me, but Douglas assured me Amery did not regain consciousness, and he didn't suffer. Maybe knowing he had a child would have made a difference, though. Maybe he wouldn't have gone on that stupid outing, maybe he would have been more careful with his equipment... Maybe, maybe, maybe..."

Astrid checked the strength of the tea three times in two minutes, put the butter away, then took it out again.

"Please sit," Andrew commanded quietly.

Astrid shot him a glower but did as bid, letting him prepare her a cup of tea.

He filled a plate for her and slid it across the table, while he took the seat on the opposite bench. "You are to eat every bit of that, Astrid, or I will tell Felicity on you, and she will tell Gareth," he threatened, earning him a slight smile from Astrid.

"She won't tell him to get me in trouble, of course," Astrid said, taking a nibble of cheese. "She'll tell him because she is *concerned* for me. Gareth won't be concerned for me, particularly, as he has oft stated faith in my resilience, but he will be irked as the devil I would give his wife cause for worry, and hence the problem will be dealt with."

She was smiling, and yet her gaze was forlorn. Had the late lord Amery ever been as protective of her as Gareth was of Felicity?

"You must promise me something, Astrid, and I

am serious about this. You must promise me to take good care of yourself: to eat, to rest, to get some fresh air and sunshine. You love the out-of-doors. You love the country. I'm sure, if you wanted to spend time at Willowdale, my mother would be happy to go with you. I know you can't lark about in Hyde Park, but you also can't expect to become happy again if you're shut up alone in your house all day."

He added a question to emphasize his point. "When was the last time you fed the ducks, groomed a horse, or petted a cat?" He let a pensive silence hang for a few heartbeats before continuing on. "You need to take better care, Astrid, and let this silly guilt go."

"Silly, is it?"

Good. She'd bristled visibly and audibly.

"Silly," Andrew said, unwilling to back down until he had her assent. To that end, he resorted to heavy artillery. "The day my brother Adam drowned, he and I had a very unpleasant quarrel. He was a difficult man to quarrel with, probably somewhat like your Amery. Pleasant, kind, cheerful, never met a stranger, that sort of fellow. He, of all people, would not want me to see that quarrel as the sum of our dealings. Amery would want you to be happy—ecstatic even—to be carrying his child."

The recitation had been unplanned—every mention of that tragic day, however oblique, was unplanned—but it was honest. The day of the yachting accident, he and Adam, for the first time in their lives, had come nigh to blows. Andrew had railed against Gareth's looming engagement to Julia Ponsonby, and Adam had defended a man's right to choose his bride. Adam would have forgiven Andrew, eventually. Andrew was almost sure of it.

Astrid looked down into her cup, as if she might see the truth of Andrew's words in her tea.

"Eat," he admonished her, though a lecture was damming up behind his teeth, about common sense and responsibility.

About babies being unspeakably precious.

Astrid slid the butter across to him. "Felicity calls me the butter thief. Gareth is every bit as bad."

"Butter is good for expectant mothers," Andrew responded. "When are you going to tell this Douglas fellow of your condition?" Because the good viscount deserved to know his title could be snatched from him by a squalling infant less than a year hence.

"I don't want to tell that man anything, Andrew."

Astrid was forthright and even brusque, but she was seldom truly difficult.

"Has Douglas Allen given offense, Astrid?"

"Good heavens, Andrew, you look quite severe. Why would you ask such a thing?"

Andrew did not resume buttering his bread. "Answer the question."

"No, Douglas hasn't given offense, unless you call an awkward kiss on the forehead offense. He did, however, offer to manage my widow's portion for me, and yesterday reminded me I have use of the dower house at Amery Hall, as well as the use of the town house for as long as I prefer."

"And you found this offensive?" In truth, it was decent of the man.

"I did, Andrew. Firstly, I am a widow now, and one

of the very few benefits of that unhappy state is the freedom to manage my own funds, to transact business, and to make contracts for necessaries. Secondly, I felt somehow that, by insisting I have the town house as long as I pleased, Douglas was hurrying me from it. Thirdly, he is a notably cold man, and any affectionate overture from him, however well intended or proper, makes me uneasy."

"I recall when affectionate overtures did not make you uneasy at all, Astrid."

Mistake. Serious, horrendous mistake, and Andrew knew it even as the words were leaving his stupid, gauche, ill-mannered mouth. He had been doing so well, taking on the role of brother-in-law and friend, and then he had to bring up their past.

"Ungentlemanly, Andrew," Astrid said mildly. "I was an inexperienced girl, and you were merely allowing me a taste of where flirtation might lead. Have you any sweets in your kitchen?"

Andrew studied the composed features on the *sweet* in his kitchen for a moment too long.

He had given her her first kiss; she had appropriated the second. He had, while Gareth and Felicity looked on in tolerant amusement, goaded her into taking her first awkward sips of brandy, he had put his life at risk for her safety, and on one occasion, he had abused her innocence terribly.

And then fled to the Continent rather than risk worse misbehavior, despite having vowed at the age of fifteen never to set foot on a sailing vessel again.

If it was friendship she sought, then despite the cost to him, his friendship she would have. As she swiped her finger over a dab of jam on the edge of her plate, he recalled her question.

"You crave sweets. Felicity sent over some muffins yesterday," he told her. "She thinks I am too thin and knows this is the staff's day off, so she sends provisions."

"You *are* too thin," Astrid said, digging through the bread box and locating the tray of muffins. "And you look tired, Andrew. Are *you* getting adequate rest and food?"

"I've gained some weight since returning. My clothes are not so loose, anyway. You are the one who is too slender, Astrid. Trust me on this."

And he ought to know, having left England haunted by the memory of intimate familiarity with her curves and hollows.

"Seeing as we're both in want of nutrition, let us have at the muffins, shall we?" she suggested, bringing the whole tray to the table.

"More tea to wash them down with, or can I convince you to drink milk instead?" She'd always favored milk, but she was no longer a young miss fresh from the schoolroom—and, damn the luck, all the prettier for her added maturity.

"A cold cup of milk has some appeal right now, though part of the reason I have lost weight is I am a bit queasy from time to time."

"You can thank your offspring for that," Andrew said, pouring the milk from a jug in the pantry and bringing it to her. "And you have to visit the necessary incessantly, have odd cravings for food, and nap at unusual hours." Her breasts might also be sensitive, though Andrew kept that possibility to himself and repaired to the far side of the table.

Astrid looked momentarily nonplussed. "How in the world do you know all that?"

They were family; she was a widow. The occasional blunt exchange between them wasn't that far outside the bounds of propriety—he wished.

"My brother, the selfsame saintly man who is now married to your sister, told me not long after I came down from university that increasing women are often available for dalliance, and with their husbands' tacit consent." He wasn't willing to say more. The look of fascination on Astrid's face suggested he'd already said too much.

"You've *dallied* with women who were pregnant?"

No, he had not, but they had certainly offered to dally with him with a regularity that had felt like the fist of fate laid repeatedly and forcefully across his jaw.

"I didn't dally with the frequency Gareth did, I assure you. I attended a birth once, if you must know. Messy business, but wonderful." He wanted her to know the wonderful part, even if it meant he embarrassed them both.

Astrid's hand went to her flat abdomen, and she looked up at Andrew in confusion. "I really am... expecting," she said, consternation in her voice.

"Which really is wonderful." He smiled across the table at her and bit into a muffin, lest he betray how earnestly he meant that sentiment. "Drink your milk."

And yet, he could be glad for her about this, which was reassuring. That he was also jealous as hell of the dear, departed, unimpressive Amery was of no moment.

She drank her milk, and they each polished off a muffin in thoughtful silence. When the remains of the meal were strewn across the table, Andrew rose to put the food away.

"I can help," Astrid said, standing up with quick purpose, then sitting down just as quickly. "As soon as my head clears."

"Botheration, Astrid." Andrew was beside her in an instant, his hand on the back of her neck as he lowered himself to straddle the bench she sat on. He scooted up, so she sat between his spread legs, and gently brought her to lean against his chest.

"Steady," he admonished, rubbing a hand along her back. "You can't move too quickly. Even if you aren't light-headed, the more the child grows, the more it will affect your balance. Catch your breath, and then school yourself to a greater display of dignity."

He hadn't meant to scold so thoroughly, but she'd gone as white as some exotic orchid. She subsided against him with uncharacteristic meekness, sending a bolt of alarm through the pleasant torture of holding her against his body.

"Andrew?"

"Hmm?"

"I want you to promise me something," Astrid said, her ear over his heart.

"I do not make promises lightly." If he could help it, he did not make them at all.

"Nor do I, Andrew Alexander, though I have promised you to take better care of myself, to eat well, to rest, to groom horses, and whatnot. I would like a promise from you in return."

He sensed impending doom, which had ever been his fate where she was concerned. "What promise would you have?"

"Don't leave again until I have this baby?"

She had no right to ask that of him, but Astrid had seldom concerned herself with rights or proprieties. As he marshaled his sound, logical arguments, she marched on.

"Until you came upon me today, I had not cried for my husband because *nobody was there to comfort me*. I had not even spoken his name to anybody, because *nobody asked me about him*. I had not eaten a meal in days because *nobody shared a meal with me*. I had not considered my fatigue and nausea were related to pregnancy because *there is no one to discuss it with*."

Andrew resisted the urge to hold her more tightly, and still, she wasn't finished with her tirade.

"Yes, I could impose on Felicity and Gareth, but I have imposed on them incessantly over the past four years, and particularly the past four weeks. Moreover, Felicity's condition is as delicate as mine, and she should not be forced to bear my worries. You are good for me, Andrew, and I am asking you not to leave England until this child is born or the pregnancy otherwise ends."

He was doomed, but then, he'd been doomed for years—for his entire adulthood at least.

"I will not leave England until your child is born. That is the only way your pregnancy will end," Andrew said, sounding like his imperious older brother. "But England is a big place, Astrid Worthington Allen."

She nestled against him, making a little sound of contentment, and doom acquired painful new depths.

"You are good for me, Andrew, and knowing you have not gone abroad somewhere to fight bears or charm snakes will help keep my mind at ease."

He had fought her memory and charmed the occasional willing woman in aid of that battle, only to lose every skirmish. "Astrid, we both know I have also been, on more than one occasion, not good for you at all, and then I left without a word."

"You had to leave," Astrid said, "though I do not entirely fathom why. And you are good for me. Do not argue with a lady, Andrew, particularly not at table."

He fell silent, knowing his next gauntlet of woes had just begun. Astrid was unwilling to face it, but a man who had treated her as Andrew had was not an honorable man. He'd known it at the time, had known it for years before, but she ignored this aspect of him.

She was pregnant, grieving, and exhausted, though she'd probably not even realized that last burden. Even as she leaned against him on the hard bench, she was dozing off. And it was sweet to hold her, sweet to be able to offer her the simple kindnesses of friendship.

Haring off to the four corners of the globe hadn't solved what was wrong with Andrew. Being a friend to Astrid for the next few months might be closer to the penance he needed to serve, but he wasn't looking forward to it.

No, he most assuredly was not looking forward to it one bit.

He let her sleep for an hour, until his behind was numb on the bench. She roused then, smiled at him brilliantly, thanked him, and stepped into the coach that would take her back to her solitary residence.

Three

Douglas Allen apparently enjoyed the entire Allen family complement of tenacity, for Astrid had not been home fifteen minutes when he reappeared at her parlor door.

"Sister." The new Viscount Amery bowed deeply. "How fare you?"

Herbert's younger brother—younger by eleven months—was a better-looking copy of the original. Whereas Herbert had been of medium height and his physiognomy merely pleasant, Douglas Allen was above average in height, and his more sharply cast features shaded closer to handsome, though it was a cold variety of handsome. His blue eyes held a depth Herbert's had lacked, and his wheat-blond hair—unlike Herbert's—showed no signs of thinning. Astrid had wanted to like Douglas—Herbert had liked him, for the most part—but Douglas took a while to warm up to.

"Douglas." Astrid offered him a curtsy. "Good of you to come. May I offer you some tea?" Interesting, how normal she could sound, how normally she could act, when her insides were still in riot as a result of time spent with Andrew.

"Tea would be appreciated, my lady, though I can't stay long. I merely thought to stop by and see how you are getting on."

Astrid poked her head into the hallway and summoned a footman to fetch them a fresh pot. Returning to the sitting room, she gestured to the couch. "Shall we sit?"

Douglas obliged her by taking the chair flanking the couch, though he courteously waited for her to be seated first.

He was like that. Courteous, deliberate, reserved, and excruciatingly polite. He would make an altogether more convincing viscount than her husband had. As that thought wandered through her head, she became aware, again, of the clock ticking and the violent impulses the sound engendered.

Though in Andrew's company she'd not felt the least bit violent.

"I am glad you have stopped by." She was not glad; she was not unhappy. She was, however, in jeopardy of losing her wits. "I've considered your comments regarding my continued tenure in this house, and you should know—"

Douglas held up a staying hand before Astrid could tell him her recently decided plans. "You became part of the Allen family the day you accepted my brother's suit, and I won't hear talk of your having to move when Herbert's death is not but a month past. You must stay here as long as you please, comforted by familiar surroundings."

More than a month. Thirty-four days ago, Douglas had stood in this very room and informed her her spouse of not quite two years had been killed in a shooting accident. She had thanked her brother-in-law politely for bringing her the news, unable to absorb it, but had been determined not to fall weeping into Douglas's arms.

As she had into Andrew's.

"Astrid?" Douglas was looking at her with concern, and Astrid had to focus to pick up the thread of their conversation. Andrew had looked entirely too thin, was the problem.

And entirely too dear.

"I've decided to accept my sister's invitation to join her when she removes to Surrey later this week," Astrid said, though she'd yet to inform Felicity of this decision. "While the surroundings here are familiar, they are also rendered... uncomfortable by Herbert's absence. I don't think I would miss him quite as painfully were I not so constantly faced with..."

With what? With the fact that she was too young to have the dream of a family of her own taken from her?

With wondering if Douglas had told Herbert's mistress of her protector's death? Had anybody told the woman?

Douglas surprised her by taking her hand in his. "Herbert was taken from you too soon, and without any chance for the two of you to make plans for the eventuality of his death. You need not worry—not about money, not about a place to live, not about your security. The dower house at Amery Hall is now yours for your lifetime, and I will be happy to manage your widow's portion as well."

Manage her widow's portion? Astrid no more wanted Douglas handling her finances than she wanted to wear mourning for the next years, or wanted to remove to the moldering confines of the Amery dower house. Legalities and trust documents notwithstanding, she would manage her own finances, thank you very much, or at the very least, consult Gareth or her brother, David, rather than turn one penny over to Douglas.

Astrid blocked out the sound of the ticking clock, murmured platitudes, and had the footman fetch her lavender shawl in hopes the combination of lavender and black with her blond coloring might make Douglas bilious. Two and a half polite eternities passed before Douglas rose and called for his hat, cane, and gloves.

"Thank you for coming by," she said, trying to appreciate the gesture.

"Your welfare is my concern, Astrid. Should you need anything, you must not hesitate to ask."

Why did he have to sound like a disapproving headmaster?

"You are kind, Douglas," she said, glad to be walking him to the door. When she thought she had him on his way, he turned to regard her once more.

"Shall I have the solicitors draw up a power of attorney? I'm sure they could see to it without delay." His expression was one of polite concern—his expression was often one of polite concern.

"Douglas, it's too soon for me to think about such things. I know the finances need to be dealt with, but I cannot make myself take such steps yet."

To her relief, he tapped his hat onto his head.

"If you are not up to making decisions, that is all

the more reason to leave troublesome financial details to me. Still, my lady, you must do as you see fit. I will see you before your remove to Surrey, and I'll have Mother join us."

"That would be lovely." *It would be hell.*

"Perhaps Henry or I will jaunt down to Surrey to check on you, if the weather's fine? I would, of course, allow my host the courtesy of notice before presuming to visit."

Astrid didn't dignify that with a reply, because it was a veiled criticism of her recent visit to the Allen family solicitors. *That* had been appallingly awkward. Without David glaring at them and making implied threats, Astrid would have fared quite poorly. Even with David's formidable presence beside her, there had been a goodly quantity of dodging, throat clearing, and paper shuffling.

"I'm sure Heathgate will always open his home to family," Astrid said, wishing it were not so.

The only time she'd felt a sense of sanctuary since Herbert's death had been when she'd been wrapped in Andrew Alexander's arms, hearing his gentle scolds, and breathing in the clean, dear scent of him.

Which meant a remove from Town and the temptations thereof was all the more prudent.

❧

"Where's the little widow?" Henry asked after he'd kissed his mother's cheek.

Urania Dupres Allen, of the Dorchester Dupres, stifled a sigh as her younger surviving son appropriated her favorite chair.

"I did not give you leave to sit, Henry, and I do believe your breath smells of spirits." His breath reeked exactly as his father's breath had usually reeked, truth be told.

"Come, Mama, you cannot begrudge me a tot now and then. The Scots prefer to start their day with a wee dram, and they're a hardier race for it."

The Scots were also impoverished, uncouth, and impossible to understand. Urania rang for the tea tray, exacting a small vengeance for the disappointment that was her surviving sons, for Henry—again like his father—despised tea. She took a seat away from the sunlight streaming through the window, a lady's complexion being one of her most important assets.

Particularly a lady of a certain age, particularly a lady with a redhead's fair skin, who used the occasional very light henna treatment on that hair.

"You asked me about Astrid, but why should I have any notion of her whereabouts? I wasn't aware she'd started leaving her house yet." The house that was a deal more comfortable than the pokey establishment Douglas provided for his mother.

Herbert had promised her better quarters as soon as the lease was up. If only dear Herbert had lived...

Henry helped himself to the lemon drops in the candy dish on the side table. "I couldn't imagine Astrid had anywhere to go except to visit you—or perhaps that sister of hers."

Astrid had said something about visiting her sister, but hadn't extended the invitation to include her dear mama-in-law.

Henry's tone suggested visiting either one's sister,

the marchioness, or one's mama-in-law, the dowager viscountess, was a dire fate, though why Astrid's whereabouts were Henry's business, Urania did not know.

"Must you take three lemon drops at once, Henry?"

He grinned. "First you complain about my breath, then you complain about my efforts to freshen it. How would I go on without your weekly scoldings, dear ma'am?"

The rascal was going to ask her for money, or an introduction, or some favor or other. He set aside his Tuesday mornings to spend time with her, but of his other comings and goings, Urania maintained a determined ignorance. Though he hardly seemed to use them, he rented rooms closer to the City, and Urania remained in purposeful ignorance of what went on there, too.

"Without my guidance, you would go straight to perdition," she said. The housekeeper brought in the tea tray, meaning scoldings—and requests for funds—had to wait a few moments. Henry did not rise to take the heavy tray from the older woman, something Douglas, for all his other shortcomings, would have done.

"What do you hear from your brother?" Urania asked as she poured out. She did not give Henry a chance to decline his tea, and skimped on his sugar. Douglas was always prosing on about economies, now, wasn't he?

"I hear a lament, Mama." Henry produced a flask from his vest pocket, doctored his tea without so much as a murmured apology, and put the flask away. "I hear from Douglas that the late viscount's men of business have much to answer for, and that we must be prepared for economies."

Urania had raised her sons to have the manners of gentlemen, though Herbert and Douglas had caught on sooner than Henry seemed to. Henry was her baby, though, and a man was entitled to grieve the loss of his favorite brother in his own way.

"Douglas has a great fondness for sermons regarding economies," Urania allowed. To her own tea, she added as much sugar as she pleased, but no milk, because a lady must be mindful of her figure.

Henry crunched up his lemon drops and drained his teacup at a gulp. "I don't think Astrid has much regard for Douglas's sermons, either. Douglas is nearly certain she dodged him when he came to call on her recently."

Dodged Douglas? Urania admitted a hint of admiration for the girl's ingenuity. "I don't think Douglas approves of dear Astrid. She is something of an original." This was not a compliment. What had Herbert been thinking to marry such a lively young woman? Other viscounts' daughters came with settlements every bit as generous as Astrid's had been.

"Astrid is something of an extravagance," Henry said, popping another lemon drop into his mouth. "Douglas cannot abide extravagances. I don't think he honestly misses Herbert as much as he resents having to deal with all that Herbert's death has thrust upon him—Herbert's widow most of all."

Urania couldn't help herself. Henry was her baby; in his way he doted on his mama, and he never preached about economies. "You would have made a better viscount than poor Douglas. He's simply not… he hasn't the breadth of view you and Herbert shared." A breadth of view that could overlook dressmakers' bills, and knew that a gentleman's turnout had much to do with his reputation in Society.

"Mama, I do love you, though I'm afraid you're not going to be very proud of me."

She'd been proud of Herbert. Sometimes. "More tea?"

"Please." He held out his cup, and Urania filled it to the brim, not bothering with any sugar at all.

"You are short of funds, Henry?"

"Just a trifle. One can't exactly ask Douglas for an advance on one's allowance, can one?"

Yes, one could, if one had backbone. Urania unpinned the brooch she'd chosen that morning from among those given to her by her late husband. She passed it silently to her son, who took it and slipped it into the same pocket where he stowed his flask.

Amethysts had never become her, and they were such small stones, too.

"Mama, what would I do without you?"

"You would have this house to yourself," she said. "Drink your tea."

Henry complied, this time without adding any wicked potation to his tea—likely because his flask was empty. Urania turned the discussion to the informal invitations Henry might accept—marrying for money was an honorable solution to many a respected family's dilemma, and it was a far less irksome path than Douglas's blasted economies.

Henry tolerated about ten minutes of Urania's gentle prodding—a man mourning his brother couldn't accept *formal* invitations, after all—and rose to take his leave. His parting kiss was a truly foul combination of spirits, lemon, and milky tea.

"I won't be in for supper," he said needlessly, because he was seldom in for supper until the weather was horrible. "Thanks much for your company."

He patted his pocket, and the brooch clicked against the flask.

"Henry, some day I will no longer have ugly brooches to pass into your keeping."

This seemed to amuse him. "Is Astrid importuning you for your ugly brooches too?"

Astrid, being in mourning, was barely permitted to wear even ugly brooches. Then the sense of Henry's question sank in.

"She does not deserve your insults, Henry. Astrid's portions were generous, and she'll manage quite well on them, I'm sure."

Urania suffered another noxious parting kiss from her son, and waited until the front door had banged closed after him before she rang for tea cakes to go with her second cup.

Astrid might manage on her portion; she might not. That was for Astrid to take up with Douglas, and if Douglas grew nigh apoplectic when dealing with a lady's inability to keep within a budget, well, that was nothing for Urania to concern herself over. Nothing at all.

❧

The day Astrid had chosen to travel out to Surrey was overcast, but the rains held off, and thus her coach tooled up the Willowdale drive less than two hours after leaving Town.

"Astrid!" Felicity came trotting from the front terrace. "I am so very glad to see you!"

"Felicity, you must not exert yourself in your condition," Astrid chided as the footman handed her out of the coach.

"Save your scolds for somebody who will listen," Felicity countered, hugging Astrid as closely as an increasing belly would allow. "I seem to have too much energy in the mornings these days, and none at all after that. Come. Gareth and Andrew are off working the hounds, so we have time to visit before they join us for luncheon."

"Andrew is here?" Warmth bloomed inside her at the thought. Friends could be glad to spend a little time together, particularly friends who were also family of a sort.

"He arrived last night, and he is staying with us until Lady Heathgate makes her progress up from Sussex. This avoids the awkwardness of having Andrew reside at Enfield with Cousin Gwen, who considers herself responsible for running Enfield."

"And how fares cousin Gwen?" Astrid asked as they gained the house and headed for the library. A statuesque redhead answering to the name Guinevere had attended Felicity's wedding, but Astrid couldn't recall much about the woman except height, a retiring quality, and vivid green eyes that had looked out on the world with both intelligence and caution.

Felicity paused outside the library. "The more time we spend here ruralizing, the better I get to know

Guinevere Hollister, and the more I like her. Still, her situation will present Andrew with a delicate challenge. She doesn't want to live anywhere except Enfield, and he won't leave her there to get by on her own much longer."

"Perhaps Andrew should marry her?" Astrid asked as casually as she could. The idea had no appeal. No appeal whatsoever, though a few years ago, Guinevere had been a handsome woman indeed—a tall, handsome woman.

Felicity led Astrid into the library, a room Astrid hadn't visited since before her wedding. Andrew had goaded her into taking her first few sips of brandy here, and the decanters still stood in a row on the sideboard.

"Most people frown on first cousins marrying," Felicity said, "though it's certainly done. And I would hope for Andrew and Gwen, if they marry, they marry someone they esteem greatly, not somebody who merely holds a property interest in common. Wouldn't you want Andrew to have the kind of marriage you had with Herbert?"

The words came out, though Astrid regretted them even as they rushed past her lips: "Merciful saints, *no*."

Consternation, then pity filled Felicity's eyes. "I am so sorry."

"I'm the one who's sorry. I should not have spoken so honestly." Though here in her sister's house, Astrid could not make herself recite the platitudes one more time:

Herbert was a dear fellow.

Herbert was taken too soon.

Herbert will be greatly missed.

And Astrid would keep the more vexing truths to herself, as well: Herbert had had a mistress he'd spent more time with than he did his wife, and upon whom he'd lavished funds he could ill afford. His mistress was probably tall, red-haired, and pretty too.

"I suspected you were putting a good face on things," Felicity said, pushing the draperies back to let the sun shine through a pair of French doors. "I feared you tolerated Herbert, and I can't figure out why you chose him. You had other offers."

"I did love him, Lissy," Astrid said, sinking down onto a couch. And why did this assertion sound so forlorn? He'd seemed steady at first, not dull. Dependable, rather than boring. Fair, whereas Andrew was dark.

Whatever that had to do with anything.

"Of course you loved him." Felicity joined her with the sort of undignified descent common to ladies on the nest. "You weren't *in love* with him."

Rather than meet her sister's gaze, Astrid instead studied Felicity's hands, and noticed the lack of a wedding ring.

"I was not in love with my husband," Astrid said, her own ring feeling abruptly tight on her finger. "I can't go around admitting that, or I will be consumed with guilt." Or possibly with anger. "I miss the man, I am sorry he died so young, and I am, in some ghastly moments, relieved, all at once—you will forget I said that. But then there is this pregnancy too, and it all gets tangled and uncomfortable. I cannot say I like being a widow any better than I liked most aspects of being a wife."

Felicity had taken the place beside her, which meant Astrid could read her sister's expression only in profile. "Will it be very difficult, putting up with me and Gareth?"

Ah, the blessed comfort of sibling honesty. "Pretending my marriage was more than it was is wearying. In truth, even David sensed my husband was, to use David's words, a crashing bore." In the drawing room and in the... elsewhere. Hadn't Herbert's mistress taught him anything?

Felicity hugged her, a tendency toward affection being another of her sister's symptoms of impending parturition. "I am sorry, for you and Herbert both. You are young, though. We can find you a more dashing fellow next time, right?"

Astrid slipped off her ring and tucked it into a pocket. Yet more honesty was in order. "None of that talk, if you please. I have something few women my age can dream of, Felicity. I have the independence of widowhood, with my whole life ahead of me. I *do not* seek to ally myself with another man in the foreseeable future, if at all."

Felicity began fussing the tea service, a pretty blue jasperware ensemble that included—thank God and the kitchen staff—a sizable array of cakes.

"Then you will allow your life to be guided by Douglas Allen's whims until such time as your child is grown to independence?"

Sometimes, one honest, insightful sister and one honest, insightful brother were more support than a grieving, pregnant widow ought to have to bear.

"My life has become complicated," Astrid said.

"This child becomes more precious to me with each passing day, but the future you describe, one as Douglas's poor relation, holds no appeal whatsoever."

"Then marry a fellow who will stand up to Douglas and protect you and your child," Felicity said. "You will esteem greatly any man who protects you and this baby from Douglas's interference."

That was the uncomplicated, optimistic reasoning of a woman happily married.

"Marriage for the rest of my life is a high price to pay for the simple privilege of raising my own child." And if the child were a boy, he could go off to public school as young as age six. The idea made Astrid positively ill, as ill as the thought of eel pie made her—also livid.

Felicity passed her a plate of cakes even before pouring the tea. "All you need contend with now is enjoying your stay here and letting us love you. You should feel free to discard your blacks, tame the squirrels, spend the day grooming horses or lying about reading Sir Walter Scott. I am thrilled you have come to Willowdale, and I know Gareth is pleased as well."

"He won't be when I've beaten the pants off him at billiards a few times."

"Oh, please," came a masculine voice from the doorway, "if anyone is to lose his pants to you, Astrid, why not me?"

"Andrew!" Astrid rose from the couch and wrapped her arms around him, unable to quell a bolt of delight at the very sight of him. "You rapscallion, lurking in doorways and sneaking up on us. I had no idea you would be staying here when I decided to visit." And this was the best of all, because *had* she known, she'd likely have declined Felicity's invitation. "I shall be ever so willing to beat you at billiards as well, or darts, or cribbage, though you may keep your pants."

"Yes, yes, or backgammon, or piquet, or what have you. I come to renew my acquaintance with my brother's family, and instead I'll get a trouncing on every hand. Perhaps I'll cut my visit short." His tone was teasing, while his eyes were serious.

"You must not."

"Shall I ring for sandwiches?" Felicity interjected. "And, Andrew, what have you done with my spouse?"

"I am here, my lady," Gareth said from behind Andrew's back. He cuffed Andrew aside and came into the room, raising a dark eyebrow at Astrid. "No greeting for me?"

"Gareth." Astrid approached her brother-in-law with the intention of kissing his cheek. She found herself enveloped in a hug instead.

"I am done neglecting you," he growled softly. "I will force you to stay with us until your spirits are restored, or Felicity will take stern measures with me." When Gareth let Astrid go, he bussed Felicity's cheek. "When is luncheon, Wife? Chasing my brother all over the shire has worked up my appetite."

"And when aren't you hungry?" Felicity asked, smiling as Andrew snitched two tea cakes off the tray and passed one to his brother. "We can eat a proper meal within the hour, but first we will let Astrid get settled and unpacked. And both of you fellows could use a bit of freshening as well."

"I can take a hint," Andrew said, snitching another

cake. "I will join you all at table and endeavor to sit upwind of my fragrant elder brother."

Astrid tried not to watch Andrew's retreating backside, though Herbert had never cut such a dash in his breeches, for all he considered himself quite the sportsman.

"I had best go start on my unpacking," Astrid said, knowing the maids would have already hung up her dresses. Gareth's voice stopped her before she made it to the door.

"I meant what I said, about restoring your spirits, Astrid. While you are with us, you must do what pleases you. If we could do your grieving for you, we would. In the alternative, we offer you whatever use of our home and our company you need."

He made this well-intended speech with his arm around what remained of Felicity's waist, forming a two-person marital bulwark of goodwill and good cheer.

"Thank you," Astrid said before fleeing the library. She was in tears within moments of shutting her bedroom door, though she couldn't have said why exactly she was crying. Rather than dwell on that question, she took off her slippers—were they also becoming a trifle snug?—eased down onto the bed, and curled up under a quilt.

Something tickling her nose awakened her. She batted the annoyance away, only to have it return moments later. When she opened her eyes, she found Andrew smiling down at her, a long stem of wild aster in his hands. He brushed her nose with it once more, bringing Astrid fully awake.

"Dratted man…" *Dear, dratted man.* Astrid struggled

to sit up, her efforts impeded by Andrew sitting on her blanket. He lifted his hips enough for her get into a sitting position, then continued to study her.

"So, Astrid, how are you?" He gently bopped her nose with the aster.

"Sleepy." Though Andrew Alexander on her bed was waking her up nicely. "What are you doing in my bedroom?" *And why must you look so delectably handsome even when you're being silly?*

He only smiled at her and bopped himself on the nose with the flower. "The bedroom door is wide open, your highness. Felicity asked me to fetch you down for luncheon. I called from the hallway, but you did not rouse, so I came in here, and was considering how best to wake you, when a toad came hopping along and stole my best idea. He left you this token of his thanks." Andrew waved the flower.

"You are ridiculous."

"And you are smiling, but also dodging my question: How do you feel, princess?"

Astrid scooted around on the bed until she was sitting beside him, hip to hip. She'd purposely put herself at his side so she wouldn't be faced with his direct gaze, lest the kindness she glimpsed there have her weeping again.

"I tell myself I am doing better, Andrew, because I am not moping constantly. But it's like swampy footing. You think you've found a solid patch, and then without warning, you are on your backside and struggling not to go under. I shift instantly from anger to sadness to indifference to relief to... anything you can think of."

He took her hand in both of his and gave her knuckles a kiss.

"You keep looking for those solid patches, princess, but it can't be easy, trying to deal with both the loss of your husband and the changes that come with bearing a child. You were smart to come out here, though."

She gave in to the pleasure of leaning into his solid warmth. Andrew had promised her, long ago, she would be *safe* with him. She still felt safe with him.

Damnably so.

"I am—*was*—an awful wife. I'm angry with Herbert, and not just for dying." She could see now that she'd been angry with her clodpated husband for most of their marriage, though his death had added sadness to her ire.

And Herbert had likely been exasperated with her, too.

"If you are angry with Herbert, you mustn't think anything of it, Astrid." Andrew spoke slowly, the flower cast aside on the coverlet. "God knows I raged at my father and brother for drowning. I still do. But you loved Herbert, though he has left you too soon. You are entitled to be peeved."

Peeved… Astrid liked that word better than the alternatives. Peeved was a playful version of anger, susceptible to humor and cajolery. And she had loved Herbert, though rather like a governess loved an indulged and not-too-bright charge.

"I shall be a peeved princess, then. I am also a peckish princess. Shall we go downstairs?"

He quizzed her on the way as if he were a midwife or Astrid's fussy old auntie: Was she eating, sleeping, getting some fresh air? Did she travel out from Town comfortably? Was there anything she needed? Astrid was relieved to reach the terrace where Gareth and Felicity were already seated at a table.

"Someday," Astrid said as they neared the table, "I am going to ask you about that giving-birth business. You said you'd seen it, once."

"Not a suitable topic for the table, sweetheart, but someday, I will tell you." Sweetheart. Andrew used the endearment so casually, and yet in two years of marriage, Herbert had never referred to her as anything other than "my lady" or, if they weren't in company, "Astrid."

Gareth stood while Andrew held Astrid's chair, and the conversation turned to the state of the approaching harvest at Enfield.

"We'll be taking the boys to play with Rose tomorrow, and that should give Gareth another opportunity to look things over. You are welcome to join us, Andrew, and you too, Astrid," Felicity said as the soup was served.

Andrew picked up his spoon. "I did not know Cousin Gwen was married, much less widowed."

Astrid slathered butter on a roll, but found it odd Andrew wouldn't know his tall, lovely cousin had a child—and a husband.

"Gwen is not widowed, that I know of," Felicity answered in the same even tones. "Astrid, you must leave some butter for the rest of us, particularly this fellow to my right, who is glowering to see someone beat him to the butter."

"Is Gwen married then?" Andrew asked.

"That blessing has apparently not yet befallen her," Felicity replied. "Astrid, you are not touching your soup."

"Sorry, Lissy. Perhaps in a moment." If her stomach would only settle. "It smells lovely." It smelled… fishy, which did not exactly appeal.

"Excuse me," Andrew interjected, "but am I to understand my cousin has given birth to a child out of wedlock, and she has endured this situation alone, without any word to me, to Gareth, or to Mother?"

"You are," Gareth said, pausing in his own diligent efforts with the butter. "Grandfather neglected to inform us, and as an adult, Gwen has always been damnably retiring. When Mother or I would pay a call, the child was simply kept in the nursery. We would still be in ignorance if my man Brenner hadn't inquired of the housekeeper regarding the child's ante-cedents, and received a lot of prevarication in reply. Because Gwen was a dependent of the late baron, and you now control the estate, I did not feel it my place to take the matter in hand, other than to see to it she and the girl were getting on well enough."

Andrew did not look mollified by this recitation, any more than Astrid's belly was mollified when a footman quietly removed her soup bowl. "I gather you also did not feel it your place to quiz Cousin Gwennie regarding the child's paternity?" Andrew asked.

Astrid admonished the two bites of roll she'd downed to remain in their assigned location, and wondered if Cousin Gwen would find Andrew's protectiveness as attractive as Astrid did.

"Gareth did not quiz Gwen," Felicity said, "and

my guess is neither will you. Guinevere Hollister is a formidable lady, and I do not think she will suffer interrogation gladly. I've already tried. Now that you have nearly scraped the glaze from the crockery, Husband, may *I* have the butter?"

"But of course." Gareth smiled at his wife pleasantly, though there was little butter left. Felicity gestured to a footman to bring a fresh pat and to remove the rest of the soup bowls.

The next offering was beefsteak, which dubious delight had Astrid studying the yellow daisies embroidered on the hem of the tablecloth.

Andrew picked up his knife and fork. "Please tell Gwen to expect me the day after tomorrow, weather permitting, and assure her she need not worry for her future or that of the child. What is the youngster like?"

Felicity obligingly launched into a description of the little girl, whose name was Rose.

"You will be pleased to know," Gareth said as he cut into a rare steak, "Enfield seems to prosper. One can make an estate look profitable on paper, while hiding a wealth of problems. Grandfather truly loved his land, though, and it shows. Gwen has stewarded the estate brilliantly since his departure."

They talked of ditches and drains, marling, and sheep pens, as each man demolished his steak, until Astrid shoved away from the table with a muttered, "Excuse me."

She moved off blindly, dashing around the corner of the house, and then she was on her hands and knees, heaving what little she'd eaten into a bed of blue pansies. When she'd lost her feeble attempt at lunch, she was treated to a bout of the dry heaves, which left her with watering eyes, sore ribs, and a burning resentment toward the man who'd brought such a condition upon her.

A white linen napkin dangled before her. "Here."

Rubbishing lovely. She took the napkin and wiped her face. A goblet of water came next, held in an elegant male hand. She held the goblet against her burning cheek as she sank back onto her haunches.

Pansies symbolized thoughts. Astrid's thoughts didn't bear speaking.

"I am feeling much better now, thank you, though I am none too pleased with my sister for allowing you to come after me."

"Up you go," Andrew commanded. He plucked the water from her hand and raised her enough to seat her on a stone bench flanking the flower bed. Then, he hunkered in front of her, surveying her as he brushed her hair back off her forehead.

"Drink something." He handed her the water, rose, and paced off a few feet.

Astrid obeyed, more to rinse the taste from her mouth than because she was thirsty or wanted Andrew getting notions about the effectiveness of the imperative voice. "I truly will feel better in a moment. Or at least it seems to work that way."

Andrew perused her as she sat sipping her water and wishing a hole in the ground would swallow her up. "You've lost more weight in the two weeks since I last admonished you to eat, Astrid, and you were no bigger than my finger to begin with. What exactly made you ill?"

Now he must scold her, because profound mortification was not punishment enough. She spoke slowly and clearly rather than start in ranting. "Bearing a child makes me ill."

"No," he countered patiently. "What food disagreed with you?"

"The butter." And the sight of those rare steaks. "I love butter, and I wanted it so badly. The soup and the rare beef, and the vegetables… It all has no appeal. In my present condition, most cooked food strikes me as slimy."

That had Andrew looking uncomfortable and his hand straying over his flat abdomen. "We have to find out what you can keep down, Astrid. You've lost flesh when you should be gaining it, and you're only, what, a couple of months along?"

"More or less."

"And this indigestion is probably part of the fatigue you're complaining of as well. You need to keep up your strength."

"Yes, your lordship," she snapped back. Since when did bearing a child mean being treated like one?

"Now, now," he chided with a grin. "Just recall all the fun you had conceiving this baby."

Astrid fisted both hands rather than pummel her dearest, densest friend in all the world—meaning no disrespect to her cat. "You are not funny, Andrew. I would like to go to my room."

His smile faded, suggesting he wasn't lost to all instincts for self-preservation. "I will be happy to escort you." He drew her to her feet and tucked her hand in the crook of his elbow, then matched his steps to hers. In an added bit of consideration, he took her into the kitchens by way of the stillroom door rather than the back terrace. "Is there anything you might like to nibble on?" he asked as they passed the pantry.

Astrid wanted to tell him she was never going to nibble on anything again, except she was, in fact, hungry. What appealed most was not food, however, but her big, soft bed, waiting for her in her nice, quiet room.

"My appetite has quite deserted me." Along with her dignity, of course.

"Let me put it differently. Is there anything you might be able to keep down?"

"Bread, and maybe a smidgen of jam. Meadow tea, possibly."

Andrew sat her on a bench in the main kitchen and gathered the items she'd named onto a tray, along with a few peppermints. He took the tray in two hands and winged his elbow at Astrid in invitation. She rose, steadied herself, and let him walk her up to her bedroom, even as she wondered how he'd known— when she had not—that peppermints would appeal most strongly of all.

Four

ANDREW KICKED THE DOOR SHUT BEHIND THEM AND set the tray on top of the bureau. His hands didn't shake, and he hadn't raised his voice even a little, though panic was rioting through his body. Astrid had gone so pale, and the defeat in her eyes…

"Do you want to eat in bed?"

"I would get crumbs all over and have even more trouble resting."

Her room was a pretty, airy space dominated by a big, fluffy bed under a white quilted counterpane. "Why not put the tray by the chaise?"

"That will do."

Her tone suggested anything would do, provided it resulted in Andrew leaving her in peace.

Andrew drew a hassock up to serve as a table beside the chaise near the window. "Your feast, my lady." He swept her a bow. He would dance a damned jig in the altogether if it would put a smile on Astrid's face.

"Thank you, Andrew. Now go away." Astrid glared at him, a true expression of displeasure. "I want to be alone, and I will never recover from the ignominy of being indisposed while you looked on. It wasn't well done of you."

And he would never recover from the sight of her distress, but Felicity and Gareth had just *sat* there, arguing over the butter as if Astrid pelted away from the table regularly.

"Astrid, it's only me, and you'd best let somebody show you some concern when you haven't a spouse or a mama to take you in hand."

"Hah," she retorted, hoisting herself onto the bed. "Do you think for one minute dear Herbert would have stood about while I behaved indelicately, much less 'taken me in hand' as you've done? You have an exalted opinion of the typical young English lord. Now go."

She was about to cry. He should have realized it sooner, because that's what all her writs of ejectment were about. He crossed the room, sat next her on the bed, and hauled her up against his side.

"Not again," she muttered as the first tears trickled down her cheeks. Andrew drew her head to his shoulder and handed her a handkerchief, turning his body so she could rest more easily against him.

"Just cry, sweetheart. You have reason enough." *And please, for the love of God, eat something before you disappear altogether.*

He rubbed her back, he kissed her hair, he prayed, and he silently cursed the departed Herbert for abandoning his wife when she needed him, and *why* had his lordship left her side? To tramp through some chilly grouse moor, half-drunk at the break of day?

"I suppose," Astrid said without lifting her head

from his shoulder, "you will make me eat something now?"

"I will ask you to eat something. I can't make you
do anything, Astrid." Nobody had ever been able to
make her do anything, but somehow, Herbert Allen
had coaxed her into marrying him.

Andrew had purely hated the man for that halfway
to Constantinople and back, even as he'd also been
relieved Astrid was safely spoken for.

Astrid got off the bed and took herself to sit on the
chaise. The bread was fresh, and the preserves were
raspberry, her favorite, if memory served. Andrew
stayed seated on the bed, unwilling to give up his
vigil until she had slowly munched her way through a
slice of jam and bread. When she would have fixed a
second, he spoke up.

"Why don't you pause there and see if it's likely
to stay with you?" he asked, setting the tray on the
night table.

"Good thought." And she looked marginally
restored, which was an even better thought. "Time
for a nap, I think." Her words were underscored by a
yawn, and Andrew took her mug of meadow tea from
her hand.

"Then a nap you shall have," he said, lifting the
quilt off the bed and bringing it to the chaise. He
draped the comforter over her, but folded the bottom
of it back to expose the hem of her skirts.

He was now going to presume significantly, but if
his various amours had been honest, Astrid would thank
him for it. Before she could protest, he removed her
slippers and dragged the hassock to the foot of the chaise.

"You nap," he said as he straddled the hassock, "while I attend your feet." He cradled her right foot in his hands—why were her feet cold on a mild summer day?—his thumbs working in circles over the sole. The first time he'd done this, the lady had asked him for it.

Her gratitude for his attentiveness had been such that, thereafter, he'd known to offer.

Astrid closed her eyes. "Nothing that feels this good can possibly be proper."

"Enjoy it anyway." For in some way, *he* was enjoying it. He enjoyed getting his hands on her in any fashion—he always would—but he also enjoyed that he could comfort her without taking anything for himself.

She drifted into sleep, and yet he lingered, knowing it was improper in the extreme and not giving a bloody damn. When Felicity and Gareth had to have long since remarked his absence, he kissed Astrid's forehead in parting, then—to comfort himself—brushed his mouth over her lips and took his leave.

❧

For the next week, Astrid tolerated ceaseless cosseting from her host's brother.

Andrew urged her to eat small, bland meals when she was neither hungry nor queasy. He read to her under the willow trees by the stream; he kept her company when she visited the stables. He complimented her attire when she ventured into lavender or gray; he challenged her to billiards, darts, and cribbage when she felt more energetic.

And gradually, she lost some of the haunted, bewildered feeling she'd borne since Herbert's death.

A day came along that was the best weather early autumn could offer: dry, sunny, warm, and with a slight breeze. Andrew appeared in the library, looking windblown and happy from a morning hacking out with his brother, a hamper in one hand, and a blanket over his shoulder.

"Time for your constitutional, my lady," he announced. "Who knows when we'll have another such opportunity? Gareth's rheumatism predicts an early, harsh winter."

"Gareth doesn't have rheumatism." Astrid set aside her Radcliffe novel, a labyrinthine Italianate tale of a heroine not worth the name who was carted from stuffy little cottages to prison cells to convents.

"Winter might still be early and harsh," Andrew said.

Yes, it might, and partly in response, Astrid allowed Andrew to stroll her down to the stream bank at the lazy pace suited to the glorious afternoon.

"Here?" He'd picked a spot in dappled sunlight, warm but private, sheltered from the errant breeze and any prying eyes.

"This will suit nicely." Astrid grabbed two corners of the blanket to spread it on the springy grass. She plopped down and began to remove her shoes— Andrew hadn't touched her feet for the past week, and she hadn't stopped thinking of the feel of his hands when he had. "A bit of wading is in order while I can still see my feet."

He followed suit, pulling off his boots and stockings, though the smile he gave her was either patient or long-suffering.

Astrid was soon in the water, her skirts bunched

up in one hand as she teetered about on the smooth limestone streambed. "This water feels so lovely. I wish I could dive out into the middle of the stream and turn into a mermaid."

"And wouldn't that make a nice mess of your pretty frock," Andrew reminded her as he skipped a stone on the tranquil surface. Skipping stones was an attractive, elementally male activity, and yet Astrid couldn't imagine her great sportsman of a late husband managing it.

"I would take my frock off, silly. How does one *do* that?" she asked as the ripples on the water spread from where the stone eventually disappeared. Andrew waded over to her and scrounged on the streambed for a small, round, flat rock.

"You want to find a rock like this." He held it out to her. "Disk-shaped and smooth. You have to sort of flick it, but get your arm into it too, like so."

This attempt bounced six times, which had Astrid peering about for a likely candidate. She, however, did not acquire the knack of "sort of flicking" even after a number of attempts, and was soon glaring at the stream.

Andrew, laughing at her frustration, found another perfect skipper and grabbed her hand.

"Here." He put the rock in her hand and fitted her fingers around it. Then he stood behind her and wrapped an arm around her waist. With his other hand, he cradled the back of her hand and slowly drew her arm back. "You let go when your wrist snaps."

When he whipped her arm forward in a smooth

arc, she released the stone, so it nicked the water three times before sinking in the middle of the stream.

"Oh, yes!" she exclaimed, leaning back against Andrew's chest. She'd been hoping for seven, but three was a nice start. "Find me another!"

But when she would have turned, Andrew did not release the arm he'd tucked against her midriff. He kept her anchored against his body, and Astrid became aware, one sensation at a time, of their position.

The cool water glided gently around her calves with the softest of laps and ripples. The ripe afternoon sunshine fell across the trees, stirred by the merest suggestion of a breeze against her cheek. The scent of a clean, well-washed male teased at her nose.

And the ridge of Andrew's erection nudged against her back.

"This is perfect," she murmured.

Andrew didn't want *her* in any special way. He wanted any willing female, of course, and he liked her well enough, but her senses confirmed what she'd known four years ago: he could desire her.

The twin demons of widowhood and impending motherhood haunted a woman sorely, and thus Andrew's desire was doubly reassuring: he could *still* desire her.

"Perishing hell," he muttered. Then he slogged his way out of the stream, leaving Astrid unbalanced and more than a little puzzled.

She tottered after him up the bank, and sat on the blanket beside him while he tried to pull his stockings on over his wet feet. "What are you doing, Andrew?"

"Getting us the hell back up to the house."

"Why?"

He shot her an exasperated look. "Because I can't *do* this."

"Can't do what?"

"God's holy bones, Astrid." He threw his stocking at his boots. "I can't keep spending so much time with you alone, acting the perfect gentleman, stepping and fetching, and behaving as if *I don't desire you.*"

The ire seemed to go out of him when his last words hung for long moments in the ensuing silence.

"I am making hash of this," he said quietly. "Look, Astrid, we both know you are entitled to more than what I have to offer, and if I were half the man you deserve—"

She stopped him with a hand on his arm. She didn't move otherwise, which left her sitting partly turned away from him. When she spoke, she adopted a quiet, dispassionate tone that she intended to land like so many hammer blows for all its calm.

"I was married for two years to the esteemed Herbert, Viscount Amery, an affable man much admired by his peers for his seat when riding to hounds and his ability to hold strong drink in great quantities. He never held his wife, however, but rather, visited her three Sunday evenings a month. His valet would inquire of her maid if such a thing were appropriate, women's bodies having inconvenient tendencies at times."

She hunched in on herself, lest she give in to the inconvenient temptation to shout, and kept speaking in the same prosaic tones because, by God's holy *ears*, somebody was going to hear this from her.

"When he came to my bed, he would creep into

my room in complete darkness and raise the hem of my nightgown only so far. At least I assume it was he—I never saw his face when he attended to his conjugal duties. He would arrive fully aroused, and insert only the tip of his member into my body, expel his seed with something like a grunt, kiss my forehead, and take himself very considerately off to his room. He never attempted to arouse me, and when, early in the marriage, I tried to encourage a more participative approach to our relations, he had his mother—his *mother*—discreetly explain that passion in a gently bred lady was a vulgar and unappealing trait."

This recitation made her feel smaller, like a seed ready to drift aloft on the autumn breeze, light and insubstantial. Because Andrew hadn't tromped away on his wet, bare, horrified feet, she took a steadying breath and went on. "A proper husband would never be so gauche as to inflict passion on his wife, but would limit such behaviors to the base vessels toward whom it was appropriate. My failure to grasp this fundamental truth could be attributed to the absence of a mother to guide me. My *dear* husband was willing to overlook my unfortunate behavior."

She was shaking, and not with cold. "Amery was being considerate, you see, by keeping a mistress, whom he visited several times a week, and for whom he paid every expense, while my pin money barely covered necessities for our household. He was being considerate by never once touching my breasts, by never kissing my mouth, by never allowing me the pleasure you gave me once long ago."

She was brittle with anger, nigh fracturing with

it, and yet her voice remained calm. Maybe her marriage had taught her something of value after all. Another steadying breath, and she hefted her verbal hammer again.

"With equal consideration, his efforts were apparently adequate to get me with child, which situation curtails most of my options and a good deal of my health as well."

A taut silence stretched when Astrid finished speaking, and she wondered if she'd destroyed the friendship Andrew had extended to her. A husband's loss she was learning to bear, but to lose Andrew…

"That miserable, arrogant, ignorant, inexcusably *inept* little prick," Andrew expostulated, seizing her by the shoulders and pressing her down to the blanket. "At least I won't get you pregnant."

To her immense, profound, *immeasurable* relief, he was all over her, his tongue tracing her lips and thrusting inside with lazy eroticism. He blanketed her with his body, letting the ridge of his erection rest along her belly. His fingers brushed at her face, her hair, her neck, and then his hand wandered up along her ribs, to settle—finally, *finally*—over one ripe, sensitive breast.

Once, at the end of a day years past, when Andrew and Astrid had faced real peril, they'd both found themselves under Gareth's roof. She'd slipped into his room, and he'd obliged her curiosity and need for human connection, petting and stroking her to her first experience of sexual pleasure, though even then, he'd been planning his travel, and she'd known it. They'd never talked about that night, but the memory of it beat in her brain in time with the rising rhythm of her heart.

What if she'd never had that experience with Andrew? What if Herbert's fumbling humiliation was all she'd ever been allowed to know of passion?

"Tell me what you like," Andrew whispered in her ear.

"Everything," she panted as she slipped her hands under his shirt. "Anything, just don't stop touching me, *please*, and clothes off, now."

Andrew lifted up enough to pull his shirt over his head, shucked his breeches in a few jerky maneuvers, then untied the bows of Astrid's bodice and jumps—her breasts were too sensitive for stays—and peeled her garments from her shoulders. She shimmied up and out of her skirt, pulled her chemise over her head, and in a startlingly short time, became, like Andrew, completely unclothed.

"This is decadent," Astrid said, her gaze sweeping the muscled expanse of Andrew's nudity. *He* was decadent, decadently beautiful, right down to the arousal that arrowed up along his flat belly.

Andrew put a fist under her chin and raised her gaze to meet his.

"We can stop, Astrid," he assured her gravely. "We can stop right now, because we both know this is not wise. I am not what you deserve."

She closed her eyes and tried for patience, but the image of Andrew in all his pagan glory would not leave her mind. "You are what I *need*, right now. *Please*."

Before she was reduced to begging—more explicit begging—Andrew again lowered his body over hers, but he changed the tenor of their coupling, his touches becoming tender, lyrical, and cherishing. His fingers brushed along her sex, and he used his mouth to bring marvelous pleasure to her nipples. When his erection probed at her delicately, she wrapped her legs around him and lifted her hips in welcome.

"Andrew," she pleaded, "I need you inside me, for the love of *God*, would you come inside me now." For years she had needed him, and that need threatened to consume her very reason.

He answered her by threading himself into her body and slowly gliding his hips forward, then retreating.

After four years without passion, without pleasure, without emotional intimacy in any identifiable form, Astrid wanted to savor the *relief* of this coupling. Later, she would grapple with guilt, shame, or consternation, but for now she wanted to savor the intimacy of it, the passion, the joy. Her body did not oblige these intentions, for she was coming in great, clutching contractions before Andrew had withdrawn for the third thrust.

He apparently understood, because he drove into her with measured force, prolonging and intensifying her pleasure, drawing out each contraction, and anchoring her as all sense of bodily orientation—up, down, prone, on earth—escaped her. When she lay quietly beneath him, he began moving once more, thrusting more deeply, setting up a rhythm that soon had her arching and groaning in his arms again.

"Let go, love," he urged. "Take all you want, and I'll still have more for you."

She could plunder his patience for *years*, and yet

she came apart again all too soon, and this time Andrew echoed the rhythms of her contractions with answering pressure on her nipple. Pleasure cascaded through her with brilliant, nigh-unbearable intensity, but true to his word, Andrew offered her still more.

She recovered enough to meet his gaze, the tenderness in his eyes registering deep in her body. Where had he been? Where had he needed to go so badly four years ago that they'd denied themselves even one more taste of such pleasure?

She could not ask him. He'd leave her naked and alone on the blanket if she tried.

"I have missed you," Astrid said, a small truth that ought to be safe, for all that missing him filled her heart even as he still filled her body. She brushed her fingers through the silky dark hair falling over his forehead.

He did not echo her sentiment, not in words. He smiled down at her crookedly, and set to kissing her, using his tongue in synchrony with his hips.

"Hold me," he whispered as he again built a rhythm with his thrusting.

She obliged willingly, joyously. Oh, how right it felt to make love with Andrew, how beautiful, and right, and loving. Tension that had built for years unfurled, as Astrid realized that not only would he shower her with pleasure, Andrew would delight in receiving it from her as well.

He moved in her with measured strokes, minutely changing the angle of his hips to effect an ever more gratifying penetration. She bowed up, trying to be closer, feeling pleasure bearing down on her again.

Andrew braced himself on his forearms, but reached both hands to cover hers where they rested beside her head on the blanket.

"Come with me, Astrid. Come with me now."

She recognized all his previous attention as so much generous teasing, because now he was moving in pursuit of mutual pleasure. He drove into her more deeply, kissed her more carnally, and laced his fingers through hers more tenderly, until she was helpless in the throes of gratification so intense she lost the sense of being in a body separate from her lover's.

Andrew groaned softly into her mouth, a sweet sound of intimacy and relief, and Astrid felt a wet heat where their bodies joined.

They lay naked in the sunshine, serenaded by the stream and the breeze for long minutes. When Andrew shifted as if to spare her his weight, Astrid stopped him with a firm hand on his lower back.

"Where are you going?" For she never wanted to let him out of her sight, never wanted this moment of intimacy and pleasure to end.

"Not far." He eased his body from hers, leaving Astrid on her back, feeling again the sunshine on her naked breasts, and a pervasive lassitude of both mind and body. Her eyes flew open, however, when she felt Andrew swabbing gently at her with a damp cloth.

"For goodness' sake, Andrew," she hissed, scrambling up to her elbows and reaching for the cloth. "What do you think you're doing?"

He regarded her curiously for a few heartbeats, a linen serviette in his hand.

"If your husband were not dead," he said quite

seriously, "I would have to kill him for his neglect of you. Lie back and let me care for you."

Confused at his irritable tone, Astrid did as he told her.

"He wasn't a bad man, Andrew, just starchy about certain things." Or thoughtless. Exceedingly, exasperatingly selfish too.

And hypocritical.

Andrew huffed—a disgruntled version of a sigh—and splashed more water onto the cloth. He surprised her by tossing it onto her stomach and lying back with an arm across his brow.

"My turn, sweetheart. You can't lie about all day when your lover needs attention." Astrid sat up and shot him a confused glance. He smiled back at her, looked pointedly at the damp cloth, and then at his own wet, softening member. "Don't tell me you're horrified at the very sight of the goods."

"The goods," she said. "Yes, well…" Horrified, she was not. "The goods," she repeated, running one finger gently over his length. She was horrified to think of two years of marriage wasted on the wrong man. What had she been thinking?

She was fascinated and appallingly grateful Andrew could be this way with her: sensual, frank, relaxed, and arousing as perdition. She indulged her curiosity, slipping his foreskin over his glans, combing her fingers through the down at the base of his shaft, and shaping him in her fingers. To her consternation, her touch was effecting *changes*.

"Andrew?" she asked, holding his growing erection straight up from his body, as if to show it to him.

"Astrid?" he replied from behind closed eyes.

"Whatever are you about?" She gave his erection a wiggle to emphasize her point.

"I am enjoying your touch, sweetheart, and thinking of swiving you again, though I shouldn't, God knows." His tone held regret, almost bitterness, which Astrid registered through a haze of curiosity.

"You mean you can *swive* more than once?" she asked, sleeving his length with the circle of her thumb and forefinger. Had she uttered the word "swive" to her late husband, the poor man would likely have swooned with shock.

"*We* can," he said, looking like some Roman faun on a midsummer's afternoon, "when you arouse me so, but only if you're willing."

"Why on earth would I not be willing?"

"Because what we are doing, Astrid, is wrong," he said with something approaching anger. "It isn't wrong for you to want to be pleasured, appreciated, and cherished; it is wrong for me to be the one to afford you those things, though I have to admit, I've never enjoyed sinning more."

How could he sermonize and incite her to argument like this? When they were naked? When she was touching him?

"I do not sin with you, Andrew. I understand you feel pity for me, or perhaps compassion, nothing more. I am grateful to you, and a woman grown. And"—she let go of him, when what she wanted was to wrap her fingers around him more tightly—"I believe—I have always believed—we are friends. Friends are kind to one another."

"We are friends," he agreed, sitting up and looping

his arms around his drawn-up knees. "But before we go back to that house, Astrid, we need to reach some kind of understanding regarding this... lapse of propriety. You, my dearest goose, refuse to see me for the scoundrel and blackguard I am."

Why must he carp on this? "You are neither, Andrew. You are a kind, honest, if somewhat troubled man."

And you do not want me to love you. *You hardly allow anybody to love you.* The irony, that she'd married a man who'd also been uncomfortable with certain varieties of demonstrative emotion, was not lost on her. Was she doomed to choose only troubled men?

"You," Andrew said, brushing a finger down her nose, "would canonize Beelzebub."

Astrid pushed him onto his back and swung her leg over to straddle him.

"I would marry him, Andrew," she said, glaring down at him, "if he made me feel the way you do."

These were the wrong words to say, though she didn't know why. Such bleakness passed through Andrew's blue eyes that she curled down onto his chest to hide her face.

"I won't be marrying you, Astrid," he said, his hands slipping around her back in slow sweeps down her spine. "If you weren't expecting, I wouldn't risk what we've done so far. You know this?"

"I do now, you awful man." Though in fact, she appreciated he was gentleman enough to spare her the fate that had befallen Cousin Gwen. "And I most assuredly do not want to be marrying again myself, thank you very much."

She would have to get into the habit of lying to him, because he physically relaxed at that pronouncement and let his hands trail down to knead her buttocks. Were she not wrapped in his arms, she'd likely find that worth crying over.

Instead, she kissed his chest. "I see now why wicked men are in such demand. You know things."

Andrew's hand on her backside paused. "It isn't wickedness to pay attention to what pleasures a lady. It's consideration and a bit of patience. These are courtesies your husband, more than anyone else, should have shown you. On his late and benighted behalf, I apologize, Astrid."

He meant the apology, she thought in amazement. The idea that Herbert could not have even comprehended what Andrew was apologizing for showed Astrid in glaring relief what a mistake her marriage had been—as if she hadn't suspected she was in trouble before the wedding night was over.

"And I should apologize to Herbert's memory for not being the wife he hoped he was marrying," she said, realizing—*admitting*—Herbert had probably sensed their mutual mistake too.

"On his late behalf, I accept your apology. Now, my *friend*, where do you see matters going from here? What are your terms, Astrid?"

The exchange, simple and odd as it was, settled something in Astrid that had needed settling. She and Herbert had meant well by each other when they'd agreed to marry, and maybe, in time, they would have been a better match. It helped, though, to realize they hadn't intended to disappoint each other.

"Terms of what?" she asked, nuzzling Andrew's ear.

He heaved a sigh that had her rising and falling on his chest like flotsam in the surf.

"Astrid, please do not fence with me. I ought not to be here with you at all, and yet, as usual, my better judgment is overtaken by lust. The decision to be made is what to do about that now."

He did not sound disgruntled, he sounded martyred, and yet his hands were the embodiment of heaven on her naked flesh.

"I would not see you unhappy, Andrew. We can consider this afternoon a stolen pleasure, a moment out of time between friends, something not to be repeated."

"Is that what you want?" he asked, toying with a lock of her hair.

He *was* brave. "No. I do not want one stolen moment. I want time with you, however much you are willing to give me. Perhaps you are a distraction from my grief and my worries. Perhaps you are reassurance after a marriage that hadn't much promise when Herbert died. Possibly you are the best friend I will ever have or something in between all the foregoing. I know I do not want only one stolen moment with you."

This virtuosic display of understatement had the intended effect of banishing more of the tension from Andrew's body.

"I suppose we shall have a small affair then." He reached his conclusion with his lips pressed to her temple. "For the duration of my enforced visit here, you may expect me to importune you for your favors, to bother you constantly with my base appetites, to jump out at you from odd corners, intent on seduction. And then we will consider our stolen moment to have run its course. Will that suit?"

They might have been discussing whether to share the polonaise or the minuet. She wanted to smack him, also to remain with him on the blanket until the sun had burned her bum pink.

The duration of his enforced visit… a few days, maybe a few weeks.

No time at all, and yet Astrid had already shared more with Andrew than she'd ever thought to have with him. On a bolt of sad insight she realized she would pack more pure, genuine loving into two weeks with Andrew than she had into two years with her lawfully wedded husband.

So she answered him with a kiss, followed by a lazy exploration of his nipple with her tongue. When they rolled up the blanket nearly an hour later, Andrew, frowning at her derriere, did indeed remark that she would suffer the effects of the sun in some unlikely places.

Five

HEATHGATE ARRANGED A STACK OF PAPERS ON THE desk blotter, likely reports from the estimable Mr. Brenner. "The Amery viscountcy isn't rolled up, exactly, but suffering an unlucky stretch. Herbert made bad investments and incurred a number of gambling losses in addition to a young lord's usual expenses. I don't envy his brother."

Andrew shoved away from the mantel he'd been propped against. "Where does this leave Astrid? I personally care not one whit what befalls the Allen family, except insofar as their circumstances affect Astrid."

The marquess and David Worthington, Viscount Fairly, who was affecting a slouch against the French doors, exchanged a look. Rather than curse the pair of them, Andrew picked up three wax seals sitting on Heathgate's desk and began juggling.

"We're working on that," Fairly said. "But what aren't you telling us, Andrew?"

There was much he wasn't telling them, much he never would. Two of the seals were silver, one gold, and the differences in weight made juggling more of a challenge.

"I've listened in low places and asked a few questions, so I know the late viscount had plenty of money to drop at Tattersall's," Andrew said, "and plenty of money to spend maintaining a mistress—though thank God the woman had modest tastes—and plenty of money to indulge the dowager viscountess in fine style."

While Astrid sat home, making do with her pin money and pretending her husband was considerate of her. Andrew caught the seals, one, two, three, and set them back on the desk in a tidy row.

"You are not entirely correct," Fairly said. "Henry, the youngest brother, came down from university only a couple of years ago and is reading law in a barrister's office. He is thus understandably dependent, but Douglas has his own investments, owns his own pleasantly situated home, and pays many of the Dowager Viscountess Amery's bills. At present, Douglas also pays the staff at Astrid's house. I gather, however, he is stretched thin, and making no headway on the family debts."

Andrew liked Fairly, mostly because the man seemed comfortable with his status as tolerated outsider to Polite Society. Despite acquiring his father's title six years after that man's death, Fairly disdained fashionable entertainments, took the management of his commercial interests most seriously, and apologized to no one for owning a brothel.

To go along with patrician features, lean height, and acceptably Saxon gold hair, he also had one blue and one green eye, which tended to unnerve the unsuspecting.

Then too, Fairly was fiercely protective of his sisters.

Gareth came around his desk to lean a hip on it and folded his arms across his chest. "Part of me wants to confront Douglas and ask him where Astrid's money is, and to please hand it over to any of the three of us. Another part of me knows if Fairly here attempted to act that way with me regarding Felicity's settlement, I would be permanently offended."

"So what do we do?" Andrew asked, because what he wanted to do would likely see him brought up before the assizes. Instead, he wandered to the sideboard and considered pouring himself a drink. "If Astrid's funds have been mishandled, Douglas ought not to have the chance to mishandle what little may remain."

"I agree with you," Fairly said, "but we don't know the funds are gone, and if they are, it was Herbert's doing, not Douglas's. We might consider giving the man a chance to redeem himself before pouncing on him."

"We might," Gareth allowed.

"We ought," Andrew agreed, hating, loathing, and resenting the dictates of gentlemanly behavior. He appropriated three glass stoppers—a Cerberus, a chimera, and a griffin—and tossed them aloft. "The issue is not how Astrid will fare financially, because any one of us would see her well set up. The issue is whether she can trust her in-laws, who will have the raising of her child."

"We're back to that," Fairly muttered.

"Invite Douglas out here," Andrew suggested, juggling more quickly, because glass in motion caught the light wonderfully.

"I like it," Fairly said. "Machiavellian, and bold.

Probably scare the poor bastard witless if we charge him en masse. I like it better the longer I consider it."

"How will Astrid feel about this?" Gareth asked.

"She does not exactly despise Douglas," Andrew said, nearly missing the Cerberus because three heads made an awkward shape. "She says he takes a while to warm up to. If she understood what we were trying to accomplish, she might support the idea. She does not talk with any enthusiasm about returning to Town, and this will give Douglas an opportunity to assure himself she is well cared for."

"I nominate you," Fairly said, his eyes alight, "to convince her on this idea."

"Second," Gareth added. "When shall Douglas honor us with his presence?"

"Have him out for the weekend," Andrew said, catching the damned dog, then the gryphon. "That will give Astrid time to adjust to the idea, and us time to strategize and gather more facts. As to that, I would invite the Allen family—you have the room here, and there's no telling what the ladies might be able to winkle out of Lady Amery."

He missed the dragon, but fortunately, the thing landed safely on Heathgate's ruby-red Axminster carpet.

Fairly regarded the fallen dragon. "Haven't you a cousin in the vicinity as well?"

"Cousin Gwen," Andrew said, replacing all three stoppers in their respective decanters, and heading for the door. "She is an utter antidote, despite the most glorious red hair. Not to invite her would be rude, though, and I am overdue to pay a call on her. Gentlemen, I bid you good day."

Andrew let himself out the French doors into a pretty autumn day, his departure a graceless and self-serving escape. Gareth, as head of the Alexander family, and Fairly, as head of the Worthington family, could credibly discuss Astrid's best interests and take action on her behalf.

Andrew was merely the cad who'd been busily seducing her for the past week, and who would be enjoying the fruits of that seduction for at least a week to come.

❧

"You wrote to me eight times in four years," Gwen said, using her best Mama is Wroth tone. "At Yuletide and on the King's birthday, and never let me know where to post a reply. How was I to tell you how matters went on with me?"

A tall woman became used to men regarding her with some puzzlement. She did not, however, become used to men taller than she regarding her with loving exasperation.

"Order up the tea tray, Gwennie," Andrew said, "and we can squabble at each other like civilized cousins."

Gwennie. Nobody had ever called her Gwennie except Andrew, and now Andrew owned the property where she'd made a home for herself and Rose. Gwen yanked the bellpull twice, then added a third yank to ensure food would accompany the tea tray.

Andrew had been slender as a boy; he was slender still. Too slender, if he intended to take over management of his estates.

"I suppose you're waiting for me to give you permission to sit?" she asked.

"I'm waiting for you to recall that I'm your cousin, I love you, and your happiness is now my concern." He leavened this scolding with a smile of significant charm.

Gwen had no patience with charm. She did, however, have many fond memories of her cousins, and of this cousin in particular. Andrew was closer to her in age than Gareth, and more tenderhearted than his older brother—at least to appearances.

"Please do sit," she said. "One's neck aches glaring up at you. How are Heathgate and his lady?"

"Thriving." Andrew folded himself onto a sofa their mutual grandfather had favored. The green brocade upholstering was wearing thin, though when Andrew crossed one booted ankle over his knee, he even looked a bit like Grandpapa. "If you expect me to endure small talk for half the day, Gwennie, it won't wash. I intend to make the acquaintance of your daughter."

And this was why Gwen had no patience with charming men, because their pretty manners and mischievous smiles usually hid some form of male resolve that did not fit with Gwen's plans at all.

"Rose allowed me to brush her hair at length this morning in anticipation of that very objective." Though the child had hardly been able to hold still, so great had her anticipation been at the prospect of meeting another "big cousin."

"If she's anything like her mother, she managed to look a fright within fifteen minutes," Andrew said. "Gareth says you run this place like a field marshal, riding your acres, meeting with your farmers, and generally saving one and all the cost of a land steward and a house steward."

More charm, to compliment her rather than lecture her. Gwen could not help a blush, but she could stall by admitting a footman with a large tray. "Enfield is a wonderful property." She gestured for the footman to set the tray down. "Will you reside here soon?"

Andrew rose and went on a tour of the parlor. "You've kept this room as Grandfather had it, except for a few touches. I like the touches." He took down a sketch in a simple oak frame—Rose and a tabby cat. "Does she have your red hair?"

She had her father's sable hair, dramatic brows, and… charm. "More like yours and Gareth's. Dark. Tea or coffee?"

He did not hang the sketch back up, but rather brought it with him to the sofa. "You drink coffee?"

"I drink both, depending on my whim." Because she was the lady of the house, and her whims controlled the domicile, *for now*.

"If it's good and strong, I prefer tea," Andrew said. "The child has your determined chin and your unapologetic nose."

Gwen fixed her cousin his tea, two sugars, a dash of cream, and let the comment pass. She'd been called much worse than determined and unapologetic, and Andrew was being observant rather than mean.

"I hear Felicity's sister is biding at Willowdale for a time." And because Astrid Allen was arguably family, Gwen really ought to have made a condolence call, though that would mean deciding whether to bring Rose.

"Astrid needs sunshine and fresh air like I need the occasional mad gallop and you need to balance your account books," Andrew said, accepting his cup of tea. "I'm curious about what else you might need, Gwennie. I'll not turn you out, you know, not banish you to some cottage on the moors, there to read your Bible and tat lace."

She knew how to tat lace, though her patience with Scripture was limited. Gwen also knew that some banishments did not require isolated cottages or visible signs of penance.

"You know Lady Amery well?"

"She's easy to get to know," Andrew said, finishing his tea at a swallow and passing his cup back to Gwen. "At first glance, you take her for a pretty little thing, and then you realize that pretty little thing is a small female tiger, with a fierce intellect, a quick wit, a keen eye, and a big heart."

Gwen poured him another cup of tea, not that he was tasting what he consumed. One of the advantages—one of the many advantages—of a marginalized existence was that others did not raise their defenses around Gwen the way they might with their peers and accepted social equals.

"How is Lady Amery managing? Her husband hasn't been gone that long, and his death had to have been unexpected." And a woman could miss a man she'd known only a season, much less one she'd been married to for two years.

"She has as much determination as you do, Guinevere Hollister. I've no doubt Astrid will come right soon. She needs only time and care, and in her sister's household, she can have both."

From the look in Andrew's eyes as he resumed

studying Rose's sketch, Gwen concluded the pretty little thing with the fierce intellect and the big heart could have more than that. Very likely, she could have anything it was in Andrew's power to give her.

"Fresh air, sunshine, and good company can set much to rights," Gwen said. They certainly had set her to rights. "Why were you gone so long, Andrew?"

Before he'd left, he'd told her the nightmares had gotten worse, but she didn't dare bring that up now.

"The world is a big, wonderful place, Gwennie, and I wanted to see it. Perhaps you'd like to see some of it, too?"

"You'd send me abroad? Have you ever traveled with a small child, Andrew? And you do recall there are hostilities on the Continent?" Because she couldn't be sure he was jesting, Gwen kept her tone more cool than teasing.

He propped Rose's sketch against a pillow on the end of the sofa, as if Rose were present in the room by virtue of her sketch resting on the cushions. "I once had the pleasure of traveling with a pair of newborns. They seemed quite portable to me."

"Then you traveled upwind of them, and slept where you couldn't hear them rousing the watch several times a night. If you're not going to eat, let's away to the nursery. Rose has had at least fifteen minutes to get her hair in complete disarray, smear jam on her pinny, and draw you pictures of every horse on the property."

For that's what Gwen had done long ago when waiting for a visit from her cousins.

Andrew escorted her through her own house, and though he did indeed charm Rose, he also glanced at the clock often enough that Gwen knew he wasn't going to tarry long marveling at Rose's drawings of unicorns and dragons.

For the fierce, pretty Lady Amery waited at Willowdale, there to be comforted in her grief. Gwen did not envy the lady her swain's devotion. That Andrew would ride off without a backward, assessing glance at the property that had claimed Gwen's heart and soul was too great a relief.

❦

"Pardon my dust," Andrew said, gesturing to the bench. "May I join you?"

Astrid scooted over and whisked her skirts aside, the gesture coming off as either indignant or insecure, she wasn't sure which.

"I didn't know you embroidered," Andrew said, stretching out long legs and crossing his booted feet at the ankles. He smelled of horse, pleasantly so, which was fortunate when a lady's digestion was given to queer starts.

"Every lady embroiders." Astrid's hoop sported a scene of rabbits peeking out from beds of pansies, which was fitting, given present company. Andrew had been least in sight for much of the day.

"You weren't so shy with me last night, dear heart, or yesterday afternoon," he pointed out, casually resting his arm along the back of the bench.

Their good-night kiss in the library had become positively incendiary, and yet, since breakfast, Andrew had been distant. Polite, smiling, charming, and in some regard, not at home to callers.

"How was Cousin Gwen?" Felicity had kindly let slip that Andrew had ridden off to call at Enfield.

"Difficult," Andrew said, tipping his face up to the sun. "She disdains the frivolous company of others, says she has farms to manage, livestock to see to. I have a fondness for difficult women, though. I will yet earn her trust."

Perhaps he was flirting; perhaps he was scolding. Two years of marriage to Herbert did not prepare a lady to distinguish between the two.

"And how is little Rose?"

"Rose thinks her big cousins are capital fellows. Clearly, I've made a conquest."

Astrid jabbed her needle into the vicinity of a rabbit's tail. "Very young women are so easily impressed."

"I rather think my horse made more of an impression on wee Rose than I did." Andrew smoothed a finger over the rabbit's abused fundament, and Astrid felt something like a shiver, though she sat in strong sunlight. "Did you sleep well?"

"Well enough." Considering she'd gotten up several times in the night to heed nature's call. "And yourself?"

"I tossed and turned all night in anticipation of further intimacies with you," he said, giving her the impression this was nothing less than the truth—a miserable truth, too.

The same rabbit got the brunt of Astrid's bewilderment. "So why didn't you come to my room?" She probably wasn't supposed to ask that, but she and Andrew had moved past *supposed to* and *should* rather decisively.

"I wasn't sure you'd appreciate it, to be honest. You need your rest, Astrid, and I was demanding of you yesterday."

She pondered that for a moment, smoothing her finger over the bunny fundament she'd just abused. "I think, Andrew, I would sleep better in your arms."

He sat beside her, close but not touching, a quiet sigh confirming that again she'd expressed sentiments one wasn't to express, even in the midst of a dalliance. "You trust me too much, Astrid. When you confide such things, you make me want to vault off this bench and sprint into the next shire."

He stayed exactly where he was, though, while Astrid reflected on how beautiful his eyelashes were. Debutantes longed for lashes like that, abundant, sensual, the perfect counterpoint to aristocratic features and glacial blue eyes.

"What else?" she asked, because he had stayed right beside her.

"You make me want to hold you and never let you go."

He spoke quietly, not a scintilla of flirtation in his sentiments. Her lover was matching her for foolishness, also for bravery and sincerity.

She ran her thumb over the bunny's satiny ears. "Is that all?"

Andrew's smile was slow and devastatingly sweet. "You make me want to swive you mindless, out here in the sunshine, up in your big, soft bed, in the hayloft, in the butler's pantry, and everywhere in between."

They had one week. Astrid set aside her pansies and rabbits and stood, taking a moment to make sure she had her balance. "It's a pleasant day. We should have some privacy in the haymow, though the butler's pantry strikes me as cozy, and the foot of the garden has some wonderful hedges of honeysuckle."

Andrew spared a glance at the discarded embroidery hoop, then rose and winged his arm at her. "Hay can be itchy, and the butler's pantry is dark. I have ever been partial to the scent of honeysuckle."

❧

"You look like hell." Gareth led a big bay gelding from a loose box as he offered his brother that cheerful greeting. "Shall I have the lads saddle up a horse for you, or can you manage on your own?"

Andrew raised one sardonic eyebrow, and grabbed a halter and lead shank off a hook near the door. He sauntered out to the individual paddocks behind the stables, his step looking to Gareth off somehow—tired, stiff, or more burdened than a young man's should be on a pleasant early autumn afternoon. Andrew came back leading a big, rawboned black gelding with a nervous eye.

"In the mood for a challenge?" Gareth asked. "I don't think anybody's been on Magic since I had him out last week. He looks full of himself, as usual."

"We'll manage," Andrew replied as he secured the horse in cross ties. He took his time, stroking his hands over the horse's neck and flanks, picking up each hoof, talking softly the whole time. "You wrote to me about this horse," Andrew reminded Gareth as he began to brush Magic's coat. "I've been curious to meet him. He's certainly handsome, for all his size."

"I bought him in part because I like his size," Gareth answered. At six feet and a few inches each, both brothers typically favored larger mounts with good bone and wind.

"But," Andrew replied, speaking to the gelding, "you are too much horse entirely when you take it into that handsome head to be naughty. We must encourage you to behave at all times as the gentleman you are." The horse flicked his big, daintily pointed ears as if he were listening.

Gareth caught the last comment as well, and wanted to broach the topic of gentlemanly behavior with his brother in the worst way. He held back, lest his brother announce a burning desire to see Cathay *and* darkest Peru.

As the horses were saddled, then bridled, Andrew continued his soothing commentary to Magic. The groom who had been mucking stalls rolled his eyes at Gareth as this homily went on, but Magic seemed to listen, the anxiety in his eyes all but disappearing by the time Andrew was on his back.

"Damned if he don't like Master Andrew," the groom commented, shaking his head.

Gareth swung up onto his own mount, a steady fellow by the name of Orion. "They all like Master Andrew, wretched beasts."

"Magic," Andrew replied calmly, "is a fellow of great discernment and sensitivity, aren't you, boy?" He gave the horse's shoulder a resounding thwack of approval, which had Magic dancing sideways and capering around the yard. "He is also," Andrew added as the horse started trying to buck in earnest, "a young man in need of a good romp." With that, he touched his spurs to the horse's sides, and Magic shot off down the drive at a thunderous gallop.

When Andrew eventually slowed Magic to the walk, the horse's coat was lathered, but his neck was relaxed, and the bucks were long forgotten.

"The trouble with that fellow," Gareth remarked, "is you think because you ran and jumped the mischief out of him today, he might be more willing to listen to reason tomorrow, but he won't be. I rode him fourteen days straight during wicked summer heat, and he came out full of the devil every time. I never found the end of his fight."

Andrew patted the horse again, this time gaining much less reaction. "It isn't fight, Gareth, it's heart that needs a little more courage. Magic needs somebody to trust."

Magic, indeed. "You want him, he's yours. Consider him a homecoming gift."

When Gareth expected an argument, Andrew saluted with his whip. "My thanks, and his."

And now, a change in topic was required, lest Gareth bring up a certain kiss he'd walked in on in the library late the previous evening. "How did you fare with Gwen?"

Andrew let the reins go slack while the horse appeared to consider the terrors lurking behind a hedge of honeysuckle. "She will not be joining our little gathering this weekend, if that's what you're asking, and she has neither love nor trust for the cousin who has come to toss her and her child out into the streets."

"She's prickly."

Magic snorted, planted all four feet, and raised and lowered his head while Andrew sat relaxed and serene in the saddle. "She's scared. She's done an excellent job with Enfield, though everyone is careful to suggest it's due to the tenants, the dairymaids, or even the damned bullocks. I suspect she was running the place long before Grandpapa died, and he was only too happy to let her."

"I can believe that."

Andrew's horse walked on calmly enough—for now. "And yet, whenever I mentioned having Gwen leave the place, even for a visit, she pokered up like a bishop in a bordello. After I'd paid my respects in the nursery, I asked her if Rose's father even knows of the child's existence, and Gwen about skewered me with her rage and contempt. Something there needs to be dealt with."

"You're a braver man than I." Or more foolhardy. "Even Felicity wasn't willing to raise that question. Do you suspect rape?"

Magic spooked at nothing Gareth could see, a nimble dodge to the side. Andrew didn't so much as pick up the reins.

"I suspect rape or ill usage or something very like it," Andrew replied, urging the beast to resume a placid walk. "Watch how she reacts when you are near, or likely to touch her in even simple ways. To see her expressions, you'd think I had nefarious designs on her person when all I do is bow over her hand."

"I can't say I like the thought of her rusticating the rest of her life away out here either," Gareth said. "But she is of age, and used to a great deal of independence."

Andrew flipped a hank of black mane from the left side of Magic's neck to the right. "But what of Rose? Is she to grow to womanhood without leaving the estate, to have no knowledge of life beyond this bucolic backwater? Rose is related to a marquess and an earl, for God's sake. We can do better for her than some simian farm boy with sweaty palms and a greasy forelock."

Felicity would counsel her spouse to restraint, but Gareth had gone for too long without a younger brother to tease.

"Such avuncular sentiments, Andrew."

Now the beast must attempt to snatch at a mouthful of leaves, an insurrection Andrew gently thwarted. "We are her family," Andrew replied. "She is a little girl, without a man's protection, and her mother is not thinking entirely clearly. Her welfare is our concern."

"So what should *we* do about it?" Gareth asked, because his brother was making too valid a point to indulge in further needling.

"I am approaching Gwen as I do a skittish horse. I am giving her a chance to see I mean her no harm, to consider how she might trust me, and to decide what use I might be to her. The lad who brings the oats can catch even the crankiest mare in the paddock."

"Granted," Gareth said, though any happily married man knew equine analogies where women were concerned were a dicey proposition. "But, Andrew, what will you do with Gwen when you've caught her?"

"I have asked Gwen to consider that," he said as they turned up the drive. "She and I are intelligent people, and we will find a solution acceptable to everybody."

"You could marry her," Gareth pointed out, because Felicity had pointed it out to him on two separate occasions. "She'd be happy with a marriage of convenience, and you could come and go as you please on the estate."

"I will not marry," Andrew said, his gaze fixed on the hills in the distance.

"Oh, for pity's sake, Andrew. Are you still clinging to the puerile notion you can't be faithful to one woman? The right woman wouldn't care, you've got titles to consider now, and sooner or later, all that hopping from bed to bed gets old anyway."

Andrew stopped fiddling with the horse's mane and took up the reins.

"I find it extraordinary, Brother, you do not use the one argument that might persuade me to consider holy matrimony: I might, against all effort and sense to the contrary, fall in love and have the great good fortune to have my sentiments returned. I surmise it was just this happy fate that impelled you to the altar at a nigh-doddering age, giving up your own *puerile notions* regarding your entrenched unsuitability as a husband. Your faith in me is truly touching."

Andrew delivered this speech in carefully amused tones, but when he finished speaking, he signaled his horse through some subtly of the seat, and rode the rest of the way up the drive in an elegant, flowing canter.

Gareth let him go, because in the course of his set down, Andrew Penwarren Alexander, swashbuckling lover across several continents, had admitted the possibility he could fall in love.

Felicity was right: there was hope for the man after all.

⌘

Astrid heard the bedroom door open and close, then lock with a soft click. A boot hit the floor, then another, followed by the rustling of cloth and a weight jostling the mattress. When Andrew spooned his warm, naked chest against her back, she reached behind her and drew his arm around her waist.

Such comfort, simply to cuddle under the covers in the middle of the afternoon. She hoped it was a comfort to him too.

They'd gone for a ride that morning to feed some ducks, Andrew putting Astrid up on a mare who looked large enough to house the entire Greek army. The outing had been lovely, and the tenderness in Andrew's eyes when he'd asked at what hour she napped even lovelier.

"Sleep," he murmured, lacing his fingers through hers, and she drifted under on a sea of contentment. The clock told her she awoke half an hour later, feeling sweet, sleepy, and warm—and in need of the chamber pot.

"Nature calls," she grumbled. Andrew held up the covers for her and kept his back to the privacy screen. She returned to the bed, resuming her place tucked against him, and wondered if she'd ever find another man with whom she could be so casually intimate.

"Your lunch is sitting well enough?" Andrew asked, notching his chin on her shoulder.

"Apparently so. If every day were as manageable as this one, pregnancy would be no burden. Feeling this good, I hardly know I am pregnant."

"I know you're pregnant."

He sounded smug, the varlet. "How would you know?"

"Your breasts have become magnificently full and probably more sensitive. Don't tell me your bodices aren't fitting more snugly, and perhaps your slippers as well." He caressed her breasts, lightly, gently—maddeningly.

"They are—bodices and slippers." And he knew exactly how to touch her *magnificent* breasts, too. "Have you made a study of this?"

"Rather the opposite, though I can tell your womb has started to increase," he said, slipping a hand down to palm her lower abdomen. "You are petite, so you will likely begin to show quite obviously in the next few weeks."

"I thought my stomach was still flat," she retorted, a bit miffed, though in truth she was not in the habit of examining her person in any detail—another gift from her oh-so-considerate late husband.

"Here," Andrew said, rolling her onto her back. "Feel here." He took her hand and splayed it under his over her pelvic cradle. "As trim as you are, this probably used to be concave, a little dish. Now you can feel it changing." He pressed down lightly, and Astrid could sense the difference he described. "Your babe is growing, Astrid," he said, a soft smile on his face.

The intimacy of that smile, of their posture, of what they discussed… Astrid closed her eyes to ensure she'd captured yet another memory to torment herself with. "When will the child quicken?" she asked, leaving her hand under his.

"You are about three months along?"

"Soon."

"Probably another month or so, but I am sure these things vary. When you were last carrying, did you ever feel movement?" He inched his hand down in small, gentle circles.

"I did not," Astrid said, loneliness pooling where their hands had been joined on her belly. And she hadn't known the absence of movement was unusual.

"I am so sorry, sweetheart," Andrew said, kissing her temple. "I said many prayers for you when I got Gareth's letter. And just because I'm aroused"—he trapped her hand on its journey south—"doesn't mean you have to accommodate me."

Herbert had never once said anything to her about the miscarriage, except, "These things happen," as if he were *forgiving* her for losing the child.

She laced her fingers with Andrew's. "I don't want to *accommodate* you." She was very sure of that. "I want to make love with you."

He settled his lips over hers, taking a teasing, tender approach to her arousal. When she was kissing him back, her hands skating along the muscles of his back, her thigh thrown across his hips, he shifted over her. She welcomed him into her body, and endured such an upwelling of tenderness and *grief* she thought she might cry.

She was going to lose him. She was going to lose him *too*, and the loss would haunt her for the rest of her life.

The pain of it wound into other griefs, and into the beauty of joining her body to his, of cherishing him with sexual intimacies she'd shared with no other, and Astrid felt pleasure bearing down on her.

"Love me, sweet," Andrew whispered. "Hold me tight and love me."

She heard the words, her hips rolling in counterpoint to his, her back arched to keep her close to him. The damned man held his own pleasure back, and waited, letting her arousal build further, giving her the solid thrusts that would allow her to join him in a mutual release.

She did not know how to hold back, not with him, not when it might be their last time. "Andrew—"

"I'm here." With languid grace, he moved into her more deeply, forcing her pleasure to such length and breadth she keened and moaned and shook with it.

When her breathing had slowed, when she could put it off no longer, Astrid opened her eyes to find Andrew looking down at her, an expression of such wonder in his eyes she could not look away.

"Andrew," she said, tears gathering, "how will I ever go on?"

She didn't elaborate—she didn't have to elaborate—but buried her face against his shoulder and bowed her body up into his. He settled a little of his weight on her, even as she felt him slipping from her body. He offered no words to comfort her, no glib answers to her question or her inconvenient emotion.

He tasted her tears with his tongue, then kissed her closed eyes and tucked her face against his shoulder until she quieted.

"Astrid, I would not cause you tears," he said, rolling to his back. "I want to bring you pleasure, dear heart, not heartache."

"I am simply emotional," she said, resting her cheek on his chest. "You need not depart again for the Continent merely to escape my tears, Andrew. I will cope."

He need not escape to the Continent *again*. That thought was too sad even for tears.

"Let me hold you." His request—despite grammar to the contrary—was silly, when his arm was already around her and her knee across his thighs. But he scooted up, to rest his back against the headboard, and bent his knees so his feet were flat on the mattress. He hauled Astrid into his arms and tucked covers around her and himself both.

She curled up in the shelter of his body and took what consolation he offered in the simple—and temporary—animal comfort of his embrace.

Six

AFTER STEALING AWAY FROM ASTRID'S ROOM, ANDREW spent the balance of his afternoon working with Magic, patiently starting the process of gaining the horse's trust.

"You're not wasting any time with him," Gareth observed when he wandered into the stables as shadows lengthened and the air grew brisk.

"He doesn't have time to waste," Andrew said as he drew a soft brush over Magic's neck. "Every day he has to shift for himself in a world where he doesn't feel safe, he becomes more convinced it's the only option he'll ever have. But he's a good fellow," Andrew concluded, thumping the horse on the shoulder. "Aren't you?"

Magic gave Andrew a disconcerted look and raised his head anxiously, but he stood his ground when he could have broken from the cross ties in an instant.

"Say, yes, Andrew, I'm a good boy," Gareth told the horse. Magic flicked an ear but kept his focus on Andrew. "And what about you, Andrew? Are you convinced shifting for yourself is the only option you'll ever have?"

Older brothers never stopped being older brothers. This was as much irritant as comfort. "I beg your pardon?"

Gareth settled himself on a trunk, much like the stable cat might settle itself outside a promising mouse hole. "At breakfast today, Astrid suggested you had always wanted to travel, but you were prevented from doing so because you were too busy keeping an eye on your errant older brother."

So they were going to air this old linen? Andrew would have to discipline himself to come down to breakfast and ensure Astrid's opinions were limited to the weather. "Is there a specific question on the floor?" Andrew asked, shifting to brush the other side of the horse.

The brush box was at Gareth's feet. He rummaged around until he found a hoof pick, and used it to scrape some dirt off his boot heel. "Is Astrid's conjecture accurate?"

"Gareth, by your own admission, until you married Felicity, you were behaving like an ass. You had no one besides me to watch your back. And I have not *always* wanted to travel. The thought of crossing the Channel makes me ill."

He should not have admitted that, but Gareth was winding up to some sort of display of fraternal pique, and Andrew was not in the mood to humor him.

"Then why the hell did you go?" Gareth asked, his sharp tone causing Magic to once again toss his head and roll his eyes.

"Not in front of the children," Andrew warned, patting the horse reassuringly. He unhitched the gelding from the cross ties and led him to his loose box. After making sure the horse had hay and water, Andrew took off the halter and bolted the door.

Gareth tossed the hoof pick back into the brush box—fired it, more like—and remained enthroned on the trunk, an inquisitor who'd chosen his moment well, for no one would interrupt.

So Andrew cast around for a suitable version of a suitable truth.

"I needed to get away," he said, busying himself with tying up Magic's bridle. "If anything, I told myself I was keeping an eye on you because it kept me from my own worst impulses. When you married Felicity, it became obvious you were no longer in need of my support, and travel seemed like an adequate choice."

"What aren't you telling me, Andrew?"

Worlds, and he never would tell his brother, either. More half-truths were in order, though, because Gareth would sense outright prevarication easily.

Andrew sank down onto the trunk, feeling abruptly old, wicked, and tired. "As long as you were cutting such a wide, scandalous swath through Polite Society, then you were also taking care of my need to be upset—about the boating accident, about the ways it changed our family, and the ways it changed things for you and me. When you found your peace with Felicity, the upset came to rest more fully on me. I do not find it a comfortable burden, but I cannot seem to escape it."

Not across twelve countries or several substantial bodies of water.

"Andrew, that boat went down thirteen damned years ago," Gareth said, clearly bewildered.

Andrew scuffed an infinity pattern in the dirt with his boot heel. "For you, perhaps, but I was on that boat, Gareth, and for me, the accident is only as far away as my last nightmare."

Gareth nudged the brush box away with a toe, out of kicking range. "Still?"

"Not as frequently as when it first happened. The fellows at school got so tired of me waking up screaming, they petitioned the master for me to have a private room. I'm better, but I will never be free of it."

Not free of the nightmares or the guilt, though his unease around expecting women seemed to have receded substantially—around one particular expecting woman, anyway.

Gareth hunched forward, his shirt and waistcoat pulling taut across broad shoulders. "I had no bloody idea. Is this why you're so determined not to marry? You think the occasional nightmare unmans you? If that's the case, then half the fellows serving on the Peninsula wouldn't—"

Andrew interrupted him with a shake of his head, and took a deep, unsteady breath.

They were to graduate to three-quarter truths.

"I watched our father drown." He'd never said those words aloud before. "I got the dinghy into the water and could throw the rope either to him or to Mother. Mother was hampered by her skirts, and Father was the worse for drink. The seas were rising all around us, and all I could hear over the wind was the screaming of the others." The ladies' distress had been particularly audible. "I saw that Papa under-stood the choice I was facing. *He swam away from the boat*, Gareth. He *goddamned* swam away from the fucking boat."

Gareth swore viciously as he wrapped an arm around Andrew's back. This reaction was so... unexpected, such a relief, Andrew dropped his forehead to his brother's shoulder—for the rest of the truth would remain forever unspoken.

For a small, painful eternity, the only sounds were made by contented horses, safe and comfortable in their stalls.

Though Andrew heard not his mother's screams, but those of Julia Ponsonby, shrill, desperate, and piercing even above the roar of the storm. Julia had cried out not only for her own life, but for that of an innocent who'd had no hand in the sins committed by its mother or father.

Andrew moved away from his brother to stand where he could watch Magic munching hay.

"I have not shared that unhappy vignette with Mother," he said. "I don't know how much she recalls. She lost consciousness the moment I got her into the boat, and she would not be comforted to know Father gave his life for hers."

"I won't be telling her," Gareth said, keeping his seat on the trunk. "Is there more, Andrew?"

Oh, damn him. Before Felicity had gotten her mitts on Gareth, before he'd become a father, Gareth would never have known to ask such a thing.

"That's bad enough, don't you think?" Andrew said, but even to his own ears, he'd failed utterly to lighten the tone of the exchange.

Andrew heard his brother march across the barn

aisle. "There is no memory you carry," Gareth said, "there is no act you've committed or omitted, no decision you've made or failed to make, no thought you've had, no impulse you've indulged that would make me love you any less." He stood beside Andrew and brought a hand to the back of his brother's neck, as if he'd shake Andrew by the scruff. "I mean this, Andrew. I cannot—*I cannot*—lose you too."

Andrew nodded once, willing the lump in his throat to subside, but keeping his gaze fixed on the big black horse.

Gareth could make such declarations, because he made them in ignorance. When Gareth withdrew, Andrew felt both relief and desolation. His brother had found a rare moment to invite honesty, and Andrew had declined the offer because no other option would serve either of them—not now, not ever.

⸎

Andrew and Gareth were both quiet through dinner, so Astrid made a bid to hold up her end of the conversation as the ladies worked out the menus for the weekend. When that topic ran thin, she engaged her sister in the entertaining pastime of listing the symptoms of advancing pregnancy before the menfolk.

"If I get much bigger, one of us is going to have to use another bed," Felicity remarked, while down the table, her husband devoured a serving of roast fowl.

"There's no possibility of twins, is there?" Andrew asked.

Felicity put down her fork. "Cousin Callista was a twin, but her sister died in infancy." She looked down at her tummy, then at her husband's face. "I had forgotten there are twins in the Worthington family."

As had Astrid. Her hand went to her belly, while her gaze was on Andrew, who'd had the boldness to raise such a potentially worrisome topic while peering so casually at his wineglass.

"Twins can be dangerous to the mother," Gareth said, scowling.

"That's not often the case." Andrew buttered a roll, all casual unconcern. Astrid focused on his hands rather than the butter. "The babies tend to be smaller, and are thus more easily delivered, if I might mention such an indelicate topic. The difficulty comes in the burden of carrying them and caring for them. The babies can be sickly because they also tend to come early."

The entire table gaped at him for a silent moment, until Astrid asked the obvious question. "And how did you come to be such an expert on this?"

"Yes, Brother," Gareth echoed. "Have you first-hand knowledge of siring twins?"

Andrew examined the roll, which had acquired something like a landscape of butter. "I have firsthand knowledge of birthing twins, well, secondhand knowledge."

"About which," Gareth said, "you will now enlighten us, within the limits of the ladies' sensibilities."

Andrew left off sculpting the butter, but kept the knife in one hand and the roll in the other.

"The Order of Saint Bernard maintains hostels for travelers who find themselves in the high passes of the Alps," he said. "Some of these hostels are quite comfortable, like mountain spas, but most are rustic: a single room, simple beds, fuel, basic provisions. They have saved many a life, nonetheless, including my own. I tried to make the trip through the mountains from Bavaria to northern Italy at a time of year when that was a chancy undertaking."

Across the table, Felicity and Gareth exchanged a look of concern while Andrew added yet another dab of butter to his roll. "I found myself in one of these hostels, keeping company with an Italian couple and the wife's old granny. The wife was quite, quite near her time, but hoping to return to Italy before the babies came. Suffice it to say, she was not successful, and somewhere in the north of Italy, there are two little fellows named Andrew and Alex, who look nothing like me whatsoever."

Gareth's expression was pure consternation, Felicity went back to staring at her stomach, and Astrid... wondered why a man purportedly traveling for leisure would attempt to cross the Alps when it was a chancy undertaking.

"Someday," Gareth said, "you should write down the memoirs of your travels, Andrew. If this is just one example of the situations you found yourself in, then the whole must be fascinating."

Andrew set what remained of the butter aside. "Lots of lumpy mattresses, boiled cabbage, and stinking cities, but some nice scenery as well."

Was *scenery* worth four years of exile?

Astrid did not add that question to her list when Andrew joined her in bed several hours later. She instead kept their conversation to safer topics.

"Screw, swive, fuck, roger... How many naughty words are there for it?" Astrid asked, exasperated.

"Lots." Andrew was curled behind her, lazily moving his hips to rub his erect cock against the tops of her thighs. If he changed the angle, he could join them in sexual union, but he apparently wasn't in a hurry.

"I dreamed of you," he murmured into her ear. "Almost made a mess of my sheets."

"Why should a dream mess up the sheets?"

And so he explained about nocturnal emissions, about the suspected causes of orchitis, and about how cold affected an erection. Her questions were avid and endless—nothing she asked shocked him. He described different positions and the diseases of vice that could bring permanent and tragic consequences, also bordellos and how multiple partners could enjoy one another at the same time.

"And you've done this, with two other men and one woman?" Astrid asked, agog.

"I have," Andrew answered through a lazy yawn.

"Did you enjoy it?"

"It was years ago, Astrid, and at the time, I fancied myself some kind of connoisseur of exotic pleasures. On my end, it was an inventive use of a woman's mouth, nothing more. As for the rest of it, I got the impression that keeping one's elbows and knees out of the other fellows' way was more of a challenge than actually screwing the wench—that and finding some leverage."

"Oh, you wicked, depraved, hopeless man." And how bored had he been to seek adventures like this? "Mind with me you don't attempt your depravities."

"I would not hurt you, you know. I would be careful with you," he said, holding her against him.

She let him make his naughty pronouncements, curiosity and trust turning her up tolerant. He would never hurt her, not bodily, they both knew that. He hinted and teased, and gently threatened, but in the end, slipped himself exactly where, in Astrid's opinion, he belonged.

"Shall you come, sweetheart?" he asked, his warm hands palming her breasts. "A sweet, easy pleasure at the end of your day?" He teased at her nipples, kissed her shoulders, and rocked himself slowly in and out of her body as if they had years, not mere days to enjoy each other.

"Andrew, I'm going to… Andrew—"

"Let me love you easy this time," he murmured. "You relax. I'll bring it to you." He set up a slow, deep thrusting; maintained a steady, gentle rolling of her nipples; a patter of words and kisses and nibbles that, indeed, brought Astrid's pleasure to her.

Andrew's loving was profoundly sweet, also heartbreaking—for her. She had no notion how it was for him, and that was yet another heartbreak.

❧

When ladies fainted in stuffy ballrooms, a bit of drama always ensued. The nearest pair of debutantes often took to shrieking, while the dowagers bellowed for their hartshorn and the hostess sent the footmen scampering to open windows that had been opened hours previous. How could passersby appreciate the spectacle of Polite Society dressed in its finest unless the windows were open and the drapery pulled aside?

Some gentleman would gently deposit the afflicted

lady on a chair, and she'd flutter gracefully back to awareness, certain her loss of consciousness would be the butt of gossip and speculation for at least two entire days.

Astrid fluttered back to awareness, certain that cat breath had to be the worst scent a lady was ever subjected to.

"I'm fine," she told her rescuer, who sat back on his tabby haunches and closed his yellow eyes. "I simply left the bed too quickly."

The beast hopped onto the bed, curled up in the warmth Astrid had left behind, and went about dreaming his feline dreams, while Astrid donned riding attire and hoped a fainting spell was not something Andrew might divine by inspecting her.

By the time she had purloined raspberry jam and toast from the kitchen, she'd concluded that the fainting spell had been an aberration, and nothing to be alarmed about. She munched her toast on her way to the stables and promised herself *nothing* was going to spoil her last day of freedom before her in-laws appeared on the morrow.

She found Andrew currying a tall, black gelding. A petite mare, already under saddle, stood sedately in her stall, lipping at hay while she watched Andrew with the other horse.

"I don't think the mare likes the thought of sharing you," Astrid observed, biting into her toast.

"Possibly, but more likely she doesn't like the thought of sharing Magic." He came around to Astrid's side of the horse, kissed her nose, and stole a bite of her toast.

How casually he charmed, and how thoroughly.

"Besides," he went on as he resumed grooming the gelding, "she knows better than to be jealous of me, for I love her dearly, don't I?" He blew a kiss to the mare, who didn't so much as pause in her chewing.

"I don't think she doubts your love," Astrid said, walking up to the gelding and reaching out a hand toward his great Roman nose.

"Of course she doesn't," Andrew said quietly. "She's a smart lady and knows I give her every bit of myself I can."

"Lucky her." To be a horse, whose heart could be broken only by an absence of oats in her bucket or grass in her paddock. "This magnificent fellow is Magic?"

"One and the same. Gareth gave him to me, probably because he didn't have the patience for him," Andrew said, placing a saddle pad across the horse's broad back.

"What's his breeding?"

"Don't know." Andrew settled the saddle over the pad. "He's twitchy enough to be bloodstock, but big enough there has to be some draft in him not too far back. For all I know, he's a reject from the Gypsy fair. But we elegant, noble fellows of good bone have to stick together, don't we?" he asked the horse as he reached under its belly for the girth.

And females intent on enjoying the morning had to take that hint. Astrid led the mare to the ladies' mounting block and climbed aboard, arranging her skirts while Andrew rechecked Magic's girth and bridle.

"Let me know when you ladies are situated, because once I'm up, we'll move off directly at the walk."

Magic looked around, seemingly ill at ease in the yard, though he'd been living on the property for months.

"We are situated," Astrid said, petting the mare.

Andrew was up in the saddle in one smooth movement, no small feat given the height of the horse. Magic danced and wheeled, while Andrew merely nodded at Astrid and followed as she moved her mare forward at the walk.

As Andrew patiently explained to Magic not every ride was going to be a tearing gallop, and the mare placidly ambled off toward the bridle path, Astrid inhaled a bracing lungful of crisp autumn air. The morning was glorious, and she was glad to be alive.

And besides, hadn't Andrew intimated that he cared for her?

Well, her, the mare, somebody… She glanced over her shoulder, to see Magic curveting and crow-hopping while Andrew sat, tall, serene, and smiling, atop the beast.

"You," he informed the horse, "are a great looby. You can see our ladies are striking out fearlessly"— Magic shot up, seemingly off all four feet at once, and kicked out behind—"but you insist on these silly tantrums."

When the horse came down, he stood still, as if waiting for something.

"Isn't that a cavalry maneuver?" Whatever it was, it was magnificently athletic. "The thing he just did, where he leaps and kicks out? It was quite grand."

Andrew patted the horse's neck. "Where in the world would you have seen cavalry maneuvers?" Magic walked forward, his antics of a few minutes ago apparently forgotten. "I do believe," Andrew addressed his mount, "the Marquess of Heathgate is going to regret the day he parted with you. But you and I will not regret it one bit, will we?"

Magic was, of course, greatly discommoded by the flapping and squawking of the ducks, and once again broke into his peculiar antics. Andrew apparently used cues known only to him—and Magic—because the horse again offered a version of the same athletic maneuver.

"Merciful heavens, you two," Astrid remarked, "would you stop showing off? We are quite impressed but would both like to see you safely home."

And if this display from the horse only entertained Andrew, what would it take to unnerve him?

"So you would care if I came to grief?" Andrew teased.

Her in-laws would be underfoot tomorrow—a matter of all too few hours. Astrid brought her mare to a halt and regarded Andrew on his skittish, magnificent black horse. "I love you, and I am in love with you. The last thing I need right now is another occasion for grief. Now toddle on, shall we?"

He had nothing to say to that, not that she'd expected anything, save perhaps some teasing. When they got to the stable yard, grooms came out to take both horses. Andrew for once did not look after his own beast, but offered Astrid his arm.

"You shouldn't say such things, you know," he chided gently as they walked toward the house.

"What you mean is that I shouldn't *feel* such things, and I agree. Loving you is a very inconvenient business."

"I am flattered." He sounded more troubled than anything else.

"You are *burdened*," Astrid retorted, giving him a sad smile. "I deem you to be a lovable man, and you cannot accept that. I don't know why, Andrew, but I know this is what you sincerely believe. And yet, your brother, who is no fool, surely loves you, as does my sister, as does your mother. I suspect every horse in that stable loves you as well, and their judgment, as we both know, is infallible."

He continued to walk beside her. Astrid expected him to explode into a display of athletics that might take him to, say, Tuscany.

When he remained quiet at her side, she forged on as they strolled through the overblown asters and chrysanthemums. "You need not fear I will importune you for a return of these inconvenient sentiments. I have already been trapped in a marriage with one man who didn't love me. You, at least, desire me, and I do not believe you are entirely indifferent to me otherwise."

"I care for you."

"Famous." The gardens were well past their prime, as was this discussion. Astrid addressed her next remark to a bed of drooping roses. "You care for me. Given the nature of my appalling admission, I will understand if you forego coming to my room, though I will certainly miss you if that is your decision."

He stood, gazing down at her, his expression pained, while the silence lengthened.

Damn her wagging tongue, damn her honesty, but mostly, damn whatever pain it was that kept him silent.

"Andrew, you needn't trouble over this, for just

as you have determined you cannot be loved, I have determined I will not stop loving you. I don't know what kind of love could be so cautious or fickle it died in the face of a challenge. I also don't know how to love carefully, which is probably the best you could tolerate from me. So will you, nil you. I will be in my bed tonight, loving you, whether you join me or not."

With that, she dropped his arm and left him standing among the exhausted flowers, staring after her and looking for all the world like he'd just lost his best, last, and only friend.

Seven

"You need to hear what Fairly has to say," Andrew told his brother, because this little after-dinner tête-à-tête among the gentlemen was not going to be about the weather and the latest gossip from the City.

"This sounds serious." Gareth went to the sideboard, where griffins, dragons, and chimeras sat gleaming atop decanters. "Brandy, gentlemen?"

When Andrew had accepted a drink he did not want, Gareth took up a characteristic perch on the edge of the desk that dominated one end of the Willowdale library.

"All right, Fairly, I'm listening."

"The bad news is that Astrid's dower funds are all but gone," Fairly began, sipping his brandy. "Heathgate, you do serve a fine drink."

Bugger the drink.

Gareth nodded graciously. "Thank you. Is there good news?"

"No, there is worse news," Fairly said, glancing at Andrew the way at an earlier time in life, his lordship might have assessed a patient suffering unpredictable fits of hysteria. "Rumors are circulating that Herbert took his own life, unable to deal otherwise with the family's debts."

Gareth peered at his glass. "Those are nasty rumors."

Bugger the rumors. Bugger dear, departed Herbert. Bugger everything.

"At this point, it's only rumor, and it might never reach Astrid's ears," Fairly said. "The state of her finances, on the other hand, is fact. The accounts are all but wiped clean. The losses can be attributed to some bad investments, and recently, to outright withdrawals."

Rage had Andrew tossing back half his drink, sorrow for Astrid the second half.

Gareth did not rouse himself from the desk to provide a refill, a small lapse in an otherwise attentive host's focus.

"That money was to have been safely stowed in the cent-percents," Gareth said. "This is going to be very hard on Astrid."

A fine bit of understatement.

"If the situation is grave enough, it might mean Astrid need not return to the Allen household," Fairly pointed out. "With a suicide in the family, and misfeasance with regard to Astrid's money, the current viscount might be open to negotiation. Suicide, if proven, is unlikely to result in forfeiture of the title but could cost the family some of Herbert's personal wealth."

Except Herbert likely had no personal wealth, if his parsimony with Astrid was any indication.

"Douglas might be amenable to discussions," Andrew said, "but if Astrid bears a male child, he'll never entrust the rearing of that child to a young widow who herself was brought up in humble circumstances. The Allens are overwhelmingly impressed with their own consequence."

And Astrid was overwhelming protective of those she loved. Andrew set his glass down a bit too hard on the mantel.

Gareth collected Andrew's glass and returned it to the sideboard, a domestic gesture that spoke to Felicity's civilizing influence. "We do not know how Douglas will treat Astrid. He has certainly been all that's proper toward her so far, and we have no proof he stole her money. We can only lay such accusations at the feet of his late, increasingly unlamented brother."

"So which of you will tell Astrid she has no money?" Andrew stared out into the darkness beyond the French windows rather than watch his relations exchange uneasy glances. And well they should be uneasy, when Astrid had no money, no husband, and no honesty from the man she insisted she loved.

"I'm her brother," Fairly said. "I'll tell her, though I will also make sure she does, in fact, have money. Enough money in pounds sterling to leave the country if necessary."

Thank God for wealthy brothers with a sense of honor toward their sisters.

"The money isn't the issue," Andrew said, turning to face the other two men.

Gareth rolled his empty glass between his palms. "Being widowed, with child, and destitute isn't an issue?"

How protective he was, and how Andrew loved him for it.

"To Astrid, certainly," Andrew said. "We need to

focus on the larger picture, however. Herbert's death has three possible explanations. The first, and the one we are asked to accept, is that an avid and experienced sportsman, familiar with the best equipment, fell victim to an accident. Perhaps his gun was defective or he neglected to clean it. Perhaps he resembled a fourteen-stone grouse to somebody else on the shoot.

"The second possibility," Andrew continued, "is that a young lord, a pleasant enough man, but more concerned with appearances than with learning how to manage his affairs, became swamped with debt, and seeing no honorable alternative, arranged his suicide to look like an accident. This course makes sense, in keeping with the family's pride and concern for social consequence.

"Again, however, many titled families are approaching dun territory, and if Herbert had sold off his stable, his art, or even his damned coal mine, he could probably have come 'round in time. Then too, what man kills himself, leaving behind a wife such as Astrid?"

What man could dally with her and then saunter on his way as if she hadn't taken complete possession of his heart years ago?

"The third possibility," Andrew said, "is that somebody who stood to gain from Herbert's death murdered him and spread the tale of suicide brought on by the man's mismanagement of funds. In addition to gaining from Herbert's death, this person would also need intimate knowledge of the family's finances. The suicide is unlikely to cost the family its title, and dear Herbert apparently had no wealth to forfeit to the Crown in any case."

"What you are implying," Gareth said, disbelief in every word, "is that we could be turning Astrid, *and her child*, over to the keeping of a man who would, with cold-blooded premeditation, murder his own brother for the sake of a title."

"That," Andrew spat as he hurled his glass straight into the fire, "is *exactly* what we might be doing."

"Hence," Fairly said quietly as the fire momentarily roared higher, "the need for precautions. I would remind you both that so far, all we have are rumors and depleted accounts. Herbert was the one who would have had access to Astrid's money, and Douglas Allen could simply be a conscientious second son who inherited under unfortunate circumstances."

"It does happen," Gareth conceded, his expression reminding Andrew that some second sons could have two titles foisted upon them, regardless that it likely took enormous influence, coin, and conniving.

"It happens rarely," Andrew growled.

"So what do we do?" Gareth used the hearth broom to sweep shards of broken glass onto a dustpan, then deposited the shrapnel in the ash bucket. "We have no solid evidence against Douglas, but it strikes me as peculiar that Herbert Allen has been gone almost three months, and we're hearing the rumor of suicide only now. That kind of speculation usually flies around before the grave is dug."

"You raise a good question," Fairly said, "and I don't have an answer. Worse, if we confront Douglas with our accusations, he could easily have Astrid shut up at the family seat, miles from help and in mortal peril. He could have her declared insane, or simply make her disappear before the child is even born."

Fairly spoke Andrew's worst fears, and probably Fairly's as well.

"We have one means of keeping Astrid safe that would also very likely protect her child." Andrew heard the words coming from his own mouth and knew they presaged something beyond a worst fear.

"Yes," Fairly said, his mismatched eyes narrowing, "we can find her someone to marry, preferably somebody whose title outranks Douglas's, and tuck her away in that person's secure keeping. We could effect this scheme before Douglas even knows she's expecting."

Damn Fairly and his nimble mind. "So we marry her to such a one. What will you have left Astrid with if it turns out Douglas bears her no ill will and her husband's death was an accident?"

Andrew posed a question that in hours of pondering had admitted of no good answer.

Gareth set the little hearth broom aside and lifted the wrought iron poker. "We will have left her in the keeping of a man who cares enough to protect her life with his own." *Again*, was left unspoken.

"I won't inflict myself on her for the sake of rumor and speculation," Andrew retorted. Not after her fierce declarations that morning. Hopefully, not ever. "She has to be told what we know, and I suspect you will want Felicity told as well."

"All we know now," Fairly said, "is that her money is missing, and since it has been missing, Douglas has offered repeatedly to manage it for her. That is what we know, no more, no less. The rumors I picked up were not being circulated anywhere near polite ears, and not loudly."

Fairly of the endless self-containment was offering Andrew a reprieve. "Saints above, man, you can be scary."

"And you've seen me only when the moon isn't full."

"As a matter of fact," Andrew said, heading for the French doors, "it's full tonight, so I'll take myself out for a gallop, gentlemen. If you'll excuse me?" He bowed and let himself out into the night rather than traverse the house.

A thoughtful silence followed the soft click of the door latch. Gareth considered following his brother and concluded Felicity would be vexed with him if he did.

"Why in the hell won't he marry her?" Fairly asked. "Astrid's adorable, she's long since had a *tendresse* for him, and by now they're probably copulating like rabbits."

Copulating was a medical term, while the consternation in Fairly's eyes was purely fraternal.

Gareth drew the curtains over the French doors because the night was nippy. And yet, Andrew had gone into the darkness without an overcoat. The saddle room held a few old riding jackets, but no scarf, no proper winter cloaks, no real protection from the elements. "I understand him, Fairly. He won't marry her, because he cares for her and doesn't feel worthy of her."

Fairly looked as if contradictory symptoms were refusing to add up to a diagnosis. "Much as you had to be convinced to offer for Felicity. What made you change your mind about yourself?"

"I didn't," Gareth said with a snort. "I just hurt too goddamned unbearably much to carry on without Felicity, and when our paths crossed again, I grabbed her literally and figuratively with both hands, and I've been holding on ever since."

"And that," Fairly countered with a half smile, "probably describes most of the happily married men on earth. It does not, however, bode well for Andrew and Astrid's immediate future."

"Perhaps not for their *immediate* future," Gareth said. "But Andrew is as smitten as I've ever seen a man, and he and Astrid, connected by marriage, will have to continue to deal with each other for years to come. I am not abandoning hope yet."

Not nearly, and neither was Felicity.

"Spoken like an older brother, Heathgate, who doesn't mind seeing his sibling twist a bit in the breeze. I remind you, though, that my younger sister has already suffered through two years of marriage to a buffoon, and I'll not tolerate anybody abusing her sensibilities further."

Unlike Andrew, Fairly was not prone to outbursts of sentiment. He set his glass down very softly and left Gareth alone, standing before the fire and wondering how to present the latest worrisome developments to his exceptionally pregnant marchioness.

❧

"I shouldn't have awakened you," Andrew said on a sigh, disentangling himself from Astrid long before she was ready to let him go. "I wasn't going to. I went for a long, hard ride. I bathed and climbed into my own bed…"

He sounded bewildered, as if his arrival into her bed, into her very body, had been the work of fairies.

"I am glad you aren't in your own bed." To her relief, Andrew settled down under the covers and spooned himself around her.

"You shouldn't be. Your in-laws will be here tomorrow, and that will put a period to our frolic, dear heart. If Douglas pressures you to return to Town with them, will you go?"

Frolic? This ache in her heart, this longing in her body was frolic? Astrid kissed the smooth curve of Andrew's biceps, grateful for the darkness. "I won't want to leave here."

Leave him.

"Astrid, listen to me." Andrew's voice did not sound like a lover's, but rather like he bore bad tidings. "I've learned things you should know, things I ought to let your brother or Gareth tell you."

"But you won't make me wait to hear it from them, because the news is unpleasant," she finished for him.

He held her fingers against his cheek, his skin both warm and rough. "I won't make you wait. The truth is, sweetheart, your funds are gone. Your widow's portion was both badly invested and flat-out pilfered. Fairly will make sure you have some cash on hand at all times, and I would not tell anyone—not your lady's maid, not the housekeeper, no one—that you have this money. Sew it into a cloak, hide it in your embroidery basket, but keep it where you alone have access to it."

As he spoke, his embrace became more snug.

"You are scaring me, Andrew. You are telling me I am *poor*?"

"As far as your widow's portion is concerned, you are destitute."

"Who took my money?"

"Herbert, as near as we can tell."

Andrew would not lie to her, and for that, as well as the security of his embrace, she loved him all the more, even as anger made her want to shout. "Why would my husband have stolen from me?"

"I don't know, love, but the family is in serious debt. According to your brother, they have enough assets to turn themselves around, but it would mean liquidating the stables, the unentailed property, that sort of thing. I don't see Douglas taking on such a project willingly, not when all of Society would be instantly alerted to his circumstances by such behavior."

"Douglas knows, doesn't he?" Hence his offers to manage her funds, the rat.

"I would guess he does, though nobody has approached him on this issue directly. The state of your funds should have come to his attention as part of his efforts to take over the viscountcy. He is, for all his faults, not a stupid man. But, Astrid, you must not fret over this money," he whispered, nuzzling her nape.

Herbert used to tell her not to fret, usually as he was on his way to go look at *another* smashing bay hunter just shipped to Tatt's from the Midlands.

Which might have been male euphemism for all manner of prurient, *expensive* pursuits.

"Andrew, all a widow has is her portion. Herbert

made no will, and I am left with only the provisions in the marriage settlements. Now you tell me those are gone and I have nothing."

"You have Gareth, and you have Fairly, both of whom can provide for you quite, quite generously."

Astrid did not, in any sense Society or the law would recognize, have Andrew. He might be her lover, her friend, and her sister's brother-in-law, but he had no right, with both Gareth and David in good health, to provide for her. "I do not want to be a poor relation to my family any more than I do to my in-laws."

He kissed her temple, likely an attempt at distraction. "Astrid, use your formidable common sense: many women are poor relations. The widow's circumstance, having her own money and her own property, is the exception. When you married Herbert, you had only what pin money he gave you. Fairly will see to it you have far more than that for emergency funds."

This conversation, about money and the lack thereof, was intimate in ways that had nothing to do with two naked bodies entwined under a blanket—intimate and enraging.

"Do you know my brother, David, the estimable and ever so self-contained Viscount Fairly, is a widower? I have no details, but this disclosure came up when he last called on me in Town. I wasn't managing very well, and David asked me what I was doing with the guilt, for I am alive and my husband will never draw breath again."

She gave Andrew a moment to absorb the news of her brother's previous marriage, then went on in quiet, clipped tones. "I am faced with a different question now, upon finding my late husband stole from funds that were to have been for my dotage, all the while telling me not to worry my head about his extravagances. I am faced with the issue of how I will deal with *his* guilt, his betrayal, his damned pride, that wouldn't allow him to practice the economies most folk observe out of sheer prudence."

Andrew rolled her to her back. "Hush. You will wake the household."

"I want to wake the household. I want to run down the drive, bellowing at the top of my lungs that Herbert was a fool, a cheat, and a lousy husband."

She also wanted to cry and to hear Andrew say he'd make everything turn out right. Flying pigs came to mind.

Andrew kissed her chin. "Herbert's brother will be here tomorrow, expecting you to do the pretty as the grieving widow, and you were the one to remind me Douglas will be your child's guardian. He is not responsible for Herbert's mismanagement and duplicity, at least as far as we know."

She wished she had more than the last of the firelight to illuminate Andrew's expression, because his tone suggested there was worse news yet. "What does that mean, 'as far as you know'?"

When he was silent, Astrid brushed a hand up along his brow, sifting her fingers through his thick locks. He did not lie to her, even when she wished he would. "Andrew?"

He caught her hand in his and kissed her knuckles, then kept his fingers wrapped around hers. "Fairly heard a rumor Herbert may have taken his own life."

Astrid's hand went to her belly, low down where

the child grew. "Andrew, no! Herbert was proud, old-fashioned, stubborn, and occasionally slow-witted, but he would not do such a thing, ever."

Defending Herbert this way—sincerely—felt good, but what a wretched accusation Andrew made.

"People commit suicide for reasons less compelling than shame," Andrew replied in the same ominously quiet voice.

Dear God, what did that tone of voice mean? "Herbert would not have wanted to shame his family." A man who indulged his mistress lavishly did not give a thought to whether he shamed his wife. Another equally bleak thought eclipsed that one. "I doubt my late husband had the courage to take his own life."

"Perhaps he did; perhaps he didn't. Perhaps he made it look like an accident, but you must consider another explanation."

This was not how Astrid wanted to spend their last night together. She laid that complaint at Herbert's sainted feet.

"What other explanation? My husband spent a great deal of time around guns and strong spirits, and one day he was unlucky."

"Astrid, I don't want to believe this, but please consider that your husband might have died at the hand of someone who would benefit from his death."

"You want me to consider that my husband was murdered?" she hissed. "That is ridiculous, Andrew. Who in their right mind would murder an impoverished, titled gentleman, particularly one as unfailingly amiable and openhanded as Herbert? One thing you must admit about Herbert, he did not have enemies."

Andrew rolled to his back, taking his warmth away when Astrid most wanted to cling to him.

"Astrid, he may not have had enemies, but he has a brother, two in fact. For a younger brother to covet a title would not be unusual. In most families, it would almost be expected. You'd not believe the number of jokes aimed at me, insinuating I wanted my brother's title, or that Gareth killed five relatives to get his hands on the marquessate." He gripped her hand more firmly. "How well do you know Douglas Allen?"

Andrew the lover was charming, dear, and heart-breaking in his determination to leave her. Andrew the warrior, hell-bent on equipping her with enough knowledge to protect herself, was daunting in an entirely different way.

"I do not know Douglas well. He is such a cold fish and even more private than David was upon first acquaintance. He is ever proper, but controlled. As if he's always standing outside himself, watching. I've never even seen him express affection for his mother or a dog or a small child. I often wished Douglas had more of Herbert's jovial social grace, and Herbert had more of Douglas's gravity."

"Do you feel safe around Douglas?"

Astrid searched in vain for reasons to give the reas-suring answer Andrew wanted to hear. She had never felt comfortable around Herbert's middle brother, and wasn't sure Herbert had either.

"Your silence speaks volumes, Astrid, and forces me to lay before you another option."

"I am not going to like this, am I?"

"No, you are not." From his tone, neither was he.

"Then at least hold me while you deliver the worst news." She made as if to wrestle him back over her, and Andrew complied.

"Your brilliant brother and your brilliant brother-in-law," he began, brushing a strand of hair off her forehead, "have come up with a way to keep you safe and to ensure Douglas does not have the raising of your child."

"I'm all for accomplishing both, so let's hear their clever plan," she said, nuzzling at Andrew's throat. "You have the most marvelous scent about you."

"As do you," Andrew replied politely, his man parts stirring back to life despite his manners. "It occurred to Fairly that were you to marry a well-heeled fellow who outranked Douglas, then Douglas's hands would be tied. He could not demand you rejoin the Allen household; he could not completely control your child; he could not control your finances even indirectly."

"Oh, that's a fine plan," Astrid muttered, dipping her head so her tongue could go questing at Andrew's throat for his pulse. "I see a small flaw or two, however. First, I do not want to be married to anyone ever again, and we have no duke or marquess hanging about the hedges, just waiting to ask for my dainty hand, not when I'm about to drop some other bull's calf."

Andrew angled up so he more thoroughly covered her. "The hedges might not hold an eligible duke or a marquess, but we could scare you up an earl."

"I don't know any earls under the age of fifty, and he would have to be handy with pistols, fists, and swords if he were to provide me bodily safety, wouldn't he?" She began to rock her hips, sliding her wet sex slowly back and forth along the length of his growing erection, and wanting desperately, desperately for Andrew to *be quiet*.

"Those skills would be important attributes, yes," Andrew said, though his voice at least had a distracted, breathless quality.

"And," Astrid went on, her hands sliding down his back to knead the muscles of his buttocks, "I am not going to marry another polite fellow who will expect me to wait patiently in the dark for his *timid… disgusting… inept… fumbling* attempts at conjugal relations." She punctuated each adjective with a roll of her hips, indignant that Andrew could even contemplate marrying her off to another man.

"No one would expect that of you," he said. "But our brothers have found somebody who meets all of your criteria: he's young enough, he is motivated to protect you and your child, he is an earl, moderately wealthy, and he manages passably well between the sheets."

"How would those two know the first thing about a man's abilities with the ladies?" she said, not quite distracted from the topic by the hard shaft nudging at her sex. "I don't believe such a man exists, anyway, and I would hardly take their word for his abilities."

"Would you take mine?" Andrew asked, teasing her with the blunt tip of his cock.

"I don't know." She would soon not know how to form words. "Who is this paragon?"

He slid into her on a lovely, deep, easy glide that gratified as it aroused.

"Me," he said as he thrust home. "They want you to marry me."

Eight

Douglas Allen, now Viscount Amery, had been taught since birth that two pillars sustained an honorable life: family loyalty and adherence to the standards of decent Society. As a grown man, Douglas had long since concluded neither family loyalty nor genteel social standards created a meaningful life—or a particularly enjoyable one. Meaning and joy, however, were luxuries the second son of an impoverished viscount could not afford.

In that spirit, the trip to Willowdale would be made to create a show of familial good feeling, to collect the young widow from the bosom of her family—and to appease the dowager Viscountess Amery's ceaseless whining.

Douglas sipped at a scant finger of brandy, feeling a passing pity for Astrid Worthington Allen, whom he liked as much as he liked anyone. She was pretty, charming, intelligent without being obnoxious, and genuinely kind. In time, she might have been the making of his spendthrift, self-indulgent older brother.

The first two years of that marriage, however, had

left Douglas with the impression his older brother, as usual, was putting a brave face on a bungled job. Herbert neglected his young wife, ignored her advice, and sought the company of muddy dogs and drunken squires—and his mistress—instead.

Douglas downed his last swallow of brandy—and it would *be* his last of the evening, economies being what they were—and prepared to take himself up to bed when the front door opened.

"Greetings, your lordship," Henry Allen called as he bounced into the library and headed straight for his older brother's brandy decanter. He poured himself a bumper, grinned, and waggled the bottle at Douglas. "May I offer you refressment… re*fresh*ment?"

"Thank you, no, though might I say how pleased I am to see you on familial territory before dawn's early light? The guest room is kept in readiness for your impromptu visits." Douglas closed the door Henry had left open, lest what meager heat the hearth produced be lost to the night air.

"Now, Douglas, don't go getting all starchy on me. I'm just nipping in between rounds, so to speak." Henry took an exuberant, audible gulp of his drink.

When had his little brother, once so merry and charming, turned into such a vapid waste of indifferent tailoring? A second son had a difficult existence, raised to understand the privileges of the title, but not to exercise them. As the third son, free of such constraints, Henry could make his way in the world however whim and fancy struck him. He chose to do so as an inebriated, skirt-chasing, utterly unimpressive excuse for a young man.

As Henry guzzled the scant supply of decent brandy, Douglas silently vowed to order the staff to leave only the cheaper offerings in plain sight.

"So, Henry, will you be in any condition to join Mother and me for our weekend call on Heathgate?"

For a moment, Henry looked confused, then his mouth creased into a smile that brought out his resemblance to Herbert. They shared the same build too—substantial and sturdy, while Douglas was taller and… skinny.

"Time to bring the little viscountess back into the fold, eh? Have to commend Herbert on choosing a right pretty thing for a wife. Do you suppose she's getting lonely yet?" Henry underscored his lascivious meaning with a wink.

"You are half seas over, Brother," Douglas observed as he put the decanter into the sideboard's cupboard. "I will thank you not to discuss our sister-in-law in such disrespectful terms. If she wishes to return to Town, we will be happy to escort her, particularly because it is Mother's fondest wish she do so."

Mother's only wish, to hear her tell it and tell it and tell it.

"And maybe your fondest wish too, your lordship?" Henry assayed such a winsome, irreverent grin, Douglas was reminded of the mischievous boy Henry had been.

"Henry, you really should be adopting a more decorous demeanor," Douglas chided tiredly. "Our brother is only three months in his grave, and you are, as long as I remain unwed, the heir presumptive to a title. You would be better advised to spend your time acquainting yourself with the family's situation than larking about with every soiled dove who waves her larcenous fingers at you."

Henry's grin broadened. "It ain't their waving fingers that makes me *come* running, Dougie." He was so overcome with mirth at his play on words, he had to sit, and still he managed to spill a few drops of his drink on the only good carpet remaining in the house.

"Henry, I will take my leave of you. Your dazzling wit is more than my feeble brain can bear. Please present yourself at a proper hour and reasonably attired on the morrow. Mother is taking the coach, and I will accompany her on horseback."

Henry gulped back more of his drink. "You would ride the distance rather than join Mother in the coach, wouldn't you? I think Herbert's death has made her worse. She's gotten downright whiney. So whiney you'll sit a horse for two hours rather than put up with her. What would my late brother say if he could see this?"

My late brother, not *our* late brother.

"Maybe he would say good night," Douglas replied, willing to leave Henry alone with the decanter if it meant Douglas could take himself off to bed.

When he gained the solitude of his room, Douglas folded his clothing into the clothes press—he did without a valet quite nicely—and made use of the washbasin before climbing into bed. One of Henry's crude remarks came back to him as he began the nightly ritual of fighting to fall asleep: "Do you think she's getting lonely yet?"

She probably was lonely. Douglas would have

wagered money he could ill afford to lose on the certainty *she* had been lonely before Herbert's death.

Viewed from that perspective, Herbert's death had probably been a blessing to his wife. Douglas rolled to his side, grateful at least one other person could feel relief that the late Viscount Amery had gone to his untimely reward.

❧

Andrew forced himself to consciousness through the cozy certainty he should remain wrapped around the delightful, warm curves sharing the bed with him.

In the next brutal instant, he stifled the impulse to scramble off the mattress, for he had fallen asleep in Astrid's bed—in her very arms. No sounds came from the lower floors, and if he'd had to guess, he would have estimated that dawn was an hour away.

So he had time, minutes anyway, to resolve what he'd been too cowardly to deal with as Astrid had drifted off in his arms hours earlier.

"Don't go." Astrid punctuated her command by taking his arm and wrapping it around her middle.

He should invite her to make a visit behind the privacy screen. She was still shy about pregnancy's effects on her body, and the idea that she'd be shy about anything with him was dear and painful.

"I'll stay for a bit." He didn't want to leave her alone in this bed, and he didn't want to leave her *alone*, but he was going to. "You did not respond to my proposal."

And because he needed to see her face when they had this most miserable discussion, he hoisted her over him so she sprawled on his chest. By the embers in the hearth, he could see her braid was a mess and her cheek bore a wrinkle from where it had been pressed to the pillow.

"Did you propose, Andrew? I heard you describing a scheme hatched by our brothers, not an offer of marriage."

Peevish. She was peevish that he'd not gotten down on bended knee and prettied things up. She was going to be more peevish still.

"If we were to marry"—not *when we marry*—"I would not get children on you."

She paused midnuzzle on his chest. "Then we won't have children. You've told me there are precautions to prevent conception. Besides, we are likely to have a brace of nieces and nephews, so it hardly matters."

The better to focus both of them on what needed to be said, he took her hand as it began a southerly peregrination. "I've told you about certain precautions. I've also told you no precautions are a perfect safeguard, and the only way to prevent conception for certain is to remain celibate. I am telling you"—he forced himself to make the words pass his lips—"if we marry, I will be your bodyguard, your friend, and until you deliver this child, I will be your lover. After that, I will not be intimate with you lest you conceive my child."

For no child should have him for a father. He'd been certain of that since before his sixteenth birthday, and he was certain of it still.

Astrid curled her fingers around his, her grip fierce. "You are saying you would be celibate rather than risk another child?" Oh, the hurt in her voice, but still he'd insist on hurting her further.

"All I can promise you is I will be celibate with you." Even if it meant more years of subsisting on thin soup, breathing the stench of cooked cabbage, and missing her.

"Andrew, why? I would gladly bear your children, and if—"

"I would not be a good father," he interrupted before the entire conversation blundered into more questions and worse pain. He kissed her knuckles and wrapped his arms around her, but being Astrid, she did not let the matter lie.

"Is it that you do not want to have children *with me*?"

He gathered her closer, hating Herbert Allen for planting a seed of self-doubt in the mind of a woman who didn't deserve that misery. He hated himself for nurturing that seed, but for the first time, and with surprising ease, he hated Julia Ponsonby too.

"If I were to have children with any woman, it would be you. I am not willing to sire children at all, though, and thus you have the terms of my offer."

Also his heart on a platter, which was no improvement on the bargain. Would that he had perished in that damned accident and Adam had survived. Would that he could assuage Astrid's doubts with tales of familial insanity or inherited weakness, but the weakness was his and his alone.

"I cannot accept such an offer, Andrew," she replied, sadness in every word. "I do not know why you have so little faith in yourself, and I know not how to argue the point. I think we are saying good-bye."

She was brave, and she deserved so much better.

"Ah, love, don't cry," Andrew whispered, shifting over her to kiss her cheeks. "Please, please don't cry. I should never have taken liberties with you, knowing it would come to this, but believe me, Astrid, it is for the best that we part now."

"No, Andrew," she said through her tears, "you do not have the right of it, not this time. You are being stubborn, misguided, and f-foolish. I am glad we took liberties with each other, but I wish you would reconsider this rule you have made, or at least tell me why it is so important to you."

She asked for so much more than she knew. She asked for him to watch the love in her eyes turn not to fond recollection or puzzled indifference, but to dismay and even hate.

He kissed her forehead as her weeping subsided. "Shall I take myself off to Enfield or disappear back to Sussex? Gareth and Felicity will understand, if it would be easier on you not to have to see me."

Astrid bit his nipple, and not gently. "You want my permission to slink away, Andrew Alexander? I think not. You have said we are friends, and that is not how I would have my friend treat me. I will go back to Town with Douglas, armed with warnings of your suspicions, and I will be careful. Once I am gone from here, I understand you will keep your distance. But you will stay this weekend, and you will be the doting brother-in-law you've always been."

"If that is your wish," he said, inordinately relieved she wasn't sending him away, equally concerned she would be going back to live in the Allen town house

while he remained in the country—of course—
thoroughly loathing himself because their dalliance
was ending exactly as he'd foreseen it would.

With Astrid hurt.

"My wish is that we remain friends," she said.
"Someday, you know, I will be too old to have children, and I am waiting to hear what excuse you come
up with then."

As an attempt at humor, her words were paltry, but
as an olive branch, they sufficed.

"You are forgiving me." He wished she wouldn't.
He wished she would make him beg and suffer, and
most of all, he wished she would make him reconsider.

"I am not forgiving you, Andrew. There is nothing
to forgive."

She bludgeoned him with her tolerance, pushed
him overboard into seas that heaved with guilt and
bewilderment. More guilt. Now he wished she'd bite
him again, this time hard enough to draw blood.

"Astrid, promise me if you feel at any time unsafe
with the Allens, if you have any evidence Douglas
means you ill, then you must allow this marriage.
Your pride, and even your feelings for me, aren't
worth your life."

"Of all the arrogance…" Astrid huffed out. "You
would ask me to be your wife, expecting me to look
the other way while you sought pleasure with others?
And what of me, Andrew? I am supposed to become a
nun, sacrificed on the altar of your antipathy to fatherhood? Do you expect me, knowing my feelings for
you, to lie with other men while you smile and wish
me best of luck?"

Astrid on a verbal tear was frightening. She wielded truth like a delicate épée, slicing cleanly to the bone with every stroke.

And yet, Andrew parried her ripostes. "If we worked at it, we could come to tolerate married life. I am asking you to put your safety *and that of your child* above your infatuation with me. In time, you will understand I'm not worth these feelings you have for me. In time, you might even be relieved I would put no demands on you. But love me, hate me, or disdain me altogether, I would very much rather have you and your child alive to do so."

She bit his shoulder in a fashion Andrew found… thoughtful. "I will promise, you misguided, *lost* man, to marry you if it becomes clear there is a threat to my life or that of this baby. I do not, however, agree to any of your other terms, and I further demand that should we marry, *you* promise *me* we will live together as if we were truly man and wife."

Andrew had long since reached a place of bleak resignation with this discussion, but rallied himself to think through that demand. He couldn't very well protect her if he was living in Italy and she was left raising a child in Sussex. And as to that, while fashionable couples often spent some of the year apart, they also spent much of the year quite publicly together. He at least owed Astrid the appearance of a true marriage—should it ever come to that.

"I accept your terms."

"Thank you," she rejoined pleasantly. "I compliment you on the first bit of sense you've shown all night." With that, she tucked herself into the curve of his body and went quiet.

In a just world, they would have had a chance at building a life together; in reality, tragedies, bad decisions, and unfairness abounded, and he would never be worthy of her.

And he would never have the balls to explain to her why.

He made love to her by way of consolation to her and penance for himself, aroused her with tenderness and care and a wealth of longing. She joined him in a sleepy haze and wrapped herself around him, apparently accepting the pleasure—and the loss—their joining signified. He couldn't bring himself to tell her good-bye, simply could not say the words.

Andrew told the woman he loved, with his hands, with his body and his kisses, that he was full of regret for causing her pain. He told her he did care for her, so very much, and he told her when his body slipped from hers and he left her bed this time, he would never, ever come back.

❧

Douglas Allen kissed Astrid's forehead in greeting. He had the sense she loathed the contact, and considered it, in some convoluted way, the least he could do for her. Anger had become his best antidote to overwhelming melancholy, and Astrid had reason to be melancholy, probably more reason than she knew.

But he had to admit as he stepped back, she looked better. Her eyes were no longer a flat mask of pain, and her face showed emotion besides sadness and bewilderment.

"The country air and the company of your sister have improved your spirits."

"Nonsense, Douglas," Lady Amery cut in. "Astrid is wan, she has lost flesh, and she looks quite worn out to me. Lady Heathgate has no doubt been at her wit's end with concern for her sister."

A slight smile flickered between the sisters, the last being no doubt true. Douglas noted the glance and felt a stab of old irritation. His brothers had exchanged the same kind of looks around him constantly.

"We shall soon have her back to Town, where she may recover from the rigors of her visit to the country." He addressed himself to Astrid, because she was a woman blessedly comfortable with plain speech. "If that is your wish?"

"Perhaps we need not make plans at this point," Heathgate interrupted, slipping an arm around his wife in a startling display of informal affection. "I'm sure you would all like to be shown to your rooms and get settled before we gather for luncheon."

"I, for one," said Henry, his grin much in evidence, "would like to see the stables. I've been told you've a prime eye, your lordship."

Viscount Fairly shoved away from the mantel where he'd been silently perusing the company with his unnerving eyes. "I'll join you," he said, "and we can leave Lord Heathgate to complete his morning's correspondence."

"Capital!" Henry rejoined.

Douglas would have liked to go with them, but

that would have left no one to escort his mother to her room. He gave the marquess a bow and offered his mother an elbow.

They followed Lady Heathgate up the stairs, Lady Amery chattering about the manor house's lovely appointments. Douglas was inordinately relieved to tuck his mother into her room and follow his hostess down the hallway to his chamber. The room was commodious and comfortable, and that was a relief too, for despite determined self-discipline, Douglas remained a man who enjoyed his creature comforts.

"Your hospitality, my lady, is all that is generous." He bowed to her formally in the corridor, seeing his valise had been brought up already.

"You must consider yourself family while you are here, my lord," she replied. "I have enjoyed having my sister's company, and thank you for your willing-ness to share her with us these weeks past."

"She seems to be doing better, and for that, you have my gratitude. In Town, she just… She was not coping well. I was at a loss as to how to assist her."

Douglas followed his words with the slightest hint of a self-conscious shrug and another bow, and withdrew into his room. Having gained the precious blessing of solitude, he opened the valise, took out a stack of letters, and prepared to bail against a tide of correspondence as endless as it was depressing.

~❧~

Dinner passed as pleasantly as lunch had, if small talk, small portions, and a small case of queasiness qualified.

Astrid had made certain to seat herself neither next to nor across from Andrew, which left her immediately across from Douglas.

While Andrew conversed, flattered, and played the part of a cheerful guest, Astrid pushed braised carrots around on her plate and thought of skipping stones. Whenever she looked up, somebody was studying her—Felicity, Gareth, Henry Allen, or Douglas.

Though not Andrew. Never Andrew.

She put a forkful of carrots in her mouth and chewed slowly, then had to pretend to sneeze into her napkin to preserve herself from swallowing food that agreed with her even less than the company who had come to call.

When Felicity rose and invited the ladies to join her in the family parlor, Astrid thought to make her escape above stairs, only to find Douglas hovering at her elbow in the corridor.

"Might I offer you a turn about the gardens, my lady?" He held out an arm and assayed what for him was probably a smile, though it looked to Astrid like an inchoate case of dyspepsia. Perhaps the condition was contagious. "The evening is cool, but there are matters I would raise with you privately."

"I'll get my shawl."

Douglas was nearly as tall as Andrew, and had an elegance to his frame neither of his brothers shared. Those attributes were none of his doing, but Astrid also had to credit the man with a curiously pleasant, cedary scent.

Her condition was making her daft, or making her nose daft. She repaired to her room, gave the quilt a longing stroke, and chose a lavender shawl. Let Douglas be warned that her mourning no longer consumed her, and she would not be a slave to convention merely to appease his sensibilities.

"Shall we use the back terrace?" she suggested, not waiting for him to offer his arm again. He stayed by her side, nonetheless, as they meandered around the side of the house to the largest terrace, the one that bordered the fading flower beds. The full moon had risen, making the whole scene eerily well lit.

"So, Douglas," she said as they strolled along, "what would you discuss with me?"

He was not like some men—like Herbert—charging ahead and leaving a diminutive lady to trot after him.

"You are my brother's widow," he began, as if rehearsing a sermon, "and as such, certain funds should now become available to you. We have, in fact, discussed these monies on more than one occasion."

He'd tried to discuss them while she'd considered smashing clocks. "We have. Briefly."

"There is no other way to say this, but your funds are sorely depleted. I do apologize to you for this mismanagement."

An opening salvo, no doubt intended to unnerve more than it apologized. "And how were my funds mismanaged, specifically?" She kept her voice pleasant, merely curious.

"I do not want to speak ill of my late brother, but his grasp of business principles was… not sophisticated," Douglas offered, as if this were the more difficult admission.

"Is ownership, then, a complicated business principle,

Douglas? As in, the dower portion of the settlements was mine, and was not his to use. That money was the one thing I, as a wife, could expect to remain in possession of, despite becoming my husband's chattel. Your brother's fault lay not in his grasp of business principles, but rather, in his grasp of morals."

They strolled along a walk of crushed white shells, which the moonlight made luminous. Perhaps the surrounding darkness enhanced her awareness of scents, for Astrid could divine the odor of rotting undergrowth beneath the fragrance of the flowers and Douglas's cedary scent.

Douglas bent and snapped off a white chrysanthemum. "I cannot know my brother's motivations." A martyr prayed for his executioner's forgiveness in the same patient, condescending tones.

"Douglas, let us be honest." Lest she spend the rest of the night among the chilly flowers and Douglas's chilly remorse. "Herbert was not a bad man, but he was self-indulgent and immature. He wasted money on himself, his leman, his dogs and horses and cronies. Your brother stole from funds that should have been saved for my exclusive use, and because *he* was head of the family, no one stopped him."

Though Astrid did not think Douglas would permit himself the same latitude.

"I can see your grief is abated." One could not tell with Douglas where thoughtful observation ended and dry sarcasm began, but he was at least trading honesty for honesty.

"Do you begrudge me an abatement of grief, Douglas? Particularly when what has speeded me

along has been nothing other than the reality of
Herbert's betrayals?"

Perhaps the full moon did incline people to lunacy,
for Astrid felt a bout of histrionics welling.

White chrysanthemums stood for truth. Douglas
tossed his into the hedge. "You speak in the plural."

"Of course I do. Tell me which of the wedding
vows Herbert kept, Douglas, and explain to me how
this frittering away of the only funds I have wasn't also
a betrayal."

They reached a stone bench that overlooked the
strange beauty of the fall garden by moonlight. Astrid
seated herself and gestured Douglas to do likewise.

Abruptly, she was tired, and tears threatened. She
missed being able to eat whatever she pleased; she
missed the simple misery of being Herbert's wife;
she missed Andrew's difficult, affectionate company.

"Sit with me a bit, Douglas. Stop looming over me
like a disappointed angel. There is more we need to
say to each other."

Nine

A DISAPPOINTED ANGEL? DOUGLAS OBLIGINGLY SAT AND waited for Astrid to fill the silence.

"My brother uses the same tactic," she said. "He sits, silent as a sphinx, unnerving people with his odd eyes, and soon they start telling him anything he asks simply to make him and his infernal silences go away."

And Fairly no doubt turned his odd-eyed stare on his own younger sibling, suggesting Astrid was due a small pang of sympathy.

"I played cards with your brother this afternoon. You would have been amused at our manly stratagems and posturing. I should hope the both of us were." He fell silent, not to make her squirm, but to give her time to collect her thoughts, because apparently, embezzlement, adultery, and bereavement were not to be the limit of their cheery little discussion.

"What would you have me do about this matter, Douglas?"

He could dither and insinuate, or he could be blunt and get them both off this cold, hard bench all the sooner.

"First, keep it to yourself, and second, allow

me time to replenish your accounts." These were commonsense responses to a ridiculous situation, but Douglas resented that they left him relying on Astrid's good graces. "The family finances are teetering somewhere between precarious and uncomfortable, but not quite dire. It is not well said of me, but if Herbert had died five years hence, I would not be so sanguine. My own investments are prospering, however, and I am hopeful in time, we will be on more solid footing."

He was not hopeful, he was bloody determined, though if he had to replace all Herbert had taken from Astrid's dower funds, he was also going to be bloody old before he achieved his goal.

Astrid scuffed a slipper against the grass. "And if Herbert had died five years ago, this whole situation would have been avoided."

Douglas maintained a diplomatic interest in the gardens rather than comment on that observation.

"Douglas, I would have truth between us. Don't hold back if you're trying to spare my feelings." She sounded like she was spoiling for an exchange of truths and wanted his magazine empty when she started firing.

"Isn't it enough your late husband abused your trust in this too?" Douglas asked, anger creeping into his voice, because as Herbert's heir, Douglas had also been bequeathed a share of ire.

She turned a pretty, sad face up to the moon. "It wasn't your fault Herbert was morally weak. It wasn't your fault he had so little self-discipline. It wasn't your fault I was so anxious to get out of my sister's household I married him. You have inherited a mess, much as Heathgate did. I will not judge you for it, nor will I judge you because Herbert betrayed your trust as well."

Douglas remained seated beside her, though the damned woman was entirely too perceptive. Herbert had betrayed them all, and it had caught up with him. Dead men tell no tales, but neither could they hide behind lies, denial, or sheer bravado when truth came for a reckoning.

"I've wondered why you accepted Herbert's suit, but it was too advantageous a match for me to question it. And Herbert's motivations were obvious."

She gathered the shawl closer. "Herbert was after two things: the marital settlements David so generously provided for me and a legitimate heir. He may well have gotten both."

"What in God's—I beg your pardon?"

"I am increasing, Douglas," Astrid said tiredly. "I appear to have conceived two weeks before Herbert's death, which puts me at about three difficult, uncomfortable months along."

Douglas said nothing, and he hoped his face gave nothing away, but inside, oh, inside his emotions were reeling. "You are sure?"

"I am." She did not sound pleased about it.

"My sincerest congratulations," he replied, but his preoccupation sounded in his voice. "This changes things." It changed *everything*.

"I know, Douglas. I know."

"No, you don't." She thought somebody had come along and moved her bishop, when in fact, the entire chessboard had been sent end over end. "Mother has it in her head you should move in with her and I should take up residence in the town house. She will be doubly insistent when she knows of this development."

"I do not want to live with your mother."

Douglas nearly snapped that nobody wanted to live with Lady Amery, but held his temper. Astrid had not had an easy time of it at the hands of his family, and besides, she wasn't done speaking.

"Your mother's house is not large, and it is dark, cluttered, and completely unsuited to raising a child. I like the town house, and you have said I might live there as long as I pleased."

Damn all logical females with accurate recall, and damn him for his misplaced generosity.

"What if Mother were to move in with you there? We are supporting three households, Astrid. Yours, Mother and Henry's, and mine. If you ask it of me, I will move in with Mother and Henry, but Mother will make a nuisance of herself with this baby anyway. You won't escape her just because she lives with me and not you."

Astrid scuffed her slippers again, both this time, while Douglas took a leaf from Fairly's book and let her stew.

"I accept your mother under my roof," Astrid said, "but you must make her understand two things: first, it is *my* roof, Douglas. I set the menus, manage the help, and keep the household accounts. Her advice is welcome, but not her interference."

Whether she knew it or not, Astrid was discussing terms of surrender.

"I can speak to her as often and as sternly as

necessary." Though with Mother, who was even less biddable than dear Herbert had been, his lectures would do no good whatsoever. "What is your other condition?"

"You and she must understand, Douglas, I will spend a great deal of time with my sister, particularly in the coming months. She will have need of me, and I will certainly have need of her."

"I would not think to keep you from her under the circumstances. As to that, your time here seems to have stood you in good stead. If we are agreed then, perhaps we can put these awkward subjects to rest?" *Please God.*

Astrid wrinkled her nose, looking young and unhappy. "You aren't getting off that easily, Douglas. We must make one further agreement. Lady Amery is not to know I am expecting until I decide to tell her."

The request was peculiar, when that child might mean Astrid had fulfilled her obligation to the succession. Most women would have been crowing over such a coup.

"Why?"

"I lost a child last year, and I was further along then than I am now. To get your mother's hopes up if another disappointment is in store would be cruel. She doted upon Herbert, and the child will be precious to her."

Herbert hadn't said anything about losing a child, but then, Herbert would not have been comfortable alluding to such a situation any more than Douglas was. He steeled himself to touch on a matter as personal as embezzlement. "How long does this business take?"

"This business," Astrid said with a small smile,

"takes about nine and a half months. I should deliver in mid-March, if all goes well."

Douglas tried to think of a delicate way to phrase his next question—and failed.

"After a certain point, I should think your condition would be obvious. Your sister, for example..." He let the observation trail off, the matter speaking for itself, though rumors abounded that Princess Caroline had hidden more than one interesting event from her royal spouse.

"Felicity is twice as far along as I am, Douglas, and first babies tend not to show as early. This is my sister's third child."

He'd already learned more than he wanted to know. Pregnant women made him nervous, particularly when their condition sailed before them like the prow of some small, feminine ship. Thinking of Astrid, as petite as she was, reaching those proportions made him...

Well, he wouldn't think of her in that condition. Would not.

"I will leave the timing of your disclosure to Mother in your hands," he said, rising. Mother would know soon enough. The household staff was not immune to her questioning and prying, as Astrid would soon learn. As Henry might realize, if he paid the least bit of attention. "Shall we go inside?"

"If you wouldn't mind, Douglas, I would like to remain out here. I value my solitude."

Douglas didn't respond to the obvious jibe: *And your mother and your thieving brother and this child growing inside me have all conspired to see to it I have no solitude.* He valued solitude as highly as anybody, so he bowed politely and took his leave of her. His most distasteful obligation dispatched—he *had* apologized to the woman—he was now free to return to his correspondence.

~~

Andrew waited in the shadows until Douglas Allen had taken his stiff-rumped, proper self back into the house, then came down beside Astrid on the bench. "How did he take the news?"

"He was his usual inscrutable, composed self." Astrid stayed right where she was, didn't scoot over or even lean in Andrew's direction. "He said the right things, but he is moving Lady Amery into the town house with me. She is not to be told my condition until the moment of my choosing, and I am to have as much time with Felicity as I desire. Finally, dear mama-in-law will not be the lady of the house, I will."

"You got all that resolved in less than fifteen minutes?" And was dear mama-in-law female company, Douglas's spy, or both?

Astrid had no rejoinder for him, which was worrisome. He'd fretted about her all day but didn't think she'd appreciate hearing that.

"What aren't you telling me?" he asked instead.

"Douglas told me my funds are gone."

"That was bold." Or conniving. "Also the only good move left to him."

"How do you mean?" Astrid was good-hearted, and good-hearted people did not naturally anticipate the deviousness of their moral inferiors.

So Andrew, who was among that number, would

explain it to her. "Douglas's solicitors have told him by now that you and your brother went nosing around, and the files have been sent to Fairly's town house. As far as Douglas is concerned, you would have found out the truth as soon as you returned to Town. He spiked your guns by offering his confession first."

Somewhere out in the home wood, an owl hooted, an eerie, lonely sound Andrew hadn't heard since he'd departed for Italy years before.

"Douglas has spiked my guns, and planted his mother under my roof, and now he knows for certain I am carrying Herbert's child. Still, Andrew, I cannot attribute foul motives to the man. He is cool, aloof, and dispassionate, but I cannot feel he is evil."

Andrew should be relieved Astrid had reached that conclusion, for otherwise, he'd be procuring a special license. He resisted the urge to take her hand.

"You have reached a Scottish verdict. Insufficient evidence—neither an acquittal nor a conviction."

They sat together, alone in the shadows, the moon appearing to grow smaller as it drifted into the sky. When he could bear the distance between them no longer, Andrew slid an arm around Astrid's waist. Astrid rested her head on his shoulder, and they stayed next to each other until the chill drove them inside.

❧

Astrid woke up one brisk fall Tuesday morning and realized she was halfway through her pregnancy. That was a relief indeed, since it meant she'd passed the point where she'd miscarried the previous year. She still had occasional bouts of queasiness—or more than occasional. At some point in each day, her stomach would signal its ability to rule her life.

Skipping meals did not help, so she headed directly for the stairs rather than get drawn into the tête-à-tête she could hear going on between Lady Amery and her youngest son in the family parlor down the hall.

And Astrid still fainted, no matter how careful she tried to be.

This unfortunate fact was borne home as she regarded the cobwebs gracing the corners of the ceiling in the octagonal entryway to her residence.

"How could you be so careless?"

That clipped, controlled voice cut across the fog in Astrid's brain like a bitter whiff of vinaigrette.

"Douglas." Why must he choose now to make one of his duty calls to his dependent females?

"Girls just out of the schoolroom know not to let their hems get tangled on a staircase. Must I assign the footmen to escorting you about your own dwelling?"

The chandelier needed a good scrubbing. Astrid could reach this conclusion from her position sprawled on the rug at the foot of the staircase. Mortification joined nausea as Douglas helped her to sit on the bottom step.

"Stop yelling at me, my lord."

"I have not raised my voice, though the notion appeals strongly. You could well be carrying the Amery heir, need I remind you, and tumbling down the steps is not responsible behavior given your condition. What have you to say for yourself?" He paced back and forth like Headmaster lecturing a class of unruly boys, his movements making Astrid's head swim.

"I have to say that you're a perfect ass, Douglas Allen." He paused to pivot at the edge of the rug, as if Astrid's words had spun him by the shoulder. "Do you think I am so stupid as to carelessly put my own welfare at risk? Do you forbid me the use of the stairs until I deliver this child? Are you determined to make me as helpless and vapid as you've made your mother?"

He came to a halt at the opposite edge of the carpet, his features dumbstruck. "What on earth are you talking about?"

"You and Henry treat the poor woman as if she is simple, Douglas. You never ask her opinion. You never defer to her judgment. Henry makes a joke of her at every turn, and believe me, she comprehends the disrespect. But at least your mother would understand that women in an interesting condition are prone to fainting."

"You are telling me you *fainted*?" His consternation was genuine, but then, what occasion would Douglas Allen have to learn of an expecting woman's tribulations?

Though Andrew had known them, had known them intimately. "I fainted. I am also frequently queasy and fatigued for no reason. I suggest you talk to your mother, who is entertaining Henry above stairs as we speak. Consult a knowledgeable midwife if you don't believe me: pregnant women faint. I didn't fall down the stairs on purpose or out of clumsy disregard for my hems, and I resent you would imply I did."

"You fainted." His brows twitched down as he applied a new theory to facts he'd already sorted and labeled. "Because of your... condition?"

The stair was hard beneath Astrid's backside, and having Douglas loom over her was intolerable. She used the banister railing to haul herself to her feet, which—thank the gods—did not try her balance further. "Douglas, what possible reason could I have for harming this baby?"

And because the front hallway was no place to have any sort of discussion, Astrid crossed to the parlor, Douglas trailing her like a worried hound.

"We are overwrought," he said. *He* was overwrought, in any case. Astrid was weary, lonely, and hungry. "I apologize for misconstruing the situation, but you have every reason to hate my late brother, and to resent bearing his child enough to wish it harm. I daresay you have every reason to hate me, Henry, and Mother as well."

Douglas and his damned barbed apologies. Astrid wanted to scream, except the parlor door was open— Douglas would be *proper* while he accused her of resorting to violence against Herbert's child.

"Why would I hate Herbert, much less his child, and his entire surviving family?" Resent, yes, but *hate*?

Douglas moved around the room, shifting the lace runner on the table so it hung exactly even on both ends, nudging a framed miniature of a hound puppy a quarter inch at one corner, and using the toe of his boot to flip a carpet tassel so it aligned with its mates.

He would have made a splendid chambermaid.

"Herbert stole from you, he paid more attention to his mistress, his horses, and his hounds than he did to you, and we both know he spent your dower funds on just those pursuits. He deserved your disrespect. He certainly earned mine."

Douglas had forgotten to mention Herbert's cronies and even Henry, who instead of reading law had been forever gambling and expecting Herbert to cover his vowels.

The present Lord Amery had many of the Allen features. Blue eyes, golden hair, a certain cast to his features, but to Astrid, he also looked like a man haunted. "Did you hate your older brother, Douglas?"

"At times, yes. Yes, I did hate him, and I'm sure he returned the favor. It is my job, in our little family, to be the lone adult, and this has earned me considerable enmity." He addressed the empty hearth, it being impractical to keep an unoccupied room warm in the Allen womenfolk's household.

Astrid refused to feel pity for a man who scolded her from coming a cropper. "Interesting."

He moved a brass candlestick one inch closer to the end of the mantel. "What do you find interesting?"

"Either you don't consider me a family member, or you don't consider me an adult."

"I beg your pardon," he said so stiffly Astrid relented.

"Douglas, may we attribute this morning's situation to a simple mishap followed by a misunderstanding? And I don't hate your late brother. He had faults, as we all do, but I console myself with the hope that in time, he and I could have grown to a better accommodation of our marriage."

Douglas peered at her as if trying to assess her sincerity. For a handsome, well-mannered gentleman, he had a positive gift for giving offense.

"He didn't deserve you," Douglas said after a lengthy silence. "And you're going to need ice on that bump." He touched a finger to her forehead, making Astrid aware that in due course, she'd be sporting a thumping bruise near her temple.

They were preserved from further discourse on that riveting topic by Lady Amery's voice on the stairs.

"Is that you, Douglas?" she trilled as she descended. "Why, so it is! How fortunate you are here. I was just telling dear Henry that Lady Porter's niece, the Honorable Miss Evelyn Buckley-Smythe, is coming to Town to share the holidays with her aunt. Why, Astrid, what is that horrid mark on your forehead?"

Douglas sketched a bow. "Hello, Mother. Astrid has had a slight mishap. No harm done."

"I fell down the stairs."

Lady Amery's face creased into a puzzled frown, but because she plucked her eyebrows into perfect, thin arches, she looked more horrified than concerned. "A blow to the head is always serious. You aren't feeling dizzy, are you?"

"Not now," Astrid said, shooting a wry glance at Douglas.

"You really ought to be more careful, Astrid dear."

"I really should, my lady." Astrid took a seat, because nobody seemed inclined to send a servant for ice and a cloth, and her head was beginning to throb. "I have particular reason to take care these days, but I have hesitated to share my news, lest it be only a temporary cause for joy."

And if dear Henry—who always seemed to pop in around meal times—would stop chasing the upstairs maid and join the assemblage in the parlor, Astrid wouldn't have to repeat her cause for joy all over again for his benefit.

"My dear, you are speaking in riddles," Lady Amery sniffed. "Douglas, can you understand her?"

"Yes, Mother. I can understand her." On Douglas, that pained expression might have passed for a smile—or an indication of wind.

"Well, what is she *saying*? Perhaps this knock on the head has scrambled your wits, Astrid."

"I believe, Mother," Douglas said in the same quiet, patient voice, "Astrid is trying to tell you she is anticipating the birth of the late viscount's child."

"But Herbert is…" Lady Amery paused, confused, then her countenance filled with joy. "Oh, my dear, dear Astrid! Is it so? This is wonderful, wonderful news."

She hugged Astrid, laughed and teared up, and hugged her again. Douglas discreetly took his leave, the sheer feminine joy of the scene no doubt inspiring his hasty retreat. Next time Astrid wanted to be rid of the man, she'd manufacture some tears.

Or maybe a lot of tears.

❧

Lady Amery's speech became peppered with phrases such as, "when you're a grandmother yourself, dear…" and "when my dear, dear grandson arrives…" Were it not for the imperative task of informing Lady Amery's every friend and acquaintance of the happy development—for what mattered the strictures of mourning compared to such news?—Astrid would have had no peace whatsoever.

As matters stood, Astrid was deliriously happy,

three days after sharing her news with Lady Amery, to
be sitting at the breakfast table *by herself.*

Since returning from Willowdale, Astrid had kept
busy by resuming her responsibilities as lady of the
house, and because Lady Amery accepted every single
condolence call, the job was not without demands.

David called every Thursday and ensured Astrid had
ample opportunity to stroll either the back gardens or
the park, and Gareth sent his man of business, Mr.
Brenner, to keep regular contact with her as well.

And she had correspondence to attend to, which was
the next thing on her morning's agenda. Every week, she
heard from her sister, who, it was confirmed, was carrying twins. Andrew occasionally added a sentence or two
to the bottom of Felicity's note, never anything more.

Astrid missed him terribly. She missed him in her
bed at night, and she missed him over the dinner table.
She missed him when she fed the ducks in the park—or
rather, scared the ducks in her widow's weeds and
veils—and when she sat out in the back garden with
a novel. And while she missed him in an adult, sexual
sense, she also simply longed for his company. He was
a generously affectionate man with her, and when her
back, her feet, or her tummy ached, what she missed
most of all was his simple caring touch.

These very thoughts were filling Astrid's mind
when Andrew strolled into her breakfast parlor unannounced and nonchalant.

"Andrew!" Astrid shot out of her chair in a joyous
leap. She was across the room and in his arms before
the dizziness hit, her vision going dark as she sagged
against him.

"Astrid?" Andrew's voice sounded far away as she clung to him in an effort to stay upright. "Astrid?" She was swung up against a hard male chest, and reveled in the knowledge she was once again in Andrew's arms.

He deposited her on the horsehair sofa in the chilly front parlor, though Astrid would have preferred he deliver her to her very bedroom.

"You know how to give a fellow a fright," Andrew commented, worry lacing his smile. He propped his hip at her waist and swept the hair from her forehead. "And what, may I ask, is this?" His fingers trailed gently over the bruise.

Astrid caught his hand in her own, and used the leverage to sit up.

"I am usually sound enough if I remember to move slowly. I am glad to see you." Glad was too small a word for the joy in her heart.

"And I you. Except for this"—he touched her forehead again—"you look well."

"I look increasingly like a walrus," Astrid rejoined, standing slowly. Andrew was on his feet instantly, a hand on her elbow as she made her way back to the breakfast parlor.

"You most assuredly do not look like a walrus," Andrew said, his grin suggesting she might inspect herself for whiskers, fins, and tusks. "Or let me put it this way: if you are a walrus, then your sister had better be on the lookout for anything resembling a harpoon."

Despite his smile, he looked tired too, and he smelled a bit of road dust and horse.

"That is an awful thing to say, Andrew Alexander. How is Lissy, anyway? Her letters are always so pleasant and lighthearted, I would hardly know she is expecting."

"I know she's expecting," Andrew retorted as he held her chair, "and Heathgate knows she's expecting. Truthfully, I think Gareth's hovering and fretting is more bothersome to her than is her condition, even with twins." He straightened and looked around the table. "Breakfast. May I?"

Anything to make him stay even a few more minutes. "Of course, but this is the last of our raspberry jam. Go near it, and I shall flatten you."

"Is that a promise?" Andrew inquired pleasantly as he dished himself up some toast, eggs, and ham.

"A threat," Astrid allowed as she slathered jam on her toast. "To what do I owe the pleasure of your visit?" And how could she induce him to visit more often?

He considered his full plate. "I could tell you I had to see for myself you are faring well, but you would probably not believe me. Instead, I will tell you I had to get away from Mother and Gwen, who are pitching a battle of their own that makes my squabbles with Gwen look paltry."

And he had come to see Astrid when he'd needed to get away. She really should not be so very, very pleased.

"That doesn't sound good at all," Astrid said, biting off a jam-laden corner of toast. "My experience suggests your mother is the singular source of that will of steel you share with your brother. Recall, if you please, she managed my come out, and my second Season as well."

And Lady Heathgate had planned Astrid's wedding

and had a great deal to say about the betrothal contracts. Though to be fair, she'd also been one of few people to understand that a miscarriage was deserving of grief rather than predictable platitudes about God's will and nature's course.

Andrew sliced off a bite of ham and skewered it with his fork. "I suppose that explains why Herbert could carry you off among the orange blossoms. You needed to get away from Mother's meddling too."

Insightful man. "What do they fight about?"

He set his utensils down, crossing the knife and fork across the top of his plate. "What don't they fight about? They fight over Rose, and what the best herb is for dealing with megrims. They fight over whether I am too polite, or not sincerely polite enough—I haven't heard such bickering since my father's family gathered in Scotland before the accident."

And the shadows in his eyes said that memory haunted him still.

"But you don't want to send your mother home," Astrid deduced, "because it would hurt her feelings, and because you would then have to share your brother's hospitality rather than live with Gwen. Or you might live with Gwen as the lady of your house, which could be awkward." She took another bite of toast and jam, though the sight of Andrew was a greater source of sustenance than her food.

"Correct," Andrew said, folding his serviette by his plate in a precise equilateral triangle, something Douglas might have done. "And I don't want to send Gwen and Rose to Gareth and Felicity, because those two need their privacy for as long as possible. *You*, however, are expected to attend your sister's confinement."

"I am looking forward to it," Astrid said, smiling at the thought that in the next five months there would be three new babies in the family—God willing.

Abruptly, her stomach gave an alarming little jump, and she felt a peculiar dry sensation in her mouth. She at least remembered to rise slowly. "Andrew, I am going to have to leave you for a moment."

He was on his feet, looking both perturbed and concerned as he blocked Astrid's path to the door. "You are still getting sick?"

"Apparently so. I will be only a moment."

She slid around him with all haste, because nothing, not nausea, not weak knees, not anything was going to keep Astrid from enjoying Andrew's company on this pretty fall morning.

Ten

ANDREW WAITED ALONE IN THE BREAKFAST ROOM FOR all of ten minutes before following Astrid upstairs, because it seemed there was not another soul in the house. Not a footman to find a maid, not a maid to look in on the lady of the house, not a housekeeper to explain why the staff was least in sight.

He came upon Astrid in the first bedroom at the top of the stairs, curled up on the floor at the foot of her bed. She clutched her stomach, her complexion dead white, her teeth clenched, but what terrified Andrew nearly beyond speech was her stillness.

When in good health, Astrid moved. She talked with her hands, she marched about the house, she *moved* through her life.

Andrew knelt beside her and pushed her hair off her damp forehead, noting again the bruise there, and hoping she couldn't tell his hand was shaking. "What's amiss, love? Did you faint again? Is it the baby?"

She shook her head and moaned as her whole body trembled and her hand flattened over the slight mound of her belly. Having learned a few things in his travels, Andrew cupped her jaw.

"Open your eyes, sweetheart. Just for a moment."

She managed this, though apparently the light hurt her eyes, and with good reason, for her pupils had dilated to encompass much of her irises.

Poison, which meant every moment counted.

Andrew retrieved a big porcelain washbasin from her bureau, rolled Astrid to her side, unceremoniously pried her mouth open, and inserted a finger down her throat. She retched violently, sprawled across his legs, her face over the basin. When he saw she'd lost every iota of her breakfast, he let her sink back into a panting crouch.

She looked dazed rather than angry, which alarmed Andrew even more.

"I'm going to carry you to the bed, dear heart, then get rid of this basin and fetch you some water. Is there a maid who can help you into a nightgown?"

"Day off. Only the housekeeper's about, and she's gone to market."

He scooped her up as gently as he could and laid her on the bed. The basin he left covered in the hallway, and from the bedroom next door he retrieved a drinking glass as well as a pitcher, basin, and towel.

All the while, Andrew prayed, prayed like he hadn't prayed since rising seas and a howling wind had threatened nearly everybody he held dear, and taken one he'd never had a chance to hold dear.

He drew the draperies over both of Astrid's bedroom windows and shut her door, then eased off her shoes and sat her up to loosen the buttons down the back of her gown. The dress came off, and then her jumps, leaving her in only her chemise.

Pale, wan, and so frightfully quiet.

One part of his mind noted the changes in her body. She was riper all around—breasts, belly, hips, everywhere, and the added flesh looked marvelous on her.

Another part alternated between prayers and curses, while he busied himself finding a clean nightgown, which he substituted for the chemise. Next he rolled her stockings off, knowing each movement was causing Astrid distress.

When he had her clothed in only a nightgown, he offered her a sip of water. She struggled to sit up, so he propped her against his chest and held the glass against her lips as she took a few swallows.

"That's enough for now, and the next order of business ought to be summoning your physician."

Astrid shivered and croaked a name at him and a direction. Andrew stuck his head out the window and bellowed for his tiger to fetch the damned doctor—the hand of Almighty God could not have forced Andrew to leave Astrid alone in that house—then pulled a rocking chair from a corner of the room and sat right next to the bed.

"Feeling better?"

"I feel *awful*," she wailed quietly. "This is not my usual bout of the queasies."

"The doctor is on his way, and he'll be able to tell us more," Andrew replied with a calm he did not feel. He smoothed her hair back and once again noted the discoloration near her hairline. "You have yet to tell me how you got this great bruise."

"Fell," she said, her eyes drifting shut. "Fainted at the top of the stairs. Douglas found me."

Andrew's hand went still on her hair, then resumed the caress meant to soothe them both. He continued to stroke her face, to hold her hand, and to offer her occasional sips of water until he heard a banging on the front door three-quarters of an hour later.

"The doctor," he told her, kissing her cool cheek before he made his way downstairs to admit a blond man who struck Andrew as entirely too young, handsome, and cheerful to be a physician.

"Dr. Phillip DuPont, here to see the Viscountess Amery. I'm told the situation is urgent," the man said as Andrew opened the door.

"Greymoor. I'm... family by marriage," Andrew said, offering a quick handshake. "She's upstairs. I suspect poison, though it wouldn't have been in her system for long."

At those words, the physician's smile fled, and he fairly sprinted up the stairs ahead of Andrew. When DuPont opened his bag and sat on the side of the bed, Andrew took up his post in the rocking chair, resisting the urge to hold Astrid's hand.

"Viscountess?" The doctor had a pleasant, calm voice, one of those voices that always sounded close to a smile. He picked up Astrid's wrist in his left hand, holding up his timepiece with his right, while Andrew wanted to kill him for touching her.

DuPont's hands moved with the deft, impersonal competence of the medical professional as he listened to her heart, peered into her eyes, and laid the back of his hand against her forehead. All the while, he asked questions: When did symptoms arise; what had she to eat today; had anything tasted off; did she use any laudanum; how long before his lordship had found her; did her joints ache; did her head hurt; and where did that nasty, nasty bruise come from?

The doctor sat back, frowning. "If you would excuse us, my lord?"

Astrid reached for Andrew's hand as he started to rise, and he promptly sat back down.

"The lady has asked that I stay." Which was fortunate, because Andrew was not about to go any farther than across the room, even when Astrid was tended by a man whose vocation was healing.

"But, my lord, I must examine the viscountess *personally*," the doctor tried again. "For you to be present, family member or not, would be highly improper."

Astrid met his gaze, silently pleading with him.

"You can leave, Doctor, or you can examine her while I sit in this chair," Andrew said. "I'm sorry, but the lady's wishes must come first. Those are your choices. And if it eases your conscience, I wasn't even in the country when she conceived."

Blond eyebrows flew up, but the doctor seemed to gather his wits as he turned his attention to Astrid.

"My lady, there are certain herbs, which when ingested, can end a pregnancy, though few of them would be effective this late in your term. Some of them, if taken in sufficient quantity, carry a risk of symptoms such as those you've experienced, though such herbs would not account for all of your symptoms." He kept his gaze on her as he blathered on, which Andrew took as an expression of the instinct for self-preservation. "Did you attempt to end your pregnancy?"

Her hand tightened around Andrew's fingers, as if she'd keep him from reacting with violence. "God, no."

"I thought not," DuPont murmured. "As I said, the symptoms are not entirely consistent with such a notion. Let's see how the baby is faring, then, shall we?"

Astrid closed her eyes, likely the better to pray for her child's welfare.

The doctor did nothing more than palpate her lower abdomen through her nightgown, gently at first, then a bit more firmly.

"Everything seems to be quite in order," he announced cheerily. "You are still carrying, Lady Amery, and there's little reason to suspect harm to the child at this point. For the next few days, you should remain quiet, though, as a precaution. If you experience any bleeding or cramping—and I mean the merest twinge, the tiniest spot—you must call me. As your activity level drops over the next few days, you may not be as aware of the child moving, but if as you resume your normal routine, you don't feel movement, you must also call me."

He sat back, still not meeting Andrew's gaze. "Any questions?"

Astrid shook her head, so Andrew escorted DuPont to the door, making sure they had gained the front entryway before posing questions.

"Was she poisoned?"

The doctor looked thoughtful. "I appreciate that you are concerned for her, and you are a member of her extended family, but I really should be discussing this with Viscount Amery."

"Amery is no more related to her than I am."

"Ah, but Amery is related to the child, is he not?"

"He might be," Andrew allowed, "but that child, if Lady Amery lives long enough to produce one, is not your patient, and the mother is."

"The Church doesn't quite see it that way."

A barrister masquerading as a physician, two reasons to rearrange the fellow's handsome face.

"And I don't see that you are wearing a collar," Andrew shot back. "Moreover, this child you are so concerned about, if male, will divest the present viscount of the title, won't he? To whom do we then attribute nefarious motives, Doctor? And do you mean to tell me you believe Lady Amery coincidentally fell down an entire flight of stairs earlier this same week?"

DuPont ran a pale hand through fashionable blond curls and eyed the door. "My practice depends on my ability to gain and keep the trust of my clients, particularly those like the viscount, who are, shall we say, *well placed*. You obviously care for the lady, so I will tell you this much: yesterday, the viscount himself was in my office, asking me all sorts of questions that sought to establish whether she might have tossed herself down the stairs in an attempt to rid herself of the child."

The doctor's expression conveyed impatience with the entire situation.

"I told the viscount, in so many words, a woman would have to be near crazed to attempt such a thing, and many, many less risky options would have presented themselves to her before now. He did seem somewhat reassured, but I can guarantee you, he will be back in my office, asking even more pointed questions after today. And unless you are the lady's husband, I really have no business talking to you at all."

When he would have turned to go, Andrew stopped him with a hand on his arm.

"You still haven't answered my question, Doctor. Do you believe the viscountess was administered a deadly poison?"

For a moment, there was little sound, except the ticking of the clock in the nearby parlor and the jingle of a passing harness.

"Yes, and no," the doctor said, his hand on the door latch. "Not a deadly poison, but a deadly combination of poisons. An opiate was involved, probably to render her unconscious, to deaden the ability to retch, and possibly to deaden the worst of the pain. In addition to that, her ladyship ingested a toxin of some sort, though there's no way to determine which one. If you hadn't been here and reacted as quickly as you did, we would be summoning the watch."

Andrew swore in Italian and German both—the doctor would likely know French—his worst fears confirmed. "And have you seen the viscountess behave in any way that suggests she would do harm to herself or her child?"

The doctor shook his head, and was gone before Andrew could ask the next question.

"He thinks you were poisoned," Andrew said when he returned to Astrid's room, "and he won't be able, in all honesty, to assure Douglas you did not administer it to yourself."

"Dear God." Astrid sank back against her pillows and turned her head, when such an accusation should have had her charging about the room and ranting.

"Astrid, listen to me. Douglas has already asked the doctor if your recent tumble down the steps could be an effort to hurt, or even lose, the baby. The doctor told him you would have to be crazy to attempt such a thing. Douglas could be laying a trap, creating a wealth of evidence to prove you unfit, if not insane, prior to the child's birth—if he doesn't succeed in killing you altogether."

She plucked at the coverlet, which was embroidered with ducks and daisies. The design was not a married woman's choice, much less a widow's, but it reassured Andrew to see it.

"Had you not come calling today, I doubt I would have survived."

"The doctor confirmed as much." And how Andrew hated to see Astrid pale and fearful. "I want you to write a note to Lady Amery. Tell her you have gone off to pay a call on your brother, and tell me which of your things you want me to gather up."

She put a hand over her belly, a hand that sported no wedding ring. "My stationery is in the escritoire, and there's a small valise under this bed."

As Astrid wrote a note to Lady Amery, her penmanship less than exemplary, Andrew wrote a different note to David, Viscount Fairly. Astrid sat on the bed and allowed Andrew to dress her—he did not want her even standing if he could preserve her from the effort. He tossed some clothing and personal items into her valise, and then made up the bed while Astrid sat in the rocking chair and stared at the carpet.

"You'd best heed nature's call," he reminded her, "and I'll get the carriage."

Andrew soon had her up in his phaeton, his tiger tearing off with the note for Fairly. Minutes later, Andrew drew his vehicle to a halt in Lady Heathgate's mews. As he escorted Astrid up the back walk, he bellowed for a running footman to retrieve Mr. Brenner from Gareth's town house, and sent another messenger on a fast horse to head for Willowdale. Both were off in their respective directions before Andrew and Astrid had gained the back entrance of the house.

With those measures taken, a bit of the anxiety riding Andrew eased.

He ushered Astrid into the house, gave orders for tea and scones to be served in the family parlor, then escorted her there, hoping to give her a chance to catch her breath.

And then he would tell her what she absolutely did not want to hear.

"How are you holding up?" he asked, taking a chair at a right angle to the couch. If he sat beside her, he would touch her, and if he touched her, he would not be able to say what must be said.

"I have a sense of unreality, of being anxious, and knowing my situation is perilous, but also feeling too tired and disoriented to do anything about it. Even thinking seems an effort, and that scares me most of all."

Astrid frightened and unsafe in her own home

was insupportable, and motivation enough for what Andrew must do.

"You were given an opiate." And a toxin—a bloody, goddamned poison. "That might account for the disorientation. But you are also, no doubt, in shock." When she would have interrupted him, he held up a hand. "Please, hear me out." Before he lost his nerve.

Now she stared at his mother's antique Axminster carpets.

"You might have fallen down the stairs, quite by accident, my dear, but if you think back carefully, can you assure me you weren't shoved?"

"The housemaids were about," Astrid said slowly, as if the words were eluding capture by her mind. "They would have had to bring the tea tray up to Lady Amery if Henry were paying his regular call on her. I have a vague recollection of starting to faint, but not quite being teetery yet when I pitched down the stairs."

That was not a denial. He'd been hoping to God she'd be able to give him a confident denial.

"And today," Andrew went on, "something you consumed at breakfast damn near killed you, under circumstances when it was likely you would have been in the house alone." Rather than watch her face, he focused on her hands, pale and still in her lap. "We have reached a point where any reasonable person would conclude you are in need of protection."

She did not launch into a lecture about him overreacting or overstepping. She didn't dismiss his fears with assurances that she'd be more careful. As

Astrid sat motionless and pale in the smallest parlor of his mother's house, Andrew battled the need to do violence to whoever had rendered her so lifeless.

"What do you propose, Andrew?"

"Marriage."

～

Andrew greeted Lord Fairly and Michael Brenner when they arrived fifteen minutes before the appointed hour, both in proper morning finery. Brenner brought the special license, and Fairly a bouquet of white roses.

"The bishop will be here on the hour," Andrew told them. Should the right reverend lord bishop fail to show, Andrew would hunt the man down on foot. "May I offer you each a drink?"

"The Bishop of London?" Fairly rejoined. "Any particular reason?"

"The haste is because Astrid was slipped a potentially fatal dose of poison today, in her own home." Andrew's hand shook as he poured drinks for his guests. "If I hadn't stopped by, completely unplanned I might add, she would have died a very uncomfortable death, alone, on her bedroom floor. The doctor confirmed that much."

He poured himself a drink and addressed the rest of his remarks to a small porcelain statute of the winged goddess Nike on the mantel.

"The bishop is because I want this wedding to be so damned official, despite its haste, Douglas will not be able to attack it from any angle."

Fairly turned his back, as if studying a portrait of

three small boys and a mastiff that hung over the side-board, though his grip on his glass looked ferocious.

"Prudent," Fairly said, sipping his brandy. "When you talk to Douglas, I would like to be present."

"As would I," said a voice from the hallway.

Gareth sauntered in, looking windblown and smelling of exertion and horse, despite the nippy day. Andrew put down his drink and reached for the decanter as Gareth knocked his hand aside and enveloped him in a hug. "To hell with the drink."

"You came."

"I am not a foolish man," Gareth said, drawing back. "Besotted, yes. Foolish, not often. Felicity saw I wanted to be here, ordered my hardiest mount saddled, then summoned me for argument. I fear I am not appropriately attired."

When a man had only one adult male relative left on earth, that fellow's presence was a bracing tonic. "You could have arrived in your dressing gown for all I care," Andrew replied. "You are here, and for that, you and Felicity have my thanks."

"Now that Heathgate has made his entrance," Fairly said, pouring Gareth a drink, "perhaps you'd care to start your tale again. You had just explained that Astrid ingested a potentially fatal dose of poison while enjoying a solitary breakfast this morning."

"Sweet, suffering angels," Gareth expostulated, scowling thunderously. "If there's more, I don't need to hear it. Marry her and move the hell out of England until the child is of age—at least until then."

Andrew felt a nudge of relief, because his brother had anticipated the next worry: How to keep Astrid and her child safe- once Andrew had guaranteed himself the legal entitlement to do so.

"Let's hope it doesn't come to that," Fairly said. "What haven't you told us?"

Andrew glanced at the clock again—he was, after all, a bridegroom—and set his drink aside. Whether it was wedding-day nerves, lingering upset over Astrid's brush with death, or sympathy for his intended's tentative digestion, Andrew could not countenance swilling spirits.

"Dr. DuPont told me Douglas had already interrogated him about whether Astrid might have thrown herself down the steps to harm or lose the baby. Astrid did indeed tumble the length of the Allens' front stairway, but her best recollection is that she may have been pushed."

"Pushed?" Gareth began. "Then why the hell would Douglas—?"

Andrew held up a hand and continued speaking. "The doctor was careful this morning to question Astrid regarding anything she might have taken, intentionally or otherwise, to induce a miscarriage. When Douglas interrogated DuPont earlier, DuPont told Douglas a woman would have to be crazy to try to lose a child by causing herself serious bodily harm."

"And there we have it," Fairly said, running a finger around the rim of his glass. "The contingency plan. If Astrid isn't killed outright, she is made to look as if she has homicidal intentions toward her unborn child. I would not put it past Douglas to raise suspicions regarding the miscarriage she had last year."

The slight uneasiness in Andrew's guts rose higher,

like seasickness as the sight of dry land receded. "I'd forgotten about that."

Gareth sat and used a handkerchief to swat dust from his boots. "And not to cheer anybody up, Douglas will have a motive for Astrid's resentment of the pregnancy when he can demonstrate the late viscount stole from his own wife."

"And did so," Andrew added bleakly, "to maintain his well-compensated mistress." In the ensuing silence, Brenner topped off everyone's glass, then put the stopper—a damned cherub—back in the decanter.

"Was there ever such a cheerful wedding party?" Brenner asked, his brogue slightly in evidence. His comment restored Andrew's balance a bit, which was fortunate, because the bishop soon joined them, eyeing their drinks with a knowing smile.

"Are we fortifying ourselves, gentlemen?" he asked genially. "I believe many a wedding is thus celebrated in advance, and wouldn't mind a tot m'self." He had no sooner downed his "tot" in a single swallow than Astrid joined them, her attire plain lavender and her complexion pale.

But, oh, she did smile when she spied her brother standing across the room. That smile helped settle something in Andrew's mind, helped him breathe more easily.

"You came," she said, hugging Fairly fiercely.

"Odd," Gareth said from his place behind her, "my sibling greeted me the same way."

"Gareth!" If anything, Gareth's hug was more fierce than Fairly's had been, fierce enough to convey both his love and Felicity's. Gareth kissed Astrid's cheek and kept an arm around her shoulders. "Felicity sends her best wishes, but she no longer hugs anyone, she docks alongside them, so great are her dimensions."

"That's quite enough!" Astrid chided, but his humor had succeeded in bringing the roses to her cheeks and the light back in her eye.

Within moments, Astrid and Andrew were poised before the bishop, and Fairly was responding to the question regarding who gives the bride in marriage. With Gareth and Fairly on either side of them, they spoke their vows, Astrid quietly, and Andrew in the tones of a man who knew this wedding was right, even if the marriage itself would suffer a world of problems.

They were pronounced man and wife together, the ring one chosen by Felicity from several owned by Astrid's mother. Documents were signed, and the bishop was sent on his way with a celebratory bottle of Gareth's finest.

"If you two can manage from here," Gareth said, "then I will return to Willowdale and report every detail of the ceremony to my lady wife. I should make it home before dark if I start now."

"I will be on my way as well," Fairly said, "though we should plan a rendezvous at Willowdale soon. Astrid, if you like, I'd be happy to pay a call on Douglas on my way home. I will deliver a letter in your hand, informing him of the nuptials."

God bless Fairly, and a mind that tended so effortlessly to strategy.

Andrew kept an arm around his wife—his *wife*—who still looked miserably pale. "We might want to create the impression we've taken a short wedding journey to my Sussex estate. I will also send a note to Douglas, explaining to him that Astrid is now in my keeping, and he needn't trouble further over her welfare."

"Fine then," Gareth said, calling for his hat, gloves, and riding crop. "I will expect you all to join me at Willowdale by week's end, and do not disappoint me, or Felicity will be unhappy. Brenner, if you could walk with me to the stables?"

Fairly made his good-byes, and Astrid and Andrew were soon left alone, seated side by side on the big leather sofa.

"I did not expect even to see you today, much less end up married to you," Astrid said. She looked and sounded dazed, not at all like the confident, articulate woman who seized life by the lapels and lectured it into submission.

"Nor I to you," Andrew replied. "I am pleased, despite all." Pleased and relieved, also furious on her behalf and rattled as hell.

She leaned her head back and closed her eyes. "I cannot think of *all* today, Andrew. I can barely form coherent thoughts, if you must know. But I am pleased as well."

Pleased was something. He took her hand, glad for the solitude that allowed him such familiarity, only to realize that as her husband, such familiarity was… permitted. "This has not been the quiet day the doctor ordered."

"Dr. DuPont? I do not want to see him again. He bore tales to Douglas, and suspected me of harming my own child. I went back to him because he attended me last year." Astrid opened her eyes and focused on

Andrew, looking more like herself—a little disgruntled and weary, her eyes not quite right, but like his Astrid. "I suppose, having dispensed with a wedding breakfast, this brings us to the wedding night?"

Eleven

"A PLEASURE, FAIRLY." DOUGLAS ALLEN, VISCOUNT Amery, bowed correctly to his guest, though he managed to convey to David that an unexpected visitor was not a pleasure at all. His lordship's sitting room was chilly, though comfortably appointed in green, brown, and cream—but then, it was public and visible from the street. The windowsills boasted no fresh bouquets; the walls were bare of domestic adornments. No paper cuttings, no watercolors from a talented cousin's days in the schoolroom, no pressed flowers as a token of Lady Amery's idle hours.

Nothing to suggest the house was anything other than a bachelor encampment with walls.

"Shall I ring for refreshment?"

"Please," David replied, relishing the thought of a hot, sweet cup of tea, but also wanting to preserve the fiction of civility.

"I confess to some confusion," Amery said, gesturing to the settee opposite the empty fireplace. "My mother stopped by only an hour or so ago and told me you were entertaining your sister Astrid. Did Astrid tire of your company?"

"I fear there has been a misunderstanding, Lord Amery," David began *pleasantly*. "Though I have in fact spent much of the afternoon with my sister. I left her in reasonably good health and in great good spirits." Two exaggerations in the name of strategy. David flipped a sealed note onto the low table before the settee. "Perhaps this will explain."

He watched Amery's features as his lordship read the brief missive, though Douglas's expression did not change.

Not in any detail.

"My sister-in-law is due congratulations," Amery said at length. "When may I call upon the happy couple to offer them in person?"

"Lord Greymoor has written to you as well," David said by way of answer. This missive he passed to Douglas, allowing their hands to brush. David had removed his driving gloves upon entering the house, and Douglas—called from his desk, if the ink on the heel of his right hand was any indication—was also bare handed. The man's fingers were like ice, and he made no reaction to the unusual, if accidental, touch of another man's hand on his.

Amery read the note, looking up only when a servant entered with the tea tray.

And again, not a flinch, not a flaring of the nostrils or a narrowing of the eyes. Over cards—or dueling pistols—Amery would be impossible to read.

"Because we have no hostess, I propose we serve ourselves," he said. "After you, Fairly, unless, of course, you are concerned I might be of a mind to poison you too?"

Opening salvo, David thought, mentally saluting.

"I am not a diminutive, pregnant, grieving widow," David said, hefting the teapot, "home alone and completely without defenses, and"—he offered his host a smile—"because I am in desperate need of a cup of tea, I will treat that remark as facetious. I gather Dr. DuPont has already called upon you?"

And there's your answering fire.

"He left a card while I was from home," Amery replied. "Do try the cakes. Cook quite outdoes herself."

"You will be interested to know Dr. DuPont will no longer be attending the countess."

Amery blinked, once. Countess—*of Greymoor, of course.*

"That is," Amery said as he reached for the teapot, "alas, no longer my concern. You are rather fond of your sugar."

"I am fond of all things sweet, Amery," David said, helping himself to a cake. "Including my sisters. When someone tries to poison a member of my family, fatally, I might add, then I take it very much amiss, as does Greymoor, as does Heathgate."

Amery settled back in his chair, his expression unperturbed. "I have been convicted of attempted sororicide by a jury of my betters, then?"

Rather than offer a snide retort, David considered a tea cake draped in lavender frosting. "I cannot speak for Heathgate and Greymoor, but as for myself, all I can convict you of is failing to keep Astrid safe, as your brother failed to keep her funds safe." *And her heart.* "In Greymoor's hands, she will be physically and financially out of harm's way. The match thus has my support," David said, popping the tea cake in his mouth.

The flavor of the frosting was lavender, and the cake itself a buttery little decadence of which Amery's cook had every right to be proud. David poured himself a second cup, the blend being a stout black without a hint of delicacy.

"Has it occurred to you, Lord Fairly, that *the countess herself* is perhaps the source of the danger to the child she carries?"

David inhaled the fragrance of his tea before adding two sugars. Greymoor had divined this line of reasoning, but when Amery presented it, it didn't sound as far-fetched as it ought.

"We did suspect that was your agenda, Amery." David gestured with the pot, a serviceable piece of blue Jasperware that was out of place in the brown, cream, and green room. "More tea?"

Amery held up his cup, and conversation paused while David poured steaming-hot liquid to the very rim of the cup in his lordship's rock-steady hand.

"Thank you." Amery sat back. "You suspect I am trying to impugn the state of the countess's mental health?"

"We suspect you, or somebody, is laying a trail of evidence that will make Astrid appear either dangerous or mentally incompetent. And of course"—David helped himself to two more cakes—"an incompetent mother is by definition a danger to her infant child. Lovely blend, by the way. From Twinings?"

"I enjoy my tea," Amery responded, his brows knit. "And Twinings's shop has the advantage of proximity.

So you don't believe a pregnant woman who would toss herself down a flight of stairs—or ingest dangerous herbs when she knows she'll be home alone—doesn't wish harm to her child?"

Douglas's expression suggested they were touching upon the variability of the weather in spring.

David closed his eyes to again inhale the fragrance of his tea—the brew was slightly abrasive, and yet, had a peculiar appeal—also to marshal his wits in the face of such sangfroid.

"Let us consider, my lord," David said when he put his teacup down. "We have two hypotheses to explain the known facts. You have seen a grown woman, one of particular grace, come head over heels down a flight of stairs, risking serious injury to herself and possible injury to her child. You also have the doctor's word that the poisons that found their way into her body could have caused the child's death, if not hers as well. You reach the conclusion the danger is directed by the mother toward the child. I see the situation differently."

Amery chose a few pretty tea cakes, his focus appearing to be on whether chocolate, cream, or pink frosting was most worthy of his notice. "Do tell," he murmured, selecting the cake with pink icing for himself.

Heavenly angels, the man was amazing. Amery bit into his confection and munched away, the picture of domestic contentment.

"I see that my sister," David said, "a woman whom I know to have been honorable under all circumstances to date, suffered a serious accident in the Allen household. As a man whose own late spouse was once in anticipation of an interesting event, I am well aware the child in the womb is, in fact, safer than the woman who carries it. Astrid could have knocked herself into a coma and very likely not have harmed her child. She would, as Dr. DuPont suggested, have to have been crazy to attempt such a stunt to rid herself of the child."

Amery appeared to be debating a second cake and declining the pleasure.

"Then we have the situation today," David went on. "Dr. DuPont was clear Astrid's symptoms could not all be explained by the abuse of herbs or drugs intended to end the pregnancy. They were, however, consistent with use of a deadly poison. I either believe my sister is making artless and painful efforts to kill herself—when relatively painless and certain alternatives exist—or I believe someone else wishes her grievous harm."

David took a steadying sip of his tea before concluding. "Knowing my sister, and knowing what I do of your family, I am not inclined to believe she is making attempts to end her own life, or that of your brother's child."

Amery frowned at his plain blue teapot. "We are at an impasse then, as we simply hold differing interpretations of the agreed-upon facts."

Rather than watch Amery demolish another tea cake, David rose to take his leave.

"Douglas," he said, clearly startling his host with the use of his Christian name, "for God's sake, use your intellect. I need not prove you wish my sister ill. You're a second son who will be disinherited of your title should Astrid have a boy."

Douglas remained sitting and did indeed help himself to another cake, this one chocolate. David forged on, when he wanted to smash his lordship's jasperware pot to bits.

"Forget the courts, Amery, for Greymoor and Heathgate will be after you like dogs on a bitch in heat if any more harm befalls my sister—as will I. Moreover, I need not investigate your theory that Astrid has been driven into a murderous rage over your brother's theft of funds Heathgate, Greymoor, and I can *each* easily replace. You are blinding yourself to the more sensible possibilities."

Amery rose and regarded David closely, all pretense of bored politesse gone from glacially blue eyes. "So you'll spend your time trying to prove I'd murder my brother's widow and his unborn child?"

The offense in those blue eyes looked genuine, and it was offense—not the feigned dismay of a murderer trying to appear righteously innocent.

Which was a relief, though a puzzling one. "If Astrid isn't trying to kill herself, and you are not trying to kill her, then at least one other person assuredly is. While we are busy pointing fingers at each other, that person will be plotting another trip down the stairs for her and for the little Amery heir, hmm?"

To that, Amery had made no answer, but merely wished David good day, and asked him to convey felicitations to the happy couple. As David departed, Douglas himself was tidying up the tea things, much as any butler or footman would do upon the departure of a guest.

❦

Astrid awoke to lengthening shadows and a sense of peace. She was wrapped in warmth and softness; she was safe and… *happy*. The child within her moved, as if waking up with her.

"Was that the baby?" asked a familiar, masculine voice. The rest of Astrid's reality snapped into place. She was burrowed against the warmth of Andrew's bare back in a bedroom at Lady Heathgate's town house. She and Andrew had been married earlier that afternoon, which meant… She was his *wife*.

"There it goes again," Andrew said, her belly still flush with his spine. He shifted to face her and covered her tummy with his hand. When the baby obligingly kicked at his hand, Andrew's smile would have lit up Mayfair.

"It's so odd," he said, "to think that there's a complete, small person in there, probably listening to your voice all day, and feeling hungry and tired or sleepy or restless. But you're used to all this." He laid his cheek on the upper swell of Astrid's breast while his palm remained on her belly.

"No, Andrew, I am not used to all this." She'd never thought to be intimate with Andrew Alexander again, and now they were man and wife for the rest of their lives. As surprises went, that qualified, and Astrid was certain it would not be an entirely happy development.

Which she would worry about later. She slid an arm around Andrew's neck and watched while he learned her new contours. The baby moved occasionally, and each time, Andrew laid his hand over the spot where the movement occurred. He'd been her lover before, and he had certainly been curious and considerate toward her pregnant body, but his touch was now that of a *husband*. And not like any husband she'd had previously.

"How do you feel, Astrid Alexander?"

Gracious, she liked the sound of that. With Andrew beside her, touching her this way, she felt *married*.

And yet, she'd decided on a nap directly after the ceremony—or her body had decided for her. "Not as tired. Still a little off, mentally. I could eat something bland."

"As could I." He took her hand and put it against his own stomach. "This is a boring comparison, is it not?"

"You are an odd man." An odd, dear man. Astrid slid her palm up to rest over his heart as she rolled against his side. "What are you thinking?"

He stared at the ceiling as Astrid let her hand drift over his exquisitely muscled—not boring at all—belly.

"I will need time to get used to being a husband. If I were more adept at it, I'd know some other way to ask this question."

"Just ask."

"I've been told women expecting a child can have intimate relations up until the last month or so, if they are so inclined."

Astrid waited, not sure where he was headed.

He turned, so they were both on their sides again, facing each other. "Are you so inclined?"

Another surprise, though Astrid knew the answer to his question, and silently thanked him for posing it. "With you?" She touched his mouth with her fingers. "Always."

"Can you still be comfortable on your back?" He kissed her fingers before trapping them in his own.

"I don't know. We'll have to find out."

❧

Six weeks ago Astrid had been a fine partner for some tender, exuberant sex. Andrew cared for her, but he'd certainly spent time with more experienced lovers. He'd had more creative partners, more sophisticated, more bold. But he didn't miss any of them the way he'd missed her. He'd forced himself to send her only one brief note a week, not flowers, not love letters, not gifts. He'd tried to convince himself he was relieved to be simply a friend to her within her own family.

He and Magic had traversed every inch of Willowdale and Enfield, and all the properties in between, by day and by night, several times over. Andrew had brought every account book up to date, met every tenant farmer, and generally worked himself to exhaustion, trying to quell a voice in his head insisting he had to go see *for himself* that Astrid was well.

The voice in his head had been so loud and unrelenting through the previous sleepless night, he'd risen with the dairymaids and tooled into Town to join Astrid at breakfast.

What if he'd been more stubborn about ignoring that voice? What if the horse had sprung a shoe halfway to Town? What if a passing shower had made the roads muddy?

What if he'd died at the age of fifteen in that boating accident and never known the glory of loving her?

He brought his body over hers, noting that her stomach was convex now, where it had been flat before.

"I have missed you, Astrid." He needed to tell her at least that.

"I have missed you as well, Andrew, terribly. And you needn't loom up there like I'm made of spun glass. I love the feel of your weight on me, particularly your naked weight."

"On your naked self." On her warm, gloriously feminine, beautiful, naked self, which he absolutely did not deserve to touch, much less claim as her husband. "You must tell me if you are at all uncomfortable, dear heart. I would not hurt you for the world."

She lay beneath him, his weight taken as much as possible on his knees and forearms, while he spent several quiet minutes kissing, nuzzling, and grazing his lips over her face, neck, and shoulders. Only when he felt her breathing slow and her body relax did he allow his mouth to settle over hers.

She opened to him on a welcoming sigh. As her tongue explored his lips and teeth, her hands gently kneaded his buttocks, urging him to rest more of his weight on her.

Carefully, he eased down, enough so his erect cock could tease and flirt with her sex. She spread her legs and brought them up to wrap around his flanks.

"Love me, Andrew," she whispered.

"Soon. Soon."

He'd dreamed this very scenario and woken up in an aching sweat more times than he could count, and he wasn't about to hurry the delectable reality. He could kiss, nuzzle, and tease her like this for hours, desire at once sustained and muted by tenderness the like of which Andrew was at a loss to explain. Astrid, however, was becoming aroused, and more than anything, he wanted to give her pleasure.

He allowed his teasing to graduate to shallow, languid penetration. "I want," he said between kisses, "to be gentle with you."

"You are unfailingly gentle with me. That isn't what I need now."

Such honesty. He deepened his thrusts, holding her gaze, willing her to see that *this* gentleness felt different to him.

"Andrew." She sighed his name, her eyes falling closed, her neck arching in pleasure. In blind abandon, her hands slipped around to his chest, where her fingers grazed across his nipples, sending tendrils of desire spiraling down to his cock, and out through his whole body. Still, he kept his rhythm slow, withdrawing and pausing before he thrust again.

A sense of burning unworthiness could give a man the most peculiar strengths.

"More, Andrew, *please*…" she crooned, locking her heels at the small of his back and pulling him into her.

He allowed his tempo to increase enough that Astrid shuddered, her breath catching, her nails digging into his hips. Her sex clutched at the length of him in hot, needy spasms as she groaned quietly into his neck. "Ah, God… *yes*, Andrew, *yes*…"

He held back. Somehow, he held back until she was easing down from her pleasure, her legs loosening their grip to rest along his flanks, her eyes again closed in repose and repletion.

And then he drove her up again, more quickly this time. His tongue thrust into her mouth, his fingers found her nipples, and his cock gave her the steady, deep thrusts that had her panting and bucking beneath him in no time. He could sense he'd taken her by surprise, and she would have been content with the softer, gentler wooing, but he kept her off balance, her defenses unorganized.

"Andrew..." she pleaded, but whether it was for relief or reprieve, he could not have said.

"Come for me, sweetheart. Come for me again."

His self-control frayed as Astrid bowed up to get her mouth over one of his nipples. She vised herself around him *everywhere*, holding on and not letting go, until pleasure bore down on him with relentless intent.

He did not deserve this, did not deserve her, and yet, she would have him.

Thank God, for however long it took to ensure her safety, she would have him.

Andrew changed the angle of his thrusting, pressing more deeply into Astrid's body and bringing a hand under her backside to anchor her against him. As satisfaction obliterated all else, he felt her shake with the force of her pleasure as well.

For a long moment, they lay together, warm and spent, breathing in counterpoint. Then the baby fluttered, and Andrew recalled himself enough to roll them, so Astrid straddled him.

"Married life with you has a certain appeal," Astrid said a few moments later, sliding down to rest on his chest. "If that didn't wake the baby, nothing will." She commenced drawing a picture with her index finger on his chest. "May I ask you something, Husband?"

Husband. "Yes, love?" Though he had the right now—the legal right—to call her Wife.

"Have you ever wished this baby was yours?"

He wasn't quick enough to cover a pause in his breathing or a momentary stillness of his hands on her back. The pain of her question was all the more brutal for being unexpected. Completely, hopelessly unexpected.

"You don't," she supplied, disgruntled. Her pointy little chin settled against his sternum. "Do you mind if *I* wish this were your baby?"

"Sweet lady, it is your wedding day, and you should be free to wish anything your heart desires. The baby is not mine in a biological sense, but the child will be mine to love and protect."

He kissed her temple, wishing he'd been able to see her face as he made his declaration. His words were a vow to treat this child as his own, and he hoped she understood them as such. He would protect her baby with his life; he would protect *her* with his life. As she leaned up to kiss him gently on the lips, he offered up a prayer that he would never have to.

❧

"Douglas, I do not understand," Lady Amery said, wringing a damp handkerchief between her fingers. "I simply *do not* understand why dear Astrid would leave us like this. Did you frighten her? You can be so very stern, you know. Not like dear Herbert, or dear Henry."

Dear Henry shot Douglas a look of fraternal sympathy. "I think what Douglas is trying to say,

Mother, is that Astrid is young, she misses Herbert, and she's overwrought with the strain of expecting Herbert's heir. She has run off and married Greymoor as a consequence, and we can do little about it."

Henry's ubiquitous grin was singularly not in evidence, which was fortunate for the state of Douglas's nerves.

"I know she's *young*, Henry," Lady Amery retorted. "But if she's so young, how could she just up and marry that man without anybody's permission?"

When he wanted to snap at someone to put some damned coal on the damned miserly fire dying on the damned filthy andirons, Douglas waded back into this most pointless discussion.

"She has achieved her majority, Mother, though barely. Unless I can prove the ceremony was a fraud, or Astrid did not consent to the marriage, our hands are tied." He'd consulted both solicitors and barristers on the matter, and had been politely prevented from consulting an expert in ecclesiastical law in the See of the Bishop of London. The Marquess of Heathgate's influence being what it was, that last was disappointing but not surprising.

His mother wagged a finger at him. "Douglas, this will not do. This will not do at all. If you brother were alive, he'd know what to do."

Oh, quite. If his bloody saint of a brother were alive, Astrid Allen would be sitting on her adorable fundament, waiting placidly to bear Herbert his precious heir while Herbert finished bankrupting the family with his horses and his whores.

Which sentiment was not permitted to disturb

the look of patient concern Douglas had affixed to his countenance.

"The best thing you could do, Mother, is write Astrid a cordial note congratulating her on her nuptials and asking when you might call on her to offer your felicitations. I will journey out to Enfield when she and Greymoor are in residence there, and you can be sure I will make pointed inquiries as to Greymoor's fitness to raise this child."

"Raise this child?" Lady Amery's voice approached a shriek. "But the child is Herbert's heir. Of course the child won't be raised by Greymoor. We're the child's family, aren't we?"

"Of course we are," Henry assured her, taking her arm and leading her toward the door of the sitting room. "You must do as Douglas says, Mother, and write Lady Greymoor the most sincere, warmhearted congratulatory note you can. We'll have a pot of tea sent up to settle your nerves."

Henry held the door for her, then stepped back and let it swing solidly shut as his mother asked, "Lady Greymoor? Who on earth…?"

Henry nearly sprinted to the decanter. "I do not envy you, Douglas. Not one bit, not one iota. And you *are* going to join me in a drink."

"I suppose I will at that." Fortunately, they were in the house Astrid had recently vacated. The decent spirits were still on display.

"So what didn't you tell our good mother?" Henry asked as he found a seat in a cushioned chair, drink in hand. "This marriage is more than a sudden affection between family members."

Douglas took a seat in the chair opposite Henry's before speaking, choosing his words and resenting the burden of even that effort.

"Our *dear* Astrid ingested poison some time this morning after Mother left for her calls and the housekeeper went to do the marketing. Greymoor happened along, just why or when we do not know, and found her in distress. Greymoor had the presence of mind to summon Dr. DuPont, who has assured me that without intervention, the situation could have been fatal to mother and child both."

Henry flicked a bit of hay off his sleeve onto the carpet. "Good God. Somebody is trying to kill us off one by one. Let's not tell Mother, shall we?"

"I must conclude, Henry, that Herbert's accident and this accident are just that—accidents," Douglas said as he poured himself a small measure of brandy. "Guns misfire, ladies occasionally tumble down steps, and food can go bad in any household. Viscount Fairly, however, paid a call on me this afternoon to ensure I understand that he, Heathgate, and Greymoor do not share my opinion on the matter."

For once, Henry was not tossing back his drink as if they could afford an endless supply. "Douglas, what do you mean?"

"Whether they are simply being prudent, or whether Astrid has embellished an hysterical tale, her Alexander and Worthington relations suspect I am trying to murder her, and, of course, the child who will bear the title in my stead."

Douglas tried to keep the indignation from his tone, but really, that all three of Astrid's titled relations should leap to such a conclusion so quickly was... disappointing.

"Of all the nerve," Henry spat, getting up to pace. "As if you *ever* had designs on the title! Perhaps Greymoor poisoned her, and now she's gone and married him. God above, what would Herbert say if he could see this mess?"

Herbert would have rung for more brandy, or gone to visit his mistress, and whiled away the rest of the day visiting with the lads at Tatt's. If in the grip of a rare bout of perspicacity, he might then have caught a packet for Calais.

"There's more, Henry," Douglas said. "Our dear brother was dipping heavily into the part of Astrid's dowry that had been set aside for her widow's portion. He all but obliterated it, and while I myself made Astrid aware of the situation, Fairly has learned of it too."

Which meant Heathgate knew, as did Greymoor. What a cheerful state of affairs.

Henry did take a gulp of his drink before setting the glass down with a decisive thump. "The little snitch told him, of course. Why should she protect the dignity of the Allens, after all? She was only my brother's choice of bride, and that couldn't have meant much to her, given today's developments."

Douglas, initially heartened by Henry's indignation, nevertheless again heard that one off word: *my* brother's choice... Not *our* brother's choice. This display of righteousness on Henry's part was not for Douglas, who was being accused of attempted murder; it was for Herbert, who had been a good-natured, immature, thieving, whoring wastrel.

Douglas wondered why it should feel good to admit that even in the privacy of his thoughts while Henry railed on against perfidious women with too many overbearing, titled relations.

Douglas interrupted when Henry paused to refresh his drink, "I will make inquiries regarding Greymoor's background in preparation for bringing suit to be appointed guardian of Astrid's child, assuming it's a boy, of course."

"You don't want guardianship of a girl? Even a daughter would be Herbert's child. Mother will feel very strongly about that."

"Of course, I would like to be guardian of Herbert's daughter," Douglas replied with the very last of his patience, "but lawsuits are scandalous and expensive and one must be practical, Henry. The primary reason for granting me guardianship of the child over Fairly, Greymoor, or Heathgate is so I might teach Herbert's heir what is expected of him with respect to the estate and the family responsibilities. A female has no need of that education."

Thank God. And yet, gently bred females were deucedly expensive to rear. Douglas silently wished Greymoor the joy of the girl's dressmakers' bills.

"You are up against a viscount, an earl, and a marquess," Henry conceded. "I know Greymoor and Heathgate both cut a wide swath with the ladies until a few years ago, but then Heathgate married, and Greymoor left the country. I haven't heard a thing derogatory about either one since I came down from university. And that Fairly." Henry shuddered dramatically. "In some ways, he's the scariest of the three."

Greymoor was the scary one, showing up at the exact moment of Astrid's peril, but Fairly was deserving of a healthy respect, too. "I believe Fairly would observe the rules of engagement punctiliously. He would give warning of his intent to strike, never fire at a man's back, and never fire on the unarmed. The most dangerous one is Astrid herself."

Henry paused, his drink—his third, and before supper?—two inches from his mouth. "You could toss her over your shoulder one-handed," he sputtered. "She's a woman, I grant you, and the whole gender is suspect on general principles, but *Astrid*?"

Henry would take convincing, but the effort was necessary. Methodically, Douglas laid out the reasoning that could lead a prudent man to conclude Astrid resented the child she carried and would take extreme measures to end its life. By the time Douglas finished speaking, Henry was reaching for the decanter yet again.

"And to think," Henry said dazedly, "my brother's helpless child is going to be born to such a one as her, and we can do nothing about it. One wonders about the unfortunate turn of events her health took last year."

My brother, again, though Henry's point supported Douglas's theory of events far better than it did Fairly's—and without Douglas having to bring up such an indelicate situation.

"We'll fight for guardianship of Henry's son, certainly," Douglas said, "and I'll do everything I can to investigate Greymoor's character. Meanwhile, there's something you can do."

Besides drink the last of the good liquor.

Henry stood straighter. "You have only to ask."

"You will be our spy in the enemy camp," Douglas said. "Whereas I am suspected of attempting to harm the mother and child, you are not. Whereas I will bring suit for guardianship, you will be the bewildered younger brother, saddened by this terrible misunderstanding, and offering Astrid a sympathetic shoulder to cry on. She is fond of you, and perhaps, if the courts are persuaded by Greymoor's money rather than my arguments, you will have secured access to the child that I could never have."

Henry finished his drink—there being no more left in the decanter—and left the parlor, apparently happily intent on his mission. Douglas, however, sat for an hour, watching the fire consume half a bucket of coal, and trying to decide for himself just what the purpose of Fairly's call earlier in the day had been. Unable to come to a satisfactory conclusion to that puzzle, he then found himself wondering how much—how much *more*—he was willing to sacrifice in the name of duty to family.

Twelve

HEATHGATE SCOWLED FROM HIS PERCH ON THE Willowdale estate desk, an unhappy raptor among the letters, reports, and ledgers of the marquessate, while Andrew wandered the room.

"Gentlemen," Heathgate began, "the morning's post has brought an interesting epistle from Douglas Allen. He proposes to call upon me as a courtesy, given that my brother has married his former sister-in-law. I know not what to make of this, but I can hardly refuse him entry."

Fairly seemed amused, or bemused. "Douglas is a proper old thing, isn't he? Either that, or he has ballocks the like of which I haven't seen before."

"He's up to something," Andrew said, picking up a pipe carved of ivory that his father had favored. He brought it to his nose, and still, after thirteen years, caught a hint of vanilla from the bowl. "I don't want Douglas anywhere around Astrid, but I expect he'll call at Enfield in due course. I am considering installing Astrid at Oak Hall instead to prevent him from seeing her."

Also to preserve Astrid from the constant warfare between Lady Heathgate and Cousin Gwen.

Fairly shoved away from his habitual post at the French doors. "I simply do not read the man as a murderer."

"That's the difficulty," Heathgate said. "It's hard to read him as anything at all, he's so damned cold."

Andrew thought of Moscow in winter, and decided Douglas was colder. "You two should know some things about the Allen family. Astrid casually mentioned that the old viscount had also died in a shooting accident. His sons were on the same shoot. My vote for the member of the party with the worst aim goes to Douglas."

Heathgate closed his eyes. "I am going to be sick."

Fairly, whose face bore no expression whatsoever, continued to stare out at the bleak, chilly day. "Why don't we just beat each other bloody, Heathgate? I was the one who approved of the match, as Astrid's older brother. Simply retching into the bushes won't answer, when Douglas is the most likely party to end up as guardian of Astrid's child."

As Andrew set the pipe back where he'd found it, the firelight winked off the decanters across the room, the gryphon seeming to laugh.

Heathgate shoved off the desk and took a seat in the big leather chair behind it, the result being a sense of enthronement, regardless that two stacks of his correspondence were weighted down with silver rattles.

He picked up one of the rattles and tossed it from hand to hand. "We come across more and more reasons to arrange an unfortunate accident for Douglas

Allen. One can't help but wonder if the world would not be an altogether better place for it."

Fairly turned, so his back was to the French doors. "We have plenty of reason to avoid the man's company, though nothing with which to convict him, or even lay charges."

Andrew had been married one week. Already he and Astrid had fallen into a pattern of assisting each other to dress and undress. She watched him when he washed off the day's dirt, and he watched her, too. He suspected she liked that he did, and more to the point, he liked watching her—somewhat more than he liked to breathe.

"I'll take Astrid to the damned Continent if I have to. I know plenty of places to bring up a child comfortably enough outside of England."

"It's an idea," Heathgate allowed, setting the rattle aside. "Felicity won't like it one bit." And anything that upset the spectacularly gravid marchioness would not find favor with her husband.

Andrew did not like it either—because Astrid would see leaving the country as cowardly, and thus rebel against the notion, and because any trip to the Continent required crossing water yet again.

And the idea of taking ship accompanied by a pregnant wife was a horror that, for Andrew, beggared description. Rather than admit that to anyone, he waited for Fairly to render an opinion.

Fairly obliged. "Even if you could convince Astrid to go, do you really think Douglas would wave you merrily on your way, the Amery heir in tow? He'd find you sooner or later."

"Maybe that is the best option, then," Andrew said. "Let him find me, posthaste, and we'll settle this once and for all."

"It may come to that," Heathgate replied, picking up a silver letter opener and testing the edge against his thumb. "But we aren't at that point, because Astrid might well bear a girl child. Take your wife to Enfield, and we'll see what Douglas brings up when he calls upon me next week."

Heathgate set aside the letter opener, swiped up both rattles, rose, and headed for the door. "If you will excuse me, gentlemen, I believe it's time I reminded my marchioness of her duty to take a damned nap."

Andrew regarded the closed door rather than heed the siren call of the decanters. "We still do not know if Herbert was murdered."

Fairly shoved away from the door and crossed to the sideboard, where he did not pour a drink, but instead began organizing the bottles: griffins with griffins, dragons with dragons, and so forth.

"I have the sense this whole business would be much clearer if we understood Douglas's motives. One hears things when one owns a brothel, and there were whispers at the time of Herbert's death that one of the Allen brothers has—or had—unusual tastes. When I delivered to Douglas the news of your recent nuptials, I all but accused Douglas of murder, and could detect no emotional response at all."

A lone chimera sat across the room on an end table. Andrew would have left him there, but Fairly collected the prodigal and placed him with his fellows.

"We are back to Douglas's motives," Andrew said,

"which remain known only to Douglas. Heathgate had the only sensible proposal at this point: watch and wait. Watch very carefully."

And the rest of Andrew's plan didn't bear repeating: spend every possible moment in his wife's company, because once he was sure she and her child were safe, Andrew would have no choice but to leave her again, even if it meant he must once again face a sea crossing.

❦

Married life was a lonely business—yet again, a lonely business—even with Andrew for a spouse. He took Astrid to Enfield, and while she loved the property, she found little to do there.

Astrid reached an uneasy truce with Gwen when it became clear Astrid had no intention of usurping Gwen's role, particularly as it related to managing the property. Not so, the formidable Lady Heathgate.

Lady Heathgate had managed Astrid's two social seasons, her wedding, and Gwen's come out. She managed her own house in town, a "cottage" on two thousand acres in the country, and numerous investments. Astrid had not yet found the nerve to ask Andrew if he'd gone on his travels in part to avoid his mother's managing tendencies—particularly her matchmaking managing tendencies—but she had her suspicions.

That Lady Heathgate's sons had inherited both her height and her blue eyes was never in doubt—also her determination and her commercial expertise.

What was in doubt, from day to day and hour to hour, was to whom the role of lady of the house would go. Gwen and her aunt bickered constantly.

They sniped, they glowered, they made veiled threats and polite insults. Their verbal battle, waged in sniffy asides and muttered ironies, might have been amusing had Astrid not felt both women were being inconsiderate of her, and worse, of Andrew.

He, smart fellow, absented himself from the manor for most of each day when weather permitted. If it was truly too miserable to be out on the property, Andrew closeted himself in the study, poring over account books, reports, and treatises.

Astrid found him there one night after yet another tense family meal, several weeks after their remove to Enfield.

He stood and held out a hand in welcome. "Hello, Wife. Are you hiding as well?"

Astrid tucked herself against him and wrapped her arms around his waist. Why did a grown man hide from the mother whose life he'd saved? Why did he hide from the wife whose life he'd vowed to protect?

"May we send your mother back to Town now that you are married and your wife is in residence here?" She'd intended to tiptoe up to that question, but pregnancy rather ruined a woman's ability to tiptoe.

Andrew sighed and rested his chin on the top of her head. Astrid was coming to understand his sighs, and that one was… dismal.

"God knows Mother is wearing out her welcome."

"But?"

"But it would hurt her feelings. The Little Season is of little interest, to hear her tell it. Then too, she is another pair of eyes and ears here at the house should you need them. Finally, I have wondered if

Mother's abrasive carping might not effect a change in Gwen's position."

Strategy. Astrid's husband had an interesting penchant for strategy—one she lacked. "You think your mother will wear Gwen down on the matter of holy matrimony?"

One did not refer to Lady Heathgate as *Mama*—at least, one hadn't been invited to do so.

Andrew patted her bottom, another aspect of his husbandly vocabulary. His bottom pats were seldom flirtatious, and he was careful not to do it when company was present. "I don't know if Gwen *can* be worn down, but I cannot deed her an entailed property, and marriage would give her options other than becoming my dependent spinster cousin. It might come down to building her a second dower house, or resigning ourselves to her company when we reside here."

Gwen had a sense of humor, and her daughter, little Rose, was a positive delight.

"I could live with that," Astrid said. "Provided we don't spend a great deal of time here. I could be happy at Oak Hall, or at Linden, for that matter, if you could content yourself at either location."

Andrew drew back, resting his hips on his desk and looping his arms around Astrid as she stood between his legs. "I am thinking of selling Linden."

This was not strategy. This was… Andrew being hard to understand and not confiding in his wife.

"That was your home, Andrew. You chose that property for yourself, and you've held it, what, almost ten years? I thought you loved it there."

Andrew regarded his wife, as if he were weighing how much of some inconvenient truth to share with her.

"I enjoyed that property, Astrid, at an age when I spent little time with my mother and brother, when I needed... independent quarters. I did not conduct myself at all times like a model squire. Some in the Linden vicinity would as soon see the land change hands again."

How many angry papas and disappointed damsels did Sussex boast as a result of Andrew's tenure there? "You were a rascal."

Andrew's laugh was dismal too. "Douglas called on Gareth a few weeks ago to inform him, should I attempt to gain guardianship of your child, he was prepared to ferret out every misdeed I ever was rumored to commit. I committed more than a few of them at Linden. Besides, I have both Oak Hall and Enfield to fret over, and those are entailed properties. I cannot get rid of either, and both are closer to Town, and to Willowdale."

Cuddling up to Andrew was delightful, despite the topic. Being near him soothed her, and Astrid felt drowsiness stealing into her limbs as she stood in his embrace.

"You must do as you see fit, Andrew. I certainly will not complain if we reside only five miles from my sister and her children, though if I had my pick, I would choose Oak Hall rather than Enfield."

"Why?"

Astrid nuzzled at his shoulder. How did he manage to always smell scrumptious? "Oak Hall is the property better suited to raising horses."

"And this is relevant because?"

"Of all the projects Gwen has put before you, you are most enthusiastic about raising horses suited to becoming ladies' mounts. You don't sit up late at night, drawing plans for further irrigation; you don't look out over the land, wondering where you might erect another hothouse; you don't wander down to the home farm to check on the lambing. You do, however, consider at length re-fencing certain horse pastures; you ponder where you might lay out a practice oval for flat racing; and you fret nightly over your broodmares. The crops, produce, home farm, and cottage industry are all well and good, but for you, the passion is the horses."

His hand went still, midpat on her derriere. "You are right." A silence ensued, and he did not resume stroking her fundament. "I enjoy the country, but I love the horses."

He said this as if something obvious to all who knew him was a revelation to himself. And then another pat, brisk and businesslike.

"I know one little broodmare who needs to find her bed," he said, straightening and grabbing a branch of candles from his desk. "It's late, and you should be asleep."

"I should," Astrid said, stifling a yawn. "I was coming to tell you I'm retiring. Will you join me?"

"I'll light you up to your room," he replied, offering his arm. "I have yet more reading to do."

Astrid made no protest, but with increasing frequency, Andrew had reasons not to find their bed until she was fast asleep. He woke at first light, and only came in to join the ladies for dinner. Thereafter, he repaired to his study or returned to the barns and stables. Slowly, inexorably, he was creating distance between himself and his wife, and he was too astute a man for this to be simple happenstance.

Astrid waited until they gained the doorway to their bedroom, though she should have waited until Andrew had escorted her inside. "Could you not do your reading some other time?"

He kissed her forehead, something in the gesture besides marital affection, something troubled. "I'll be up soon enough." He entered the room only long enough to light candles for her, then left and closed the door behind him.

Astrid got her clothes off, and brushed out and rebraided her hair before climbing into the bed. She wished she had Felicity to talk to, but that would mean ten miles of travel, round trip, and burdening her sister with her petty troubles. Felicity wrote frequently, and Gareth had been over twice since Astrid had come to Enfield, but he spent his time with Andrew, and that meant Astrid had seen little of him.

She had, however, had two visits from Henry Allen. Andrew had left her strict orders not to receive Douglas Allen unless Andrew was with her, but he was less concerned about Henry.

To her surprise, she had enjoyed the time spent in Henry's company. He seemed to be a genuinely nice man, as Herbert had also seemed to her on first acquaintance. Henry, however, did not take himself nearly so seriously as either of his elder brothers, and he was more than ready to poke fun at them on occasion.

"Douglas has his underlinen starched and ironed," he'd announced. "That explains a lot, you know."

Henry could say such an outrageous thing in good fun, meaning harm toward none and bringing Astrid a smile. Henry also assured her Douglas did not have the blunt to pursue a costly lawsuit, and neither did he see his brother taking on the gossip and censure litigation would generate.

But as Astrid tossed about, alone in her bed, visits from family were no comfort. She drifted off, determined to confront Andrew regarding his schedule. They were newlyweds, for pity's sake. She wished her husband would start acting like it.

❧

Andrew put aside the treatise on contour plowing he'd been staring at for the past twenty minutes. More and more, he was making excuses to avoid his wife. Oh, he rode about the property with Gwen, commenting repeatedly on the fine job she did as de facto steward. He spent time training the few young horses on the premises, and he spent time with Magic.

But he actually *did* little. He was waiting for Douglas Allen to make another move, and patience was by no means his forte—particularly not when Andrew was trying to wean himself from his wife's company, and from her intimate attentions. Having to remain close to her for the sake of her safety, while trying to maintain an emotional and physical distance, was beyond nerve-wracking.

So Andrew kept close to the manor, made sure he fell into bed each night exhausted, and met frequently in the stables with the informants he employed to watch Douglas, Douglas's finances, his comings and goings, and his family members.

While Andrew slowly went insane.

Sometimes, in the drowsy place between sleeping and waking, he reached for his wife. She came into his arms with a sweet, openhearted eagerness, and loved him within an inch of his life. Each time he slipped like that, he told himself one more encounter surely wouldn't make much difference. He told himself he would break her heart regardless of how often they coupled, and broken hearts didn't come in degrees.

He told himself the memories of her passion would be enough, when the time came. They would have to be.

Feeling exhaustion and despair in every bone and muscle, Andrew took himself up to the bedroom, praying Astrid had fallen asleep.

He undressed as quietly as he could, made use of the wash water she had considerately left by the hearth, and climbed into bed, stretching out on his back. In the darkness, his wife rolled toward him, then climbed across his body to straddle his hips. His arms came around her before he could remind himself he was not—absolutely was not—going to encourage her affections any further.

"Husband," Astrid greeted him, curling up against his chest.

"Wife."

She was silent, but Andrew could feel her thoughts whirling, and hoped her concerns were simply those of the new housewife: the maids and footmen

misbehaving, his mother bickering with Gwen, the
laundress not getting along with the housekeeper.

"Andrew, what is troubling you?"

"I am simply tired," he replied, running his hands
over the fine bones of her back. Her stomach, now
more than five months distended with child, was
folded against his, warm and oddly comforting.

"You are tired because you charge around all day,
inspecting what has already been inspected. Gwen tells
me this, you know, and she is puzzled. I believe you
are avoiding me."

He wouldn't lie to her, they both knew that, so he
kept his silence, his hands resting on her hips.

"You are," Astrid concluded. "Why?"

Astrid would not be put off. In hindsight, he
was surprised she'd let matters go this far without
making comment.

"The purpose of our marriage," he said, hating
himself and his words and his life, "is to keep you and
your child safe. It is serving that purpose."

"I see. You will explain yourself further."

"I will not." He swooped up to kiss her into
silence instead.

He taught her then, about sex that attempts to
substitute for communication. She wrestled him at
first, bending herself away from his mouth, away
from his hands, and most especially, away from his
body. But she didn't try nearly hard enough to thwart
his advances, and Andrew knew it for the symbolic
protest it was.

Had she spoken even the single syllable, "No," he
would have desisted and likely quit the room, not to

return. But she kept her silence, kissing him back, and allowing him to enter her in a single, hard lunge. He held her to him, not letting her move as he set up a rhythm as relentless as it was vigorous.

"Come for me," he rasped, locking his arm at the small of her back. But she resisted even in that, and he redoubled the intensity of his effort.

"Astrid, please…" He did not know what he was asking her for, but she relented, and was soon shuddering around him. He exploded inside her, his harsh groan mingling with the single sob that escaped her.

As the last tremors receded from her body, Astrid lifted away from him, fetched a damp cloth, and swabbed herself clean. Andrew heard her movements in the dark room, and wondered if she was going to take herself off to a guest room.

"Astrid, shall I sleep elsewhere?"

His answer was a wet rag, tossed unerringly and with some force onto his chest despite the dark.

"You awful, odious, foolish man," she spat. "Do you think I would make it that easy for you?"

She bounced back onto the bed, pausing to give Andrew a moment to use the washcloth before she flipped the covers back up over them. To Andrew's surprise, Astrid lifted his arm and tucked herself under it against his side.

"In your present state of stubbornness, you do not deserve me," she informed him, "but you have me, and I will not give you the satisfaction of excusing you from this marriage. I did not agree to your silly terms, Andrew Alexander, and I did not agree to stop loving you, wroth with you though I may be for the rest of my natural days."

After that speech, they lay together, thinking separate thoughts, being separately miserable in the same bed.

Their confrontation marked a turning point, one likely noticeable to the other members of the household. Andrew's good cheer, a hallmark of his personality in the eyes of those who knew him, faded, and the three women came to appreciate it in its absence.

He left Gwen to manage the estate as she saw fit. He no longer used humor and gallantry to divert his mother from her carping. He stopped observing even the domestic civilities with his wife, addressing her only when necessary, and touching her as little as possible. He became a much closer approximation of his older brother in earlier years.

Silent, broody, and withdrawn.

Andrew continued to sleep with his wife, or to occupy the same bed at night. On the bad nights, they lay side by side, not touching, each willing sleep to come, each usually failing.

On the worse nights, Astrid would lace her fingers through Andrew's, or curl up with her head on his chest. Sometimes she was bold enough to kiss his cheek or slide a hand down his torso, stopping short of his genitals. He would lie, silent and unmoving for long minutes, until the backs of his fingers stroked Astrid's cheek, or his lips tasted her wrist.

On those nights, they would make love tenderly, yearning beyond words in their touches and sighs and silences.

On the worst nights, Astrid would awaken in deep

darkness to find her husband curled around her or carefully crouched over her, nudging at her body with his erection. He would hold on to her, loving her silently, his arms wrapped around her in an embrace so desperate and tender it brought tears to her eyes.

But regardless of the night—bad, worse or worst— they arose in the morning without indulging in meaningful conversation, each going alone into the day.

Thirteen

NOTHING WOULD DO BUT HENRY MUST JOIN ASTRID on the platform adjoining the haymow while she watched Andrew and Magic in the arena. Horse and rider had been in fine form, until Andrew had apparently realized she'd brought a guest. He'd left the arena, telling the grooms he'd cool the horse out with a hack.

"I have never seen the like of that gelding," Henry said as Astrid poured out for him fifteen minutes later. "That last fence was five feet if it was an inch!"

His enthusiasm was jarring, reminding Astrid of the way Herbert had come home from two weeks of hunting, stories of mud and gore and freezing mornings somehow able to light up his eyes in ways his wife could not. She really had not understood her husband.

"More tea?" she offered automatically.

Henry smiled, an expression that made him look more like his late brother. "Well, perhaps just a spot. So, old girl, how are you getting on?"

"Well enough." Nobody, but nobody, had ever called her "old girl," and that jarred too. She was all of two and twenty, for pity's sake.

"Come now, Astrid," Henry chided, "you know Dougie is going to interrogate me proper when I get back to Town. I can't tell him you're doing 'well enough.' Does married life agree with you?"

She regarded him quizzically over her teacup, and he had the grace to look chagrined.

"I suppose you are no stranger to married life, are you? My apologies."

Astrid let a silence take root, wanting to be rid of Henry and not caring particularly why.

Marriage to Andrew was eroding her manners. "How is your mother, Henry? I've written to her, but she makes no reply. I suppose she is disappointed in me for not serving out my year of mourning."

Henry swilled his tea in one gulp and set the cup down a bit too hard on the saucer. "You say that like mourning Herbert is a prison sentence."

"Mourning is not a happy time, Henry." Astrid refilled his cup, thinking she should not have to tell him about the realities of mourning. He'd lost a brother, hadn't he? "Should I stop writing to your mother?"

He stirred his tea the same way Herbert had, quick little circles in the center of the cup that resulted in the occasional messy saucer. "Heavens, no. I've every suspicion she's written to you, but Douglas has probably refused to frank the letters. We three live in the town house together now, and Douglas's own house is to let. The situation isn't exactly comfortable, though I still have my rooms in the City for when it gets too awful at home."

Andrew had spared her joining that household, and for all the tensions at Enfield, it wasn't as bad as what the Allen family would have offered. "I am sorry. I know your mother can be a challenge."

"Mother, I can handle," he said, oddly bitter. "It's Douglas, with his endless economies and his grim pronouncements I can hardly tolerate. But I mustn't complain. I have a roof over my head and decent prospects, which is more than many others have."

"It is. You are sweet to take the time to come visit me."

He folded two tea cakes into a serviette, stuffed them into his pocket, and rose. "Visiting you is a pleasure, though the interrogation when I get home isn't."

"What will you tell Douglas?" she asked, taking his arm as they walked toward the front of the house. And thank the Deity that Henry was not inclined to overstay his welcome, though he'd taken the last chocolate peppermint cakes, and those were Astrid's favorites.

"I will tell him you are in great good health and tolerably good spirits, but your new husband is not as courteous to you as he could be."

Courtesy. Herbert had been courteous, and Andrew was the soul of courtesy, not that courtesy mattered much compared to respect, trust, or love.

"Greymoor is a good man. I am content with him. How is Douglas, by the way? We've heard nothing from him since his call on Heathgate some weeks ago."

"Now that is odd." Henry took his hat, cape, and gloves from a footman. "I thought he was going to pay a call on you following your nuptials. Appears he changed his mind. Consider yourself lucky."

He grinned, bowed, patted his pocket, and took his leave.

As Astrid listened to the clatter of his horse's hooves cantering down the driveway, a choking sadness welled up. She had lied to Henry, and Henry had probably sensed it: Andrew was a good man, of that she had no doubt, but she was most assuredly not content.

"What did the puppy want?" Andrew asked from a perch halfway down the stairs.

"I beg your pardon. I did not know you were in the house." Did not know where he was in any sense.

"I came in to change." Andrew prowled down the steps, and if a man could do such a thing peevishly, he did. "You'll forgive me if I did not join you for a polite chat over tea. I assume he is reporting everything you say and do to Douglas?"

"He did say Douglas will question him upon his return."

Andrew studied her as if she were a crooked painting of a peculiar subject, badly executed. "You are pale, Astrid. Did the puppy upset you?"

He was standing so close she could smell his cologne and the soap he'd just washed with, but she kept her expression bland and did not allow herself to lean closer.

"Astrid?" His voice was quiet, caring. Not the terse bark he'd adopted of late when necessity dictated they converse.

She did look at him then, knowing her eyes were bright with unshed tears.

"Whatever he said—" Andrew began fiercely, but Astrid shook her head.

"It isn't Henry who upsets me."

She did not—could not—say more but advanced

past him, her spine straight, her gait dignified as she left him standing on the stair.

Andrew stood at the bottom of the steps, feeling as if Magic had just delivered a kick to his chest. He contemplated ferreting out Douglas Allen and slapping a glove across the man's face. A duel would resolve the entire situation, and Astrid would be left in peace to raise her child in safety.

Possibly.

Andrew was lethal with a sword, and a good shot, but he wasn't the kind of marksman the Allen men were. With his dying breath, Andrew would know he'd left Astrid unprotected and widowed again.

"What are you scowling about now?" Gwen asked, coming down the stairs with Rose at her side.

"I can scowl too," Rose said, frowning with exaggerated ill humor. Andrew scooped the child off the stairs onto his hip.

"You will scare me, Rosebud, if you don't stop looking so ferocious. I am scowling because it is nearly luncheon, and I am quite hungry."

"I am hungry too," Rose said. "Where is Cousin Astrid?"

"She was here a minute ago," Andrew hedged, but he caught Gwen's eye, and the rare compassion he saw suggested she'd overheard, or even seen, some of his exchange with Astrid.

"Cousin Astrid is sad," Rose said. "I wish she would be happy."

Gwen's expression went carefully impassive, but she retrieved Rose from Andrew and set the child back on her own two feet.

"We will go find Cousin Astrid and cheer her up," Gwen said. "There is nothing *worthwhile* for her to be sad about."

They turned their backs on Andrew and went off to enjoy their meal, while he... sat down, pulled on his muddy boots, and returned to the stables, there to muck stalls until the ache in his chest subsided and his hunger was nearly forgotten.

✎

Arabella Antoinette Hollister Alexander, Lady Heathgate to the tedious nincompoops of Polite Society, hated autumn, for it was the season of her failures. Thirteen years ago, she'd failed to talk her husband into ignoring a summons from his papa, the marquess, to attend a doomed family gathering in Scotland.

Who in their right mind traveled north as winter approached?

Six years ago, she had taken until autumn to realize her niece Guinevere's abrupt withdrawal from her first social Season had been a harbinger of disaster, though Rose herself had been more of a salvation than a disaster.

Andrew had departed for the Continent in autumn, and now, autumn found not only Andrew, but his entire household lost at sea.

A lady could tolerate just so much of failure, however, and now that the anniversary of the accident had come and gone—remarked by nothing more than a short, determinedly cheerful call from her older son—it was time to set Andrew's household to rights.

"My son is due for a review of his domestic

accounts," Arabella remarked after Rose had said the blessing over another meal from which Andrew had absented himself.

Astrid and Gwen looked askance at her, then at each other, suggesting Arabella's efforts to foster an alliance between the young ladies had borne some fruit, at least.

"What are 'mestic accounts?" Rose asked from around a mouthful of bread, jam, and butter.

"A discussion of his expenditures and assets in the marital realm," Arabella explained. "Astrid, you are letting Andrew get away with poor manners and all varieties of inconsideration. He walked right past me this morning, not so much as a 'good day' to his own mother. He has no conversation anymore, much less any wit, and his gallantries are all wasted on those horses of his. What will you do about this?"

For Arabella's notions of how to go on with the boy—stern lectures and dire warnings delivered in the privacy of his study—had had no effect.

Gwen busied herself arranging a serviette as a bib for Rose, while Astrid considered a slice of pear.

"I quite frankly don't know what to do," Astrid said. She set the pear down without taking a bite, and fired off something like a glower at her mama-in-law. "The two of you leave me nothing meaningful to see to under my own roof, and if my husband has no use for me, I can hardly take exception to his behavior without taking the two of you to task as well. Rudeness and inconsideration are not such unusual behavior in this household."

Clearly the girl had surprised herself with her

honesty, and she had relieved Arabella, for those dreadful Allens had nearly crushed Astrid's spirit. Now this spark of forthrightness must be fanned to a flame that might illuminate the shadows still clouding Andrew's eyes.

"Sweet heavens!" Arabella exclaimed in her best Offended Dowager tones. "Andrew's foul humor is contagious. This, my dear, will never do."

A tense silence spread, with even Rose apparently comprehending something had gone amiss.

"Astrid is right," Gwen said, pushing her spoon around in her soup. "And I am at least partly to blame."

Guinevere was brave to a fault. Of course she would join this affray and try to protect Astrid from a scolding. As Gwen set her spoon aside, Arabella noticed a hint of her own late father about Gwen's chin and jaw.

"I am so unable to consider any life for myself other than the one I've made here, that I see Andrew as the enemy," Gwen said. "I see you all as my enemies, and I know I have been… difficult. I am sorry."

Rose took another bite of bread and jam, her gaze bouncing among the adults seated at the table. Clearly the child sensed that the ladies were spading fresh turf, and clearly, she relished her bread and jam.

Andrew used to love bread and jam, too. Now, his own mother could not have said what or whom he loved, other than the small blond lady sitting across from her.

"I believe, my dears, I should return to Town," Arabella said, though the words were difficult. "I was here to smooth the way between Andrew and Gwen, but you are in residence now, Astrid, a widow and a wife, and you are right: this household should be yours to run as you see fit. Besides, come the holidays, I will be staying with Heathgate and Felicity to assist with the care of my new grandchildren."

Both young women looked at her as if she'd just announced an intention to emigrate to the Antipodes. Young people could be so predictable—and so dear.

But these young women were bright and brave, too, and Arabella was leaving her son in their care, so she did not abandon the table to deal with a sudden tightness in her throat. Years ago, Andrew had pulled her from the waves, but in many ways, Arabella had been the only one to make it to shore.

Astrid took a nibble of her pear, chewing thoughtfully. "For a time, Andrew's conversation, wit, and manners allowed all of us to continue bumping along, though not happily. Perhaps his ill humor is a blessing in disguise, but ladies, I honestly do not know what to do about my husband. I will happily take over the household management, Gwen, and I will understand, my lady, if you want to return to Town, but neither of those changes will make Andrew any happier with me."

Rose stuck a finger in the jam pot and smeared the results on a piece of bread. Andrew had perfected the same maneuver before he was three. Now he'd perfected the art of being a ghost in his own home, and Arabella had had enough of it.

"My dear girl, you are no more able to *make* Andrew happy than your sister could have *made* Heathgate admit he loved her. Men are stubborn about the simplest things."

"She's right," Gwen added, wiping Rose's finger off on her bib and giving the child's hand a light smack. "Andrew cares for you. You have only to catch him watching you when he thinks he's unobserved. Whatever troubles him is something he has to resolve, Astrid."

"But why won't he let me help him? Why won't he let anybody help him? Talk to him? Carry his burdens with him?"

How often had Arabella asked herself the very same vexing questions. She suspected Heathgate plagued himself similarly where Andrew was concerned.

"Maybe he thinks you'll be disappointed in him," Rose piped up. "Cousin Andrew is a grown-up. He wants to do things himself."

She went back to munching on her bread and jam, having stated the obvious, after all, while the adults exchanged bemused smiles over her head.

Astrid dipped her slice of pear into the jam pot, leaving a smear of red over creamy white fruit. "Please don't feel you must go back to Town, my lady."

"Nonsense, my dear," Arabella said, scrounging up a smile. "I have overstayed my welcome. Seeing a growing unease between you and Andrew, and foolishly thinking I might be of some help. All I've done is aggravate everyone around me."

Which at least had given the young people a common complaint, and that was a start. That Arabella had for once been with Andrew as the anniversary of That Awful Day had come and gone was a private victory, but a significant one.

Arabella steered the talk thereafter to pleasantries—

the increasingly cold and gray weather, the prospect of Felicity's confinement in the coming month, the approach of the holidays.

"We haven't resolved your situation, Astrid," Arabella said, lest the girl feel her woes were ignored. "The only advice I can give you is to be patient. Andrew is a good man, if stubborn and proud. His father was the same way, and I can't tell you the number of times I threatened to take my boys and go home to my mother."

Gwen passed Rose a slice of white cheese flecked with caraway seeds. "You still miss him, your Robert?"

Need she even ask? Privileges had courteously decided that Arabella's menfolk had died in order of the succession, the marquess, his son, his grandson, then Robert, and finally Adam, so Arabella might have the courtesy title of Marchioness of Heathgate.

The title was not a courtesy, but rather a curse to a woman who'd much rather have remained simply the wife of Lord Robert Alexander.

"I miss my Robert every day," Arabella said as Rose made another raid on the jam. And because the child would not understand, but the young ladies would, she added, "and every night."

Astrid set her pear down, probably realizing belatedly she'd set a bad example for the child. "I cannot see Andrew ever pining for me that way, though I can see him taking ship for darkest Peru without a backward glance."

"But you would pine for him," Gwen said, rising and holding out a hand to Rose. Rose and her mother left, with Rose munching on her cheese and nattering on about why lessons after lunch were not a good idea.

Now it was safe to smile. "That girl…" Arabella reached for the teapot.

"Rose?"

Rose, too, who was at risk for growing up exactly as independent and lonely as her mother—and her great-aunt.

"Guinevere. If only I knew which of her admirers had taken such shameless advantage of her, I'd turn both Gareth and Andrew, not to mention your lovely brother, loose on the scoundrel. But she's never said a word."

They finished their meal in quiet, companionable conversation, though Astrid glanced repeatedly at the door and at the clock. No doubt she worried that Andrew was out in the barn, starving himself—as his mother worried—and not for food.

Arabella announced an intention to depart the very next day, lest anybody waste effort trying to change her mind.

"You'll miss Andrew," Astrid said, demonstrating the perceptivity Arabella was counting on to salvage a young and troubled marriage—and a young and troubled husband.

"I have been missing Andrew for thirteen years," Arabella said. "In some ways, he was the worst casualty of the accident. I don't recall many details of the entire incident. I doubt Andrew can forget any of it."

"I hate that accident," Astrid said. "I never knew those who drowned"—a less forthright woman would have used a gentler phrase for death—"but I know that because of that day, Andrew does not intend to remain a proper husband to me. I might well be missing him myself, every day and every night, even thirteen years from when he leaves my side."

"Then you must not allow him to slip out to sea, lest he take your joy, your meaning, and your heart with him."

Arabella ran her finger around the edge of the jam pot, and let a dab of strawberries and sunshine grace her palate before leaving the dining parlor in search of her maid.

And a quiet corner, in which a lady might say a prayer or shed a few tears.

A few more tears.

❧

The dream started the same way it always had, with the frigid sea air whipping a stiff, briny lock of Andrew's hair against his mouth. He didn't bother brushing it away, and beside him, his brother Adam waved off a footman who would have teetered and plunged across the pitching deck to offer yet another dram of Heathgate whiskey.

"At least we're getting close to shore," Adam muttered. "Bloody, infernally stupid of Grandfather to keep us out in this weather."

Adam rarely used foul language around his younger brother, and that as much as the heaving seas made Andrew uneasy. "We'll be on shore soon." Part prayer, part wish, because progress toward shore was hampered by the wind, the waves, and the whiskey Grandfather and the other adults had been swilling all morning.

"I'm glad Gareth isn't aboard to see that." Adam's

scowl took in the sight of Julia Ponsonby, standing at the captain's wheel with Grandfather, the damp wind plastering her dress to her body to an indecent degree.

Andrew looked away, whereas five weeks ago, he would have shamelessly gawked. "She seems to be enjoying herself."

"That damned woman has a penchant for enjoying herself, but Grandfather needs to be minding the tiller, not Julia's wares."

Another wave lifted the small pleasure vessel higher, which meant the plunge down the trough—

I'm scared. Andrew was fifteen, and a man at that age did not admit such a thing, even to a trusted older brother whose expression suggested he too was at least uneasy.

"You can swim, right?" Adam asked.

"Like a fish. Anybody who wants to row crew has to be able to swim." Though the sea was only part of what frightened Andrew. Julia Ponsonby and her penchant for enjoying herself was a large part of the rest of it.

On the quarterdeck, their father was also watching the goings on at the wheel with an uneasy eye, while their mother stood clutching the taffrail, her expression shuttered, her gaze on the shore that hadn't come closer for the past half hour.

"If we come a cropper, you swim for shore, Andrew. You don't bob in around the wreckage, hoping for survivors, understand?"

"Stop being dramatic."

"Gareth is alone on shore, and he'll need you."

The peculiar gravity in Adam's tone had Andrew

turning to argue with his brother, only to lose what was left of his digestive fortitude. "Adam!" He pointed at the wave coming toward them, a huge wall of dark-green water with a rabid froth of brine cresting along the top.

Inside the wave, serpents of seaweed and two enormous fish were trapped like souls caught in hell, even as the wave raced closer to the boat.

Adam produced a knife and several colorful curses. "You head for shore, Andrew. Promise me." He slashed at the moorings holding a small rowboat fast. "I love you, and you'll be fine if you head right for shore."

Panic gripped Andrew with a cold fist to the guts, and like a frightened boy half his age, he wanted to scream for his papa. Up on the quarterdeck, Julia's laughter went silent, then turned to screams.

"I can't swim! We're going to die, and I can't swim!"

Hands slack on the wheel, Grandfather stared at the approaching wave, while Papa shouted over the wind and Julia's screaming, "My lady! To the boat! Adam, Andrew, the boat!"

Papa struggled against the wind and the pitching of the boat to make his way to the steps to the lower deck, but Julia shoved him aside. "Andrew, Adam, you have to save me! I cannot swim!"

With one hand she clutched the rail, with the other she clutched her belly. For one sick, eternal instant, Andrew felt the boat sink lower than all the seas around them. He had time to hope they'd ride up the swell and pitch into the trough behind the wave, when an avalanche of water crashed over the rails, sweeping Julia from the steps.

A great crack sounded, and her screams echoed as she was carried overboard. "Andrew, please! I cannot swim! *Andrew! Please!*"

"Andrew, please. *Wake up.* You'll do one of us an injury with all this thrashing about."

Lungs heaving, the sting of salt water in his eyes, Andrew came awake sitting bolt upright in bed. The covers were a tangled mess, and Astrid was frowning at him by the last of the firelight.

Astrid, the closest thing he had to a friend, his wife. *His wife.*

"You nearly pitched me overboard, Husband. Have you no sense that a woman in my condition needs her rest?" Her words were tart, while the hand she used to brush Andrew's hair from his eyes was gentle. "Sir, this will not do."

She slogged over the side of the bed, and Andrew wanted to call her back. "I was dreaming."

"You've had this dream previously, you know." She moved across the room with the ungainly dignity of the expectant mother, nightgown billowing in the darkness. Andrew heard glass clink and liquid slosh. Each sound was distinct, and each one brought with it relief.

He was not on board a doomed pleasure yacht; he was not going to die by drowning, or have his life dashed to pieces on the rocks. Not tonight.

Astrid came to his side of the bed, a half-full glass in her hand. "This is not water. You will drink it in the interests of settling your wife's nerves."

He reached for the glass, his hand shaking. Astrid held the drink until he had a firm grip, then kept to her place until he'd downed the entire contents in one swallow.

Brandy, not whiskey. Never whiskey. "My thanks."

She put the glass aside and climbed into bed. "You were having a nightmare. Talking about these things sometimes helps."

Her practical, tart, intimate presence helped. Normally, Andrew would have been getting dressed, preparing to roam the house, the streets, the park, anywhere to work off a convincing case of mortal panic.

But talk to *her*, about *this*? Never.

"Everybody has the occasional nightmare. I'm no different." Now, that might be so. Thirteen years ago, he'd had nothing but nightmares.

Astrid budged up against his side, belly and all. "You dream of the accident."

Nine souls had lost their lives when the boat had foundered and gone down, including five Alexanders, Julia, and two crew members. "Not so often anymore. You should get back to sleep."

He wanted another soothing tot of brandy, but wanted more to hold his wife.

"It was bloody awful, wasn't it?"

"Such language, Lady Greymoor."

She scooted higher in the bed, got an arm under Andrew's neck, and tried to wrestle him against her side. "You are in want of cuddling, you great looby. My condition is delicate, so you will indulge me in this."

He didn't smile, but simply by being Astrid, she pushed the panic away and calmed the roiling in his belly. "If I must."

Nothing, not even Astrid on a tear, could banish the guilt.

"I hate that you're tormented by something that happened nearly half your lifetime ago."

He pillowed his cheek on the slope of her breast as her arms settled around him. "When you next see the sea, you must share your displeasure with it, Wife. Perhaps your sentiments will meet with more respect than my own, but Astrid?

She kissed his temple. "Hmm?"

"You must promise me never to travel on the water."

Her hand went still midstroke over his brow. "So you can hare off to the Continent, secure in the knowledge I can't give chase?" She sounded more exasperated than offended.

"So you don't die, screaming for rescue, knowing your child will never draw breath and your family will be driven insane with grief."

He had not planned those words, had not mentally braced himself against the desperation with which he meant them. Astrid's hand resumed its soothing progress over his features, bringing him a faint scent of lavender and lemons.

"I will not chase you, Andrew. Drat you, you have been honest with me regarding the metes and bounds of this marriage. I wish you'd tell me about the accident."

"Promise me."

She heaved up a sigh, a soft, fragrant swell of the bosom upon which Andrew's cheek rested. "I will not travel upon the water without you, Andrew. I can swim, though. Felicity and I both can swim like ducks—or perhaps like hippopotami, given our present dimensions. Go to sleep now. This bed holds no sea monsters, other than your damnable pride and perhaps my own."

Andrew closed his eyes but did not expect to sleep. Astrid would make a wonderful mother—practical, loving, patient, insightful, and good-humored. That she would never be the mother of his children was only part of the price Andrew would extract for what she called his pride.

When sleep did come stealing up to him, bringing with it the echoes of Julia's screams, Andrew instead focused on the sound of his wife's breathing, on the feel of her hand in his hair, on the scent of her.

And for the first time following that particular nightmare, despite all deserts to the contrary, Andrew slept the remainder of the night in peace.

Fourteen

MORNING DAWNED SUNNY, DRY, AND SURPRISINGLY mild, a parting gift of autumn as winter tried to elbow its way in the door. The pleasant weather was fortunate, because seeing his mother off in a storm would likely have been a greater trial than Andrew's nerves could tolerate.

He should not have come back to England in autumn.

He should not have come back to England *at all*.

When Lady Heathgate had taken her leave of the ladies, she asked Andrew to walk her to the coach.

"I am not a demonstrative woman," she said, turning worried eyes to him. Andrew steeled himself for some display, because her words were nothing less than a warning shot. "And yet, I think you need to be reminded that I love you. Do you know, Andrew, there is nothing I would not do for you, nothing I could not eventually learn to accommodate, should you ask it of me. I have always been proud of you and considered myself fortunate to be your mother."

Andrew felt as if his mother had doubled back her fist and ploughed it into his belly, much as he felt when the nightmare plagued him. Scolding and criticism he could handle; a disapproving silence would have been within the ambit of his tolerance, and even a relief.

But this... loving kindness was unbearable. In the years he'd been gone, Andrew's mother had changed subtly. A touch more gray fringed her dark hair, a touch more sadness lurked in her blue eyes. She was still a tall woman, but not so tall as she'd been four years ago. And yet, like Astrid, she was fierce.

"I am fortunate to be your son," he said, wishing he were *worthy* of it as well.

But her ladyship had merely fired her opening salvo.

She laid a hand on his arm. "Your brother is concerned for his wife, but you know he would also make every effort you might ask of him. If you had seen the way he anticipated your letters, read them to one and all, and reread them and reread them... We missed you so."

His throat constricted around a painful lump, his vision blurred. He bent to kiss his mother's cheek, inhaling her signature lilac scent as if it could make him a small child again.

Thirteen years ago, he'd hauled her from the waves that would have taken her from him, and yet, even saving her life could not excuse the other choices he'd made the very same day.

He bowed, the universal gesture of respect. "You had best be on your way, Mother. Safe journey."

She patted his cheek and allowed him to assist her into her cavernous traveling coach. As the coach rumbled off, Andrew was mortified to feel a tear slipping from the corner of his eye.

Christ above, what was wrong with him?

He stalked to the stables, intent on using the rare sunny day to good advantage with his horses. He began as he always did, with a treat and a pat to little Daisy, the wizened pony he'd ridden as a child, who now creaked up and down the lane with Rose bouncing on her back.

He worked in hand with the young stock next, and by the time he'd brought out his riding horses, Astrid had taken up her perch above the schooling arena. After that parting scene with his mother, Andrew was comforted to know Astrid still took an interest in this aspect of his life. He was about to call up to his wife, when the groom led Magic out, ready for work over jumps.

Andrew swung up and kneed his horse out into the arena. "Mustn't let a pretty set of quarters distract us from our work, my boy." Or a pretty smile. Or a sad one.

The horse was his salvation, a beast who could not be ridden with anything less than a rider's full attention. Andrew put Magic through exercises intended to loosen the gelding's neck and back, and to sharpen his attentiveness to his rider's aids. The next step was a series of poles on the ground, gradually raised to form low jumps, then higher jumps.

Magic was enjoying himself, working in good rhythm, and ready to take on the progressive challenges before him. Pleased with and proud of his mount, Andrew had the grooms set the last jump up to about four and a half feet, a height Magic had certainly done before, but beyond the abilities of many horses.

They bounded through the gymnastic, only to finish with a tremendous clattering crash as they landed after the last jump. Magic burst forward, then shied and bolted across the arena in a blind panic, Andrew struggling to bring him under control.

Andrew first thought they'd simply caught the top rail with a back leg and brought the whole jump down behind them, but Magic was still prancing and snorting when Andrew slowed him to a halt.

And then he saw why the crash had been so loud.

The balcony upon which Astrid had been sitting lay in matchsticks on the ground. His heart in his throat, Andrew galloped Magic back to the end of the arena, coming to a rearing halt beside the pile of lumber that had been a dozen feet in the air moments previous.

Andrew pitched boards aside, his heart thumping against his ribs. An odd, tense quiet descended as the grooms watched him searching through the wreckage for his wife. A groan directed him, and he found her, prone under yet more boards. He had them cleared away in moments, and knelt beside her.

"Sweetheart?" He felt at her wrist for a pulse as he pushed her hair back from her eyes. She had a nasty cut on her arm, a long, bloody laceration that would need stitches, at least.

"Perishing, blighted… Andrew…"

Andrew could hear the pain in her voice, but she was alive, cursing, and she knew him.

"Don't move, dear heart. We'll get you out of here, but you must lie still." His voice was calm, much calmer than he felt. He told himself she had a strong, steady pulse, and she was conscious, but God help her, she had fallen a considerable distance.

And the baby. What about the baby?

He barked an order, and the grooms fell to, lifting off and stacking boards without a word. In minutes, they had the wreckage cleared, but when Andrew tried to lift his wife, her scream had every man blanching white.

"Where does it hurt?" Andrew asked around a rising sense of panic.

"Head," Astrid said between panting breaths. "Fire in my arm, and my shoulder."

"I'll carry her," Andrew said. "Somebody run up to the house and tell Gwen to get out the medicinals."

Andrew noticed only then that Magic had come to stand near Astrid, his great long face gazing down at her worriedly.

"Watch that dratted beast!" Ezra spat.

At the sharp tone of voice, Magic looked even more worried, but he flicked his gaze from Andrew to Astrid and didn't move a hoof.

Andrew lifted his wife carefully, then quietly told the horse what to do. Magic, having learned this command easily, knelt in the sand, waiting until Andrew had settled both himself and his wife into the saddle.

"Up," Andrew commanded, and Magic rose gracefully to stand and wait for further instruction. The reins hung slack, because Andrew's arms were full of his injured wife, but his seat and legs were adequate to guide the horse up the driveway to the front terrace. Ezra sent a stable boy ahead at a dead run to warn the household, and walked a few paces away from the horse.

As Andrew approached the house, Gwen emerged, her apron knotted in her fists. She kept her questions to herself, however, and sent a footman for the medical supplies as Andrew once again ordered the big horse to kneel.

Andrew swung a leg over the withers, then gave Magic the signal to rise so Ezra could take his reins.

"Magic loves you," Astrid said, as Ezra led the horse away.

"Hah," Andrew retorted, making his way up the front steps and into the house, Astrid in his arms. "He loves his oats. He thinks I am a member of his herd, and you too, apparently."

"You are an idiot, and your horse has more sense than you do."

How reassuring to hear her scold like that, and he *was* an idiot. "If you say so."

"My shoulder still hurts, but not as badly. I'm afraid to look at my arm."

"You're bleeding a bit," Andrew informed her as he took the stairs with her still in his arms. And the sight of blood had never made him ill—before. "I think a knot on your head, the cut on your arm, and a wealth of bruises will be the extent of the damage to you, but I would like to send for Dr. Mayhew."

"Don't," Astrid said as he set her down on a sofa in the sitting room of their suite. "I am sure the good doctor will be looking in on Felicity regularly. He can add me to his usual list of calls at that time."

"Astrid," Andrew began as Gwen joined them, "you may have internal injuries." He remained standing over her, unable to move away even a few paces.

"*Andrew*," she shot back in the same repressive tone he'd used, "if I have internal injuries, and if I lose the baby, there is nothing the doctor, or anyone else for that matter, can do."

She'd put it into words, matching him bluntness for bluntness, which reassured on some level.

Gwen stepped between them and bent to look at Astrid's arm. "Why don't we tend to this first, look you over for other injuries, and then you can decide what the next step should be?"

So reasonable, her suggestion, and yet Andrew wanted to pitch his dear cousin through a window and bolt the door.

They were joined shortly by a maid carrying the medical supplies, and another carrying bandages and hot water.

Andrew stayed beside Astrid—and she didn't ask him to leave—while Gwen cleaned the wound on Astrid's arm. No doubt it stung, it burned, it ached, it throbbed, and it just plain hurt. When Gwen threaded her needle, Andrew wanted to be sick.

Instead, he laced his fingers through Astrid's and tucked his arm around her more securely. "Do you want me to hold your arm still?"

"No," Astrid said, as Gwen knotted the thread, "but don't let go of my hand."

As if he could have. When Gwen finally snipped off the last knot and sat back, every freckle across Astrid's cheeks stood out against her pale complexion, and Andrew's hand had deep crescent marks where her nails had bitten into his flesh.

"A bath is on the way up," Gwen said as she

sprinkled a white powder on Astrid's arm. "I'll
wrap up your arm, but you must keep it dry. The
dressing should be changed every day. With luck, as
much as it bled and as carefully as we cleaned it, it
shouldn't become infected. Shall I stay to assist you
with your bath?"

"No need," Andrew said, cutting off Astrid's
reply. The servants began to troop in with the bath
and a dozen buckets of steaming water. "I will see to
my wife."

Gwen shot Astrid a questioning look, but withdrew
without further comment.

"My cousin has allowed me the privilege of privacy
with my wife," Andrew said. "So, come along,
you." He rose from the sofa and extended a hand to
Astrid—a hand that, to his surprise, did not shake. "I
want to assure myself you are not injured elsewhere,
and get you into the bath while the water is hot. Shall
I wash your hair?" he asked, coming around to the
back of her to start on the hooks of her dress.

∽⊛∽

Andrew's competent fingers began the process of
undressing her, and just like that, Astrid suffered an
upwelling of self-consciousness. A blush crept past her
neck, one Andrew could not fail to see.

They had made that reluctant, desperate sort of
love in the darkness, doing things with each other
that required trust and intimacy under the blankets.
But it had been weeks since Andrew had seen
her naked, and in those weeks, Astrid's body had
continued to change.

Andrew's hands paused on her shoulders. "You are shy of me."

Of course she was shy of him. He was the only man ever to see her naked, and in his own way, he rejected her daily.

"Ah, sweetheart," Andrew said on a sigh, "I am sorry." He brought her against his chest and used the embrace to complete the process of unfastening her dress. She sensed his apology was general, for transgressions past and present, but also future, and that hurt worse than all her injuries put together.

"Shall we consign this to the ragman?" Andrew asked, tossing her dress across a chair.

"The maids might want it."

Andrew's eyes were tired and not only in a physical sense. When had that happened? And he did not argue with her, though Astrid suspected he'd have the dress burned.

He untied the ribbons on her chemise, one by one, and she made no move to stop him as his strong, graceful fingers unraveled bow after bow.

"I don't deserve the privilege of assisting you, Wife, but if you will allow it, I would be appreciative."

He would not plead with her. She didn't want him pleading with her, for that matter, so she remained silent as Andrew finished with his task.

Which left her naked before him for the first time in weeks.

His gaze traveled over her, pausing at an angry contusion at her shoulder. He stepped around her and ran his fingers over the darkening flesh.

"You have a terrific bruise coming up here," he said,

stroking gently. "Another one here." He trailed a finger from the bottom of her back over her right hip. "A quite respectable, though slightly smaller one here." He brushed fingers down the back of her right thigh. He touched several more before coming around to her front.

"All in all, you are going to be more than a little uncomfortable for at least a few days. Shall I have Gwen send up some laudanum?"

"No, thank you," Astrid said, taking her naked self over to the tub. He'd looked at her bruises; he hadn't looked at *her*—and how symbolic was that?

Andrew was beside her in an instant. "Let's prop the arm on towels and let the rest of you soak."

She lowered herself carefully into the delicious, soothing heat of the water, as Andrew held her bandaged arm aloft. He arranged towels so she could prop her arm on the rim of the tub, and then stepped back, his expression hooded.

"You are comfortable?" He looked like he wanted to kick something. "Stupid question. Is there anything I can do to make you less uncomfortable?"

"You offered to wash my hair." She wouldn't ask either, and a lump in her throat joined her other aches. Delayed reaction, no doubt.

"I did offer." He dragged a stool over to the tub and settled himself on it. "Would you like to soak a bit first, or shall I be about my appointed labors?" His voice wasn't flirtatious, not for Andrew, but it wasn't combative either.

"Soak." He could not walk away, not with her injured and unable to dress herself, so Astrid seized the initiative. "And talk."

"What shall we talk about?"

"About this attempt on my life?" Astrid suggested pleasantly. She picked up the soap in her left hand and realized one needed two hands to raise a lather. One needed two hands for many worthwhile undertakings.

"Let me." Andrew came off his stool to kneel by the tub. He took the soap from her, and was soon sliding his lathered palms over Astrid's uninjured arm. His touch, while far from lover-like, was gentle and soothing. He attended her arm, back, neck, legs, and feet, but avoided her breasts and genitals. With her belly, which protruded noticeably, he was particularly tender.

And while he bathed her, they did talk—or their version of it.

"I wish I could argue with you," Andrew said as he lathered her hair some minutes later. "I wish I could assure you this was simply an accident, an unfortunate mishap, but I suspect otherwise."

Astrid closed her eyes, enjoying the feel of Andrew's fingers massaging her scalp. "I am the only person who uses that platform as a balcony," she said. Used it as often as she could, because watching him ride was one way she could be with her husband. "I sit up there almost every morning you work the horses, not just every once in a while."

His dug his fingers into the muscles of her neck and applied a luscious pressure. "Why do you do it?"

"I love to watch you doing what you love. To work with a beast who does not particularly choose to work with you can be frustrating, I know, but you win them over, Andrew, and the results can be beautiful. Look at your gallant steed, and how he behaved today. Gareth despaired of that horse ever being safe under saddle."

"Thank you. Your words mean… a lot."

They weren't words about horses, but Astrid doubted Andrew grasped that.

He rinsed her hair, wrapped a towel around the heavy, wet mass, then knelt beside the tub, crossed his arms on the rim, and rested his chin on his wrist.

"Astrid, would you consider traveling with me to the Continent?"

"To hide me from this menace?"

"Yes. I have failed to keep you safe, even here, on our own property. That platform was built to hold great quantities of hay, as well as the weight of a grown man. I know it's as old as the rest of the barn, but I am sure I will find that a saw was taken to the supports. I don't know how on earth you survived the fall, as well as the weight of all the lumber that landed on you."

She'd landed in the muck pit, that's how, a fitting analogy for her circumstances generally. The sturdy sides had kept the lumber from landing on her, and the contents of the pit had cushioned her fall.

Which would be funny in some metaphorical sense, except…

"If Gwen were laying my body out in the parlor now, Andrew, would you be relieved or sorrowing or both?"

He pushed away from the tub and paced across the room.

"I would be insane with grief and guilt," he bit out, snatching a large towel off a pile on the clothespress.

He came back to the tub as she rose from the water, opened the bath towel, draped it over his shoulder, and held out a hand to steady her as she stepped from the tub.

"Allow me," he directed when she would have taken the dry cloth from him.

She allowed him to gently towel her body dry, then sit her down, back to him, on the sofa. He brushed her hair dry then dropped a nightgown over her head, working carefully to avoid movement of her throbbing shoulder. With equal attention to her comfort, he wrapped a night robe around her.

When Gwen brought up a very late luncheon tray, Andrew joined Astrid in a meal, making her a sandwich and cutting her apple into quarters, so all she had to do was eat one-handed.

He could not have been more attentive. Astrid considered planning an attack on her life every few weeks to keep him at her side and civil, but discarded the notion. As much as her shoulder hurt and her arm throbbed and her head ached, the hurt she saw in Andrew's eyes was the far greater source of pain.

Fifteen

In the ensuing days, Astrid suffered no cramping, no bleeding, no signs of internal ill effects whatsoever, while the child continued to move and grow within her. She was stiff, sore, and scared, but above all, she was grateful her child yet lived.

About a week after she'd sustained her injuries, Astrid lay in bed, spooned with her husband. They had not made love since she'd been hurt, but in the intervening days, she'd seen the hungry look in Andrew's eyes and been heartened by it. Maybe these injuries were a blessing in disguise. Maybe Andrew was resolving whatever doubts had been haunting him.

Though Dr. Johnson's observation about second marriages being the triumph of hope over experience came to mind.

Andrew's hand splayed across her belly, his touch familiar and comforting. "Somebody is up past bedtime tonight."

"Lying down seems to provoke a time of moving about," Astrid replied, drifting her fingers across the back of Andrew's hand. "It has been thus for the past few weeks, and Felicity has written it was thus for her as well."

· And Gareth had loved to spend the time marveling at the child's movement, but she didn't voice that confidence to the man's brother. Instead, she wrapped her fingers around Andrew's and deliberately moved his hand up over her breast.

He kissed the nape of her neck on a sigh. "I am not a saint, Astrid. If we couple again… It changes nothing."

Astrid wrestled herself onto her back, finding Andrew propped on one elbow, looking down at her gravely. His eyes by the dying light of the fire conveyed a wall of sadness banking a burning desire.

"I want to make love to my husband," Astrid said, her voice surprisingly even given the desperation she felt.

Andrew brushed his fingers across her forehead, smoothing her hair back in one of the touches she loved best. "You are sure?"

"I am sure," Astrid said, turning her face to the muscular plane of his chest. "Andrew, I miss you so."

He closed his eyes, as if sustaining a blow, but he had spoken honestly: he wasn't a saint, and the next thing Astrid felt was her husband's mouth, open and tenderly ravenous against hers.

He shifted over her, enfolding her in his arms. "If I am careful, can you be comfortable on your back?"

"Don't, for the love of *God*, be careful. Just love me, Andrew, please…"

He apparently couldn't talk to her, couldn't tell her what demons drove him, but he could offer tactile consolation, with his hands, with his mouth, with his hard male body. He offered his mouth, to cover hers when she cried out. He offered his hands, to arouse and soothe by turns. And he offered himself, thrusting into her eager heat with endless, determined patience.

But as passion built, and built some more, Andrew held himself just above her. This *consideration* drove Astrid mad and had her clutching at his back, his shoulders, his buttocks.

"Andrew, I can't…" She levered herself up against him, interrupting his rhythm in a desperate search for the satisfaction of his intimate weight. "Please, Andrew… oh, God, please…"

He groaned something unintelligible, shifted them to their sides, cupped her buttocks with one large hand, and buried his face in the crook of her neck. She gave a panting sigh, then a low keening moan of satisfaction as he drove her into a release all the more powerful for having eluded her.

When she lay sated and boneless against him, Andrew resumed moving in her slowly, each thrust and withdrawal lazy and thorough. He kissed her eyes, her cheeks, her forehead lingeringly, as if memorizing the feel of her features with his lips.

Astrid's hands trailed languidly along the muscles of his back, then into his long, thick hair. Any pretense that they were merely coupling was shattered by the tenderness of Andrew's attentions. He was making love with her, making love like a man going off to war, storing up the feel, the scent, and the taste of her the way she'd stored up the same memories of him.

Or perhaps, like a man coming home from war.

Heartened by that possibility, Astrid moved with him, undulated in counterpoint to his thrusts, focused her awareness on his scent, on the feel of his sighs against her skin, the soft, intimate sounds their bodies made in the darkness. He laid his cheek against hers, a gesture of intimate surrender.

"Sweetheart... I can't..." he rasped.

Whatever he'd been about to say, whatever thought he'd been able to form dissipated as Astrid felt a wet heat deep inside her body. He dropped his forehead to her shoulder and remained still, while she savored the pleasure of stroking her fingers over his nape.

He was hers. For these few moments, he was hers and hers alone. The thought encouraged her, and the way he wrapped her in his arms as she eased into dreams gave her hope.

In the morning, she rose to the news that he was sending her away.

❧

"You knew." Astrid fired the words across the breakfast table. "You knew you were sending me to your brother, and yet you said nothing to me last night."

Andrew, usually so handsome and attractive, looked haggard in the morning light. She half hoped he'd indulge in some sniping or grouching that would gratify her need for... meanness.

Instead, he regarded her with patient, unhappy eyes. "Would it have made a difference if you'd known my plans?" he asked gently.

He seemed to think she would have withheld her favors, the idiot. "Yes, it would have made a difference.

I would have imposed on your generosity until neither one of us could have kept our eyes open."

When she wanted him to launch into an argument, Andrew covered her hand with his. "I am sending you to Heathgate because you will be safer there, nothing more, nothing less. He is the marquess, he has held Willowdale for more than fifteen years, and our papa held it before that."

Andrew did not let go of her hand, which was prudent, because many small objects lay within Astrid's reach. Her husband had considerately allowed her to heal, and considerately ensured the child had not been harmed. Now, he was considerately sending her away.

Husbandly consideration was apparently to plague her in both of her marriages.

"Astrid, do not be wroth. Heathgate's people are loyal to us, whereas here, I am still viewed as an interloper. Somebody very cleverly weakened the supports to your viewing platform, and the only thing that saved you and the baby was that you landed on a week's worth of old straw and hay. Any other day of the week, any other time of the day, and the muck pit would have been empty."

She'd landed on a week's worth of manure, fortunately; otherwise, she would be dead. He didn't need to say that, and he didn't need to admit *again* that her death would devastate him. His eyes were that haunted.

"Andrew, I do not want to go," she said, all pride deserting her.

"And I," he said quietly, "do not want to let you go, despite all, Astrid."

Despite all. That covered a lot of nameless misery

and loneliness caused by a man she thought she'd known, and known she'd loved.

"But you will send me away."

"I must," Andrew rejoined. "Besides, Felicity's confinement draws nigh, and she needs you. Gareth needs you too, as do our little nephews. I've sent word to Fairly he might find you at Willowdale as well."

"That's lovely." Astrid pushed cold eggs around on her pretty blue plate and wondered why Gwen had known to dodge breakfast today, of all days. "You have decided I am needed by my sister, my brother, my brother-in-law, and my nephews, so off I go. Was it my imagination, or did you fail to mention *I* might need my husband, or—just possibly—*he* might have need of me?"

Andrew shoved tiredly to his feet—had he remained awake while she'd slept in his arms? "He does need you, Astrid, but he needs you safe, whole, and out of harm's way. Please, I beg of you, do not fight me on this."

He stood by the window, looking out over the bleak, gray morning he had chosen for her departure. His back was to her, the set of his shoulders grimly determined. His complexion this morning was as gray as the clouds lowering over the hills and fields, fatigue etched in every line on his face.

Andrew was suffering. He had stopped trying to antagonize or avoid her, almost as if he had no energy to spare for such pretenses. He truly did want her safe, and that goal was directing this decision. His recent weeks of dodging her and barking at her had taken a toll, one Astrid was not happy to acknowledge.

He does need you, Astrid... The words brought her

strength, for they were an admission beyond that niggardly business of simply caring for her.

She took a place beside him. He neither looked down nor made a move to touch her, until she rested her head on his shoulder and slipped an arm around his waist.

"I am as afraid of losing you, Andrew, as I am of losing my own life. I will do as you ask today and go to my sister's household, but I fear what the future holds for *us*. I am afraid if I go today, you will believe you have won in your efforts to destroy the hope I have for our marriage."

His arm came around her shoulders, and his lips brushed against her temple.

"If you go today, you do so simply to respect my need to keep you safe," he said, relief evident in his voice. "I will visit when I can."

Oh, what a lot of comfort that wasn't. He would always find some horse to ride, some pamphlet to read, some ledger to stare at. He'd send her little notes, and she'd try to answer them…

She pulled away, the pain in her heart making her reckless.

"Perhaps you should not visit. You say I am being sent away simply as a function of my safety, but, Andrew, a part of you wants this too, and not because Gareth has the better, more trustworthy staff. You are confused about your reasons for marrying me. Maybe if I am not underfoot, your reasons will become more clear to you."

He continued to stare out at the bleak, dreary day for a moment, then nodded.

One nod, and yet it was a death knell to Astrid's hopes. If he'd had any intention of making a real marriage out of their situation, he would have argued with her. He would have put up a fight to see with his own eyes that she fared well; he would have made at least a pretense of remaining in her life.

Was this how it felt to drown, to struggle and struggle as the waves closed black and heavy over one's head? No air, no light, no hope?

"Come," he said, steering her toward the door. "The coach will be ready shortly, and we have preparations yet to make."

The preparations consisted of an elaborate ruse that had short, pot-bellied Ezra sashaying up to the house in Astrid's good cloak and bonnet, while Andrew, to all appearances, escorted Gwen over to Willowdale. In old breeches, duster, and floppy hat, Astrid took a place on the box between John Coachman and Andrew.

She steadied herself against the rocking of the coach by bracing herself against Andrew as they traveled the five miles to Willowdale. She did not cry, and she did not argue, but instead considered the man who'd made such tender, heartbreaking love to her the previous night.

Andrew had treated her to her second experience with parting sex, good-bye sex. She nearly hated him for it, except in hindsight, she could recognize the wellspring of the tenderness he had shown her. Andrew had been drawing upon anticipated sorrow and regret, and a man did not regret parting from a wife for whom he felt only a duty to protect.

❦

Andrew followed his brother into the Willowdale library, feeling an incongruous sense of homecoming. He'd fallen a little in love with his wife in this room more than four years ago, when she'd tried her first sips of brandy, while Andrew, Gareth, and Felicity looked on.

"You are offering libation this early in the day?" Andrew asked as Gareth went to the selfsame decanter and poured them both a couple of fingers of spirits.

"To the health of our wives." Gareth lifted his glass. Andrew did likewise, and savored the smooth burn of good brandy.

Gareth set his glass down barely touched. "I need fortification, because my wife's circumstances trouble me. She is so consistently uncomfortable these days, anything I can think of to pass the time, I offer to her. I read to her, rub her back, rub her feet, play the guitar for her, or brush her hair until she falls asleep. I stroll with her morning, noon, and night. I get up in the middle of the night to stroll with her yet more. I have never done so damned much pacing about in my life, and all at the speed of a drunken turtle."

When was the last time Gareth had confided his woes this way? Not since he and Felicity had faced all manner of difficulty on their road to the altar.

"Confinement is hard on a fellow."

"Just wait until it's your turn," Gareth retorted. "You wonder how in the hell you'll mount your wife again, knowing the misery your rutting could bring her."

The truth will out. "You are worried for her." Approaching panic, if Andrew's guess was correct.

"Worried sick," Gareth said, marching across the room to the errant chimera again holding vigil on his end table. Rather than return that sentinel to the company of his brothers, Gareth opened the stopper and sniffed the contents. "Felicity is so uncomfortable, Andrew, and there is no relief for her. She doesn't complain, but whether she's sitting or standing or lying in bed, she can find no ease."

When had his brother, the marquess, the man about town, the imposing, intimidating, surviving scion of the Alexander family, turned so… shamelessly besotted.

"Felicity looks different to me," Andrew noted after a pause to sip his drink. "Her shape is different."

"The babies have shifted, meaning her time draws near. The doctor claims it is part of the normal progression, and Felicity reminds me this happened with the boys—who, by the way, will not rest until they see Uncle Andrew. I believe they mentioned something about a tiger under the bed."

"So that's where the blighter got to?" Andrew pretended to admire the view out the mullioned windows as a pang assailed him. He had nephews and thanked God for them. He would never have sons. Worse yet, he and Astrid would never have sons.

"If we had more time, and if I thought it would help," Gareth said, "I would suggest we get thoroughly inebriated. You, little Brother, look as tired, irritable, and out of sorts as I—and my wife—feel."

Andrew sat on the hard stones of the hearth, knowing this interrogation—this confession—was unavoidable. "Married life does not agree with me."

Gareth left off sniffing at spirits and leaned a hip

on his desk. "Astrid seems to be in reasonable charity with you."

"She, silly little twit, thinks she loves me," Andrew said, bitterness creeping into his voice. "And I have been unsuccessful at disabusing her of that notion, despite a good faith effort on my part."

"Take a lover," Gareth suggested laconically. "She'll hate you something fierce then. A mistress in Town, a night or two with a toothsome opera dancer, a receipt for a bracelet or a necklace given to another. It isn't hard to break the heart of a good woman, Andrew. I should know."

Gareth was taunting him as only an older brother with a thorough grasp of strategy might. Andrew shot him a disgusted look.

"Dear me," Gareth replied innocently, "not the advice you sought? Hmm. Let's see… you could try loving your wife, Andrew. The concept is novel, and not favored by titled Society, but it has, I can tell you, much to recommend it."

Return fire was expected, but the entire discussion curdled the drink in Andrew's gut. "Like you're so happy pacing about and drinking at midday over this wife you love?"

"Unworthy of you, Andrew," Gareth said mildly. "I am happy with Felicity, and well you know it. She is… the home my heart has longed for. At present, however, I am also quite concerned for her. The two conditions—love and concern—are occasionally found in proximity to one another. I believe"—his eyes narrowed—"you know this already."

"To my everlasting sorrow."

Rather than needle him further, which Andrew would have welcomed, Gareth sat beside him on the hard stones. "Is there anything I can do?"

"Keep her safe. For the love of God, keep Astrid safe. She won't take stupid risks, but she won't cower, either. My wife has an appalling abundance of courage."

"She'd have to, to take you on. But something about this whole situation… rankles badly."

"I know." And thank heavens that Gareth's instincts matched Andrew's. "Something doesn't add up. Something feels like it's missing my notice. Douglas has done nothing since Astrid married me but meet with solicitors and barristers and even bankers. I cannot believe he will be content merely to bring a lawsuit when the baby arrives. He doesn't strike me as a man who would trust his ends to the ponderous whims of the court. Moreover, you and I and Fairly are in a much better position to buy the outcome of any litigation, and Douglas is not stupid."

"He most assuredly is not, and that is part of what bothers me."

A rap on the door had both brothers looking up as David Worthington, Viscount Fairly, let himself into the library.

"Time was," Fairly observed cheerfully, "one never knew what one might interrupt waltzing into this room unannounced. Part of the charm of the household."

Gareth rose and scowled at his guest. "You are an unnatural brother."

"There you would be wrong," Fairly replied. "I am nothing if not a natural brother. I thought we had decided to be discreet about it."

"Sit," Andrew growled at him. "We were discussing Amery's doings and the present state of his mischief toward the family."

Fairly's smile vanished, leaving in its place a coldly polite mask. He sat on the sofa, facing Andrew's perch on the hearth.

"Amery has been a busy fellow," Fairly said. "He conducts business with a dispatch that would impress even you, Heathgate. He has also, to my surprise, paid a call on the Pleasure House, though he remained below stairs for the duration."

"So we must conclude he knows you own the place?" Andrew asked.

"We must. I've warned the women if he does ask one of them upstairs, to be very, very careful. We don't know that he's ever abused a woman outright, but there were rumors, and that reassures me little."

That they were monitoring another man's traffic with Fairly's ladies did nothing to calm Andrew's nerves. "He's repaying Astrid, with interest."

Gareth shoved back to sit on his desk, which on this occasion, sported no rattles. "He's paying her back? With what money? The man was all but done up."

"Not quite." Andrew considered another drink and decided on a sharing of intelligence instead. "The family was all but done up. Herbert had the handling of the family finances, and those are in sad disrepair. Douglas's personal wealth, however, has been growing steadily since he attained his majority."

"Where did he get his start?" Fairly asked. "He's only the spare, and he hasn't married money."

"His maternal grandmother left him her modest

fortune when he was nineteen, and tied it up so his family could not relieve him of it. He has made steady progress restoring the sum taken from Astrid's dower account. She is not aware of this, but she will be when the funds are repaid entirely."

Or when Andrew quit England again, whichever should first occur.

"I take it," Fairly said, "you are also not supposed to be aware of this, but rather, the account, whole and hearty, will be produced as evidence should we attempt to disparage Amery at trial?"

"I can think of another explanation, one that fits most of our facts."

Gareth glanced pointedly at the clock. "Because luncheon and a resumption of the ladies' charming company looms, I hope you will share that with us."

"Douglas was a year behind me at university," Andrew said. "He always struck me as a tediously upright fellow, but also rather his own man. He never rode to hounds with his brothers and father. He shoots well, but not for sport. He is, above all, pragmatic. When you, Gareth, were cutting such a wide swath as a newly minted marquess, Douglas did not join in the gossip or the teasing."

"Luncheon," Fairly reminded him, shooting a cuff.

"My point," Andrew said with some exasperation, "is that it could be Douglas is not our man. Viewed objectively, if he is not the one out to harm Astrid, then his theory that she seeks to harm herself also fits the available facts. He simply has to ignore what he knows of Astrid's personality, just as we are ignoring what we know of his. We know Herbert was a weak-kneed, self-indulgent nincompoop, but we have little evidence of that same character in Douglas."

Fairly toyed with a gold sleeve button nearly the same shade as Astrid's hair.

"Who else has all the right motives, Greymoor? Who else would want Astrid and her child disposed of? I've made the acquaintance of Herbert's former mistress, and I can assure you Mrs. Banks is not a woman afflicted with jealousy toward her late protector's wife."

Respect for Fairly twined with something else. To follow up with the mistress was prudent, a loose end Andrew had not considered. That Fairly should take it on without saying anything to anybody else was… sad.

"We are not going to settle this by argument, gentlemen," Gareth said, pushing to his feet. "You raise a good point, Andrew: Douglas is either not our man, or he is making a very careful case for not looking like our man. I vote the latter."

"As do I," Andrew said, "because I cannot afford to do otherwise."

"Perhaps our malefactor is not a man at all," Fairly said, his peculiar eyes focused on some aspect of the problem Andrew could not see.

Felicity interrupted at that point, calling all hands to the table, though all too soon, luncheon was over and Fairly taking his leave. The coach was ordered around from the stables, and the time for Andrew to bid his wife farewell—yet again—drew nigh. He chose the library for that purpose.

Astrid watched him close the door the way another might watch a physician who could only bear bad news. "I feel as if by complying with this scheme of yours, Andrew, I am somehow abandoning you, and thus I am going to cry."

Abandoning him. She offered the sweetest, most daft sentiments. "Come here, then," he said, holding out his arms. "You needn't cry all by yourself over there." Astrid went to him, but she'd doubted her welcome in his embrace, and that was nobody's fault but his.

"Andrew, why does it have to be like this?"

He rested his chin on her crown—she fit him perfectly, in so many ways.

"It has to be like this, Wife, so you may be safe, and that is all that matters for now."

"What about after this *now* you speak of? Why must we have this awful distance between us? Oh, don't answer me," she said, sniffing into his handkerchief. "You will give me some drivel about expectations and happiness, and more nonsense than I can stand."

An accurate summation. Andrew wasn't going to admit to her that her husband was a conscienceless bastard who would betray his brother, his honor, his birthright, and his own child. Not yet, and maybe not ever. Better she hate him on general principles than have the burden of that knowledge.

He kissed her temple and tried for something—anything—honest. "I did not set out to make you unhappy, please believe that."

"And I," she said, stepping back, "did not set out to love you, Andrew, but there it is. I will miss you."

She delivered that observation like the slap that conveys a challenge, then ruined the effect by wrapping herself against him again, clinging fiercely.

Andrew, despite his best intentions, was gratified by the desperation in her embrace. It nearly matched his own, and so he held on to her just as tightly, until long moments later, when she again found the strength to step back.

"I love you," she said, tears spilling down her cheeks.

Andrew caught a tear on his index finger and brought it to his lips.

"Be well, Wife," he said, bowing, "until next we meet."

⟿

"He told me," Astrid fumed, "to be well. *Well*, Lissy, and I let him walk away while I cried like the greatest fool God ever created from the rib of Adam. How can I *be well* when he leaves me to hide in your house while Douglas skulks about Enfield, lying in wait?"

Felicity threaded an embroidery needle with purple thread as Astrid paced the library where only hours earlier, she'd bid her idiot husband farewell.

"Gareth says Douglas is not the only suspect, Astrid," Felicity said, knotting the thread. "Douglas does not appear to have the requisite dishonorable character, though he certainly has motive and opportunity."

Astrid whirled in a swish of skirts, paused to assay her balance, and glared at the sister who sat so serenely behind Gareth's desk. "I am talking about my husband here, and you are going off about Douglas and his schemes. You are as bad as the men in this family."

Felicity looked nonplussed. "That bad?"

"That bad," Astrid said, unwilling to be teased.

"Worse, because you are my sister, and I expect you to support me in my marital difficulties."

Felicity fastened her hoop onto a pillowcase that was acquiring a border of hyacinths the same color as Gareth's eyes. "I do support you. When Gareth told me you and Andrew were marrying, my first reaction was glee, because I love you both, and I know you had a great *tendresse* for Andrew before he went traveling. But upon reflection, the idea troubled me, Astrid, for this very reason you allude to. Andrew is…"

"Andrew is lost," Astrid finished the thought, plopping down into a reading chair far too large for her. "He always was, I think, but compared to Gareth, who was even more lost, Andrew appeared the more reasonable of the two. I believe Andrew merely became more adept at hiding his true nature. Gareth, bearing the title, was allowed and even expected to behave outrageously."

"And look at him now." Felicity scooted forward to adjust a pillow at her back. "My dear husband is nigh unmanned to see me this gravid. He is full of talk about waiting at least two years to have more children, if even then, and so forth. I argue with him that one of the pleasures of marriage is the conjugal bed, and I will not be denied my husband's affections because nature takes its course. Sometimes, I even win this argument."

"I suppose you won it last, oh, about eight months ago?" Astrid replied, though she wasn't nearly finished ranting about Andrew's stubborn, misguided, infernal, pestilential pigheadedness.

"About eight and a half months ago, we did indeed

have a memorable skirmish." Felicity's smile was naughty. "I would I did not win it quite so effectively."

Twins. Twins was a very effective victory, provided there were no casualties. "Are you afraid?" For Astrid was afraid. Afraid of childbirth, afraid of losing her husband, afraid of accidents that might be planned for her by Douglas Allen or his minions.

"Terrified," Felicity said, blinking at her embroidery. "Twins are always complicated, and the babies are usually small, and… I am not worried for myself, but I am worried for my children. For these two, but also for my dear little boys, who can barely understand what's going on with their mama. And Gareth… I worry most for him."

"Heathgate? Why would you worry for him, Lissy? He's as stubborn a man as I've ever met." Though not as stubborn as Andrew.

"He is such a *good* man, Astrid, an honorable man," Felicity said, smoothing a finger over glossy hyacinths. "And he has lost so much. How will he bear it if he loses these children, or me, as well?"

Felicity started to rock back and forth on the seat of her chair, then, on the upswing, heaved herself to her feet.

"I have no dignity," she said dryly. "For the hundredth time this hour, I must use the blasted chamber pot. I see it is also nap time, and so I take my leave of you."

A knock on the door heralded Gareth's arrival, and he entered the library scowling. "What are you doing on your feet?"

Felicity held up a staying hand and toddled past

him. "I am marching myself right up to our bedroom, where I will obediently subject myself to more rest, though I hardly do enough to tire myself to the point of needing any rest. Then I will careen myself out of the bed, perhaps bellowing for my husband to apply shoes to the feet I haven't seen for months, and lumber back down here, to sit on that dratted sofa and read some more dratted novels."

She swayed from the room with ponderous dignity; her husband followed meekly after, while Astrid contemplated stubbornness and love.

Sixteen

As November trudged toward December, winter clamped down with unusually early ferocity, bringing bitter cold, stinging wind, and day after day of gray skies. Andrew forced himself to continue working with his horses, but most days, he took Magic for a gallop that inevitably ended up on the hills over-looking Willowdale.

"The weather will warm up and snow," Andrew informed his horse as they came down to the walk. "And I suspect it will be more than a pretty dusting."

His fingers, toes, and lips were numb from their gallop. If only his emotions could be numbed as well.

"I miss my wife." He wiped his eyes on the back of his glove. "As much as you ache to gallop across these hills, as much as you hate being tethered in a stall, that's how much I goddamn miss my wife."

He missed her sunny, irreverent humor; he missed her casual affection; he missed her tart rejoinders; and he missed—like an ache in his chest—her intimate companionship. This missing wasn't merely erotic, but bore a resemblance to homesickness and desire swirled together, a hollow, restless, unsettled, anxious, incomplete feeling.

Gareth's words came back to Andrew as Magic plodded across the frozen ruts of the road, words Gareth had used to describe his love for his marchioness. "She is the home my heart has longed for." Gareth's heart deserved a home, while Andrew's...

His litany of self-castigation was interrupted by the sight of another traveler trotting along the main road from Town, something familiar about the big bay gelding.

Douglas Allen pulled up and nodded curtly. "Greymoor."

"Amery." Andrew's nod was even less civil, but rather than sit in the frigid air and provoke a staring battle, Andrew let Magic resume his progress toward Enfield. "Bit chilly to be so far from home, isn't it?"

"Chilly seems to be the order of the day, considering you've not replied to my last two letters."

Shite. Andrew had neglected his correspondence, true enough, but saw no need to admit that to Amery. "Perhaps, Amery, my silence was intended to be a reply."

"Am I to assume, then," Douglas said as his horse fell in beside Magic, "you have no interest in conveying the bank draft I bear to your lady wife?"

Only something as plebeian as money would have Douglas riding this distance in this weather.

"I'll take her your draft, and you'll have no need to travel on to Enfield, how's that?" Andrew smiled at his opponent—for that's what Amery was—while a wish sprang up that Douglas would haul him off his horse for his rudeness and indulge him in a bare knuckle discussion of men who sought to harm Astrid.

"Let us at least repair to the village tavern," Douglas suggested. "I would not conduct my business on the open road, even though it appears deserted."

Deserted. Subtle—Douglas was subtle, and Andrew was nigh freezing.

"As you wish." Andrew nudged Magic into a trot, but reined in as he approached the local tavern. The establishment was cozy, served a decent pint, and was reasonably clean. At mid-to-late morning, the common would also be devoid of custom.

Douglas took his bay around to the stable in back, which was more consideration than Andrew would have thought the man capable of.

"Come along," Andrew said to Magic. "You can cadge secrets from Douglas's horse while I ply his owner with winter ale."

Douglas paid a groom to unsaddle his horse, while Andrew merely loosened Magic's girth and slipped the bridle from his head.

"He's a lovely animal," Douglas said. "One hopes you appreciate him."

His lordship did not lack for balls. "Shall we trade our insults over a tankard of ale?"

"Tea will do."

His primness brought Andrew a reluctant smile. If Herbert had been anything like his brother, Astrid would have seen to his demise inside of five years. When they gained the common, Andrew ordered tea and two tots of brandy, then made his way to the snug tucked into the back corner.

"You have business to transact with me?" Andrew asked, sliding onto the bench along one side of the table.

Douglas took his time, unfastening his greatcoat, removing his riding gloves, and removing his hat. Andrew, bare headed and long since divested of his gloves, watched these maneuvers with amusement.

"I have business to transact with my former sister-in-law," Douglas said when he'd hung his greatcoat on a peg, tucked his gloves in his pocket, and set his hat on the table. "Because you are her husband, I suppose... you will do."

Such exquisite condescension befitted a duke, at least.

"You have reconciled yourself to the legality of our union?" Andrew asked as the serving girl brought them their tea and brandy.

"I have. Shall I pour?"

The viscount's manners were the outside of too much, and yet, somebody had to pour the damned tea. "Please."

"I should say, rather"—Douglas daintily poured them each a mug of tea—"I am convinced of the legality of your union, until further evidence can be gathered."

"Brandy?" Andrew asked, holding up a glass.

"No, thank you. Feel free to enjoy my portion."

"As you enjoyed Astrid's portion?" Andrew replied politely.

Douglas looked pained, and also, now that Andrew studied him, tired. "If you familiarized yourself with the timing of the embezzled withdraw-als, Greymoor, you would see my brother was the one enjoying his wife's money, and for that, Astrid has had my sincere apologies."

Andrew dumped the brandy into his tea, though the resulting combination had never appealed to him. "My error. I'm afraid the details of the crime would be more familiar to you than to me."

"I suppose if one considers stupidity a crime, then my brother must be convicted of same," Douglas said, sipping his tea with just the smallest grimace.

Sitting across from the man, it was hard to like him. He was fussy, cold, and bearing a bank draft Andrew had never expected to see.

And yet, it was also hard to believe Douglas had murdered his older brother and attempted to murder Astrid. Hard, but not impossible. "The brandy might be an improvement."

"The tea is hot," Douglas replied, adding more sugar. "I would probably drink pig swill right now if it were served hot."

He'd have the patience to lie in wait until timbers could be sawed through, one by one in the dead of night, but would he have been able to push Astrid down a flight of stairs then pretend to scold her for her clumsiness? Would he have arranged to poison her when she dwelled in the same home as his own mother?

"I would be happy to order some pig swill for you, Amery."

"No doubt, your manners would extend that far," Douglas remarked dryly. "Shall you accept this draft on your wife's behalf?" He tossed a document across the table, as if the bank draft were distasteful to him.

Andrew unfolded the paper, raising an eyebrow at the

amount. "You truly are out to impress the courts, aren't you?" he said, any sympathy toward Douglas evaporating.

"I beg your pardon?" Douglas's tone was as chilly as the Channel wind whipping snow flurries across the fields and hedges.

"You are paying Astrid back with more than token interest, Amery. I can only surmise this is your attempt to create evidence favorable to you when you seek guardianship of your brother's heir. I should toss this money back in your face."

"Then toss it," Douglas said with exquisite indifference. "I shall invest it on Astrid's behalf, if her husband is too busy strutting and pawing to look after it for her."

Andrew's temper snapped, the relief of it enormous.

"By God, Amery"—Andrew rose from the table—"you tempt me to call you out. This"—he waved the draft contemptuously—"does not disguise the fact that yet another attempt has been made on Astrid's life, and the only person motivated to harm her sits before me now, oozing manners and restitution."

"Sit down," Douglas growled as the serving maid paused in her scrubbing at a nearby table. Something in Andrew's eyes must have promised imminent doom, because Douglas added, "Please. Please sit down."

Andrew had to again give credit: Douglas appeared convincingly disconcerted.

"What is this attempt at further harm to Astrid you refer to?"

"What's wrong, Amery, won't your spies talk to you anymore?" Andrew asked—and he did not sit down, but he did keep his voice down. "Know this:

Astrid is safe enough, despite your schemes. And I plan for her to remain that way. And as for this"—he gestured with the draft—"it is not mine to refuse or accept. I will pass it into my wife's keeping, and she will decide what to do with it."

Andrew tossed a handful of coins on the table, snatched up his coat, and stalked from the room, leaving Douglas staring into his tea and the serving girl ducking back to the kitchen.

As Andrew trotted Magic homeward through a snowfall growing more purposeful by the minute, he mentally reviewed the meeting. Douglas could have been lying in wait for him, because Andrew had made a habit of riding over to Willowdale at this time of day.

Which would have to change, effective immediately. Andrew might miss his wife, but he would be damned if he'd leave such an obvious clue regarding Astrid's whereabouts. No more excursions to sit on the hill and pine for her, not if he valued her safety.

❦

Despite the storm outside, dinner concluded pleasantly, with Gareth consuming two large pieces of spice cake. Astrid had seen a few winces cross Felicity's face, but attributed them to the simple challenge of remaining seated through the meal.

"I'll go up to the nursery and check on the children," Felicity said, setting her teacup down and struggling to her feet.

"I'll join you," Gareth added, his hand under her elbow.

"No, you will not," Felicity replied. "You got them so wound up this morning, that one glimpse of you, and they'll be galloping around the room on another fox hunt. Astrid, if you wouldn't mind?"

"I will be in the library then," Gareth informed the ladies. "Please tell my sons I love them, if you can manage it without waking them up."

Astrid linked her arm through Felicity's and escorted her from the room at a particularly deliberate pace. Astrid held her silence, knowing Gareth might well be lurking in the door to the dining room, monitoring their progress.

When they reached the darkened nursery, Felicity went to the small bed where her older son slept, his boneless sprawl a deceptive variation on his usual boundless energy. She lowered herself to his side— slowly, carefully, the way a stately vessel might glide the last few yards into its slip in a calm harbor—and smoothed a hand over his forehead.

"Your father loves you, and so do I. Never doubt that," she said softly. She repeated her words to her smaller sleeping son while Astrid looked on in growing dismay.

Felicity was terrified, mortally terrified. This fact—for it was a fact—hit Astrid like one of those lengths of lumber that had left bruises all over her body. Felicity was saying a good-bye, in case these twins cost her her life.

The child in Astrid's womb chose then to kick hard, provoking a longing for Andrew more intense than any to date. She didn't care why he'd put distance between them, didn't care she should be angry with him. She simply wanted to be *with* him, on any terms he'd consider.

"Lissy?" Astrid called softly.

"Help me up, please," Felicity replied in the same subdued tones. Astrid complied and kept an arm around her sister's back.

When they had gained the corridor, Felicity paused, her lips thinning. "I wish I could tell you to send Gareth off to Willowdale to fetch Andrew tonight, but he'd see through the stratagem. Get me undressed and into bed, then tell my husband to send for the doctor."

Astrid had her sister into a nightgown and tucked under the covers in no time.

"David was able to keep Gareth from the room during my previous birthings," Felicity said, "but I don't think my husband will be as easily distracted this time, and neither David nor Andrew is here to make the attempt. It will be up to you, Astrid, and Dr. Mayhew to keep my husband under control."

"You know that's not fair. Gareth will listen to you, and you alone. If you want him from the room, you must be the one to tell him." Did she expect Astrid to toss the marquess bodily from the room?

"I can't." Felicity went silent, and Astrid could feel the pain resonating through her sister's body. "When Gareth looks at me, his anxiety so carefully hidden, I haven't the heart to send him away. In truth, he steadies me."

"That's not all he does to you."

"Well, please fetch him," Felicity replied. "He will be furious I've done this, gone into labor right as the weather turns nasty. Dr. Mayhew will be none too appreciative either."

"Then let them be the ones to birth the children while we stand around, swilling brandy, and cursing the weather," Astrid replied staunchly. That inspired a smile, so Astrid left the room and went to fetch her brother-in-law.

"Gareth?"

Wire-rimmed glasses were perched on his nose, and he held a small silver rattle in his big hand while he read at the desk in the library.

"Hello, Astrid." Gareth rose, taking his glasses off and folding them into a pocket; the rattle went into a different pocket. "Did you leave Felicity upstairs?"

"I left her in bed." And abruptly, it was hard to say what needed to be conveyed. Fear was contagious, apparently. Astrid shoved it aside with a confidence she did not feel and a prayer she did not voice. "She asked that I fetch you, and that I further ask you to send for Dr. Mayhew."

Gareth sat right back down, as if his knees had simply given out.

"I was afraid of this," he muttered. "The damned weather... The goddamned bloody weather has brought this on." He crossed his arms on the desk and momentarily rested his forehead on his forearms.

He was praying. Astrid was sure she was witnessing the Marquess of Heathgate in a sincerely prayerful moment, and that frightened her too.

"I rather think the weather is only one factor, Gareth, but we waste our time here, and it is going to be a long night. You go up to your wife and act pleased with this turn of events, or I will personally use a horsewhip on you. First you should send a rider for Dr. Mayhew and one for the local midwife as well."

"Felicity doesn't like the midwife," Gareth said, getting back to his feet. "She interviewed her, but said only dire emergency would justify relying on her."

"So we don't like the midwife," Astrid said, "but she is much closer to hand than Dr. Mayhew and will be a source of some experience until he arrives. Now pull yourself together and go to your wife."

He left, so Astrid penned the requisite notes, put Heathgate's seal on them, sent for the grooms, and prayed the snow would ease off.

❧

Five miles and one universe of misery away from his wife, Andrew stood at his library window, watching the snow come down by the light of a lantern hanging outside the stable doors. He knew Astrid loved snow, but this had all the look of a true winter storm, one that would leave roads impassable, travelers stranded, and Andrew unable to join his wife, even if he wanted to.

And he did want to. He wanted to wrap her in his arms and never let her go; on that much, at least, he was now clear. Astrid had been right to insist on a separation, because Andrew had been forced to confront his feelings in a way he wouldn't have otherwise.

He loved his wife, and he wanted her to be happy; it was that simple, and that difficult. He would have to accommodate himself to whatever wishes she expressed that supported her happiness, even if it

meant she sent him away. The difficulty lay in the
nature of the truths Andrew was honor-bound to
share with her before she made such a decision.

Were it not pouring snow, he would saddle
Magic up and make his way to Willowdale. He
hadn't mentally arranged all the hard truths that he
must convey to Astrid, but a lonely and very likely
condemned husband could visit his wife while he was
considering his next move, couldn't he?

※

When Astrid returned to her sister's side, Gareth lay
curled on the bed with his wife, his hands pressed
against the small of Felicity's back.

"Heathgate, what *are* you doing on that bed with
my sister?"

"I am comforting my wife," he observed, rolling
over and sitting up.

"Here." Astrid tossed him a thick towel. "Get that
under your wife, then, and don't wrestle her around
in the process."

Gareth looked puzzled. "What's this for?"

"When my water breaks," Felicity explained gently,
"it could be untidy."

"I knew that," Gareth reminded himself, folding the
towel several times. "Up you go." Felicity struggled to
comply and asked Gareth to arrange her pillows and
then to fetch her a book from the library.

"Astrid," Felicity began when Gareth had reluc-
tantly left the room, "I suggest you get some rest. Dr.
Mayhew won't arrive until well after midnight, and
Gareth is determined to keep me company. If this

takes more than a few hours, somebody will have to spell Gareth with the bedside duties."

"You want to be alone with your husband this evening," Astrid concluded. "I think he would like that too, and I would not want the task of separating him from you. I will go, but I will sleep in my dress and expect to be wakened when the doctor gets here."

And for all the prosaic, practical nature of their exchange, neither of them had raised the real issue: Dr. Mayhew might not be able to come, not with this snowstorm, and the village midwife might not be able to come either.

The next thing Astrid knew, Gareth was shaking her shoulder none too gently.

"For God's sake, Astrid, *wake up.*"

If Gareth were in her bedroom in the dead of night, then matters were dire indeed.

"I'm awake," Astrid muttered, sitting up. "Is the doctor here?" she asked, swinging her legs over the side of the bed.

"The damned doctor," Gareth growled as he handed her a shawl, "is not coming. The roads are barely passable, and this storm has apparently provoked half of titled Society into whelping their little ladies and lordlings. Better yet, the damned midwife is apparently halfway to the South Downs, attending somebody or other's ill-timed birth. Your sister needs *you.*"

"I'm on my way," Astrid said, suppressing a shudder. She hurried from the room, Gareth following with his branch of candles. When she reached Felicity, her sister was in distress but hiding it as well as she could.

The room was hot and stuffy, Felicity's forehead damp, and her hands clammy.

"Shall I open a window, Lissy?" Astrid asked in as normal a tone as she could muster.

"Please. And I need some water."

"I'll fetch it," Gareth said, disappearing out the door.

"If he'd stood there two more seconds, I could have told him to bring a basin and towel," Astrid muttered. "Let's get you walking, shall we?"

"Yes. I've sweated all over the sheets, and I am *sick* of this bed, but, Astrid?"

"Yes?" Please no last wishes, not so soon. Not ever.

"Gareth is terrified. You must be patient with him."

"I will be the soul of forbearance." Provided Gareth was the soul of accommodation. "Now, are you having contractions?"

"They started around midnight, real contractions, not just twinges and grabs and pains, but my water still hasn't broken." Felicity paused beside the bed and drew in her breath on a hiss.

"How far apart are they?" Astrid asked, glancing at the mantel clock.

"Sometimes they are five minutes apart. Sometimes they pile up, one right after the other. This isn't like having James or William, Astrid. It isn't like them at all," Felicity said, resuming a ponderous walk around the room.

"I suppose twins will be different," Astrid observed, trying to mask a growing sense of distress. She'd attended a few births, and she'd read some treatises in preparation for the delivery of her baby, but compared to a doctor or midwife, she knew little.

And Gareth knew even less.

"I'm back," Gareth said, "and I am not leaving this room for another fool's errand, you two."

"Fine, then you can walk with your wife while I change the bedsheets," Astrid suggested. When she'd completed that task, Astrid tarried in the hallway, the load of sheets balled up before her. She'd been present at William's birth, but so had Dr. Mayhew, and it hadn't been snowing.

"I want my husband," she informed the cold, dark corridor. She added the sheets to a growing pile of soiled linen, found a footman to deal with it, and sent up a prayer for her sister.

When Astrid returned to the bedroom, Felicity was looking tidier, but no more comfortable, and Gareth looked quietly panicked.

"Shall we get you back into bed, Felicity?"

"Not bed, please. I am already sick unto death of that bed, and labor has not yet begun in earnest. Let's walk."

So she walked.

She walked with her husband.

While he read to her, she walked with her sister.

She rested on the chaise lounge, and she walked a bit more. By dawn, Felicity was too tired to walk, and she reported that her feet ached as badly as her back. She'd had one period of strong, regular contractions, but they subsided as weak light suggested that somewhere beyond the snowstorm, the sun had gained the horizon.

And still, her water hadn't broken.

Seventeen

"I MISS AUNT ASTRID."

In Rose's voice, Gwen heard the telltale whine of a child confined to the house for too long. "I miss her too, but eat your toast and eggs, poppet. If the snow lets up, we might make a snowman later today."

Rose did not eat her toast. She kicked the rungs of her chair, sending an air of discontent wafting through the breakfast parlor. "Aunt Astrid likes snow. She would play with me in the snow if she were here."

Across the table, Andrew stirred his tea. He'd put a piece of toast on his plate ten minutes ago, and it sat there, cold, unbuttered, not boasting even a smidgen of jam. That he was awake at such an hour was a testament to the way a storm could put one bodily at sixes and sevens.

"I miss her too," Andrew said, surprising Gwen. He rarely came to the table anymore, rarely contributed to conversations. He shaved only often enough to avoid scaring Rose.

"You should go see her," Rose said, plucking the toast from Andrew's plate. "This needs butter and jam."

Andrew stared at the child as if she'd spoken in Hottentot. Gwen wrested the toast from Rose, slathered both butter and preserves on it, then set it back on Andrew's plate. "Don't pester Cousin Andrew, Rose. The weather is dangerous, and I'm sure your aunt will be fine. You were born in the middle of a snowstorm, you know."

The natural self-absorption of the young took over. "I was? Did it snow this much?"

"Almost, and your great-grandfather said it wasn't unusual to have the first crop of lambs come during a good storm. Nobody stirs around much when the weather's acting up, so the little ones can arrive safely."

Across the table, Andrew paused with his teacup halfway to his mouth. He set it down untasted and rose to go to the window.

"You didn't say excuse me," Rose informed him. "Can I have your toast?"

"May I," Gwen corrected. Something about Andrew's posture was alert though, alert in a way she hadn't seen since he'd sent Astrid away. The day was bleak, the kind of day when everything was hues of gray, white and frigid.

"Andrew, at least drink your tea."

"Mama, you didn't say please. Cousin Andrew should *please* at least drink his tea," Rose instructed from around a mouthful of Cousin Andrew's toast.

Andrew glanced over his shoulder, not at Gwen, but at Rose. "She was born during a snowstorm?"

Gwen nodded, the memory made vivid by the heavy snow blanketing the gardens beyond the window. "Grandfather was right, too, about the lambs. When a storm's coming, it often provokes the livestock to bearing their young. It doesn't make sense, what with the cold, but sometimes, it has to warm up to snow, you know? In that sense—"

Andrew was already headed for the door. "I'm going for a ride. If I don't come back, assume I'm at Willowdale with my wife."

About damned time. "I'll fetch you a flask," Gwen said, rising and following him. As she left the breakfast parlor, Gwen heard Rose scrambling down from her chair.

"Mama, you didn't say excuse me either."

Astrid's concern mounted as the morning wore on, both for Felicity, who was tiring markedly, and for Gareth, who was becoming equally exhausted. The close air of the birthing room reeked of sweat and desperation, and the servants had learned not to linger anywhere nearby.

"Heathgate," Astrid interrupted his reading, "would you be good enough to order us a tea tray?" He went without protest, having taken on the post of drudge-at-large, likely because it allowed him to feel useful. As soon as he'd quit the room, Felicity sank back against the pillows on a sigh.

"Thank you," she said in a low, tired voice. "Astrid, listen to me, please, because he'll be right back in here in a moment, pacing and fussing. If things get bad, I want you to send for Andrew."

Astrid swallowed past the lump of fear stuck in her throat—*things* were already *bad*—and opened the drapes enough to see that... she couldn't see anything, save a white landscape as bleak as it was beautiful. "Why send for Andrew?"

"Gareth will need him if matters continue in the present vein," Felicity said, fingers plucking at the counterpane. They'd graduated from the embroidered, monogrammed sheets to everyday sometime during the night. "I'm tiring, Astrid, and these children are not nearly close to being born. If anything should happen to me, Gareth will need his brother, but he won't send for him if he thinks it would create awkwardness for you."

Astrid left the drapes open, some daylight being better than none. "If anything happens to you, *I* will need Andrew. But you mustn't think like this. Sometimes birthing takes its own time."

"That might be true," Felicity allowed, smoothing a hand over her belly, "but this birthing isn't *right* somehow."

Gareth came in, not bothering to knock. "What plots have you two been hatching?"

"I have been asking for Felicity's permission to order you off to bed for a nap, but she won't give it—yet."

"Damned right she won't. The tea tray will be up in a bit."

He went to the window, the one that had periodically been opened to clear the air in the stifling room, the one that admitted such feeble light, and stared out into the pale gloom.

"Still snowing, and there's at least a foot on the ground already. We haven't had snow like this in several years, and *now* it won't stop."

"It will be beautiful," Astrid asserted. "And the sun will come out, and these babies will be safely born. But right at this moment, I need to excuse myself, so both of you behave in my absence."

She let herself out into the blessed cold corridor and collapsed against the wall, despair swamping her last reserves of strength.

I am going to have to send for Andrew and hope he can—and will—come here. Even if Astrid could get word to him, and even if he were inclined to come, Andrew would be risking his life to attempt to cover five miles in such a storm.

The horse was crazy. Andrew had no other explanation for the enthusiasm with which Magic trotted—actually trotted—down the driveway. Granted, the riding stock had been stall-bound for the past day, and some excess energy was likely to have accumulated, but Magic was churning through the snow like an exuberant colt.

The result for Andrew was a stinging headwind, but he knew better than to try to overpower the will of a horse intent on movement. Besides, they needed to make use of the daylight, or the journey would turn into a suicide mission after all.

Fortunately, the wind was working for them, sculpting drifts on one side of the road, while creating troughs on the other. This boon proved invaluable, and after the second mile, Magic had apparently fixed his internal compass on their destination. Traveling in this direction, they also cleared the longest stretches

of open road first, when Magic had the most energy.
The closer they got to Willowdale, the more thickly
the trees bordered the road.

By the three-mile point, Magic was willing to
proceed at a walk, and by four miles, he was down to
a plodding crawl through a sea of white. In the saddle,
Andrew had lost feeling in all of his extremities, and
had begun to consider he might not ever see his wife,
his brother, or his mother again.

When faced with the possibility of death, he found
dying had no appeal.

None.

This conclusion hit him like the proverbial bolt
from the blue when Magic took a misstep and
plunged to his knees in nearly four feet of drifted
snow. The horse was oddly still for a moment, and
Andrew had a sick premonition his flighty, neurotic
gelding was about to roll in the snow, complete with
saddle and rider.

"Up," he commanded quietly. Magic heaved
himself to his feet and waited for the command to
walk on.

In hindsight, Andrew acknowledged that his own
fears had nearly drowned his common sense. Magic
had merely been waiting for the command—patiently,
obediently. The neuroses and insecurity resided with
the rider.

But in that moment, when Andrew had contemplated three-quarter ton of horse rolling over his
chilled bones, he'd felt a panicked desire to live, and
live happily, if that were possible. And if it weren't,
he'd find a way to live contentedly and *gratefully*.

Somewhere, he'd find the courage to face his demons and make peace with them.

The alternative, letting his fears and regrets submerge any hope of a decent future, certainly hadn't borne useful fruit, he admitted as Magic began to move as if aware he was approaching a familiar stable. The horse kept to a walk, but it was an enthusiastic, businesslike walk that made short work of the remaining mile, despite the gathering wind, stinging snow, and miserable footing.

Andrew had to bang on the barn door and holler at length before old Bekins peeked out from the smaller door.

"Saint Scholastica's bones, lad," he exclaimed. "Get ye and that damned beastie in here!"

Magic, of course, had to shy and attempt a rear when the door rolled back before his eyes, but it was a tired, halfhearted display brought on by proximity to his former surroundings.

"None of that, you," Andrew admonished. "You've done well thus far. I am inclined to let the lads spoil you rotten."

Bekins shot a skeptical look at the horse. "You want me to look after the beast, then?"

"Look after him like the prince that he is, Bekins. He kept his head when I was losing mine, and comported himself like a perfect gentleman when any other horse would have tossed me into the nearest drift."

"Master Andrew?" Bekins said, when Andrew would have left for the house. "Tell her ladyship we're all pulling for her."

Andrew had guessed rightly then. The shift in

weather had brought on Felicity's travail, and Andrew had arrived nearly too late to be of any use.

❧

Gareth closed Mrs. Radcliffe's novel, the heroine having once again been carted off to some unlikely location, there to languish and pray in hope of rescue. "I wouldn't be eager for birth if this were the sort of drivel I could expect outside my mother's womb."

Felicity shot him a glare, while Astrid pushed away from the window and headed for the door. Even a potentially tragic birthing did not overcome some bodily necessities.

"I will leave your wife to your tender attentions, Gareth, but be warned, the pains are getting worse. I'll be back shortly," she said, closing the door softly behind her, knowing Gareth and Felicity wanted the privacy, and knowing—more to the point—Astrid's nerves were frayed past endurance.

Her feet hurt, her back ached, her eyes were gritty with fatigue, and still, the wretched weather meant no help would be forthcoming. None.

The air in the corridor was cold enough that the chill penetrated Astrid's clothing. She made her way to the kitchen, where she found not one soul, not even the pantry mouser, with whom to share her fears.

Astrid sank onto the hearth, no prayer occurring to her, save for a prayer that her husband might be faring better than she.

"My sister is going to die," she whispered to the empty room. Dried herbs and limp curtains obscured what little light might have penetrated from the window, and likely to conserve fuel, the hearth gave off only meager heat. The empty kitchen felt more like a crypt than the thriving center of a busy manor house.

"She's weak, she's made no progress for the entire night, none of the learned treatises have anything useful to impart, and I am no use to her at all."

Worry was making Astrid sick, oppressing determination every bit as thoroughly as grief had once upon a time oppressed all hope of a happy future. "I want my mother." Then more softly, "I want Andrew."

Wanted him with an ache as great as any Felicity was enduring.

Astrid did not dare close her eyes, lest she fall asleep on that hearth. A commotion from the back hallway gave her the impetus to struggle to her feet, for the servants must not see that she'd lost heart.

"Halloo the house! Has everybody deserted their post because of a bit of snow?" That voice, the sardonic confidence of it, sent sunbeams of sheer gladness piercing the fatigue and worry darkening every corner of Astrid's soul.

"*Andrew.* Thank God you are here." Astrid was across the room and wrapped in his arms in an instant. Tears started, much to her horror, but Andrew only held her more snugly in his embrace, bringing with him the scents of damp wool, husband, and hope. He kept his arms around her, stroking her back gently, until she could muster her dignity.

"What could you be thinking?" She took his proffered handkerchief as he unbuttoned a cloak that still had snowflakes melting across the shoulders.

"You must have been mad to attempt this weather. I could spank you, do you hear me? What are you *doing* here?"

"Thawing out, firstly," he replied, finishing the process of removing his coat, hat, scarf, and gloves. "Where can we set these things so they'll dry?"

Astrid bellowed for a footman from the servants' hall to deal with the wet garments, then made a tray of hot tea, hot soup, fresh bread, and butter.

"Talk to me," Andrew said, slapping butter on his bread. "And be blunt, as only you can be."

"Felicity went into labor last night," Astrid said, so grateful for the sight of him she could start crying all over—even if he was skinny, tired, and haggard. "It isn't going well, and I am afraid for her."

"Who is with her now?"

"Gareth. He hasn't left her side all night unless it's to see to her every comfort."

"I might have known. What seems to be the difficulty, and where is the damned fancy doctor Heathgate lined up?"

"Dr. Mayhew is stuck in Town because of the snow, or because a lot of babies decided to come all at once, the midwife is similarly detained, and I don't know what the trouble is," Astrid replied miserably.

"I wouldn't give much for Dr. Mayhew's reputation once it's known he let Heathgate's marchioness down," Andrew observed as he poured a second cup of tea. "What are Felicity's symptoms?"

"She has contractions, but they are not regular, and they haven't started coming in any predictable pattern. She says it doesn't feel right, and while I'm no expert,

I have to agree. She's in a lot of pain, very tired, and there's little progress."

Andrew polished off his tea in gulps and then started on Astrid's. "Is the opening to her womb dilating?"

This went beyond blunt, and yet, that Andrew knew what to ask was an enormous relief. "Only a doctor would be able to determine that, and I am certainly not a doctor."

"Has her water broken?"

"It has not," Astrid replied, a hot blush creeping up her neck.

"That might be part of the problem. If you break her water, the whole business might get under way in earnest, though some think it can hasten infection."

"And if I break her water, assuming I could figure out how to do that safely," Astrid replied, "and that doesn't get the whole business under way, might it not hurt the babies?"

"Astrid," Andrew said gently, "you've likely read the same treatises I have nearly memorized. Labor might not be progressing because the babes are dead. Breaking Felicity's water will not make them any more dead."

Astrid sat back, breathing having become a challenge. "You mustn't let Gareth hear you talk that way, and I can't say I like it much myself."

"Nor do I. You look exhausted. Why don't you rest while I look in on Lissy?"

"I'll rest later." She didn't want to let him out of her sight, and she didn't want to rest while her sister's life might be slipping away.

❧

Andrew gave in to his tired, beautiful, gravid wife, and let her accompany him as he marched himself up to Felicity's room. He knocked once, then let himself in.

The stench nearly gagged him.

Felicity lay in the big bed, her great belly mounding up under her nightgown. The room was hot, the air foul. Gareth sat by the side of the bed, holding his wife's hand. While Andrew stood just inside the door, Astrid slipped her hand into his, and despite the heat, Astrid's fingers were cold.

This wasn't the reception Andrew had expected, not by a long, wide shot, but Andrew squeezed her fingers gently. Hope lanced through him, hot, light, and irrepressible. He savored it as he held his wife's hand, then tamped it down to be examined later, when less trying circumstances might reveal it for folly.

"Andrew," Gareth said quietly. "I suppose Astrid sent for you." His voice was devoid of emotion, but his face told a tale of exhaustion, bewilderment, and grief.

The staff would be of no help, it being rare for servants to marry, much less marry, have children, and know enough of childbirth to be of use in this situation. Hence, Gareth's unwillingness to abide by convention and leave Astrid to contend with Felicity on her own.

"I was about to send for Andrew," Felicity said, her voice scratchy with fatigue. "For Astrid," she clarified.

She was conscious, at least, and that counted for something.

"I'm here now, Felicity," Andrew said, "and I see there is much to be done, so let's be about it, shall we?" He slipped his hand from his wife's grasp and approached the bed.

"*Don't you touch her,*" Gareth snarled.

"Gareth…" Felicity chided quietly.

"He'll hurt you if he touches you," Gareth said, not taking his eyes off his brother.

"And you will hurt her if you insist she continue to lie in those soiled sheets," Andrew shot back. "Her own mother did not die in childbirth, you know. That poor lady died of the ensuing infection caused, no doubt, by the unclean conditions of the birthing chamber."

"I tried to tell him that," Astrid murmured. "We have to keep things clean here, but he doesn't want Felicity to have to move."

"What is the damned point?" Gareth bit out.

"The point," Andrew said gently, "is that your wife would be safer and more comfortable if you would let us see to her hygiene. Astrid, open the window, please, would you?"

Astrid hopped to comply, and then stood by the window, her arms crossed over her chest, glaring at Gareth like a particularly determined female terrier might regard a tomcat.

Heedless of his brother's scowl, Andrew came around to the far side of Felicity's bed and propped a hip on the mattress. Her lovely face was drawn in exhaustion and pain; her hair was matted to her temples. Her complexion was worse than pale.

"Felicity, do I have your permission to try to help here?" Andrew said, taking her free hand. "You should not lie in these damp sheets, breathing this nasty air, and allowing the situation to overwhelm your determination. But I will defer to your wishes."

Andrew kissed her hand, but saw her glance over at

Gareth, who was scowling down at her from the other side of the bed.

"I am not asking Heathgate," Andrew said gently. "His fatigue and his love for you have put him beyond reason." His grief, too, which Andrew did not dare mention.

"And he can still hear you perfectly well," Gareth said, turning his back on his wife to sit on the bed near her hip. "Help Felicity if she will allow it, but I will not leave her."

Felicity reached out a hand to touch her husband's back. "Gareth…"

He turned to face her. "I won't leave you. I cannot. Not this time."

"You can," Felicity said, holding his gaze. "I need to talk to Andrew and Astrid for a moment in private, Gareth, just for a moment."

The look he sent Andrew promised slow, painful death to any who troubled his wife, but he kissed her hand and left the room.

Felicity closed her eyes and sighed, whether in relief or despair, Andrew could not tell. "Talk to me, Andrew," she said, her voice holding a spark of determination. "Tell me what you're contemplating."

"Astrid is expecting, and thus I've made it my business to read every medical treatise I could find in French, English, Italian, Latin, or German on the subject of childbirth. I've talked at length to Fairly on the same subject, and even discussed this scenario exactly." An awkward, fraught, frankly frightening discussion, though Fairly managed it with brisk applications of Latin and a few peculiar sketches.

"The first thing I'd like to do is investigate the positioning of the babies. If they are not lying properly, then the solution might be easy, if a bit uncomfortable to effect. Prior to that, we need to get you cleaned up."

He gave directions to Astrid regarding the latter necessity, and left the sisters in privacy to see to it. When he exited the room, he was surprised to see Gareth slumped against the wall, sitting on the floor, fast asleep.

Thank ye gods. Andrew fetched a blanket from a spare bedroom to drape over his somnolent brother, and went in search of the housekeeper. When he returned, he brought clean sheets, clean towels, and two empty buckets.

"Gareth has been gone for some time," Felicity said, her gaze on the cracked window. A sliver of cool, fresh air eddied around the room, and the fire danced higher in the hearth as a result.

"Your husband, God bless him, has fallen asleep at your threshold," Andrew said, setting down his burdens. "I propose we leave him there for now."

"My husband will not thank you—"

"Felicity," Astrid interrupted. "Gareth would not let me open the window, for pity's sake. He isn't thinking clearly, and he needs rest."

And Gareth shouldn't be in the damned birthing room in any case, while Andrew felt... as if this were the one place he should be.

"You need to know, Andrew," Felicity said, "my body has given up. I haven't had a strong contraction for more than an hour, and my lower back is one unending ache. I have made my peace with the probable outcome here."

Had he ever been that brave? No, he had not. Not yet.

Andrew did his best impersonation of the Marquess of Heathgate in a royal taking. "Then shame on you, because what you call making your peace, I call giving up, and I won't allow it. You may be quite sanguine about the notion of seeing your babies in heaven, but you would leave me on earth to contend with my grieving brother, and that is a task I will not take on willingly."

He left her to ponder that, while he explained to Astrid what needed to be done.

"We are going to turn a baby? You and I, who have little in the way of medical training or experience?" She leaned against him then, and he savored the trust of it. "I cannot do this, but I shall do it, regardless."

Perhaps they'd adopt that as their family motto. "That's my lady. Get out of your gown, put on a clean shift, and scrub your hands with lye soap."

"I can do that."

"I am going to fetch more hot water, so be quick about it." Because Astrid was as much in need of rest as Gareth or Felicity, and the babies needed to be born sooner rather than later.

Andrew returned, bearing ten more gallons of hot water and sheets that had been recently washed and bleached. He spread a sheet on the birthing stool with a thickness of towels underneath.

"Time to get busy, Lady Heathgate. Up you go, and all that."

Moving Felicity from the bed to the birthing stool took considerable effort. The slightest change in position, and she was in agony, leaving Andrew and Astrid on either side of her to half carry, half walk her across the room. Just as she lowered herself to the stool, a contraction hit.

"It appears," she gasped, "they aren't quite done yet."

"No," Andrew said, "and that is very encouraging." He took most of her weight in his arms as she carefully lowered herself to sitting. "And now we have to see if the babies need to be turned."

One baby did need to be turned, exactly like one of Andrew's small namesakes in northern Italy. The process was uncomfortable, so uncomfortable, Felicity passed from consciousness, and that was probably all that allowed Andrew and Astrid to align matters properly.

Astrid sat back on her stool, surveying her sister's pale face. "Andrew, I think we did it… The baby has moved."

Andrew eased his grip on Felicity's belly, expelling a breath he'd been holding for far too long.

"Good work, Astrid," he said, offering an encouraging smile. "I suspect there are children to be born here very shortly."

"Hurts," Felicity said, opening her eyes moments later.

"Yes." It hurt Andrew's heart to see such suffering and courage, hurt him to think of his brother exhausted in the hallway, hurt him to know Astrid was dealing with all of this, when her own time wasn't far off.

"You moved the babies," Felicity said, frowning.

"You can tell?"

"Oh yes, I can tell. Holy smiling Jesus, Andrew…"

Before that contraction had passed, her fingernails had dug crescents into the back of his hand.

"This is right," Felicity said wonderingly when the pain had passed. A smile bloomed on her tired face. "Oh, Andrew, this is right. This is like when James was born. It feels like the pain is pushing the babies *down*. I want to push the babies down."

"Fairly said you might," Andrew replied. "Is it time to summon the nursery maid?"

"Yes, please. And open the window more. I need air. The babies need air."

When Astrid was in position to assist with the next contraction, Andrew went out into the hallway, sent a footman trotting for the nursery maid, and squatted beside his sleeping brother.

"Gareth." He shook him by one muscular shoulder. "Heathgate…" Then more loudly, "*Brother…*"

Gareth's eyes flew open, and Andrew could see the moment when reality intruded on waking awareness. "My wife?"

"Is busy right now, delivering your children. She'll soon be asking for you." Andrew stood and extended a hand to his brother.

Gareth let Andrew pull him to his feet, but stood as if dazed. Andrew turned him by the shoulders toward the master bedroom. "Tidy up, Heathgate, and pull yourself together. You will soon be introducing yourself to my newest nieces or nephews."

He gave his brother a small push, then watched as Gareth squared his shoulders and marched off in the direction of clean clothes, a hair brush, and a few minutes of privacy in which to compose himself.

Felicity was far from out of the woods. She'd lost blood, and infection was always an issue. But she and Gareth had both been spared the awful choices Fairly had described, and for that Andrew would always be grateful.

And gratitude was something he hadn't felt in any unreserved sense for almost half of his life, though it flooded every corner of his heart now.

Eighteen

"GARETH, WAKE UP." A VOICE AT GARETH'S EAR roused him from the daze he'd been in, for he'd refused to let sleep claim him again. His hand remained wrapped around Felicity's fingers, his face pressed to her shoulder.

Her chest still rose and fell with slow, shallow breaths.

"She's asleep," Astrid said, "and you need to rest as well, or you'll be no use to either her or those children." Astrid's voice was gentle, a light of compassion and sorrow in her eyes.

Gareth scorned Astrid's forgiveness, and he would not tolerate any from his wife, for he had been *no use* to Felicity. No use at all.

"I love her too," Astrid reminded him. And he heard what she mercifully hadn't said: I need to say good-bye to my sister, just as you need to say good-bye to your wife.

After the hell of the past twenty-four hours, he owed Astrid that much. "I will be back."

He rose from the bed, feeling aged and hopeless at the sight of his sleeping wife, so pale, but at least at peace. The emptiness that threatened him was beyond tears, beyond sorrow. Felicity had held on, and fought, and fought, finally bringing their children into the world. But she'd labored in vain for too long first, becoming dangerously exhausted and offering up too much of her life's blood to bear their children.

He kissed Felicity's cheek, then made himself walk away from the bed. When he gained the chilly corridor, the house was dark, the servants abed. A few candles had been left lit in sconces, but silence, cold and oppressive, pressed in from all sides.

He moved toward the stairs, thinking to walk out the front door and breathe in the cold night air. To perhaps keep walking, until he could walk no farther, breathe no further.

But someone sat near the top of the stairs, hunkered like a child intent on spying on grown-ups in the entryway below.

Andrew, waiting for him, with the patience and selflessness Andrew had shown him in years past. His brother, his friend, his entire surviving adult male family. The sight made Gareth even more sad, his heart more leaden. He got exactly one step past Andrew on the stairs before sinking down on the step below him, exhaustion and sorrow colluding to halt all progress toward the oblivion and darkness beyond the door below. Gareth wrapped his arms around his knees and bowed his head.

❧

Andrew waited in the gloom, dreading to hear what his brother would tell him. The euphoria of having assisted with the birthing had faded as the nursery maids had scurried in to help Astrid with the new arrivals, and Andrew had been left alone in the dark to wait and pray.

"My dear wife," Gareth began in a rusty whisper, "has given me…"

Gareth's breathing hitched, and Andrew's heart broke.

"She has given me," Gareth went on, "two beautiful, fat, squalling babies. The younger, a daughter, we have named Joyce… in honor of my unworthy self…"

Another pause, while the silence of the house absorbed these quiet, desperate words.

"And a son, named Penwarren, in honor of the boy's dear uncle… I am much concerned…"

Andrew waited, fearing to hear the worst, wishing he could spare his brother the words, knowing it was Andrew's place, his burden, and his privilege to be the one Gareth spoke them to.

"I am much *afraid*," Gareth corrected himself, "that my wife is soon to give her life, so I might have… our children… to love."

He had pushed the words out, spoken so Andrew would know the terrible pain to befall the household, but he was still laboring to form more words. "Andrew…"

Andrew reached out, unable to let his brother grieve in isolation. He settled a hand on the back of Gareth's neck, trying to communicate whatever paltry comfort his love for his brother might be.

"Andrew… if it hadn't been for my selfish, thoughtless pleasures…"

"Hush. Just hush." Andrew slipped his arm around Gareth's shoulders while Gareth began to shake with silent, shuddering sobs. Andrew wrapped him tighter then, a fraternal presence the only rope he could throw to his weeping brother.

No words could comfort a sorrow as deep as this, a regret as deep as this. Andrew had lived with regret and sorrow for thirteen years, and he knew better than anybody the futility of comfort, the burden of despair, but he held on to his brother and hurt for him and cursed a God who would allow a man to love, then punish him for it so bitterly.

The heat that came from Gareth's body enveloped Andrew. His brother's weight at last grew heavy against his shoulder, and his body seemed to ease.

"Gareth, you love your wife, and she loves you." Andrew's chest constricted, for he'd nearly said: she *loved* you. Past tense. "She has no regrets, save that her health was not equal to this task. She does not blame you, and you must not blame yourself."

"Ah, but I must," Gareth said, easing away. He sat up, but he did not take himself from the circle of his brother's arm. They sat thus, once again sharing grief.

"Listen to me," Andrew began quietly, for now it was his burden and privilege to speak, while Gareth must listen. "The woman you love yet lives, and your children, thanks to her, live as well."

Gareth shook his head, but Andrew hadn't finished. He went on in a detached tone, but settled his arm more snugly around Gareth's shoulders.

"I told you, not long ago, that when the accident occurred, I faced a decision."

It was Andrew's turn to pause, to gather the strength needed to push heavy, hurting realities into spoken words, and to labor those words into the darkness he shared with his brother.

"When the boat foundered, I faced a decision," Andrew said. "I could throw the rope to either Mother or Father, but Father made that decision for me, at least."

Another silence, laden with grief, pain, and despair.

"There were others in the water, however. Our uncle, our cousin, our grandfather... They were not close enough that I could have reached them. I am almost sure I could not have reached them."

Andrew's throat ached with dread, as if he could choke the words off at their source. Beside him, Gareth had gone still.

"Your fiancée, however, was within the range of my assistance, and screaming for help. Mother was swimming, while Julia had already begun to sink. I made a choice, Gareth, a deliberate, conscious choice to save Mother before Julia, to let Julia die, as it turned out, knowing..."

When Andrew was sure his brother would turn from him, Gareth shifted so he sat on the step above Andrew, and then Gareth's arm came around Andrew's shoulders.

"*She carried my child, Gareth. Your fiancée carried my child*, and I let them both drown." Andrew tried to turn from him, but Gareth wouldn't allow it. He vised his arm around Andrew with a soft, bitter oath, and wouldn't let go.

Andrew had thought himself beyond tears, beyond the ambit of regret and grief, but they rose up to drown him, just as surely as the sea had engulfed his unborn child. His body would not hold the despair inside him; there was neither air enough to breathe through the despair, nor light, nor love enough to heal it, and there never would be.

When he attempted again to escape his brother's hold, Gareth let him go, but only far enough to sit up and fish out a handkerchief. Gareth's arm stayed around his shoulders, and Andrew had the sense when Gareth withdrew that support, he, Andrew, would die. He would simply cease, collapsing from the weight of his guilt, weakness, and utter failing as a man, as a brother, a son, a father.

As a husband and a lover.

"I let the woman you were to marry, and my own child, die," he repeated, contempt rising into his voice.

"I did hear you. I do not understand you."

Gareth wanted to hear mitigating circumstances; that was why this companionable arm remained around Andrew's shoulders, why the warmth of Gareth's body still kept the chill and darkness of the night at bay. Andrew could offer no mitigation, but he could offer an explanation.

He needed to offer it, in fact.

"That summer, I was fifteen," he said, struggling to reclaim an earlier tone of detachment. "Mother and Father marched me around to the usual series of house parties, in the hopes I might meet some of the fellows who would be in my form at university the next year. I found, to my surprise, I enjoyed these gatherings, because they were planned to allow the young people plenty of socializing. I polished my manners, and for the first time, the ladies—not the dairymaids and laundresses and more generous tavern wenches—but the ladies were susceptible to my flirting."

"You were a lamb to slaughter," Gareth bit out.

Andrew went on as if his brother hadn't spoken.

"I began that summer as a virgin in the most literal sense. I met Julia and was delighted, delighted beyond my wildest dreams, to find she was willing to accommodate me in the loss of that burden. At twenty years of age, she was to me a sophisticated lady, and that she'd bestow her favors upon me, miraculous.

"Imagine my surprise, when that selfsame woman appeared with her parents at our family gathering in Scotland, claiming she was pregnant with our cousin Jeffrey's child. Of course, she soon took me aside and explained it would be better for all were my son to be raised as the heir to the marquessate, and I, craven, witless, conscienceless coward that I am, said nothing. I *did* nothing, not when talk arose of wedding her to you, not when she let Jeffrey believe the child was his, not when Jeffrey protested that he could not be the father. There was never a man who behaved as dishonorably as I."

Still, Andrew felt the weight of his brother's arm around him, the quiet bulk of Gareth's presence at his side.

Soon would come the stiffening in outrage, the drawing away in horror.

"Gareth, don't you understand what I am telling you? I dishonored a young woman, allowed her to lie about whose child she carried, failed to take responsibility when she became your chosen bride, and then committed murder, with the result that my perfidy might go unnoticed."

"You intended to leave Julia floundering in the water once you got Mother into the boat?"

"Of course not, but by then…" Nothing but frigid green-black water, towering waves, the roar of the wind, and wreckage in all directions. "I no longer knew where to throw the rope, and I have no memory of how Mother and I made it to shore."

In contrast to the mayhem of Andrew's memories, Gareth's voice was calm. "For half your life, you have thought yourself a conscienceless, rutting coward who murdered his own unborn child?"

"For half my life, I have known the truth about myself," Andrew replied. To say it though, and to Gareth, had made a curious change. Andrew could finally breathe. He could draw air all the way into his lungs in a manner that had slipped from his grasp so long ago, and so subtly, he hadn't noticed.

"Adam told me," Gareth said. "He told me that woman had been after him and every other man in the family, including our grandfather. Grandfather was not affronted by her behavior, Andrew, why should you have been? Why did neither Adam nor I, nor Grandfather, nor Father, for that matter, think to protect you from her?"

Shock went through Andrew, a physical sensation not unlike an electrical spark. The shock of revelation, of learning something so far outside his imagined universe, his very body had to react. "What… are… you… saying?"

So Gareth repeated himself, his voice more firm.

"She as much as offered to bed down with the old marquess, and did with you, probably with Jeffrey, and who knows how many others. She certainly made a play for Adam, and for me. Adam told me I ought to bring it up with you, since he suspected she'd gone after you as well, but I argued with him, bitterly, thinking Julia would not have preyed on a mere boy. She wasn't right, somehow, wasn't... natural."

"She claimed Jeffrey had enticed her with promises of marriage, but she assured me the child was mine. Adam and I argued over your betrothal to her, but even then..." Andrew had not told his oldest brother the truth in the course of that protracted altercation, but Adam had apparently had his suspicions.

Suspicions that cast Andrew as a *victim*.

"Had she been with child, Brother, as often as she spread her legs, she could not possibly have given you that assurance." Gareth gave Andrew's shoulders a shake for emphasis. "She apparently tried that ruse with Jeffrey, among others that we know of."

Andrew seized on the single word: *ruse*. "What ruse? What do you mean?"

"She was no more with child than I am."

"But, Gareth, there she was, the waves dragging at her, screaming to save our child, begging me..." Andrew's breath constricted again, and vertigo threatened.

"I am telling you," Gareth said, shaking Andrew's shoulders again, harder this time, "*there was no child*... You did not murder your unborn child, you did not betray me, you did not commit murder. You made mistakes, Andrew, mistakes common to adolescents the world over. And no one, not your own father, not your brothers, not the head of our benighted family, made any attempt to protect you from them."

The very irascibility of Gareth's tone was as reassuring as the weight of his arm across Andrew's shoulders, and yet, comprehension would not coalesce into acceptance. "I cannot understand this. I cannot get my mind to absorb this version of my history. I cannot."

"There's more," Gareth said, "but it will keep. I cannot believe you lived with these lies and falsehoods for this long. I am sorry, Andrew. I am so sorry."

The arm around Andrew's shoulders became a hug then, a simple, affectionate embrace Andrew found he wanted never to end. His brain could not focus enough to sort out the ramifications of what his brother had shared with him, not yet. But his heart felt lighter, able to beat freely, unburdened save for the task of sustaining his own life.

Andrew loved his brother again; he simply loved him, openheartedly, joyously. It would take time for the guilt and shame to fade, but if he and Gareth had time, they could arrive to that.

"This stair," Gareth growled, "is giving my arse a pain. I am going to shave, eat something, then chase your wife out of Felicity's bedroom, so I might pray my marchioness back to a semblance of health. Where shall I chase her to?"

"Bed," Andrew said. "She's been up far too long, and she needs her rest."

"I am getting old." Gareth rose stiffly and extended a hand down to assist Andrew.

"Yes. You are, old and wise. Gareth…" He dropped his brother's hand. "Thank you."

"Now you grow tediously maudlin. Good night, little brother."

But as they turned to go to their separate rooms, Gareth grabbed him in one more hug. "And thank you too."

They walloped each other on the back, once, hard, and went to face their separate challenges.

⁓

The marquess's household remained unsettled, the marchioness's health precarious at best, and the addition of two newborns upsetting established routines. Worse, neither the lord nor the lady of the house was available to reestablish order, because Heathgate spent almost all of his days with his wife.

Felicity slept. She slept for much of three days, rising to a stuporous wakefulness only to nurse her children, use the chamber pot, and drink either beef tea or sugared hot tea. While she suffered no fevers, she did continue to bleed heavily.

So Andrew did not leave, given that the servants were turning to him and to Astrid for guidance. Moreover, his original purpose in joining the household, to talk to his dear wife, remained a priority.

"Come, your lordship," Andrew said irritably to an equally annoyed brother, "your eldest has not seen you yet today, and your wife is sleeping. Leave this room for at least the next five minutes, or I will haul you away bodily."

"You can bring James down here," Gareth argued.

"Gareth?" Felicity's voice from the depth of the huge bed silenced both men, and Gareth was beside his wife in an instant.

"Right here, beloved."

"Go with Andrew. If you keep arguing, you'll wake the babies." *In addition to me*, she left unsaid.

Gareth scowled but kissed her cheek. "I will be back shortly."

Andrew walked with him up to the nursery, mostly to make sure he went. Andrew himself had spent considerable time with James and little William, and had carried them down to see the new arrivals while Felicity and the babies napped, oblivious to the visitors. James had yet to visit with his mama, however, because she was still terribly weak and rarely awake.

And when they arrived to the nursery, they found James's nanny had bundled him up for a brief outing in the snowy back garden.

"She'll lose him in this damned snow," Gareth groused.

"If she does," Andrew replied, "he will howl loudly enough to summon the watch clear from Town."

"And wake his mother, brother, and sister," Gareth agreed, his expression lightening marginally. "I have been an utter ass, haven't I?" he said, settling on James's low bed.

"Yes—but you have also been enduring heart-breaking circumstances better than I would." Andrew rummaged through a carved toy chest and found a ball he and Astrid had used to amuse James a lifetime ago. He tossed it to his brother, who caught it deftly in one hand.

Gareth tossed the ball back to Andrew, who perched on the toy chest.

"I tell myself if there's no infection," Gareth began, "then Felicity should rally and eventually recover. But then I look at her, slumbering in that bed, hour after hour. She forces herself to stay awake long enough to nurse the babies, but drifts off before she herself has anything to eat. She is not rallying, and she is still bleeding."

Andrew tossed the ball to Gareth again.

"Fairly said it might take several weeks for the bleeding to subside entirely, and certainly a week of heavy bleeding is normal."

"And what would *he* know of such things?" Gareth said, lobbing the ball back to Andrew.

"*He* has been trained as a physician," Andrew said as he continued their game of catch. "Astrid told me Fairly lost a spouse who had borne him a child."

"Fairly? The mercantile shark, the self-contained, brothel-owning, dapper, articulate, odd-eyed, insufferable, pain-in-the-arse brother of our respective wives was a *physician*?"

"I don't know that he practiced, but when I asked it of him, he filled my head with more detail about women's, er, plumbing, than any man should know. He endorses breast-feeding, by the way, and says it might help the womb heal and return to its original contours, so stop arguing with Felicity about it."

"And does he endorse having a mother starve to death so she can nurse her babies?" Gareth shot back. "And he's a widower who has buried a child?"

Andrew held the ball for a moment, looking Gareth

straight in the eye. "Yes," he said, firing the ball. "He has lost both a wife and a child."

Gareth absently threw the ball back. "Shite."

"Probably as accurate a summation as any."

"Are you making headway with your wife yet?" Gareth had turned his attention to something besides his marchioness for the first time in days, and yet it was a subject Andrew wished he'd not brought up.

"My wife has been sleeping nearly as much as yours, and when she isn't sleeping, she's taking care of her sister or the babies, or answering the servants' questions so we will continue to have clean laundry and hot meals."

"Coward."

"Quaking in my perpetually soggy boots," Andrew agreed mildly. "I can't find a good time to approach her."

"You aren't even sleeping with her, which is pure foolishness. Women like to cuddle, and you're the creative sort. You should be able to work with that."

Andrew fired the ball at Gareth's chin. "So women like to cuddle, do they? Imagine the opportunities I have missed because this subtlety eluded me."

"Let me put it this way," Gareth said, matching the force Andrew had applied to the ball. "If my wife were not bleeding her life away, I'd be sharing that bed with her every spare moment I had, even if it were simply to hold her."

Andrew caught the ball and held it. "I take your point, Brother, but I have not yet accepted that your wife is bleeding her life away, and neither should you. Though now that I have you alone, I have a question for you."

"Ask," Gareth said flatly. "If it's a question about funeral arrangements, be warned I am up for a bout of mean, bare-knuckle fisticuffs."

A tempting offer.

"The other night, you told me Julia was not expecting, not my child, not Jeffrey's—I believe your words were, there was no baby."

Andrew had repeated those words over and over in his mind, the relief of Gareth's pronouncement renewed each time.

"Those were my words, and I meant them. When we realized four years ago some aspects of that accident hadn't been fully resolved, I had Brenner go back and talk to anyone we could find who'd been employed on our Scottish property that summer. Brenner interviewed Mother, Julia's parents, and as many of the servants as he could locate."

"That must have been some undertaking."

"It took weeks, and more than one trip North," Gareth said, "and he would have interviewed you, but you had already taken yourself off to foreign shores. In the course of his efforts, he came across the woman who had been Julia's lady's maid. She had since become a nanny to a cousin of a cousin and so forth, but she recalled the whole summer quite well."

Why had Andrew never thought to do this? Why had he thought exile on the Continent his only option? "And?"

"Julia's courses had arrived the morning before we went out on the boat, Andrew. The maid recalled how irritable and difficult her employer had been in the days leading up to the accident, knowing full well

Julia had been swiving anything in breeches to try to conceive her much-vaunted child. The maid knew Julia's patterns, however, and dreaded the tantrum that would ensue when Julia realized she wasn't pregnant."

Andrew tossed the ball from one hand to the other. "And that was the *more* you referred to?"

"Not all of it. Brenner uncovered evidence Julia had paid one of the local sailors to tamper with the rudder."

"What in the bloody hell could she have been about?" Andrew said, standing and pacing to a dormer window, because tampering with a rudder was tanta-mount to… *murder*. Cold-blooded, premeditated, malice aforethought *murder*.

"Even her maid had no conjecture as to why Julia would have sabotaged a boat she herself was on, but the tampering would not have been evident except in heavy seas. If enough force were applied to the guides and cables, they would have snapped, but not in calm seas. And if you'll recall, Julia was not sanguine about joining the outing."

Gareth had carried her up the gangplank bodily, her objections peppering the air.

"Jeffrey loved to take that boat out," Andrew recalled, facing his brother, "and the seas were calm when we cast off."

"They were, so perhaps she was merely laying a trap to rid herself of Jeffrey at a later date, should he have been her spouse. She resisted my insistence she join the outing, if you'll recall. Resisted bitterly. But then, Grandfather also considered himself quite a yachtsman, and Julia's fatal trap could have been intended for him."

"But you were prepared to spare Jeffrey the chore of marrying her, and Grandfather was happy to let you do it," Andrew reminded his brother as he tossed him the ball.

"The offer I made to Julia was to marry her and to live with her in the household of my choosing. She did not accept that offer, because she 'wanted to raise Jeffrey's child' at the family seat, where she knew Jeffrey would be forced to reside at least some of the time. I believed Jeffrey's protestations regarding the child's paternity, and would not capitulate to Julia's conditions. So at the time of her death, she was not, in any sense, my fiancée, despite press and portraits to the contrary." He punctuated that statement by aiming the ball straight at Andrew's chest.

Andrew caught it and tossed it up into the air.

"These things you tell me…" he said, heading for the door. "I feel disoriented, as if I've taken a bad fall from a fast moving horse."

"Give it time," Gareth said as Andrew tossed him the ball one more time. "Where are you off to?"

"Going to ride my horse," Andrew said, because a man needed to plan his strategy if he were to reclaim his wife's affections—and her trust.

"There's nigh two goddamned feet of snow on the ground, or hadn't you noticed?"

"You know how some horses are mudders? Most horses don't like sloppy footing, they hate the mud hitting their bellies, and they don't have the knack of keeping their feet under them in bad going."

Gareth shoved up from the small bed. "And others

bestir themselves to a decent effort only if they're on a muddy track," he finished the thought.

"Well, Magic is a snow horse. He marched right over here through more dirty footing than I've ever asked a horse to negotiate. Five miles of it was nothing to him, thank God."

Gareth considered the little rubber ball in his hand. "I haven't thanked you yet for making that journey, Andrew. It was inexcusably risky of you, but I appreciate it all the same."

A little scold made the thanks go down more easily. "I needed to be here."

"Yes, you did, but I've been meaning to ask you: What exactly did you and Astrid do while I was taking my nap in the freezing hallway?"

"Astrid didn't explain it to you?" Andrew said, his hand on the door latch.

"She evaded the question, which I will not tolerate from you, so talk."

"Why not browbeat her?"

"Because I can beat the stuffing out of you," Gareth replied in the same pleasant tone Andrew had used.

"If you must know, all we did was turn one of the babies in the womb," he said. "I'll just be off now…"

But before he could get the door open, a rubber ball hit his backside with stinging force, and his brother's "You did what?" roared through the nursery. By the time Andrew turned, Gareth had launched himself across the room and effected a neat tackle, bringing himself, Andrew, and a shelf full of toy soldiers crashing to the floor.

Nineteen

FELICITY KISSED THE SMOOTH BROW OF THE TINY infant in her arms. "What is that sound?"

Astrid glanced upward, only to hear another loud crash, followed by a series of bumps and thumps. "Our husbands went up to visit James in the playroom."

Though Andrew did not keep her informed of his comings and goings, and Astrid lived in fear of a note telling her he'd decamped for Town—or Sweden or the Antipodes.

"If these babies had been sleeping…" Felicity muttered darkly. One child was at her breast; Astrid was returning the other—already enjoying a postprandial nap—to the bassinet.

"But we're all awake," Astrid pointed out, smiling, "so let the boys play. It's hard on Andrew being cooped up in the house and being away from his horses. I can't imagine Gareth is used to this much inactivity either."

Another sharp thump had both ladies peering at the ceiling.

"Gareth needs to quit fretting," Felicity said. "I am

stronger by the day, and there have been no fevers. Here." She held Pen out to Astrid, wiped off a damp nipple, and fastened the bodice of her nightgown. "Pen was slurping and dreaming and slurping some more. My arms are too tired for that."

Astrid cuddled the Mad Slurper to her shoulder. "Maybe when you are not too tired to hold a baby for more than a feeding, your husband will be less inclined to fret."

Felicity flopped back against her pillows. "You know, Astrid, when people say they are tired in their bones?"

"Yes." Astrid's burden emitted a tiny burp, sending his aunt into a round of appreciative cooing.

"Now I know what that means. I am so utterly fatigued, even breathing is an effort. If I stand to use the chamber pot, I get light-headed. At least I'm getting out of this bed, though."

"It will take time," Astrid chided gently. She tucked Pen in beside his sister in the bassinet and sat on Felicity's bed. "You lost a lot of blood, and you are still bleeding."

"I bleed, and I use the chamber pot, and I leak milk… I feel like a human drain, Astrid. And my poor stomach will horrify Gareth out of any amorous thoughts he's ever had about me. I look like the world's largest prune."

Astrid was saved from casting about for a diplomatic rejoinder by a knock on the door. She hopped off the bed, then grabbed the bedpost to steady herself.

She went to the door at a more careful walk and opened it a crack.

"David!" She threw the door open the rest of the way and wrapped her arms around her brother. "Oh, it is so good to see you," she said, drawing him into the room. "You've arrived at a good time. Felicity is awake, and the babies are asleep."

"And best of all," David added, "Heathgate is not straining on the end of his chain, threatening to breathe fire on all passersby. Hello, Sisters." He returned Astrid's hug, then kissed Felicity's cheek. "How are you?"

"Tired," Felicity said, smiling up at him. "Relentlessly tired. But alive."

"Of course you are," he replied, propping a hip on the bed and giving her a pensive look. "You are much, much too pale, Lissy." He put the backs of his fingers against her forehead. "No fever, though. Well done of you."

"I had help."

"Really?" David raised an eyebrow at Astrid. "I handed my horse off to a groom at the foot of the steps, so you'll have to enlighten me. And ladies, do not even think to dissemble."

"Astrid and Andrew had to turn one of the babies," Felicity said. "Heathgate, fortunately, was felled by exhaustion for those few moments and spared us his presence for the actual deliveries, though it was a near thing."

"Divine providence, though there's doubtless a part of him that would delight in shocking the gossips." He ambled over to the bassinet and picked up one bundle. "What unbelievably lovely little babies these are. Be proud of yourselves, ladies.

When God wants to add to Creation, he chooses only the most worthy assistants."

"What a lovely sentiment," Felicity said.

Astrid remained silent but thought of Andrew, of his calm in the birthing room, of his methodical study of childbirth—in multiple languages—when Astrid had mentally accused him of hiding in his study by the hour.

"Babies," said David, picking up the second child, "make everything lovely."

He kept the child—Pen—in his arms when he came back to sit on the bed.

"Now," he said, "pay attention, Sisters, because Heathgate will soon come through that door like a jealous horse and shoo me off to drink brandy with Greymoor in the billiards room. Felicity," he continued, "you are to eat red meat at every meal until the bleeding stops, and then twice a day until your energy is back where you need it to be. Liver or other organ meats would be best. Some Spanish oranges would be well advised too. You are to drink as much as you can stand, because you will be nursing two babies, not one, and you are to get out of this bed for a few minutes at a time, starting immediately."

His tone dared either sister to argue with him, but they merely exchanged a look of sororal curiosity.

"You are justifiably exhausted, Lissy," he pointed out. "But for the past week, you haven't even gone up and down a flight of stairs. Soon you will lose the strength you had when you climbed into this bed, and thus you will invite more fatigue. I will take my leave of you now, but I sincerely hope that before you blow out the candles tonight, you will consider reading for a few minutes by the window, sitting by the fire while Astrid changes your sheets, or taking a turn about the room."

David glanced at the ceiling, then looked at them askance. "What *is* that noise?"

"The playroom is directly above us," Felicity said. "Gareth and Andrew went up there to visit him."

"I will offer mine host a proper greeting," David said, kissing each sister on the cheek. He handed Pen to Astrid before adding, "Remember: red meat, fluids, and moderate activity."

When the door closed behind him, Felicity flopped the covers back and wrestled her way to the edge of the bed.

"I feel like Dr. Mayhew's younger, better-informed assistant paid me a call," she said. "Dr. Mayhew said to remain abed for at least a week after James was born, and mentioned neither fluids nor red meat."

"David has medical training," Astrid replied. Also good timing and a way of dealing with the difficult topics directly. "Could I talk you into some cold slices of beef, perhaps taken by the fire?"

Felicity pushed to her feet. "I suppose so. After which, by God, I am going to read something besides that dreadful Mrs. Radcliffe."

"She awaits you by the fire. I'll order you a tray, then, and see what all that rumpus was about in the playroom."

Astrid made it as far as the hallway before a footman stopped her with a note.

Meet me in the stable in twenty minutes.
Greymoor

Now this was interesting—Andrew hadn't, apparently, decamped for Sweden without notice.

Astrid and her husband had developed a cordial, superficial means of communicating over the past few days. They had worked as a team when Felicity had needed them, and Andrew exhibited better spirits than when Astrid had left him at Enfield.

But he was too thin, and he avoided her by day and slept elsewhere at night, suggesting they were in the midst of a cease-fire, not a rapprochement. Astrid wasn't about to question him directly regarding his preferences for their next move.

But neither would she run from a confrontation, so she made her way downstairs to the kitchen entrance fifteen minutes later and retrieved her old, heavy cloak from a peg by the door. When she was bundled up against the cold, she grabbed a few lumps of sugar and eschewed gloves, mittens, scarf, or hat.

The stables were deserted when she gained the door to the barn. The grooms had done their morning chores, fed the midday meal, and repaired to their quarters over the carriage house to clean harness, play cards, or nap. Fairly's mare stood in a loose box, demolishing a pile of fragrant hay, Andrew's gelding doing likewise in the stall beside her.

Andrew's timing, at least, would guarantee them privacy.

And what, in fact, did Astrid want to tell her husband?

That she loved him, of course, but love to Andrew was apparently no inducement whatsoever.

"Greetings, dear Astrid," a cheerful male voice called from behind her.

Astrid whirled in surprise then had to grab an empty saddle rack to catch her balance. "*Henry?*"

He grinned and bowed. "Your most devoted and doting caller, in the flesh. I understand felicitations are in order, if what Lady Quinn told my mother is correct."

"Felicitations are in order," Astrid said, smiling. "The marchioness presented her husband with a healthy boy and girl just three days past. It is good of you to call." Though unusual, given the weather, the state of things between their families, and the normal restrictions on a new mother's social calendar.

Henry pulled off riding gloves, finger by finger, and stuffed them in his pocket. "Lady Heathgate was waving the note from Heathgate around at some tea or other yesterday, letting all and sundry know exactly where you bided. If her coach weren't too heavy for this snow, she'd be here, I'm sure."

Unease prickled up Astrid's neck. "I don't see your horse."

"Tied him at the bottom of the drive," Henry said, fingering a bridle that hung by an empty stall. He took it off its hook and fiddled with it, which was presumptuous, riding equipment being among a gentleman's more personal property.

"I'll summon a groom to fetch him," Astrid said. "I'm sure, after toiling all the way out here from Town, you don't want to leave a valuable animal standing in the cold."

Henry shook his head as he unfastened a buckle. "Can't let you do that, Astrid dearest." He hung the bridle back on its hook, though he'd unfastened the thin snaffle reins and was drawing them across his palm in an odd, repetitive motion.

And Astrid *dearest*? Unease lurched closer to dread.

"Whyever not? A decent horse is worth quite a sum, and even the worst shouldn't be left to stand in the weather."

She started to walk past him, intent on summoning a groom, but Henry's arm snaked out to catch her in a punishing grip above the elbow.

"Henry, turn loose of me this instant."

He grinned at her again, and the light in his eyes made Astrid's flesh crawl. "Struggle," he challenged her softly as he tightened his grip. "Please."

"What are you about?"

"You won't struggle," Henry said, pulling the sort of face a doting swain made when a lady's dance card was full. "Alas for me, but I suppose time being of the essence, it's for the best. Still, I've never beaten a pregnant woman before—might have been fun, you know? One usually has to pay for that variety of sport."

He shot a speculative look at the bulge of her stomach, and when his gaze dropped, Astrid wrenched away. She got all of two steps before Henry's fist grabbing her voluminous cloak stopped her progress. He wrestled her around to face him and delivered a stinging backhand across her cheek.

"Naughty, naughty," he crooned, raising his hand for another blow.

❦

Andrew made his excuses as Fairly dragooned Heathgate off to the library for a celebratory tot—and wasn't it a relief that somebody else was on hand to keep Gareth from hovering over his wife even as she slept?

Life was, in fact, full of relief. Relief that Felicity was slowly, slowly rallying. Relief that Andrew again dwelled under the same roof as his wife, and relief that Astrid's tracks through the snow were singular, suggesting she'd hared off to the stables without maid, footman, or groom in tow.

Good things had been known to happen in stables, and at this time of day, the barn would afford Andrew privacy with his wife, so he followed her there, pausing outside the barn door for a moment to gather his courage.

The sun shone with the relentless brightness of a snowy winter day, the eaves dripped with a promise of moderating temperatures, and all was right with the world—or soon would be, if luck was with him.

On that fortifying thought, Andrew grasped the door latch.

The sound of a blow, flesh on flesh, rent the winter stillness, followed by a male voice, soft, snide, the words indistinguishable.

Astrid was in that stable.

Andrew's entire life was in that stable.

Her voice came to him, defiant, bothered, not the least afraid, then more snide male taunts.

Andrew had no weapons, but *Astrid* had no weapons either, save her wit and courage. He crept closer and cracked the door.

✵

Astrid cringed, her arms wrapped around her belly, as Henry cocked his arm back for a second blow.

"Touching." Henry smirked, lowering his hand. "You protect my brother's heir rather than yourself. Did you know"—Henry wrapped the reins tightly around Astrid's wrists—"Herbert refused to share you with me? I had it all planned, the pitch darkness, the dressing gown, slipping up the back stairs of a Sunday night like a marital thief—what fun, eh? It wasn't as if Herbert actually enjoyed servicing you, but that damned title does put certain requirements on a fellow. He wasn't as stingy with some of his other toys though, or with your money."

A pang of sympathy for Herbert's hunters pierced Astrid's ire, for a man who'd strike a petite, defenseless, pregnant woman would delight in abusing a helpless beast with whip and spurs. "What are you talking about?"

"My brother," Henry said, giving the leather a vicious yank, "or should I say my late brother, was becoming too headstrong. He begrudged me the occasional loan from your funds, but then, he'd also married you against my wishes. He got you pregnant against my wishes, telling me it was what Father would have wanted. Bah! All Father wanted was to tramp around in the mud, shooting at anything that moved—a convenient propensity, in the end."

Henry put a tight knot in the reins, painfully binding Astrid's wrists.

"Is that snug enough for you?" he asked oh-so-pleasantly. "Such a shame we don't have time to play..."

She needed to keep Henry talking. Sooner or later, somebody would check on the horses, or on her— wouldn't they?

"You sent the note telling me to meet you here, didn't you?" She was damned if she'd let Henry know how much her bindings hurt.

"Clever of me, wasn't it?" Henry yanked on the trailing ends of the reins, pulling Astrid toward the door of the saddle room. "You see, I am the clever one in the benighted Allen family, but by definition, that means my parents and my dear siblings were unable to appreciate my superior intelligence. While that allows a fellow a certain freedom, it does grow tedious, always having to manage every detail oneself. Come along."

Astrid weaved on her feet, half in earnest. "I'm dizzy."

"Come anyway, bitch," he growled, "or I'll drag you. And right now, you don't particularly want to be on the floor, much less on your back, do you?"

Astrid stumbled along behind him, her sense of balance hampered with her hands tied in front of her. The saddle room loomed at the end of the barn aisle like a crypt, with doors opening both onto the aisle and onto the outside wall of the barn. If Henry got her in there, he could easily kill her and leave the building unseen.

"So it was you who poisoned me? And was it you who pushed me down the stairs?"

"Now that's exactly what I mean," Henry said, reverting to eerily pleasant tones. "I did indeed put the poison in your raspberry jam. Mother wouldn't have gone near the stuff, but as for that, Mother nearly caught me giving you a little push down the steps. I do this for her, too, you know, dutiful fellow that I am. She doesn't care for Dougie. Doesn't appreciate nipfarthing, pompous condescension, doesn't realize the poor boy can't help himself. Douglas was due to join us for our weekly tête-à-tête, and it should have been he who was suspected of pushing you down those stairs, but alas, spontaneous schemes are sometimes not the best. Tell me you did suspect him, just a bit, hmm?"

Nausea rose, for once having nothing to do with Astrid's condition. She considered bolting while Henry fumbled with the latch on the saddle-room door.

"How does pushing me down the stairs harm Douglas?" Though accusations of murder would rather hamper a man's prospects.

"Foul play would appear to be in his interests rather than mine at present, though Dougie, I regret to inform you, is not long for this world." He peered into the saddle room. "Damn it. It's black as Hades in there."

Henry Allen, cold-blooded murderer of innocents, was apparently afraid of the dark, thank God.

❧

Astrid conversed with a homicidal lunatic, as if the man had come to call at teatime. Through the cracked door, Andrew had a narrow view of the barn aisle and could see his wife tethered by the hands as she was dragged toward the saddle room. Her captor was solidly built, though not as tall as Andrew.

Not as tall as Douglas Allen either. The dim lighting

of the barn's interior shrouded the man's features when he turned to head down the aisle toward the saddle room, hauling Astrid behind him.

The saddle room held weapons—knives for trimming and repairing harness, farrier's tools, and other items a man might use to take the life of a small, defenseless woman.

Astrid stumbled, and Andrew nearly bolted through the door to catch her. She righted herself, grousing at the fellow who dragged her through the gloom.

Andrew considered working his way around the barn from the outside, but the door from the saddle room on the outside barn wall might well be locked. The element of surprise was his only advantage, and he could not squander it. When Andrew might have slipped into the barn, the fellow contemplating Astrid's murder yanked the saddle-room door closed and came stalking back up the aisle, forcing Andrew to give up his vantage point as well.

He eased the barn door closed the two inches he'd dared open it, just as the crunch of snow behind him warned him he was no longer alone.

"Greymoor, what in God's name is going on?"

The voice was clipped, irritated, and far from welcome, for what murderer ever worked alone when he might recruit a willing accomplice?

❧

"Your immediate family seems to suffer from a propensity for fatal accidents," Astrid observed. Henry tugged her along, and she had no choice but to trot along behind him, like an obedient dog.

"They do, bless them. Father was my first stroke of genius, and then when Herbert became too... obstreperous, he was the next to go. I blush to admit I started a few rumors suggesting Herbert might have taken his own life—a diversionary tactic, of course."

Henry passed the reins to one hand to fiddle with a lantern hanging from a crossbeam. "You are the first person to connect those two deaths, and they occurred in exactly the same fashion. Herbert moved, damn him, and ruined my shot, but it did the job, nonetheless."

"And you think you can also murder Douglas, leaving you with the title?"

"Not a doubt in my mind—this one's empty, bugger it." Henry tossed the lamp aside, the resulting crash making the horses restive. "I will be creative, maybe sabotage his curricle, though I rather fancy it myself. I might hire somebody to call him out and anticipate the count just the least, most unfortunate bit—that sort of thing happens all the time."

Something nudged at Astrid's awareness, a flicker of light near the barn door, a shift in the air. Magic peered at the door too, suggesting Astrid hadn't imagined whatever caught her eye. The horse also ignored his hay. Despite the cold, despite being as devoted to his fodder as any equine.

Keep talking.

Henry straightened and gave her his boyish smile. "You know, Astrid, the most difficult thing for me has been managing this whole business without having anyone—not one soul—to appreciate the genius of it. You should consider yourself honored. I would not be surprised if intelligent younger sons weren't getting away with murder much more frequently than the world suspects. Now where"—he gave the reins a savage yank—"will I find a damned lantern with oil in it?"

"I don't know, Henry. I am not familiar with Heathgate's stables. When I need a mount, I summon a groom to fetch me one."

Henry leered at her and stroked himself through his breeches with his free hand. "And do you need a mount now? We probably have time, and I can assure you, my attentions will make you forget Herbert—or that strutting pain in the arse, Greymoor—ever touched you. You complicated things too much when you married that one, Astrid."

Her life had been saved at least twice over when she'd married Andrew—Astrid was more sure of that now than she'd ever been.

Henry stroked himself again, and nausea welled anew. Astrid could contemplate death more easily than she could defilement by this incarnation of evil, but if Henry wasted only ten minutes raping her, that was ten more minutes when a groom, stableboy, or somebody else might come along.

"Ah-hah," Henry cried as his gaze lit on another lantern, this one hanging on the ladder that led up to the haymow. He hauled Astrid to it and crowed with pleasure when he saw the lantern had plenty of oil.

"We're in business, dear Astrid," he said cheerily, lighting his prize from the single fixed lantern burning low halfway down the aisle. "Come along."

She did, but stumbled when he pulled too sharply on her wrists.

"Isn't it enough," she hissed, "that you're going to kill me, Henry? Must you abuse me in the process?"

That struck him funny as he hauled on the reins again, sending Astrid careening into the unused saddle stand. As she righted herself, the main barn door cracked open.

"Henry!" she bellowed. "You need not jerk my wrists, for God's sake. I'll follow you to the saddle room readily enough if you'll be patient."

"It really, *really* is a shame we don't have time to play," he observed, proceeding more quickly.

"So how will you kill me?" Astrid asked, using her two remaining wits to not look in the direction of the barn door.

"Interesting question. Do you have a suggestion? Firearms are my preference, as you know, but a gunshot would bring a crowd a bit too hastily for my convenience. I've a knife in my boot if all else fails."

Oh, the preferences she had. To see Andrew again, to see the last of Henry in this life, to keep her child safe. To keep Herbert's child safe from a menace poor Herbert hadn't recognized. "I don't particularly want to suffer."

Though to reach his knife, Henry would have to take his attention from her, which gave Astrid a glimmer of hope.

"Reasonable enough, I suppose, but we must bear in mind your death cannot appear to be murder, which leaves only accident or suicide. Suicide would fit in nicely with Douglas's theory, though his conviction regarding your inclination toward self-harm is wavering. What say we start a fire in the stables?"

And then nip 'round the pub for a pint? "That won't answer. I'd simply run out of a burning building, Henry."

"Same thought occurred to me," Henry replied genially as he unlatched the saddle-room door. "That leaves us with suicide, which will have the advantage of being relatively painless for you, though messy for your family. My apologies and condolences."

"So you'll simply cut my wrists and leave the knife by my body?" Astrid asked, hanging back at the saddle-room door.

"He will not," Andrew hissed, brandishing a pistol. "Run, Astrid!"

She bolted for the far end of the barn aisle, jerking the reins from Henry's grasp in the instant it took him to realize that his ingenious machinations would again be foiled. Astrid flung open the door and pelted out into the bright sunshine.

Her balance and her nerves failed her then, and she ended up floundering to her knees in the snow a few feet from the door.

"Astrid!"

Douglas Allen hissed her name from beside the door. He put a finger to his lips, motioning for silence. "It's Henry, isn't it?" he whispered. He drew a knife from the folds of his cape and freed her wrists with one slice.

"With Andrew—Henry has a knife. Henry was going to murder me, and… oh, Douglas…" She hung her head and tried not to retch.

"I know," Douglas said softly. "But it's dark in there, and Henry is distracted by Greymoor. I'll have the advantages of stealth and surprise." Only then did Astrid see Douglas, too, had a gun, a long-barreled pistol that would be lethal over a goodly distance, likely half a matched set of Mantons. Before she could say another word, Douglas hoisted her to her feet, nodded briskly toward the manor house, and slipped into the barn.

Get help, Astrid thought desperately, trying to draw air into her lungs. Go to the house and get help. Feeling returned to her hands in stinging agonies, and she wasted precious moments trying to push away the dizziness and the roaring in her ears.

The barn door burst open, and Henry stumbled out, his knife in his hand. Before Astrid could scurry to safety, he hauled her up against him and raised the blade against her throat.

"That's far enough, Greymoor," Henry panted. "Toss your gun out here into the snow, and then come out slowly with your hands behind your head."

Nothing moved in the darkness within the barn, prompting Henry to jam the blade tighter against Astrid's neck.

"Quickly, man! No tricks, or I cut her throat," Henry cried.

A gun the exact match of the one Douglas had held came sailing through the door, landing in the snow at Astrid's feet.

"Now out!" Henry barked.

After a long moment's pause, Andrew slowly emerged from the barn and stood in front of the door, his hands raised and clasped behind his head. The posture was humiliating, one forced on soldiers taken prisoner.

"You have only one blade," Andrew pointed out. "You might as well bury it in my heart, Henry.

There's no love lost between my wife and me, and I doubt she'd testify against you. In fact, you could probably depart the scene and blame my death on her."

"Oh, Greymoor." Henry sounded positively gleeful. "I do admire this display of coolheaded reason, but it won't serve. Astrid, I'm afraid we're back to setting the barn on fire."

"Henry…" Astrid raised her left hand, as if fending off a swoon. She sagged against his arm for further effect, but as her hand approached her face, she opened her fingers and flung a handful of sugar directly into Henry's eyes.

"Astrid, down!" Andrew bellowed.

She rolled herself into the snow as Andrew dove at Henry and wrenched the knife from his hand.

"Hold still!" Andrew roared, sending the knife sailing across the stable yard. "Hold still, or by God I'll murder you with my bare hands."

He had Henry in a choking hold, his elbow hooked around the shorter man's throat.

"Andrew, you can't kill him," Astrid panted, struggling to her feet. "He's Douglas's only brother, and he's not—"

"He's not sane," Douglas said, emerging from the barn, his pistol cocked and aimed at Henry. "He's cheerful, charming, good company, and willing to kill for the privilege of a viscountcy I neither need nor want."

Henry seemed to grow smaller as Andrew dropped his arm and took a step away. "Douglas. You weren't supposed to find out. You were supposed to be dull old Douglas, until—"

"And *you* weren't supposed to leave Mother alone. I am slow, Henry. A plodding embarrassment of a brother, I know, and a pathetic excuse for a viscount, but the staff at least follows my directions when I tell them to report to me the comings and goings of family."

While Astrid watched, Henry's bewilderment shifted, his expression lightened, and foreboding gripped her by the throat. "Andrew, watch—"

She'd left the warning too late. Henry darted forward, snatched the gun from Douglas, and as Andrew bundled Astrid off to the side, the sharp report of a sizable pistol reverberated through the stable yard.

Douglas's tortured, "Dear God, no," reached Astrid's ears while Andrew's arms tightened around her.

"Don't look," Andrew rasped as he pushed her face against his shoulder. "Dear heart, please spare yourself and don't look."

Twenty

"WHAT MADE YOU COME OUT TO THE STABLES?"
Astrid asked.

She feared Andrew's reply, because when one
person asked a question and the other provided an
answer, it could be construed as a conversation,
particularly when those two people were alone before
a roaring fire in the Willowdale library.

Since Henry Allen had... *died* earlier that day,
Andrew had not left her side. He'd kept an arm
around her, a hand on her arm, or his fingers clasped
with hers. He reminded her of a wolf, bedding down
with its mate to maintain bodily contact through the
long, cold night.

But they'd spoken little. Andrew had summoned
Gareth and told him in terse language what had trans-
pired. Gareth, after a few moments of outrage that
his household would be further troubled while the
marchioness's health was imperiled, had calmed down
and set about dealing with the practicalities.

Andrew had sent for the magistrate and the estate
carpenter, who would measure Henry for his coffin.

With Douglas's consent, he'd directed that a place be made for Henry's remains in an unused, unheated parlor, and dispatched notes to Lady Heathgate and to the Allen solicitors. A groom tore off for London to fetch changes of clothing for Douglas and David, and to determine the whereabouts of Lady Amery.

Douglas had been assigned a guest room, and David had been assigned to watching over Douglas, lest the events of the day result in any more pointless tragedies.

Between Andrew, Gareth, and David, it was agreed that Henry's death would be labeled an accident, rather than a suicide, damp weather being notorious for making guns unreliable, even in the hands of men accustomed to their use.

Andrew seemed to share Astrid's reluctance to begin a dialogue, for he took his time forming an answer to her inquiry regarding his trip to the stables.

"Gareth and I had been roughhousing in the play-room," he said slowly, "and talking. Talking about… the past. I wanted to be in the saddle, wanted to go for a good gallop and clear my head. Cook told me you'd taken yourself out to the barn, but what about you? What drew you to the stables?"

He wasn't telling her half of what she wanted to know, but neither was he lying. "One of the footmen had a note for me. I thought it was from you. Henry likely slipped it to a groom, and the rest of the house-hold knows I'm happy to go visit the horses."

Astrid laced her fingers through her husband's. How long would it be before she had the courage to visit the stables without an escort? What if Douglas had not brought two pistols—because by all accounts, Andrew had arrived to the stable unarmed? What if Henry had seen his brother lurking in the shadows of the barn? What if Henry had pitched that knife at Andrew? What if Andrew had not felt the need for time in the saddle?

"I like to visit the horses too," Andrew said. "They can help a man sort himself out. These past few days have been so…"

"At sixes and sevens," Astrid supplied. "So happy, so sad, so tense, so tiring… I have wanted to talk to you too, Andrew, but I haven't known what to say."

"Hush," he replied, looking at their linked hands. "Never let it be said Astrid Worthington Allen Alexander was at a loss for plain speech."

Rather than admit she was at a loss for much more than that, Astrid concentrated on the feel of his hand, warm and secure around hers. *This is where he tells me, so gently and regretfully: we really cannot continue like this, and he will be leaving me soon.*

"Astrid," Andrew said as a shower of sparks disappeared up the flue, "we cannot continue the way we've begun in this marriage." Her worst fears, put into words, but Andrew wasn't finished. "I love you—"

She dropped his hand. "*What?*"

"I love you." He eyed her hand but didn't make a grab for it. "I've loved you since you were a girl of seventeen trying not to cry because you'd beaten out a fire with your bare hands. I've loved you across three continents, several years, and more stupid behavior on my part than I can recall. I love you, and I've done a damned poor job of owning up to it."

"Yes, you have." Astrid subsided against him, at a loss to label what she was feeling beyond… shock.

"You don't have to choose now to be agreeable."

"Civil and agreeable are two different things," she retorted. "So why have you gone to such great and unpleasant lengths to convince me my husband did *not* love me?" Because that question desperately needed an answer if she was to maintain her sanity.

He was silent for a moment, while Astrid contemplated smacking him.

"It's complicated."

She mashed her nose into his shoulder. Love was *not* complicated. "Then you'd best have a good explanation."

"I have for many years been under a serious misapprehension," he began. "I was wrong about myself, among other things, and I want to choose my words with utmost care, Astrid, because I doubt you'll give me a chance to refine on them."

She did not tell him he likely had the right of that, for his tone was too grave.

Haltingly at first, then more easily, Andrew related to Astrid the events of his fifteenth summer. About the accident, Astrid had thought she'd been well informed, but about Andrew's involvement with Julia Ponsonby, she'd had no clue—neither, apparently, had Gareth, at least not until it was too late.

When Andrew paused to pour them both a tumbler of brandy, Astrid was aware that she'd rather he not have left her side even to cross the room.

"I had clues as to this misapprehension of yours," she said, considering a drink she did not want but probably needed. "I once overheard Gareth wondering why you never entertained women he'd been involved with, despite their many attempts to gain your notice, but you didn't mind in the least where your castoffs went for consolation."

Andrew's expression was... bewildered. "You consider that a clue?"

"Of a sort. Or there's the way you would not allow Gareth to help you, not with your property, not with your various scrapes and peccadilloes—why did it never occur to you, if you're going to fight a duel, your brother should have been your second, not the last to know?"

Andrew sat beside his wife, his drink untouched.

"I did not want my brother to be as ashamed of me as I was of myself. I did not want him to ever, ever find out what a weak, immoral, dishonorable man I was."

This reasoning was flawed. Understandable, but badly, badly flawed. "If anybody knows about being immoral with women, it is your brother. He convinced himself he could misbehave with Felicity, a spinster virgin if ever there was one."

Andrew settled his arm around Astrid's shoulders, a warm, welcome weight. "Gareth apologized to me. It about broke my heart. He said my brothers ought to have protected me." Now he slugged back his drink, a gesture that struck Astrid as despairing.

"I've seen him looking at you lately with an odd expression on his face. Was this a recent discussion?"

"Shortly after the babies arrived," Andrew replied. "I waited for Gareth to come down the stairs, knowing he'd have to get something to eat or drink eventually. When he found me, he was a man who believed his selfish rutting had cost his wife her life. I thought to comfort him by confessing to costing my own child—conceived with Gareth's fiancée—his or her life. In hindsight, it was a deuced odd sort of comfort to offer, but under the circumstances, it made a kind of sense."

Astrid was silent, feeling utterly weary. Andrew's revelations explained a lot, but she wasn't ready to believe their marital problems were solved.

She squirmed down to lay her head on his muscular thigh. "Something bothers me."

His hand settled on her hair, the near reverence in that simple touch making Astrid's heart beat harder. "Tell me, love."

"You believed you were responsible for the death of an unborn child, but now you know there was no child. Morally, is that a material distinction to you?"

Andrew put his drink on the end table and let his hand drift from Astrid's hair to her face. She had asked the ultimate difficult question, but she was also coming to know her husband, and the matter had to be faced:

How was Andrew to reconcile himself to the fact that he'd been *willing* to put the life of that unborn child second to his mother's welfare, and in his own eyes, second to his own convenience? Had there been a child, the child would have died with Julia, and by virtue of Andrew's choice.

"I made a mistake," he said. "I made a selfish mistake, the results of which are no more than I deserved for having slept with a woman who was, as far as I knew at the time, otherwise chaste. Had there been opportunity, I would likely have slept with her again at other times and places."

Such remorse would have felled a lesser man, and

yet, the conversation could not end with that guilt-wracked recitation. Astrid covered Andrew's hand with her own, lest he try to extricate himself from the discussion.

"Let me put a question to you, then, Andrew," she said. "Why do you define your entire self, your entire life, in terms of those mistaken moments?"

Andrew's hand went slack in hers.

A silence grew, punctuated by only the crackling of the fire.

"Why do I...?" Andrew repeated slowly, stupidly, as if drunk.

"Why do you define yourself, your entire life and worth, in terms of the mistakes you made with Julia?"

"Because some mistakes are so great as to define one."

Astrid sat up, hoisted herself off the couch, then turned and lowered herself to straddle his lap, her tummy bulging between them.

"You listen to me, Andrew Penwarren Alexander. You are a *good* man, an *honorable* man, and a *loving* man," she pronounced slowly, as if he might have trouble comprehending her. "You faced a decision when you risked your life charging over here from Enfield. You could have let my sister quietly die, and her children with her, but you did not. You took a chance, you made an effort, and now Felicity, James, William, Pen, Joyce, and Gareth all have a chance to enjoy long, happy lives as a family."

She framed his jaw in her hands. "Why don't you allow those moments—those moments when your courage carried the day for all of us—to define you? Why don't you allow the moments today when you *again* risked your life for me to define you? Why don't you allow the moments years ago, when you also risked your life for me, to define you?"

She lowered her forehead to his and let her tears trickle onto his cheeks.

"I am not finished," she admonished him, though where the fortitude to persevere would come from, she did not know.

She laid a hand over his heart, as if she'd prevent him from setting her aside and leaving the room, the property, her life.

"You were a friend to both Felicity and Gareth when they had no friend. You behaved honorably with respect to me when I was a girl, even if your notions of honor were misguided. You danced attendance on your mother when his blooming lordship, the marquess, couldn't pause in his wenching long enough to notice she was lonely for her sons. You took yourself off to God knows where, Andrew, to try to protect the people who love you from yourself…"

She was crying openly now, but wasn't sure all the tears on his cheeks were hers.

"You make me out to be some kind of bloody knight in shining armor," he whispered, his lips seeking hers for a quick kiss.

"You hopeless man," she said, kissing him back, "you *are* some kind of bloody knight in shining armor. You were prepared to let Henry m-murder you today, and I thought I would die right there with you if he did."

He enfolded her against his body, letting her cry out all the fear and upset and loneliness and sorrow that was in her. She cried for him, and for Douglas, and even some for Henry, miserable, murderous, and mad though he'd been. She cried for Felicity and Gareth, who had come through such a frightening situation. She cried for the children who would have lost their mother, as Astrid had lost hers, and thus lost a part of their father...

And she cried for herself, finally. For her miserable excuse of a first marriage, for Herbert, so misguided and manipulated. For the child she might yet not safely bear. In the end, Astrid cried herself to sleep, her husband's arms around her, his lips murmuring comfort against her hair.

Nonetheless, despite the revelations of the previous evening, despite Andrew's presence beside her as she'd drifted off to sleep, when she rose the next morning, Astrid found she had, again, slept *alone*.

❧

Douglas was escorted to the library the next morning by Fairly, who'd forced hot tea and buttered toast on him, then valeted him into proper morning attire. Greymoor and Heathgate were waiting for them, and to Douglas's surprise, Astrid was also present, sitting beside her husband on the hearth.

Immediately beside him.

Douglas bowed to each, greeting them in turn. Fairly took up a post by the French doors, his back half-turned to the room, a clear reminder to Douglas he had no ally among the assemblage. Not now.

Heathgate perched on his desk, a particularly undignified choice for the marquess, but no more informal than Greymoor, hunkered beside his wife on the stones of the raised hearth.

Greymoor stood and gestured to the sofa.

"Have a seat, Douglas," he said, the use of Douglas's Christian name apparently deliberate. There were two explanations, of course, the first being that Greymoor intended humiliation by assuming an ungranted familiarity; the second, possible in theory, was that this was a family gathering, where one needn't stand on ceremony.

Douglas took his assigned seat and waited, deciding silence was to his advantage. Though it ought to be beyond him, he could yet feel humiliation, whether Greymoor intended it or not.

"We have matters to resolve in this room," Greymoor said, "and they are best resolved by consensus, but my wife has also requested an opportunity to put some questions to you, Douglas. I believe you owe her that."

"Of course." Douglas likely owed the woman his life. He'd not begrudge her a few painful answers.

"Did you know Henry killed your father?"

Astrid's soft words landed with the force of a blow. Across the room, Fairly had turned, resting his shoulders against the doors likely the better to view the proceedings. Douglas's gaze swept the room, and on each face he saw more patience than curiosity.

That puzzled him on the level still capable of thought after Astrid's terrible revelation, but he marshaled his resources to address the question.

"No," Douglas said. "I never even suspected, not before yesterday, for which I must bear the blame. Henry would have been an adolescent, but he was always keen for weaponry. I should have realized…"

Those words ought to be engraved on his tombstone.

So much he *should have realized*. Douglas remained silent, the confirmation of every dark thought about his family he'd ever attempted to deny battering at him. Greymoor—a man whom Douglas would never understand—chose that moment to sit beside Douglas on the sofa.

Greymoor glanced at his wife before he spoke. "Did you know the missing funds were loans Herbert made to Henry? We think Herbert might have suspected Henry's patricidal tendencies, and yet feared Henry could engineer things such that blame might fall on Herbert as the one in line for the title."

Worse and worse. "I did not know anything regarding Astrid's funds until Herbert's death. I can understand, though, why you would make the mistake of misreading Henry. To my everlasting sorrow, I read him no more accurately."

Everlasting being the operative word, for how was a man to transcend scandal and heartache of this magnitude?

Greymoor's expression became terrifyingly compassionate. "Henry told Astrid he had killed both your father and your brother."

Douglas had to stand, had to move, had to do something to avoid the truth of Greymoor's words.

"I can't—" He wanted to say he couldn't believe it. But the brutal, unbearable truth was that he *could* believe it. He had overheard Henry in that stable and slapped a weapon into Greymoor's hands, then allowed the earl to court death by entering the barn first.

Douglas had been stunned and sickened, listening to his younger brother chatter blithely with Astrid about murder and worse. Through the long, cold night since, Douglas had done nothing but think of all the signs he'd missed, all the clues he'd ignored.

"I don't know what to say." He came to rest like a rudderless ship against the end of a long set of shelves. The smell of books came to him over the pleasant scent of the wood fire. What would prison smell like? What was the scent of complete social ruin, and did Douglas care either way?

The assemblage seemed to expect more words of him, and his fool mouth obliged. "I simply do not know what to say. I had suspicions Henry was up to no good when he didn't stay put with Mother, and he didn't tell me he was leaving Town. Details, such as motive and opportunity, began to fall together, so when I got word he'd taken a notion to travel through deep snow in this direction, I trailed him here. Then I found his horse at the bottom of the lane, shivering, in a sweat such as a decent animal ought never to be left... But about all this... I am at a loss for coherent speech."

Greymoor resumed his place beside his wife, a cozy couple in an informal posture before the hearth. Thank God they, at least, were alive.

Greymoor took his wife's hand and kissed her knuckles. "If you want my suggestion, Douglas, you say as little as possible. We will inform the magistrate Henry's gun, damp from the snow, misfired while he was cleaning it out in the stables. The magistrate can be given to understand Henry was not coping well with his beloved older brother's death, and might conclude we are putting about a polite fiction—unless you would prefer to tell the magistrate something else?"

Douglas heard the words and comprehended them. Across the room, Fairly was once again studying the view toward the stables, as if covering up attempted murder and suicide were all in a morning's work. Douglas reviewed the words Greymoor had spoken, and found they held the same meaning, still, and yet his mind must continue to examine them.

"Come on, man," Heathgate growled from his desk. "We need to decide this before the bloody magistrate comes bumbling up the drive."

Fairly didn't turn, but rather, drawled over his shoulder, "The bloody magistrate can bloody wait in the bloody guest parlor, swilling your finest gunpowder and chatting up the rather buxom maid. Astrid, my apologies for the language."

Douglas paid attention to not a word of that exchange—though Fairly was being protective of him, and that was remarkable—because he'd found a name for what was being offered here: sanctuary.

A safe place, a place where one need not be always on guard. He didn't want to trust it, but his defenses were in shambles, and he frankly lacked the strength of will to resist the lure.

"That plan should suffice," he told Greymoor, his voice shaking a bit. "What of my mother?"

"Mothers," said Greymoor with a glance at his wife's belly, "are always a complication. I see no need to provide the dowager Lady Amery any details at variance with what's told to the magistrate."

A look passed between members of the Alexander family, but Douglas was at a loss to interpret it. Pity, maybe? Dismay? His mental faculties had become like those of some mute beast, capable of observing human behaviors, but unable to make sense of them.

"All right," Fairly said briskly, again facing the room. "If that's settled, then what say I found the body? Went out to check on my mare, and alas, tragedy had struck."

That turned the discussion to the story to be prepared for the magistrate. When that matter had been dispatched, the next order of business became Henry's final arrangements.

"We have a family plot on the estate," Douglas said, drifting back to the sofa. "I can deal with it there."

Greymoor glanced at his wife again, an assessing glance the lady probably didn't even notice. "I'd rather you held at least a memorial service in Town. Henry was well liked among the hunting set, and it would save both my wife and my brother the journey to your estate."

The sense of sanctuary, of being protected, swelled again in Douglas's chest. "You really need not make that effort."

"Oh, yes, we really do," Heathgate said. "The man we bury would have been uncle to Astrid's child, and there will be no taint on the family honor if we can manage it."

Douglas felt a faint inclination to smile at the fig leaf Heathgate had extended. This great effort, this show of solidarity and civility, wasn't for him, it was for the child.

Of course it was.

"A memorial service, then," Douglas said, "and a funeral at the estate. I will take my leave of you once the magistrate has finished, and you have"—he paused to look particularly at Astrid and Greymoor—"you all have my sincerest thanks."

"One more thing," Fairly said, pushing away from the French doors and taking a seat beside Douglas on the sofa. "Who shall have guardianship of Astrid's child?"

Astrid's husband squeezed her hand before turning his gaze on Douglas. In the two years Herbert had been married to Astrid, Douglas hadn't seen his brother so much as touch the lady's hand once.

"You, Douglas, are head of the Allen family," Greymoor said. "What would your decision be regarding the child?" The use of the conditional was not lost on Douglas, who heard the question as: What would your decision be, *had you the authority to make it*?

For there was no Allen family worth the name. Perhaps there never had been.

Douglas opted for honesty—no point in abandoning that course at this late stage.

"I want no responsibility for any child, ever." A man who could not sense a murderer in his own family dared not assume such responsibility. "If this child is a boy, and Greymoor had the raising of him, it would relieve me of having to deal with the succession, and that would be the answer to a prayer."

Fairly's expression went carefully neutral, but Greymoor and Heathgate exchanged a relieved glance. Astrid's head was bowed, but Douglas could see she, too, had been prepared for him to fight on this.

Fight them, with what? Funds, truth, and honor resided on their side of the ledger.

"I guess that's settled then," Greymoor said.

"Douglas should at least be the child's godfather," Fairly interjected musingly. "Appearances, you know."

Douglas stiffened, resisting the notion he should have anything to do with a child others were better suited to nurturing, but he found Fairly staring at him with particular intensity.

This idea of Lord Fairly's was a challenge, and a chance to make some small reparation for the harm Douglas's family—and Douglas—had done to the child's mother. Moreover, the light in Fairly's eyes guaranteed Douglas would be given no opportunity to harm the child.

"Very well," Douglas conceded. "I shall be a devoted, though lamentably distant, godfather."

"My wife will stand as godmother," Heathgate added thoughtfully. "That should serve well enough. And if it comes down to it, Amery, even if the child is a girl, you might petition Privileges to have her offspring inherit the title. Your family has had a run of... bad luck, with respect to its male line. In our case, a similar lack of surviving adult males resulted in tremendous leniency when it came to imposing the barony and earldom on Andrew."

"That," said Douglas slowly, "is an encouraging thought." Though leniency tended to show up where coin had been bestowed, and Douglas had nowhere near Heathgate's resources.

"Are we finished then?" Greymoor asked. "Anything further from anyone?"

"Yes," Astrid said firmly. "Something needs to be said, and I will be the one to say it."

Douglas braced himself for the tirade she was due to unleash, the invective he and his brothers had earned, the scathing denouncement she would ring over his head. To feel the lash of her scorn and rage would be a relief, provided any feeling at all penetrated the numbness enshrouding him.

"Douglas," Astrid said, tears filling her eyes, "we are all so sorry for your loss. For your losses..." She went to him and put her arms around him in a swift, fierce hug.

He was so stunned, so unable to comprehend the gesture, he simply sat for a moment, blinking rapidly. He might have eventually mumbled his thanks, but he was saved from worse mortification by a servant announcing the arrival of the magistrate. The gathering broke up, but Douglas only knew Fairly shoved a drink in his hand and got him back to his room before he embarrassed himself.

Twenty-one

ANDREW STARED AT HIS WIFE, INCREDULOUS. "YOU are *leaving* me?"

She shot him a pitying look and continued tossing clothes into the valise sitting open on the chest at the foot of her bed.

"For God's sake, why?" Andrew yelled. "You said—"

"Yes?" Astrid gave him that same look, laced with mild curiosity. With *only* mild curiosity.

"I said," Andrew began again, lowering his voice, "I said I loved you. You seemed to take that sentiment to heart."

Her eyes narrowed, but she merely tossed another pair of shoes into a trunk made of dark wood, like an old coffin.

"And you said I was a decent enough sort of fellow…"

Apparently, those were not the right words, if right words even existed. She slammed the lid on the valise and folded her arms, her mulish expression speaking volumes.

"You said…" Andrew turned his face toward the ceiling and closed his eyes, the pain of this parting lancing through him and lodging in his chest. "You said I was… honorable, and good, and… loving."

"I did say that, but I don't think you heard me, Andrew Penwarren Alexander."

Oh, she was mad, all right. Use of his middle name meant matters were serious with Astrid.

"I heard you." He shifted to stand before her, but using the advantage of his height was not appropriate somehow, so he sat on the bed and put himself below her eye level.

"I heard you," he repeated more softly.

Astrid latched the trunk, the little snick of the locks sounding like manacles closing around Andrew's heart. "Well, Andrew, what are you going to do about these words you heard from me?"

"What am I going to do?" Begging came to mind, but some stray male intuition suggested this was not what she sought from him.

She pushed past him to go to the wardrobe, and began pulling dresses off their hooks. "You are hopeless, Andrew, and I wash my hands of you."

"You can't," he said, panic clawing at him. "I won't allow it." Inspiration struck. "You *love* me." He seized her gently but firmly around the middle—she'd long since lost her waist—when she attempted to reopen the valise, and caused her to drop her load of dresses.

"Damn you. Take your hands off me," she spat, plucking at his fingers.

"*You love me*," Andrew growled now, his hold more firm. "You can't just say those things, Astrid, not to me. A woman who loves her husband doesn't leave him."

"And a husband who loves his wife," Astrid said in low, vicious tones, "doesn't leave her."

"I'm here, for God's sake," Andrew said, holding her more firmly still. "I'm not going anywhere without you."

"You *went to bed* without me."

He went still, insight rendering him mute and paralyzed. He'd made the Dreaded Worst Mistake; he'd committed that single unforgivable blunder every male with sense worries about. Not in his words, apparently, but in his deeds, or in what he'd failed to do.

"I see," he said, turning Astrid loose and locking the door. As he crossed the room back to Astrid, he picked up the pile of gowns on the floor and tossed them over a chair. Then he stood before his wife, directly before her.

"I was trying," he said in clipped, frustrated tones, "to be considerate of my exhausted, sleeping wife. The same wife upon whom murder had been attempted, if I recall. The wife who had borne the burden of a series of uncomfortable revelations from me just before weeping her heart out on my shoulder."

Astrid's gaze remained fixed on that shoulder.

"I awoke alone," she said in a small, broken voice. "Again, Andrew. I fell asleep in your arms, and I awoke alone, *alone*. I can't be married to you like this, I cannot."

"And I," Andrew said softly, "don't want to be married to you *like this* either."

She raised tortured eyes to his, and he feared— feared—what might come out of her mouth.

"For God's sake." Andrew's right hand moved as

if he would touch her, but then dropped back to his side. "Astrid, don't go, please. I love you, and I want to make love with you. Always. I don't want you to wake up without me—I don't want to wake up without you. I don't ever want to wake up without you again."

He let her see into his soul. He let her see the vulnerability, the hope, and most of all, the love she'd found in him. He loved her, and a man who loved and who was loved was not at liberty to wander his existence away on foreign shores.

It was the hardest truth he'd faced, but he bore her scrutiny without flinching.

"Say it again, Andrew," she said softly. "If you mean these words, prepare to say them often for the rest of your life."

For the rest of his life…

Relief coursed through him, and joy—and lust—and love.

Most especially, love.

"You, Astrid Alexander, are the home my heart has longed for, and I would be the home your heart has craved as well. I will be the father of your children and your partner in all that life holds in the years to come."

More poetry welled up, but he fell silent as Astrid studied him at interminable length.

"You want more children, then? Children of your own?"

"Every child you bear will be a child of mine," Andrew said, because it was a simple truth, easily given. "If God wills, we'll have a large, happy family." Though based on the way Astrid's lips turned up at the corners, her will would have something to do with the size of their family too.

Her smile died aborning, and Andrew felt as if his heartbeat suspended with it.

"You must not make love to me as another farewell, Andrew. Not ever. I cannot bear it."

He sat on the bed and steered her by the hips to stand between his legs. She'd put her finger on a truth. All of his lovemaking with her had borne an element of parting, of loss, and acceptance that she would soon be telling him good-bye, because good-byes were all he'd thought he deserved.

"I could learn from you how to make love as something other than a farewell, Wife, but you must be patient with me, for I can be slow to learn the most important things."

She wrapped her arms around him, bringing him the flowery fragrance of her person and the sweeter scent of welcome. "We will learn together, Husband, and be patient with each other too. We will be patient with each other quite often."

❧

Three months later

"Andrew?"

Three pairs of male eyes riveted on Felicity's smiling face.

"You can go up now, and congratulations on the birth of a fine, healthy daughter."

Andrew was out the door like a shot, leaving Heathgate and Fairly to call for the champagne, while he bounded up the steps two at a time.

"What are you doing out of bed?" Andrew asked, closing the bedroom door quietly behind him.

"I have spent the past six hours getting in and out of the bed, Andrew," Astrid replied. "Unless you are prepared to share the bed with me, I have no intention of wasting any more time there."

"That's all right then," Andrew said, slipping the sleeve button from his right cuff.

"Andrew, what are you doing?"

"If I have to spend the next week in bed with you so you'll take care of yourself properly, then into bed I go," he said, freeing the second sleeve button.

"Stop that, Husband. I was being ridiculous."

Astrid was whole, she was scolding him, and he could breathe for the first time in weeks. She could be as ridiculous as she pleased. Andrew crossed to the window seat where Astrid was perched and sat down beside her.

"Are you all right?" She looked tired, but exultant too, with a luminous quality that was more than the late-afternoon spring sun on her hair.

"Andrew, I am…" She leaned on him, and Andrew felt his heart turn over with joy. "I am in awe…"

"May I see her?"

"No," Astrid teased. "You have to wait until she's eighteen, at least. Of course you may see her." She carefully unwrapped the tiny bundle she held cradled in her arms, and a small, sleepy face emerged. The baby sported a golden-blond peach fuzz of hair and a tiny rosebud mouth.

"She's *perfect*," Andrew said, stroking a finger down the baby-fine cheek.

"Here." Astrid tucked the blanket back around her daughter—*their* daughter—and handed the child to Andrew.

Andrew accepted the baby, accepted the implicit trust with which Astrid had handed her over—to him. "I am overwhelmed by her... by you."

Overwhelmed was accurate, Astrid thought, smiling at her husband and daughter. In the past few months, Andrew had struggled to become a more communicative, trusting husband. For him, it was hard work. He tried Astrid's patience, and she tried his, bludgeoning him with sentiment and argument and a relentless pursuit of his honest involvement in their marriage. Sometimes they got it wrong, and each had to retreat and reconsider, until the other could be approached again more thoughtfully, or more overtly.

But more and more, they got it right. And as the weeks had gone on and the winter had turned to spring, their love had blossomed like the verdant, well-tended land they lived on.

Andrew wrapped one arm around his wife and kept the baby cradled in the other. "I feel an instant willingness to slay dragons and smite griffons and otherwise take on any challenge for our daughter. This is amazing..."

"Were you concerned?" This was, after all, not his biological child—whom he could not take his eyes off of.

"A bit."

Which meant he'd been terrified.

"Me too," Astrid said, resting against him again. "I love my nephews and my nieces, but I wasn't at all sure

I would immediately take to someone who did her level best to split me in two on her way into the world."

Andrew kissed the baby's cheek, the tenderness of the gesture threatening to tear Astrid's heart asunder. "You were concerned I might not be smitten with her at sight?"

"Of course not. She's a pretty girl, Andrew. You didn't stand a chance."

"I suppose not," he agreed, a smile spreading to his every feature. "What shall we call her?"

"Well, we are not calling her Herbertia, or anything ridiculous like that. No *H* names at all, if you please. I'm surprised we didn't consider this before—babies do need names."

"What about Lucy?" Andrew suggested, snuggling his wife and daughter to him more closely.

"For the light she brings? I like it—today is the equinox, isn't it?"

"It is. Maybe Lucy Elizabeth?"

"I can live with that. I am not sure, however, I can live with waiting three months before starting on the conception of her first sibling."

"But wait we shall," Andrew said, smiling ruefully. "And what did you mean her *first* sibling?"

Astrid kissed him on the cheek. "I meant exactly what I said. Exactly."

They lasted nine weeks.

Acknowledgments

First, I would like to acknowledge my dear mama, whose initial experience with childbearing involved the procedure now referred to as a manual version. As if that challenge weren't enough, her obstetrician had not wanted to upset his patient, so he kept his suspicions about twins to himself. Mom did not learn she was carrying twins until the nurse told her, "Keep pushing, Mrs. Burrowes. You're still in labor." My brother Dick showed up three minutes after John's arrival in the world, though both have ever known how to make a noteworthy entrance.

Second, thanks are due in another direction. When I wrote this book, life was handing me a few lemons. Beloved Offspring's efforts to leave the nest were not going well, my law practice was reeling from the effects of some nasty, awful cases, and the economy seemed to be doing much of its contracting right in the neighborhood of my checking account. I still had the means to regularly ride my horse, Delray the Wonder Pony, a 17.1 hand Oldenburg gelding who was and ever shall be one of the Good Big Things to happen in my life.

I'd show up for my riding lessons feeling like crap, eighteen child abuse cases in my head, my dear daughter in distress I could not help her with, and no relief in sight. My instructor, Todd Bryan, would not ask me about that stuff. Todd's a smart guy (and a helluva horseman); he could probably see the alligators riding right behind me on Delray's croup. Instead, he would ask me "How's the writing going?" and between playing with flying changes in our warm up, and eventually getting down to business at the trot, all the bad things would go away, and the stories and the ride would take their place.

In every riding lesson, I was reminded of two things. First, in Todd, his wife Becky, and the other folks at the barn, I had friends who knew what I was dealing with—riding buddies who honestly did not care if I ever learned to sit the trot (and I still haven't, not properly), provided I kept showing up for the ride. Second, the writing was going well.

When I write, I'm happy. I needed my friends, my horse, and my riding to remind me of that, and they did. And when the writing goes well, much else in life takes care of itself.

May you have riding buddies, and may your writing always go well.

Read on for an excerpt from
Douglas, Lord of Heartache

Coming January 2014 from Grace Burrowes
and Sourcebooks Casablanca

THE CHILD WAS SMALL, HELPLESS, AND IN HARM'S WAY.

As Douglas Allen drew his horse to a halt, he absorbed more, equally disturbing facts:

The grooms clustered in the barn doorway would do nothing but mill about, moving their lips in silent prayer and looking sick with dread.

A woman—the child's mother?—unnaturally pale at the foot of the huge oak in the stable yard, was also likely paralyzed with fear. The child, standing on a sturdy limb of the old tree, thirty feet above the ground, was as white-faced as her mother.

"Rose," the woman said in a tight, stern voice, "you will come down this instant, do you hear me?"

"I don't want to come down!" came a retort from the heights of the oak.

Douglas was no expert on children, but the girl looked to be about five years old. Though she stood on one limb, she also anchored herself to the tree with a fierce hold on the branch above her. When she made her rude reply, she stomped her foot, which caused the branch she grasped to shake as well.

Douglas heard the danger before he saw it. A low,

insistent drone, one that would have been undetectable but for the stillness of the stable yard.

At Rose's display of stubbornness, the woman's hands closed into white-knuckled fists. "Rose," she said, her voice an agony of controlled desperation, "if you cannot climb down, then you must hold very, very still until we can get you down."

"But you *promised* I could stay up here as long as I wanted."

Another stomp, followed by another ominous, angry droning.

Douglas took in two more facts: The child was unaware of the hornet's nest hanging several yards out on the higher branch, and she was not at all unwilling to come down. She was *unable*. He recognized a desperate display of bravado when he saw one, having found himself in an adult version of the same futile posturing more than once in recent months.

He stripped off his gloves and stuffed them into the pocket of his riding jacket. Next, he shed his jacket, slung it across the horse's withers, turned back his cuffs, and rode over to the base of the tree. After taking a moment to assess the possibilities, he used the height of the horse's back to hoist himself into the lower limbs.

"Miss Rose," he called out in the steady, no-nonsense voice his governess had used on him long ago, "you will do as your mother says and be still as a garden statue until I am able to reach you, do you understand? We will have no more rudeness"—Douglas continued to climb, branch by branch, toward the child—"you will not shout"—another several feet and he would be on the same level as she—"and you most *assuredly* will not be stamping your foot in an unladylike display of pique."

The child raised her foot as if to stomp again. Douglas watched that little foot and knew a fleeting regret that his life would end now—regret and resentment.

But no relief. That was something.

The girl lowered her foot slowly and wrinkled her nose as she peered down at Douglas. "What's peek?"

"Pique"—he secured his weight by wrapping one leg around a thick branch—"is the same thing as a taking, a pout, a ladylike version of a tantrum. Now come here, and we will get you out of this tree before your mama can devise a truly appalling punishment for your stubbornness."

The child obeyed, crouching so he could catch her about the waist with both hands—which did occasion relief, immense relief. The droning momentarily increased as the girl left her perch.

"You are going to climb around me now," Douglas instructed, "and affix yourself like a monkey to my back. You will hang on so tightly that I barely continue to breathe."

Rose clambered around, assisted by Douglas's secure grip on her person, and latched on to his back, her legs scissored around his torso.

"I wanted to come down," she confided when she was comfortably settled, "but I'd never climbed this high before, and I could not look down enough to figure my way to the ground. My stomach got butterflies, you see. Thank you for helping me get down. Mama is very, very vexed with me." She laid her cheek against Douglas's nape and huffed out a sigh as he began to descend. "I was scared."

Douglas was focused on his climbing—it had been ages since he'd been up a literal tree—but he was nearly in conversation with a small child, perhaps for the first time since he'd been a child.

Another unappealing aspect to an unappealing day.

"You might explain to your mama you were stuck," he said as they approached the base of the tree. He slipped back onto the horse, nudged it over to where the woman stood watching him, and then swung out of the saddle, Rose still clinging to his back. He reached around and repositioned her on his hip.

"Madam, I believe I have something belonging to you."

"Mama, I'm sorry. I was st-stuck." The child's courage failed her, and weeping ensued.

"Oh, Rose," her mother cried quietly, and the woman was, plague take this day, also *crying*. She held out her arms to the child, but because Rose was still wrapped around Douglas, he stepped forward, thinking to hand Rose off to her mother. Rose instead hugged her mother from her perch on Douglas's hip, bringing Douglas and the girl's mother into a startling proximity.

The woman wrapped an arm around her child, the child kept two legs and an arm around Douglas, and Douglas, to keep himself, mother, and child from toppling into an undignified heap, put an arm around the mother's shoulders. *She*, much to his shock, tucked in to his body, so he ended up holding both females as they became audibly lachrymose.

Douglas endured this strange embrace, assuring himself nobody cried forever.

EDWARD LINDSEY *m.* CAROLINE PIERCE

HARLAN HADDONFIELD *Earl of Bellefonte* *m.* DARLA DANAHER

NAOMI GREY

TRENTON LINDSEY Book Ten, *Trenton* *m.* ELEGY HAMPTON

DARIUS LINDSEY Book One, *Darius* *m.* VIVIAN LONGSTREET

LEAH LINDSEY *m.* NICHOLAS HADDONFIELD Book Two, *Nicholas*

ETHAN GREY Book Three, *Ethan* *m.* ALEXANDRA PORTMAINE

NITA

SUSANNAH

BECKMAN HADDONFIELD Book Four, *Beckman* *m.* SARA HUNT

KIRSTEN

DELLA

ADOLPHUS

GEORGE

ANDERSON HUNT *m.* ALMA SHAY

GAVOTTE HUNT (deceased)

POLONAISE HUNT *m.* GABRIEL NORTH Book Five, *Gabriel*

Lonely Lords
Family Tree I

About the Author

New York Times and *USA Today* bestselling author Grace Burrowes hit the bestseller lists with her debut, *The Heir*, followed by *The Soldier*, *Lady Maggie's Secret Scandal*, *Lady Eve's Indiscretion*, and *Lady Sophie's Christmas Wish*. *The Heir* was a *Publishers Weekly* Best Book of 2010, *The Soldier* a *Publishers Weekly* Best Spring Romance of 2011, *Lady Sophie's Christmas Wish* won Best Historical Romance of the Year in 2011 from RT Reviewers' Choice Awards, *Lady Louisa's Christmas Knight* was a *Library Journal* Best Book of 2012, and *The Bridegroom Wore Plaid*, the first in her trilogy of Scotland-set Victorian romances, was a *Publishers Weekly* Best Book of 2012. All of her historical romances have received extensive praise, including starred reviews from *Publishers Weekly* and *Booklist*.

Grace is a practicing family law attorney and lives in rural Maryland. She loves to hear from her readers and can be reached through her website at graceburrowes.com.